Sunris ay

The Sunrise Coast Series

New Beginnings at the Harbour Inn

The Secret of the Summerhouse

The Cottage by the Sea

The Guest House at Shingle Cove

The Houseboat by the Quay

Return to Willow Tree Cottage

The Bookshop of Memories

The Beach House

A Summer to Remember

Sunrise Over Seashell Bay

The Secrets of Somersby Hall

Sunrise Over Seashell Bay

A Novel

ELISE DARCY

Penny Lane Press

ISBN 978-1-913147-41-9

"Every moment is a fresh beginning." – T.S. Eliot

1

The first light of dawn filtered through the thin curtains of Hannah's modest bedroom, casting a gentle glow on the worn-out furniture. The alarm clock buzzed incessantly on the bedside table. Hannah groaned and reached out a tired hand to silence it. She lay still for a moment, staring at the ceiling, gathering the strength to face another day.

With a sigh, she swung her legs out of bed and padded softly across the creaky floorboards. The small apartment was quiet, save for the hum of the refrigerator in the kitchen. She moved quickly, knowing she had little time before Maisie woke up.

In the kitchenette, Hannah set the kettle to boil and prepared breakfast. She buttered toast and poured cereal, her mind already racing through the tasks ahead. She glanced at the pile of bills on the counter, anxiety tightening her chest. The shop had to start making money soon, or she didn't know what she would do.

'Mum?' a small voice called from the hallway.

Hannah turned to see Maisie, her nine-year-old daughter, standing in the doorway, rubbing sleep from her eyes. Her heart softened at the sight. 'Good morning, sweetheart. Did you sleep well?'

Maisie nodded, her hair a wild halo around her face. She shuffled over to the table and climbed into a chair, stifling a yawn. 'I'm hungry.'

'Breakfast is ready,' Hannah said, setting a bowl of cereal in front of her. She poured herself a cup of tea and sat across from her daughter, watching her eat.

Maisie chattered about her plans for the day, excitement in her voice as she talked about seeing her father, Nate, her half-brother William, and of course Lili.

'Are you excited to see Daddy and Lili?' Hannah asked, forcing a smile.

'Yes! Daddy said we might go to the park. And Lili promised to bake cookies with me, although she said she's not a very good cook, but we can have a go together,' Maisie replied, her eyes shining with happiness.

Hannah's smile faltered slightly. She couldn't help but feel a pang of jealousy and inadequacy. Maisie's joy in spending time with Nate and Lili only highlighted the things Hannah felt she couldn't provide – a stable, happy home and a big, loving family.

'I'm sure you'll have a great time,' Hannah said, trying to keep her tone light. 'Finish your breakfast, and we'll get you ready.'

After breakfast, Hannah helped Maisie get dressed and gather her bag. They left the flat above the shop in Cobblers Yard where Hannah worked. Previously she had rented a small cottage for herself and Maisie in Aldeburgh, along the high street, one street over from the promenade and the beach. Although they'd been very happy there, the dwindling shop profits had meant giving up the cottage and returning to the small flat. This felt like a significant setback. If her situation worsened, she might face homelessness. Hannah shuddered at the thought. But at least Maisie would not be without a home. She could go and live with Nate, Lili and William in their beautiful home. Hannah forced herself to avoid dwelling on such bleak prospects.

They walked out of Cobblers Yard and along Aldeburgh's high street to her car, which was parked a short distance away by the kerb. The morning air was crisp and cool. The blue skies signalled the start of another lovely early September day. As they drove to Nate's house, Maisie continued to chat excitedly. Hannah listened, her thoughts drifting to the shop and the mounting pressure to make it a success.

When they pulled up in front of Nate's house, a four-bed detached Georgian house set back from the road, Maisie unbuckled her seatbelt eagerly.

'Mummy, can I go in now?'

'Of course, sweetie,' Hannah said, turning off the engine. 'I'll walk you to the door.'

Maisie bounced out of the car and skipped up the path to her dad's front door. Hannah followed more slowly, her heart heavy. Nate's house was large and welcoming, with a well-kept garden and a sense of stability that Hannah's own life seemed to lack.

Nate opened the door with a broad smile. 'Hey, there's my girl!' he said, scooping Maisie into a hug. 'Hi, Hannah.'

'Hi, Nate,' Hannah replied, her voice strained. 'She's got her things for the weekend in her bag.' Although they shared custody of Maisie, and originally it had been agreed that she would live part of the week with Nate, in practice this had changed; Maisie stayed with her dad every other weekend instead.

Lili appeared behind Nate, smiling warmly. 'Good morning, Hannah. How are things?'

Hannah forced a smile. 'Yeah, things are … great.' By *things*, Hannah knew that Lili meant the shop. It had been Lili's idea to hand over the lease of the old antiques shop in Cobblers Yard to Hannah, Lili's best friend. It had been Nate's grandfather's shop, but Nate was too busy with his job and Lili was too busy with The Potting Shed – the flower shop in Cobblers Yard – to run another shop too. And, of course, Lili and Nate now had their relationship too; a relationship that Hannah had had no way of knowing would spark off when Lili had taken a holiday to the Suffolk Coast without her then boyfriend, Alex.

Nate and Hannah had a history: a one-night drunken teenage romp that had resulted in little Maisie. They had parted ways after that night, thinking their paths would never cross again. The teenage Nate had had no clue that Hannah had been pregnant. He'd gone on to marry and have another child, William, four years later. Unfortunately, his wife had died, leaving him a widower with a son to raise. He'd returned to the Suffolk Coast, where he'd found a position working as a doctor in A&E at Aldeburgh Cottage Hospital. It was there he'd met Lili one day during the holiday she'd taken with Maisie.

Perhaps if my daughter had been on holiday with me, instead of with my best friend, who took her while I swanned off abroad with yet another new man, I might have met Nate again, Hannah thought to herself. *Perhaps we'd have fallen in love this time. Perhaps William would have been my stepson, and we'd all be living in the house Nate inherited from his grandparents.*

Hannah shook her head. The thought had crossed her mind so many times. If she could go back in time and change just one thing, her life might have panned out differently. But there was no point wishing. She had the opportunity that Nate had given her – the shop. It was up to her to make a success of that opportunity. So far, things had not been going well. She didn't want to tell Lili and disappoint her.

Lili said, 'Oh, don't rush off. Come in and see what we've done with the house.'

Hannah felt a pang of discomfort. She followed them inside, feeling like an outsider in their cosy, well-decorated home.

Inside, the house was even more inviting. Soft light filtered through the long Georgian windows of the old white brick detached property, illuminating the freshly painted walls and the tasteful decor. Lili led Hannah through the living room, pointing out the new light oak furniture, L-shaped sofa, large wall-mounted flatscreen TV, and family photos adorning the walls.

'We've been working on making it more of a family home,' Lili explained, her voice full of pride as they made their way upstairs to look in the bedrooms too.

Hannah smiled tightly, trying to hide her envy. 'It looks wonderful, Lili. Really.'

Maisie followed them upstairs. She tugged at Lili's sleeve, her eyes wide with excitement. 'Lili, can we tell Mummy our secret now? I can't keep it any longer!'

Hannah's heart skipped a beat. 'Secret?' Since when did her daughter keep secrets from her?

Lili laughed nervously. 'Alright, Maisie. But remember, it's meant to be a surprise.'

Hannah's mind raced. Was Lili pregnant? Upstairs, they stopped in the open doorway of another newly decorated room with soft pastel colours and a box of baby's toys. But it was the crib that immediately caught Hannah's attention.

'That was William's crib, and his toys from when he was a baby,' Lili explained.

Hannah's throat tightened. She felt surprise mixed with a bit of hurt. 'Ready for when the baby comes,' she said.

'What baby?' Lili turned to her. 'Oh, you thought …? I'm not pregnant, Hannah. Nate is just storing the crib and toys in this room. I know Nate would love us to have more children, and this room would make a lovely nursery, but I've got my business, and he's super busy working at the hospital. Right now, two children are enough – don't you agree?'

Two children? Hannah couldn't hide her frown. William lived there, but Maisie did not. However, what Lili had just said made it sound as though it was Maisie's home too.

Lili must have caught her frown. She touched her arm. 'Oh, I didn't mean anything by that comment. I wasn't saying that having two children around was enough in a negative way. Not at all. I love having Maisie to stay.' Lili turned to Maisie standing beside her and ruffled her hair, smiling down at her affectionately.

Lili had looked after Maisie so much in the past when Hannah had been off gallivanting with boyfriends that Hannah knew it was understandable that her best friend loved having Maisie to stay. She supposed she should be thankful that Nate's girlfriend was Lili – someone Maisie had known, and loved, all her life.

'She knows she's always welcome to stay with us and her little brother. We all miss her so much when she's gone.'

'Well, so do I,' Hannah blurted. She looked away, embarrassed, even though that was how she was feeling. She said,

'What's the secret, anyway?'

'The secret is that Nate and I have finally set a wedding date.'

'Oh, I see.' Hannah said. She knew they were engaged, and it wasn't really a surprise that they'd set a date. Lili's life was moving on. 'That's … that's wonderful news. Congratulations.'

Lili smiled. 'Thank you. We're really excited, but we haven't figured out where to have the wedding yet.'

Hannah nodded, her thoughts drifting to her own failed relationships and the struggle to find stability. She felt a pang of envy but pushed it aside. 'I'm sure you'll find the perfect place.'

They walked back to the front door, where Nate and his son William joined them. Maisie hugged Hannah tightly. 'Bye, Mummy! I'll see you on Sunday!'

'Bye, sweetheart. Have fun.' Hannah watched as Maisie disappeared into the house, her heart aching.

Lili said, 'You must come for Sunday lunch with us all when you come and collect Maisie tomorrow.'

Hannah didn't really want to. Of course she wanted to spend time with Lili, but not with Nate, although they did get on amicably. She tended to avoid spending time with them as a family, especially when invited to their lovely home. It would just rub the reality of her situation in, especially now she'd had to move out of the rented cottage and return to the flat above the shop.

Hannah had sworn Maisie to secrecy about their move back to live above the shop, even though she was aware that Lili would find out soon enough. Just then, she didn't want Lili to be aware that things weren't working out with the shop, despite all the hard work and effort she had put in to set it up.

'Oh, please say yes, Mummy! Then I can show you my new

bedroom that I'll be moving into when they've finished decorating.'

Hannah raised her eyebrows. 'Your new bedroom?'

Nate stepped in. 'Maisie wants a bigger bedroom.'

'Yes – it's huge, Mummy.'

'I bet it is,' Hannah replied, forcing a smile. She looked at Nate, at his dark hair falling into his brown eyes. 'When were you going to tell me this?'

'I don't need to discuss giving my daughter a bigger bedroom with you, surely.'

Hannah looked away, embarrassed. The phrase *making a mountain out of a molehill* came to mind. She shook her head.

'I was going to tell you, Mummy. Promise.'

Hannah smiled down at her. 'Of course. I'm just a bit surprised, that's all. I thought you liked that little room overlooking the garden. Is it because you're the eldest? Is that the reason you want a bigger room?'

Maisie shook her head and frowned. 'No.'

Lili said, 'Maisie likes to get up really early sometimes and paint, so she could do with the extra space.'

Maisie smiled up at Lili. 'Do you remember when you brought me on holiday here, and we stayed in that big, old hotel on the seafront? I used to wake up really early to paint the view from the window.'

'How could I forget?' Lili rolled her eyes, even though she wasn't cross; she was smiling. She pulled Maisie towards her in an affectionate hug. 'That's when I discovered I had a prodigy on my hands.'

'My hands, you mean,' said Hannah.

Lili stopped and looked at Hannah. 'Well, of course. It was

just a figure of speech, Hannah.'

Hannah pursed her lips and looked at Maisie, who was staring up at Lili. *She doesn't smile at me like that.* Hannah dismissed that thought. *Of course she does.* Hannah still couldn't shake the feeling of envy over having to share her daughter, not to mention seeing everything that she couldn't give her – a house, a brother, a dad.

Nate said, 'It just made sense for her to move into a bigger room, with two windows for the natural light. And that way she won't disturb any of us when she's awake at the crack of dawn, running down the stairs to the artist's studio at the back of the house.'

'She has an artist's studio?' Hannah said, taken aback. She turned to Maisie. 'You didn't tell me that.'

'I didn't want you to feel bad.'

'Why would I feel bad?' The moment those words were out of her mouth, Hannah knew what was coming.

'Because there's no spare room in the flat to paint – not like at the cottage,' said Maisie.

'The flat?' Lili and Nate said in unison.

Hannah breathed a sigh. This was all she needed. If she didn't feel bad enough, now she had to tell them on the doorstep of their ridiculously lovely family home that she'd moved out of the cottage and taken a big step backwards. 'I had to give up the cottage and move back to the flat.'

'Oh, Hannah. What happened?'

'Just had a couple of not-so-good months.' That was an understatement. Hannah inwardly cringed at the lie. A couple of bad months? If only. How about the last six months – although she didn't want to admit it to herself. She blamed it on the location. The trouble with Cobblers Yard was that it was down a narrow lane in between two shops. Unless you knew the lane opened up into a cute little cobbled yard complete with old-fashioned store fronts with bowed, small-paned windows like something out of Dickens novel, and even an old streetlamp, you were more than likely to just walk on by than venture in, despite the little sign in the high street.

And yet all the other little shops seem to be thriving – Thea's bookshop, The Bookshop of Memories; Lili's flower shop, The Potting Shed; Reggie's music shop next door to the charity shop; the solicitor's office next door – although Hannah thought that didn't count because his business was purely pro bono work; Joss offered a free walk-in legal service for local people. *That will be me next*, thought Hannah, although it wouldn't be legal advice she'd need, but financial.

Free legal advice. It was little wonder the footfall next door was always tremendous. Hannah could do with a few of his clients popping into her art and craft shop. But they didn't. Why would they? It was a rather specialist shop, unlike the bookshop, the flower shop, or even Marjorie and Mabel's charity shop across the yard. *Perhaps I shouldn't have changed over completely to an art and craft shop*, thought Hannah.

Originally, she'd renamed the shop *Hannah and Maisie's Art and Antique Emporium*. She'd thought it was a good idea at the time as there were still a lot of old antiques left in the shop to sell, and it did seem to attract more customers in, but since running down that side of the business and changing over to just an art and craft shop, things weren't going well.

I'm in the wrong business, thought Hannah. Perhaps she should have left the shop as it was – an antiques shop – when Nate had passed it from his grandfather over to Hannah as an opportunity to put her past behind her and start afresh with Maisie, away from London and all those bad relationships she'd got involved in. Hannah did not want to think about what had happened, how she'd betrayed Lili's trust, and still she and Nate had given her this opportunity to start over.

She owed Lili and Nate.

Hannah thought of the other shop in Cobblers Yard that had closed; the one where Joss had taken over the lease to set up his solicitor's office. It had been an art and craft shop run by Maisie's grandfather, Ray, a retired police officer, as a bit of a hobby.

The writing was on the wall, thought Hannah sadly. She knew one of the reasons Ray had parted with his art and craft shop; it had been haemorrhaging money. Hannah had considered starting another business in her shop, but it was always Maisie who stopped her in her tracks. She'd wanted to do something for Maisie, and running a shop that was bound up with her daughter's gift for painting had just seemed like a lovely thing to do. If you were made of money. But Hannah wasn't. She couldn't afford to run it just as a hobby. It needed to make money. And it wasn't. She just didn't know how to tell her best friend that she'd done it again – made a mess of things and failed.

Hannah unsuccessfully stifled a yawn. The worry of it was understandably keeping her up at night. What should she do? Where would she go?

'Now, I know you're probably working hard in the shop to turn it around, and you've got a ton of things to do, no doubt,' said Lili.

Hannah didn't. Her overstocked shop was lying idle, the books didn't balance, and she spent most days staring out of the window, getting ridiculously excited every time someone wandered into the yard – even though they rarely looked in her window, let alone ventured into her shop.

'I won't take no for an answer,' said Lili. 'We all expect you tomorrow at noon.'

Hannah felt she had no choice but to accept. Even though she had considered opening the shop open on a Sunday, just on the off-chance that someone might wander in and actually buy something, she thought, *what the hell – I might as well come over to their place and sit here and have a nice meal, and chat about their wedding, rather than waste time in the shop*.

That was what she realised she was doing each day; wasting time on a business that was just never going to amount to anything. And besides, she couldn't go on as she was. Soon, the small amount of savings she had managed to put by in the beginning, when Lili and her friends in Cobblers Yard had encourage their friends and family, and friends of friends, to look in on the new art and craft shop, was dwindling fast. They mainly bought the amber bracelets and necklaces that she and Maisie had made out of the amber they'd collected from the beach.

But Maisie didn't have time to make those anymore, and Hannah had lost interest in spending the hours after manning the shop scouring the beach for the pieces of amber to make the jewellery that she'd realised was just a passing fad. If you really wanted a proper piece of professional amber jewellery, there was a jeweller in the town with the most beautiful pieces Hannah had ever seen.

Hannah decided that the time had come to tell Lili the truth about what was really going on. The next day at the dinner table in their beautiful home was not ideal, but she couldn't keep putting it off. She'd rather Lili and Nate found out in advance that the shop was likely to close rather than close the doors of Nate's grandfather's old shop for good without giving them any warning.

Hannah said, 'Don't worry, I'll be here.'

Maisie turned to her mum, giving her a quick hug. 'Bye. See you tomorrow!'

'Bye, sweetheart. Have fun,' Hannah said.

Nate and Lili stood at the door with William and Maisie, all of them waving goodbye to Hannah.

The image of this perfect family, standing together in front of their beautiful home, made Hannah feel even worse. Maisie looked so happy with them. Hannah couldn't shake the fear that one day Maisie might ask if she could live with Nate and Lili permanently.

She couldn't help but compare her life to Nate and Lili's. They had a solid relationship and the ability to provide Maisie with the stability that Hannah desperately wanted to offer but felt she could never quite achieve.

Back in her car, Hannah took a deep breath and started the engine. She needed to focus. She was determined to prove to herself and to Maisie that she could be successful and create a good life for them. But how? The shop was failing, and she didn't know what to do about it.

She sat in the car and couldn't shake the feeling of being left behind. Everyone else's lives seemed to be moving forward, but hers felt stagnant, stuck in a rut she couldn't seem to escape.

She glanced in the rearview mirror, watching the house

disappear into the distance. It was a new day, and she had to believe that things would get better. For Maisie's sake, she had to keep trying. Her luck had to change, surely.

2

The bell above the door jingled as Hannah stepped into her art and craft shop in Cobblers Yard, the familiar sound a small comfort amidst her worries. The little shop with its old bowed, leaded window was a cosy space brimming with art and craft supplies that Maisie had helped her order – she was the artist. Hannah wouldn't have had a clue.

The shop was stocked with everything a budding artist, or a child who just wanted some crayons and colouring books, would need. But it hadn't been enough to make the shop a success. Despite its charm, she knew that unless something changed drastically, and quickly, the shop would continue struggling to attract enough customers to stay afloat. *I'm not a businesswoman*, Hannah thought. *I haven't a clue what I'm doing*. She couldn't help thinking that Lili's faith in her was misplaced.

She set her bag down behind the counter and took a deep breath, surveying the space. She had poured her heart into the shop, thinking it was just what was needed after everything that had happened in her past. The shop was her dream; a fresh start after a series of bad decisions that had landed her in prison. But the dream had turned into a nightmare. She looked at another bill on the counter that she'd picked up from the doormat on her way in.

Hannah sighed and cast the bill to one side. She saw no way out of the financial mess she was getting herself into unless the shop miraculously became very profitable. She knew she could ask Lili for help, but this shop was meant to be the end of her relying on Lili for support.

Hannah walked over to the shop window and rearranged some of the items on display. It was silly, really, thinking that it would make a difference to the footfall that day. It was the weekend, a Saturday, and should be her busiest and most profitable day of the week.

The trouble was that on those weekends that Hannah didn't have Maisie around, when she was with Nate and Lili, her daughter's constant chatter and happy carefree disposition wasn't there to take her mind off her troubles. The fact was that if she closed early, which she often did on the weekends when Maisie was with her, she knew she wouldn't lose any money. There was little point sitting around waiting for an elusive customer if she could be having fun with Maisie, buying fish and chips in one of the local chip shops in the high street and sitting on one of the benches on the promenade overlooking the little fishing boats and the pebble beach.

Hannah stared out of the window. She watched a young man cross the yard and glance in the charity shop window before stepping into Lili's flower shop. Lili had an assistant who worked in her shop when Lili wasn't there. Her business had flourished, branching into landscape gardening too. She had done very well for herself.

Before Lili's move to the Suffolk Coast, Hannah had thought

her best friend's life was coming together. Lili had been living with her last boyfriend, Alex, in a lovely apartment near Kew Gardens, where Lili had worked at that time. But things hadn't worked out, and Hannah knew that it was in no small part due to her own actions – regularly crashing on their sofa with a young child, sometimes just leaving Maisie with Lili and disappearing.

Lili hadn't been able to say no to looking after her best friend's child – but it had come at a price. Hannah was sure her dependence on Lili had contributed to the breakdown of Lili's relationship with Alex. Things had come to a head when Alex had planned a surprise break away to the Suffolk Coast, staying in a plush hotel right there in Aldeburgh on the seafront. Hannah rolled her eyes. It had been the day that Alex and Lili had been leaving for that unexpected holiday that Hannah had turned up out of the blue to offload Maisie on to Lili so she could fly away on holiday herself with her new boyfriend. Back then, selfishly, all Hannah had been able to think was that her child would cramp her style and get in the way of her new relationship. She hadn't even bothered to ask Lili if it was convenient. *It was all me, me, me back then*, thought Hannah sadly.

Lili's surprise holiday with Alex hadn't been what she'd thought. They weren't getting engaged. Alex had been celebrating a promotion, and a move to Washington, and had been expecting Lili to drop everything – her job at Kew, her best friend, Hannah, and little Maisie – to go with him. If Hannah had known, she would have told Lili to go. But she knew her best friend. She always put others first – and in that case, it had been her and Maisie. Alex had refused to go on the break away with Maisie, effectively making Lili choose.

Lili had chosen Maisie, and took her away, just the two of

them, to stay in the grand hotel instead of going with Alex. That had marked the beginning of the end of their relationship.

After everything Lili had done for her, Hannah didn't begrudge Lili's success with her flower shop business or her happiness in meeting Nate. It was just she wanted a bit of that success and happiness too, and perhaps a little bit of luck.

Luck. She glanced out of the window, willing the young man with the bouquet of flowers to come into her shop. She imagined those flowers were for his love. Maybe he'd think to make a homemade card to go with them. *Of course, he won't come in here*, thought Hannah, watching him. He seemed to stand for a moment looking indecisive before heading across the yard and into the bookshop.

Thea. She ran the bookshop with a young man, a stranger who had arrived in town not that long ago. They'd fallen in love, and despite the secret he'd kept from her regarding his connection with her father's bookshop, when it was revealed, everything had worked out for them.

Hannah sighed when she thought of Lili's other good friend, Abigail, who had settled in the area after inheriting a cottage right by the sea. Of course, that had not made up for losing her husband, who had died tragically young, leaving her a widow, but at least she had the cottage. And she'd fallen in love again too.

Hannah stared out of the window, feeling sorry for herself and wondering why things seemed to work out for the other people she knew who'd gone there to start again. There were quite a few young women she was aware of who had found themselves there on the Suffolk Coast and had never left – who had forged new lives and found love.

'Why not me?' Hannah asked as her eyes locked for a

moment with those of the good-looking guy, who was carrying a beautiful bouquet of flowers and a small paper bag with the name and logo of The Bookshop of Memories.

She smiled his way, thinking stupidly that catching his attention might entice him into her shop.

Her eyes dropped, embarrassed, when he did look her way and caught her staring at him. Of course, he didn't head into the shop. She sighed and looked at her watch. Normally she made it to lunchtime before she closed up and took the afternoon off. Today barely half an hour had passed since she'd opened the shop.

'I am *so* bored.' She looked across the yard at the charity shop. She was always tempted to pop in there and have a look around, knowing that if she did find something of interest – some clothes, or a trinket, or something she fancied treating herself to – it wouldn't exactly break the bank. She could spare a couple of pounds, just.

So far, Hannah had done her best to steer clear of the other shops in Cobblers Yard, especially the charity shop. She'd heard from Lili that Mabel and Marjorie, the two octogenarian sisters that ran the shop, were quite the local gossips. The last thing she needed was for them to find out about her past, and what she'd done in Cobblers Yard, leading to her stint in prison.

Hannah did not want to think about that. Who would have thought that she'd end up running the very shop that she—

The bell tinkled above the shop door, startling her. She'd been so lost in thought, staring at the new set of paintbrushes she was about to put out on display while she ruminated over her past, that she had no idea who had ventured into the yard, let alone her shop.

'Penny for your thoughts?'

Hannah stared at the old lady, who said, 'I was in the shop window, fiddling about with the display, hoping to entice some more customers in, when I saw you doing the same.' She paused. 'You do know who I am – don't you?'

Of course, Hannah did know who she was. 'You're … er … Marjorie?'

'Ah, I see Maisie has mentioned us.'

Hannah nodded. Of course, Maisie had mentioned the friendly old ladies across the yard, but it was their reputation as the town's gossips that had really caught Hannah's attention.

'But no, that's my sister. I'm Mabel.'

In all the months that Hannah had been there, neither of the sisters had ventured over to her shop, even though Maisie had, under Hannah's watchful gaze as she crossed the yard and disappeared inside, run over with her pocket money and looked around their charity shop on plenty of occasions, returning with all manner of bits and pieces that Hannah was convinced her daughter hadn't had the money to buy.

Whilst she'd been considering nipping across the yard and having a browse herself that morning, she hadn't expected one of them to come into her shop. 'Can I help you with something?' Hannah asked expectantly, anticipating that Mabel was there to buy something. After all, what other reason would she have to venture in? She had wondered why neither of the town's gossips had yet come over to introduce themselves and find out about their new neighbour. She could feel the colour rising in her cheeks at the thought that maybe they didn't have to because Maisie had told them everything about her past.

She wouldn't have – would she? Hannah hadn't thought to

tell Maisie not to talk about their private lives. She had just assumed that Maisie wouldn't have reason to talk about their past. She was a child; she lived in the moment.

Hannah eyed Mabel, wondering if they'd asked Maisie any questions.

Mabel said, 'Yes, you can help me … us … with something.'

Hannah's mood brightened considerably. 'Yes?'

'We've had a rather large, bulky item donated. Now we've cleared a space in the window, we're afraid we can't lift it by ourselves. We might put our backs out trying or drop it and damage the item.'

'Oh, right. I see.' Hannah's shoulders sagged. Mabel hadn't visited to buy anything.

'Well, if it's that heavy, why don't you ask Joss next door, or Thea's partner in The Bookshop of Memories?'

'Oh, we couldn't do that – they're far too busy.'

Hannah frowned, thinking, *Of course they are.*

'Well, I'm far too busy too,' said Hannah haughtily, annoyed with Mabel for pointing out how busy the other shops were.

Mabel peered at her. 'Busy doing what – exactly?'

'Rearranging my window display – just like you.'

'Ah, but there's a difference between our window display and yours.'

Yeah – you sell second-hand tat. Hannah didn't voice that thought. The second-hand tat Maisie had brought home with her from the charity shop made her very happy, even though Hannah thought the trinkets were worthless. Maisie spent hours polishing her little ornaments from far-flung places that people had bought in flea-markets or gift shops on their travels, probably in the heat of the moment on fantastic holidays. Hannah guessed that once they returned home with what they thought were their prized possessions from their travels, the novelty quickly wore off, and suddenly the souvenir and the holiday became quite forgettable – at least once they were booking the next getaway. And so the trinkets were given away to Mabel and Marjorie's charity shop.

Hannah imagined there were loads of similar things left at the doors of charity shops up and down the country. Maisie loved nothing better, apart from nipping across the yard to see what new treasures awaited her, than spending her time painting her discarded treasures.

Hannah looked at Mabel, aware that Maisie didn't have the money to buy all those items. Helping them out was the least she could do. 'Perhaps I can spare a moment to come and give you a hand,' she said. She could spare all bloody day, and they all knew it. The Gossip Girls, as they were known, weren't stupid. They had a clear line of sight from the charity shop window straight across the little cobbled yard to her shop. They knew the comings and goings – or lack thereof. She imagined nothing much escaped their notice.

'Let me just get my keys.'

Mabel said, 'You won't need to lock up. I doubt very much anybody will venture in while you're gone.'

'Thanks a lot.'

'For what – speaking my mind and telling it how it is?'

Hannah pursed her lips. 'Can you tell me how to attract more customers?' Hannah asked hopefully.

'Nope.'

Hannah had thought that as an elderly lady who had been running a shop for many years since being widowed – Lili had filled her in about all the other shopkeepers in Cobblers Yard –

Mabel might at least have some words of business wisdom, or even offer some friendly words of encouragement.

Hannah sighed. 'I'm going to grab my handbag.'

'Why?'

'Because I keep meaning to venture over to your shop. Who knows, perhaps, like Maisie, something might catch my eye while I'm there.'

Hannah closed the shop door and locked up. She turned to Mabel, who had left the shop before her, and caught her expression. *What did you bother locking up for?* It was written all over her face. Hannah had a good mind to head off to the high street and do some grocery shopping instead.

'We've got lots of things for sale, from second-hand clothes, bags and shoes,' said Mabel, 'to books, trinkets from far-flung places, and even a bear.'

'A what?'

'Oh, it's not a real bear. It's a rug, actually, with a stuffed head.'

'Urgh! I wouldn't have that if you paid me,' Hannah exclaimed, having second thoughts about having collected her purse on the way out.

'Well, you know what they say,' Mabel continued, as they walked across the yard together. 'One man's trash is another man's treasure.' She opened the door to the charity shop.

As Hannah stepped inside, she couldn't resist saying, 'I'm interested to see all the trashy things in your shop then.'

Mabel smiled at the joke.

Hannah wandered through the shop, her fingers brushing lightly over the various items. She loved the eclectic mix of treasures the charity shop offered, from vintage clothes to old records. As she turned a corner, something caught her eye – a painting, partially hidden behind a stack of books.

Mabel called for her sister. 'Marjorie? Hannah is here to help us.'

'Who?'

Hannah stepped into the shop behind Mabel, not a bit surprised at Marjorie's question. Hannah kept herself to herself. It wasn't even as if the art and craft shop had made a name for itself.

Hannah frowned, thinking that actually, it *had* – just not in the way she would have liked. Not like Thea's bookshop. She remembered how she'd done up the shop, and had a grand reopening party, even inviting a famous local writer to sign her new book at the bookshop. It wasn't fair, how some people just seemed to have luck on their side.

Why can't I have a little bit of luck – like Thea? she wondered.

'You know Hannah – Maisie's mother,' Mabel replied to her sister. 'I told you that I was calling on her across the yard.'

Hannah stood in the doorway.

Mabel turned around. 'Don't dawdle. Let's get this done.'

3

'This is Marjorie.'

Hannah greeted a large, rather overweight woman. Taller than Mabel, she had her sister's eyes, and a kindly, round face. 'I'll go and put the kettle on.'

'Marjorie …' Mabel's voice held a warning note.

Marjorie was already heading to the back of the shop. She turned on her heel and glared at her sister. 'Mabel, you know me better than anyone. I can't do anything without a sweet cuppa first.'

'And a chocolate digestive biscuit,' mumbled Mabel.

Hannah couldn't help but smile.

'All right,' said Mabel. 'I'll show Hannah what we need help with.'

Hannah heard the kettle boiling from somewhere in the back of the shop and the tinkle of a spoon against crockery.

'So, this is it.'

Hannah looked at the back of what appeared to be a framed painting or print. It was quite large with a worn, old-fashioned gilt-edged frame, reminding her of the paintings by the Old Masters she'd seen hanging in art galleries.

Hannah had never visited an art gallery in her life until the discovery that her young daughter was a prodigy. She had a gift for painting that no art school could teach. Hannah didn't know where the gift came from, although she now knew that Maisie's paternal grandparents were artists, so she imagined Maisie had inherited their artistic bent. Her daughter could see a famous painting hanging in a gallery and copy it convincingly, apparently. Hannah didn't know anything about the art world. What she did know was that if she exploited her daughter's gift, told the world about her, it would be the answer to all her financial problems.

Hannah might not know about the art world, or paintings, apart from what she'd learned from Ray and Sarah, but she knew she wanted her daughter to have a normal childhood for as long as possible. She wanted her to go to school, get qualifications in lots of subjects, as Hannah never had herself, and then decide whether she wanted to be an artist when she grew up. She'd even turned down Lili's offer to pay for a private education for Maisie, sending her to a school with an emphasis on the arts. Lili had inherited a substantial sum from her late great-grandfather in the form of a valuable art collection which had been hidden away for decades. Hannah knew that Lili didn't want to sell the paintings to a private art collector but wanted to gift them to a museum instead. Lili would have sold one of the paintings to fund Maisie's education, but Hannah didn't want Maisie to have any preferential treatment. She wanted her daughter to attend the local school with her brother and her peers. And she wanted Lili to follow through with her original plan for the art collection.

Hannah already knew that it was a foregone conclusion – art was Maisie's world, and her talent was innate. But still, she wanted her only child to go to college and have the student experience she had missed out on herself because she'd got pregnant and had a child as a teenager.

Once the art world discovered Maisie, there would be no going back. Their lives, especially Maisie's little life there in Aldeburgh on the Suffolk Coast, going to the local primary school, visiting Nate, Lili and William, and helping her mother in the shop would never be the same again if it became known to the world that at nine years old she could paint like the Old Masters.

Hannah wanted Maisie to have a nice home, like Nate's and Lili's, and nice things – pretty dresses and designer trainers – but she wanted to earn the money to give Maisie those things, not for them to come at the expense of Maisie's simple, carefree, idyllic little childhood on the Suffolk Coast.

Hannah had thought about it when they'd had to move out of the rented cottage and back into the flat over the shop. Was it time to start selling Maisie's paintings? Perhaps she could approach a gallery in London, or an art dealer. She imagined people would pay very good money for an exact copy of a Picasso, or Rembrandt. Maisie could solve all their financial problems – Hannah knew that. But just because she could, it didn't mean she should.

Hannah could just imagine the clamour for a painting from a nine-year-old prodigy. The orders would fly in, and with them the pressure for Maisie to produce painting after painting. She loved to paint. Maisie would happily paint all day and all night if Hannah let her. But she was painting what interested her, painting for fun. She was playing, but instead of with toys, it happened to be with paintbrushes on canvas, creating masterpieces. But it was still play.

What if she *had* to paint? What if she was told *what* to paint – then what would happen? Hannah had no clue, but she could imagine Maisie would get tired, burnt out, and disillusioned – much like an adult upon finding out their dream job wasn't what it was cracked up to be.

And Maisie wasn't an adult; she was still a child. Hannah knew her daughter shouldn't be supporting her financially. She felt enough guilt as it was over how she'd always put her own needs, and those of her past relationships, above those of her own child. Hannah realised she'd acted like a child herself. It was Lili who had been the adult and had taken on her responsibility to look after Maisie whenever Hannah had felt like going off somewhere and it was inconvenient to have a child in tow.

Hannah sighed. She'd put Maisie way down in her list of priorities in the past. And if she now used Maisie as a source of income, exploited her gift for money, what sort of parent would it make her? She wanted Maisie to decide on the direction of her life. Perhaps she'd grow up and forget about art; do something else. Maybe she'd marry, and have children, and become a stay-at-home mum.

Hannah's thoughts were interrupted by Marjorie handing her and Mabel a mug of tea and a chocolate digestive each.

'Thank you,' Hannah said, genuinely appreciative.

Mabel looked at the packet of digestives in Marjorie's hand and said to Hannah, as her sister returned to the back of the shop, 'She must have taken an instant liking to you.'

Hannah looked at her. 'How do you know?'

'Ah, that's easy. Marjorie is rather possessive over her chocolate digestives. She won't offer them to just anybody, I can tell you.'

Hannah thought she was having a joke until she saw Mabel's expression. 'To tell you the truth, I like you too. I think it's rather brave of you to return to the scene of the crime.'

Hannah nearly spluttered in her tea. 'I'm sorry – what did you just say?'

Mabel turned her head in the direction of the front window.

Hannah followed her gaze as Mabel said, 'Joseph's old shop, which you now run.'

Hannah felt blood rushing to her head, her face growing hot with embarrassment. So, they knew what had happened in the shop, what she'd done.

Mabel touched her arm. 'But we don't need to talk about that. You've done your time, and now you're doing your best to make amends.'

Hannah stood stock still. She couldn't believe she was having this conversation. She'd had no idea they knew. She wanted to run right out of the door, but her legs were like jelly and wouldn't move.

'Now, we won't hold it against you. Everybody deserves a second chance, even—'

Hannah somehow brought her eyes to look at Mabel, wondering what she was going to say. Even bad mothers who should have thought about their child before listening to their then boyfriend and ending up getting themselves in big trouble? Hannah didn't know how much they knew – probably just what they'd read in the local newspaper. She suddenly felt very foolish for thinking that avoiding The Gossip Girls, or anybody in Cobblers Yard, would mean they wouldn't know about her background.

'Even the likes of me?' Hannah said.

Mabel squeezed her arm. 'Like I said, everyone deserves a second chance. Now, drink up – we've got this painting to shift.'

Hannah gulped down her tea and passed Mabel her empty mug. She was still feeling embarrassed that they knew about her past, and she couldn't wait to get the task over with. Hannah had already decided that her shop was now closed for the day. She was going to find something better to do, out of Mabel and Marjorie's watchful gaze.

Mabel handed Marjorie the two empty mugs.

Marjorie said, 'I'll just wash these up, and then I'll come and help with our newest donation.'

'We want it in the window,' Mabel said. 'It's not particularly heavy, just quite large, and the frame is bulky. Like I said, we don't want to risk dropping it and damaging the frame. Would be a shame if that happened – then no one might buy it.'

'What's the painting like?'

'Let me move some things out of the way, and we can turn it around.' Mabel carefully moved a stack of books aside.

Hannah took one end of the painting, and Mabel took the other, to turn it around. 'Let's lean it against the wall again,' Mabel suggested, 'Then when Marjorie has finished washing up the mugs, we can all help shift it into the window display.'

As they held on to one corner of the frame each, and moved the painting, Hannah realised it wasn't half as heavy as she thought it would be. She could manage it by herself.

Mabel said, 'We have no idea who the painting belonged to. When we arrived, we found it outside wrapped in old sacking. No note or anything.'

'Just left outside your shop?' Hannah said in surprise.

'Oh, we get all sorts left outside. It's quite normal.'

'But a painting … what if it had rained?'

They'd started turning it around. Mabel said, 'Hmm, I guess that would have been the end of the painting. We've had lots of old framed prints donated, that sort of thing, but never a painting. It's very exciting.'

They carefully propped the painting back up against the wall.

'There now,' said Mabel taking a step back, revealing a beautifully painted canvas. The scene depicted a serene bay at sunrise, the sky awash with soft hues of pink and orange. Seashells lined the shore, glistening in the early morning light. Hannah felt an instant connection to it.

'That's a lovely piece, isn't it?' Mabel said, appearing beside her.

Marjorie joined them, peering at the painting. We were thinking of putting it in the window for the right person to find it.'

Hannah smiled, feeling a strange sense of destiny and thinking *I'm that person.*

4

Hannah stared at the oil painting of a stunning windswept beach with sand dunes and a VW camper van parked on the dunes. But what caught her attention was the focus of the painting – a woman on the beach. She appeared to be collecting seashells which were scattered by the shore and were glistening as though the tide had just come in and washed over them. She was barefoot and dressed in a long, flowing white dress, one hand holding her fly-away golden hair from her face, the other hand full of seashells. Her dress and hair were battling against the wind. Hannah could just imagine it was a beach in Suffolk.

'Oh, my god,' breathed Hannah.

'What is it? Do you know this painting?'

'Not at all. Never seen it before in my life. But I love it. I adore it.' Hannah stared at the painting. She was mesmerised. The light captured in the painting was exquisite, the orange hues capturing a stunning sunrise.

Of all the art galleries she'd visited with Maisie since learning of her daughter's talent, she'd never seen anything quite like this. She wondered if it had been painted by a famous painter. 'Do you think you should consult an art expert or something? What if you've got a masterpiece on your hands and you don't know it?' Hannah had read about instances where people had parted with a few pounds for an item in a charity shop and discovered it was an antique or a famous painting worth thousands.

'Ah, we've already done that. Phoned him first thing this morning, but our resident art expert has never heard of the painting. He suggested it sounded as though it was perhaps painted by a local amateur artist. You know Ray?' Mabel shook her head. 'Of course you do, silly me, he's William and Maisie's grandfather.'

Hannah nodded. That had been a surprise. It was Lili who'd first met Ray. When Lili had taken Maisie on holiday there from London while Hannah had been off on holiday with her new boyfriend, inevitably Lili had visited Ray's shop to buy art supplies for Maisie. Soon after, she'd met Ray's son, Nate. Eventually, Nate had discovered that Maisie was his daughter and Ray's granddaughter. At first, Nate had assumed that, like himself, Lili was a single parent. Hannah had never told Lili who Maisie's father was, so she'd had no idea it was Nate. When Hannah had unexpectedly returned from her holiday abroad, she'd discovered that Lili had taken Maisie on holiday to the Suffolk Coast. When Hannah turned up in Suffolk to take Maisie home, Nate had recognised Hannah and found out the truth; Maisie wasn't Lili's daughter, but Hannah's. He remembered the night he'd spent with Hannah at a party when they were teenagers, but he'd had no idea she'd had a child, his daughter, as a result.

'Anyway, he's quite an art expert – isn't he?'

'Yes.' Hannah knew all about Ray's career in the London

Metropolitan Police, tracking down stolen art. He had been delighted to discover not only that he had another grandchild but that she was an artist with a talent for painting far, far beyond her years. Maisie's half-brother did not share her talent. His drawing and paintings were very sweet, and just what you'd expect a child of six to produce.

God knows where she gets it from, thought Hannah. *Certainly not from me.* Hannah would not embarrass herself by picking up a paintbrush, let alone trying to paint something. But since moving to Suffolk with Maisie, and getting to know Nate's parents – both Ray, and Maisie's grandmother, Sarah – she'd learned a lot more about art and the art world, which she thought stood her in good stead to understand and chat to her daughter about her passion in the future.

Maisie's grandparents had met at university, both studying art. How peculiar life was sometimes, Hannah mused, that Lili's then boyfriend had randomly booked a few days away at a posh hotel on the Suffolk Coast only for Lili to end up taking Maisie instead, and meeting Maisie's father, and grandparents.

Fate. That's what it was, Hannah had decided. She was grateful that she had reconnected with Maisie's father, and that Maisie had loving grandparents who also understood her love of art. Hannah had thought she'd never quite understand it fully – until she'd set eyes on this beautiful painting that had taken her breath away, and made her feel quite emotional, as though she was going to cry. It felt very silly, but she couldn't help it.

'It looks like a beach in Suffolk, don't you think?' Hannah said.

'I do indeed. That's what I said to Marjorie.'

Marjorie came slowly down the shop and joined them in

front of the painting.

Mabel said, 'Hannah is admiring the painting.'

'I'm not surprised. It's quite something, isn't it? The way it depicts the sunrise, with those gorgeous orange hues. Never seen anything quite like it. Not that I'm exactly an art connoisseur – like some people we know.' She winked at Hannah.

Hannah knew Marjorie wasn't referring to herself but her daughter. Cobblers Yard was just too small to keep that sort of secret, but unusually for The Gossip Girls, they had kept it to themselves.

'Still, I expect there's going to be a lot of interest once we put it in the window, don't you agree, Mabel?' Marjorie asked, turning to her sister.

Mabel nodded enthusiastically. 'If nothing else, it's certainly going to attract a lot of attention, and I imagine encourage more footfall into our shop.'

Hannah turned her head and stared wistfully towards the charity shop window, thinking of her empty forgotten shop across the yard and wishing she had something she could put in the window to attract people into her shop.

I could put one of Maisie's paintings in the window, she thought, although she didn't want to attract that sort of attention. And it went against her decision that she would not sell Maisie's paintings and make money from her daughter's talent.

'Does it say which beach it is?' Hannah asked, crouching to look at the inscription in black lettering at the bottom of the frame. She'd been to lots of art galleries with Maisie, and seen countless oil paintings on canvas, so she knew where to look.

Hannah read the inscription. '*Sunrise Over Seashell Bay*.' She stood up, smiling. 'Seashell Bay. Is there such a place in Suffolk?'

Mabel and Marjorie shook their heads.

Hannah looked up at them. 'Are you sure?'

'Positive,' said Marjorie.

'We've lived here all our lives,' Mabel said. 'We should know.'

Hannah stood up disappointed. 'I would love to see this place for real.'

'And there's no reason you can't.'

'How?' Hannah furrowed her brow. 'It's likely a figment of the artist's imagination.'

'But is it?'

'Ah,' Hannah said. 'That makes sense. It feels like the painter was sitting right there among the sand dunes painting his love.'

Marjorie rolled her eyes. 'Oh, not you as well!'

Hannah turned to her, wondering what she was talking about. 'Huh?'

Marjorie sighed. 'My sister. She's always been such a big, soppy romantic, just like you, apparently.'

Hannah had never thought of herself as a romantic.

Mabel looked at Hannah. 'I think that too – about the painting. I can just imagine a man sitting outside the campervan, sketching this scene while his sweetheart walks down barefoot to the water's edge, looking for pretty seashells. I imagine him calling her name, and that moment—'

'Is captured in the painting,' Hannah said enthusiastically.

'Yes, yes,' said Mabel. 'She turns at the sound of his voice, the fresh morning wind catching her nightdress …'

'Oh, you think she's still in her …'

'I think they were staying the night in the campervan parked up amongst the dunes.'

'How could you possibly know that?' Marjorie interrupted.

Mabel ignored her sister. 'The wind caught the dress and her lovely golden locks.'

Hannah looked closely at the figure of the woman, her hand holding her long hair back from her face. She looked like she was maybe in her thirties, although it was hard to be sure. Now Mabel had mentioned it, the figure in the painting looked as though she had just turned at the sound of the painter's voice. And the long flowing white dress could be a nightdress. Although now Hannah was looking at the dress doubtfully.

Mabel noticed her expression. 'What is it?'

Hannah was rather enjoying the story of the two lovers from the campervan enjoying the secluded, deserted beach at sunrise. It was just so romantic – the thought of them waking up to the sound of waves lapping on the shore, and the most beautiful sunrise. And there was something about the thought of the woman getting straight up and running down to the beach without getting dressed that added credence to the wonderfully romantic nature of the painting. Until she saw an obvious flaw in their assumption.

'She can't be wearing a nightdress,' she said.

'Why not?' Mabel asked.

Hannah didn't want to sound mean, but said, 'It might be something someone your generation would have worn – a long nightdress.' Even the word nightdress was old-fashioned, out of another era. She said as much. Nowadays, the woman would be in pyjamas or perhaps something silky, lacy and revealing. Hannah knew all about those slinky little lace numbers, which she'd worn to impress her boyfriends in bed. Although there had been none of that lately. Since she'd moved there, she'd sworn off having another relationship until Maisie was eighteen and had gone to college. She was determined she'd never look at another man until then. Well, she might look, but that was as far as it would go.

Lili had told her that was ridiculous. What if she met someone really lovely, and wanted to settle down, and even have more children?

Hannah remembered her response. Every relationship she'd ever had always went wrong. And when that inevitably happened, it wasn't just her that suffered, but Maisie too, having these guys in and out of her life. And now Maisie had her real dad around, things had worked out surprisingly well without the complication of another man in either of their lives. And Hannah wasn't after having more children. Maisie was her life now. And it wasn't as though she had to feel somehow responsible for giving Maisie a sibling. Maisie already had a little brother.

If Hannah needed any confirmation that she was doing the right thing, she only had to look at her daughter. Maisie was happier than she'd ever been. Hannah knew the reason. For once in her life, Hannah was giving Maisie all her attention – something she'd never, ever done until she'd moved to the Suffolk Coast.

Hannah realised in that moment that when she thought of all the people she knew, or knew of – all the young women who'd gone there for a fresh start, and whom she was rather envious of because their lives appeared to have fallen neatly into place, especially when it came to love – she'd lost sight of something: none of the other women who'd arrived on the Suffolk Coast and had ended up staying and making a life for themselves had gone there as a single parent with a child in tow.

That hadn't stopped Hannah in the past, meeting a guy and

starting a new relationship. So, why was it stopping her now? Hannah realised that for the first time in her life, she had *not* put herself first. This wasn't about her happiness; it was about Maisie's.

She stared at the painting and smiled. It would have been nice if the shop had turned out to be a success. And yes, it would be lovely if she did meet the love of her life there in Suffolk, where she was putting down roots. But she was comparing her life to the lives of Thea, and Lili, and Abigail, and a couple of other young women she'd heard about – one who was living on a houseboat, and another who had moved into her grandmother's beach house.

She realised she couldn't compare herself to them. She may not have had luck with her business or relationships since moving there like the others, but she had made a big success of something she'd been failing at, and which had been the most important thing she'd needed to fix in her life and be a success at – being a mother. And luck had been on her side – she'd found Maisie's father, and they'd succeeded in becoming friends for Maisie's sake. It meant that Maisie had both her father and her paternal grandparents, who meant the world to her.

Maisie. That was where her luck and success had happened. She just hadn't realised it until now. She just couldn't win it all. She didn't have what she believed the woman in the beautiful painting had – the love of her life. After all, who else could have painted such a beautiful, heartfelt painting? It was painted out of love. It shone through the painting. That was what she felt. She said as much to Mabel.

'Oh, for goodness' sake, Hannah! Don't encourage her,' said Marjorie, rolling her eyes.

Of course, the icing on the cake would be to make a success of the business, but just then she was happy with what she had achieved – being the sort of mother that she'd never previously been to Maisie.

5

Mabel said, 'I still think it's a nightdress.'

Marjorie clucked her tongue. 'Didn't you hear what Hannah just said?'

'Yes, but you see, the woman in the painting *is* around our generation – well I would say about ten years older.'

Hannah looked at Mabel.

'How could you possibly know that?' said Marjorie.

'Because there's a date.'

'A date?' said Marjorie indignantly. 'Whatever do you mean?'

'Look here …'

All three bent down and peered at the painting.

'I had a good look at the painting with my magnifying glass after we brought it in. That's when I saw it – right there.'

In the top left-hand corner, where the sky was a dark orange, the painter had dated it, in a slightly darker brush stroke. It was very faint.

'It *is* a date!' said Marjorie, looking surprised.

'See, I told you, Marj.'

'Why didn't you tell me before?' said Marjorie.

Mabel shrugged, and continued, 'I was seeing if I recognised the woman in the painting.'

Hannah turned to Mabel with interest.

So did Marjorie. Raising her eyebrows. 'Well – did you?'

'Did I what?'

'Recognise the woman?'

'Oh, I know that was silly thing to do. It's only a painting, after all.'

Hannah had Googled on her phone, and there was no beach called Seashell Bay in the UK according to the search results. She put her phone away.

'But you do think it's real, don't you? The woman in the painting, and Seashell Bay, even though that's probably a made-up name. But the place isn't made up,' Hannah said, almost pleading. She so wanted it to be real. She wanted to find that beach and see the beautiful sunrise.

'Yes, I do think it's real,' replied Mabel.

Marjorie sighed heavily. 'Oh, really. And next you'll be telling me you recognise her.'

'Oh, but I do, Marjorie.'

'Really, Mabel,' Marjorie put her hands on her hips. 'You've got such an imagination.'

'Alright, perhaps I can't remember her by name, but she does seem familiar.'

Marjorie stared at her sister.

'Vaguely familiar.'

'Oh, Mabel. You're seeing things that aren't there. You want her to be real because you like the painting and the love story you just made up.'

Mabel frowned at her sister. 'I did not make it up.'

Marjorie cocked her head to one side and folded her arms.

'Oh, all right, I did make it up, but that doesn't mean it isn't possible that she is real, and the beach is real, and they were there together on that date, and chose to spend their final hours together there.'

Final hours together? Hannah had resumed studying the painting. She turned to look at Mabel. She was about to ask what she'd meant by *final hours together* when Marjorie piped up, 'Well, if this painting is real then she's braver than us. Do you remember what we were doing, Mabel?'

Mabel creased her brow. 'Of course I do. How could anybody forget that date – I was on my hands and knees, hiding under the kitchen table.' Mabel shook her head. She stared at the painting. 'I think if it had happened, I would rather have been on a beautiful Suffolk beach, collecting seashells with the wind in my hair, and the sound of the waves in my ears, and seeing one final amazing dawn, than on my hands on knees, hiding under a table – the last thing I saw would have been dirty linoleum kitchen flooring.'

Marjorie looked at her sister, and for the first time in the whole conversation, she did not disagree. 'If she was a real person,' said Mabel, 'If I had known her, I think I would have liked this woman.'

'Me too,' Hannah agreed.

Even Marjorie agreed.

'But I don't understand. What you were just talking about – *final hours together*, and *hiding under the kitchen table*?'

Mabel looked at her sister. 'Do you want to explain?'

Marjorie smiled. 'Not really. Who wants to be reminded of that dreadful month?'

'But that's just it, Marjorie. We *have* been reminded.'

Marjorie nodded. 'Yes, the date on the painting. I thought it was familiar.' She looked at Hannah. 'Ever heard of the Cuban Missile Crisis?'

'I remember we vaguely touched on it during history at school. Wasn't it the closest the world ever got to a nuclear war?'

'Yes, and let's hope it stays that way,' Marjorie replied. 'You see, events unfolded rapidly on the world stage during October 1962. We were told that if the sirens went off, we were to get under our desks, or if we were at home, we were to get under the kitchen table.'

'Well, that's ridiculous,' Hannah said.

'Yes, isn't it?' Mabel agreed. 'We're not talking about protecting ourselves from falling debris after a bomb is dropped, we're talking annihilation, and if you do survive a nuclear detonation, then chances are the radiation will get you in the end. But of course, back then, what did we know – or our parents, for that matter?'

Marjorie said, 'Makes you wonder what other things people did when they thought it was the end of the world … unlike us, practising diving under the table.'

'Marj, we should have all done what this couple did – found a beautiful spot in our lovely country and just watched one last sunrise.'

Hannah turned and stared at the painting. If that were true, if that was what the couple had done, and they had captured the moment in a painting, then it just made her love the painting – and them – even more. She stared adoringly at the scene.

Marjorie asked, 'Why are you smiling after we told you that, Hannah?'

Mabel smiled too. 'Marjorie, I think we've found a buyer for our painting already.'

Hannah whirled around to see who had walked into the shop.

Mabel and Marjorie exchanged a glance before Mabel said, 'Would you like the painting, Hannah?'

'Me?' The shop was empty of customers save for her. 'Oh, I'm afraid I couldn't possibly afford—'

'It's a charity shop, Hannah. We are grateful for any and all donations.'

Hannah looked at the painting as she opened her bag and got out her purse. 'A donation,' she repeated. All she had was a twenty-pound note, which she had planned to spend on a bag of grocery shopping. If she spent it on the painting, her dinner that evening would be beans on toast. But Maisie was staying over at Nate and Lili's house that night, so it would only be herself going without. And besides, perhaps Mabel and Marjorie were right: the painting in the window would attract customers. And if it was displayed in her window, perhaps it would attract people inside.

Hannah was about to hand over the money when she realised that she might be depriving the charity shop of more money than she was handing over.

Hannah sighed, explaining why she was putting the money away in her purse. 'You said yourself that it's bound to attract interest. You'll make more money with it in the window.'

'That's as maybe,' said Marjorie, 'but it will sell eventually, and I think we're both agreed that we'd rather see it go to a friend, and a fellow shop owner.'

'A friend?' Hannah hadn't expected them to call her a friend.

'Well, I don't hand my chocolate digestives out to just

anyone, you know,' said Marjorie, holding her chin up and looking down her nose at Hannah before offering her a wisp of a smile.

Hannah smiled too. 'So I've been told.'

'Now, hand us over your money, and the painting is yours.'

'I'm going to display it in my window,' said Hannah, thinking she ought to tell them in case they thought she was trying to fleece them, and their charity, then sell it on for money and make a big profit. 'But it won't be for sale.' Hannah had this notion that the painting she had fallen in love with was going to bring her luck. 'I'm hoping it will entice customers inside.'

'We do normally have customers call in our shop regularly; some come every morning just to see what new things have arrived and to have first dibs. Today, of all days, that hasn't happened. It must be your lucky day.'

Hannah grinned, her smile faltering as she handed over her last twenty pounds. As she watched Mabel and Marjorie wrap the painting carefully in loose bubble-wrap, saying they didn't want anything to happen to it on its travels across the yard to its new home, she prayed that it would attract new customers that day.

'Can you manage, or do you need us to give you a hand?'

'No, I can manage.' Hannah picked it up and carefully held it under her arm. The only disadvantage was having to give up her last twenty-pound note. She didn't want Maisie returning on Sunday to an empty kitchen cupboard that she had no way of stocking. At least they'd have a big slap-up Sunday roast before they headed back to the flat. And then, tomorrow, she might have to ask Lili if she could borrow some money, admitting that things weren't going at all well with the shop.

That had been her plan all along, anyway. She didn't think the shop would miraculously become profitable, with oodles of customers, in one day. She'd been putting off telling Lili the true extent of her financial troubles. She was not looking forward to Sunday lunch and telling Lili what had really been going on in their lives. She'd made Maisie promise not to talk about their move from the cottage back into the flat above the shop. It had been their secret – until Maisie had forgotten to keep quiet.

'But why?' Maisie had asked.

'It's adult stuff,' she'd told Maisie, only for Maisie to surprise her when she said, 'You're embarrassed. I understand, Mummy. But when the shop makes money again, we can get the cottage back.'

Hannah didn't know how she'd kept it together and not dissolved into tears in front of Maisie. Instead, she'd smiled and given her a big hug. She hated herself for then telling Maisie a big lie: that yes, they would be moving out again soon, so there was no need to tell Lili about their temporary living arrangements.

Hannah feared were not temporary at all. Perhaps it was just as well that Maisie had told Lili they'd moved back to the flat. At least it wouldn't come as such a shock if she had to close down the shop.

She walked to the charity shop door, carrying the painting, feeling like she'd won the lottery. Perhaps the painting would bring her luck. Then she saw the easel in the charity shop window upon which the painting would have stood, and the price tag they'd already decided upon. Ten times what she'd paid. Two hundred pounds? Oh dear. It was what she had feared – that the charity shop would lose money because of her.

She stopped at the door, put the painting carefully down by her feet, and turned around.

Mabel held up her hand in a stop sign. 'Don't even think about changing your mind.'

'But the price tag …'

'Oh, ignore that,' Marjorie said with a wave of her hand.

'But I can't!' Hannah thought quickly. She didn't want to give up the painting, but she did have an idea. 'Look, what about displaying a different painting?'

The sisters exchanged glances. 'What did you have in mind?'

Hannah had vowed never to sell one of Maisie's paintings, but it was different if she wasn't making money for herself, and it was for a good cause. 'You can have one of Maisie's paintings. I will ask, but I know she won't mind. She loves coming here. And I know what you two have been up to. She comes back with all sorts of things which I know she hasn't had enough money for.'

Mabel said, 'Whatever do you mean?' She was avoiding eye contact.

Hannah shook her head. 'You know very well. Now look, I'll bring one of the paintings right over when I've taken this—'

'Oh, dear me, no,' said Mabel, glancing at her sister. They both shook their heads.

'Absolutely not,' agree Marjorie.

'Oh,' Hannah was quite taken aback. 'But you know about Maisie and how good she is at painting.' She realised it was a stupid thing to say. Of course they knew.

'That's the point,' Mabel said, chuckling. 'And I think *good* is a bit of an understatement – don't you?'

'So, why wouldn't you want one of her paintings to sell and make a bit of money for charity? In fact, I could give you more than one. I know Maisie won't mind.'

'I've seen what Maisie paints,' said Marjorie.

'You don't like her paintings?'

'Don't be daft,' said Marjorie. 'She paints like … like …'

'An Old Master.'

'Yes,' Marjorie eyed her sister before she turned to Hannah. 'You see, that's rather the problem.'

'Are you saying she's too good?' Hannah looked at them in surprise. 'I don't understand.'

Mabel stepped forward and affectionately squeezed Hannah's arm. 'Now, picture the scene. Someone comes along and sees Maisie's painting in the window. Now, I know she loves to copy the Old Masters – and it would take a professional to tell the difference …'

Hannah had an idea where she was going with this.

'So, picture the scene,' she said again. 'A customer walks in and thinks we've had an original painting by an Old Master handed in. This customer imagines it was probably a probate thing – that someone had cleared out a relative's house and hadn't realised the value of the painting. So, they buy the painting, giving us a few quid and not telling us what they think they know – that they've got a real Rembrandt or Picasso, or any other painter you can think of that Maisie has copied. So, off they go to an auction house, thinking they are in the money, I mean *really* in the money. And then they discover it's fake.' Mabel's eyes went wide. 'Sorry, I didn't mean to lessen Maisie's ability as an artist, but you know what I mean.'

'I do. If I wanted to make pots of money from art forgeries, you've certainly come to the right place,' joked Hannah. She quickly added, 'That was a joke.'

'We know,' Marjorie said, smiling. 'If you'd wanted to make money out of your daughter's exceptional talent, you'd have done it by now. We noticed you are all keeping her talent firmly under wraps – as are we.'

'Yes, it was agreed within the family. It's what I want, for her to have a normal childhood.'

'We guessed that. And that is why we cannot, under any circumstances, display her painting here. You see, and I know this is all in theory, but if a person were to discover such an expert copy, the next question would be – who is the artist? And the discovery that a nine-year-old child had such talent would, well … she'd be the biggest thing since sliced bread in the art world.

'And our lives would never be the same again.' Hannah knew Maisie painted when she spent every other weekend with Nate, but they were both in agreement that Maisie got away from behind a canvas and did normal things for a child her age. Having a little brother helped enormously, and she was always joining in playing games in the garden and throwing a ball with their dog.

'I imagine everyone would want to know the little girl who paints as though she has decades of knowledge and experience.'

'I imagine she – you – would make lots of money.'

'Yes,' Hannah said. 'But that would be the end of her idyllic little childhood in Suffolk with her family and friends, and her little trips across the yard to see you both.'

Of course, it wasn't that idyllic now she was stuck back in a flat above a shop, but if she couldn't turn things around soon, then Maisie would have to go and live with Nate in their lovely house until things changed. That was the last thing Hannah wanted, but she was clear on her priorities. 'Maisie comes first,' she said. 'She's too young to decide on this sort of thing – fame and money. So right now, I'm protecting her from all that.'

'As are we all,' said Mabel. 'Now, take that the painting you have fallen in love with, and we wish you lots of luck with your shop.'

Hannah gave them both a hug, surprising the sisters and herself. She realised that quite unexpectedly she'd made two life-long friends.

Marjorie said, 'When you have another spare moment, we hope to see you back – with Maisie, both of you – for tea and biscuits and another browse around our shop.'

'But we can't promise you another painting like this,' Mabel joked.

'Shame,' Hannah replied, but she wasn't joking. She'd have loved it if there was another painting by the same artist.

'That's if she has the time with all the new customers she's going to attract, Mabel.'

Chance would be a fine thing, thought Hannah. But she felt a flicker of hope. Maybe this painting was the key to turning her fortunes around. She thanked Mabel and Marjorie and headed back to her shop, eager to display her new find.

6

Hannah walked over to the window display, straightening the crafts she had arranged the day before. Her eyes fell on the centrepiece of the display: the beautifully painted canvas titled *Sunrise Over Seashell Bay*. As soon as she'd returned from the charity shop with the painting, she'd place it prominently in the window display, standing back to admire her handiwork.

The vibrant colours immediately brightened the display. She hoped it caught the eye of anyone passing by and enticed them into her shop. She looked out on to the empty yard and admonished herself. The painting had only been displayed in her window for ten minutes. What was she expecting – a sudden stampede of new customers?

Mabel and Marjorie were in the window of the charity shop across Cobblers Yard removing the easel now they had no painting to display.

They saw her in the shop window and waved. Hannah smiled and waved back. She sighed. It was only half past nine on a Saturday morning. She'd have to wait until people ventured into the yard for Joss's free legal advice next door, or to buy a book from Thea's bookshop, or maybe some flowers from Lili's or to have a browse in the charity shop. There was Reggie's music shop next door to the charity shop too. She'd just have to be patient and see if anyone paused outside her shop to admire the painting and – if she was lucky – it enticed them inside.

As she adjusted the painting, the bell above the door jingled. Hannah's heart leapt at the thought of a customer. It would be quite unusual to have a customer so early in the day.

Hannah stepped out of the window to see who it was. 'Oh, Lili – I didn't expect you this morning.'

Lili walked into the shop carrying a bouquet of fresh flowers. 'I know it's my day off, but we've brought William and Maisie to the beach this morning for a walk. We're going to paint some stones. Then we're going to have fish and chips on the beach.'

'Where are Maisie and William?'

'Ah, they're with Nate, having fun on the beach. They didn't want to come with me while I looked in on my shop.'

Hannah did feel sad that Maisie hadn't want to come with Lili and say hi to her. She knew it was a silly thought, but she couldn't help feeling excluded.

'It goes without saying that you could join us for lunch, and if you wanted to close early, you could meet us in the cinema at half past two. They're showing a children's movie.'

On any other day, that would have been very tempting, considering that by early afternoon, she would normally have given up on having any customers and shut the shop to spend time with Maisie instead. She glanced at the painting. But today would be different – at least that was what she was hoping.

Hannah smiled. 'That's really kind of you to offer, especially as it's your weekend to spend time with Maisie, but I need to keep the shop open.'

'Ah, yes, I didn't think you'd want to close early. After all, it is Saturday – busiest day of the week.'

It is for some, thought Hannah, frowning when she glanced across the yard and saw several people walk into Lili's flower shop.

'Hey, what's the matter?'

Hannah forced a smile. 'Nothing.'

'Now, don't tell fibs to your best friend. I know when something's up.'

Hannah was just preparing to tell Lili what was going on with the shop when Lili said, 'I know what's going on.'

Hannah looked at her, eyes wide in surprise. 'You do?' *Of course she does*, she thought. There were no customers in the shop.

'It's Maisie. She didn't want to come and see you this morning.'

'Yes, that's it,' Hannah replied, heaving a sigh. That wasn't all of it, but it certainly hadn't helped.

'If it's any consolation, it certainly isn't me and Nate that she wants to spend time with instead – or William. We bumped into one of her school friends taking a walk with her parents.'

Hannah felt her mood lifting when she heard that. 'Maisie loves her school friends,' she commented.

'Yes, I know. We were understandably disappointed that we weren't spending the afternoon together as a family.'

A family. Hannah pursed her lips, trying to keep her emotions in check when she thought of Maisie with Lili, her dad, and her little brother – a *proper* family.

She knew that if she'd voiced that thought, Lili would have admonished her, reminding her that just because she and Maisie were not in a traditional family structure – if that was still a thing, even – it didn't make their little unit any less of a family.

'She's getting to that age, isn't she, Hannah?'

'How do you mean?'

'Wanting her friends. Soon, she probably won't want much to do with any of us – she'll just be on her mobile arranging to see her friends.'

'I'm not buying her a mobile phone.' Hannah didn't want to hear that. It was something she knew was coming but tried not to dwell on – the thought that Maisie would have her teenage friends and do her own thing at the weekend. Just then, Hannah had a focus – to take care of Maisie, and take her out, spending time with her; something she'd rarely done with her daughter when she was young. Now that she was doing things properly, there was niggling question: what would she do when Maisie didn't need her anymore – when she left home for university, if that what she chose to do? Hannah had thought she had years before she felt that aching loneliness for someone to be in her life. But Lili had just made her realise that she might be alone sooner than she'd thought. Not in terms of Maisie going to live with her father – although that was always a possibility – but because in a few years' time she'd be a teenager, and her mum would be the last person she'd want to spend time with.

'Look, I wish I hadn't said anything, Hannah. Here, I'm sure this will cheer you up. I've brought you something …' Lili thrust the gorgeous bouquet of autumnal flowers in Hannah's direction. 'I brought you these.'

Hannah looked at the large colourful bouquet. 'Oh, Lili, you shouldn't have. You know I can't pay for them.'

'How many times do I have to tell you that they are a gift?'

This wasn't the first bouquet she'd given Hannah and wouldn't be the last. Hannah knew what she was up to. She always popped in on the pretext of delivering a bouquet of flowers after Maisie had stayed at theirs to check she was all right.

'I'm perfectly capable of spending the night on my own,' Hannah had said the first time, guessing that Lili had used the flowers as an excuse to check up on her. 'Those flowers look very expensive.' She hoped that someone had reneged on their order, and that was why Lili had decided to give them to her.

'Oh, these?' Lili said. Do you know how many flowers don't make the grade and end up on the cutting room floor?'

Hannah did not. But what she did know was that these flowers did not look as though they were rejects. The expression on her face must have given her away.

'Besides,' said Lili in a small voice, 'they're wilting a bit. Not any good for a fresh bouquet.'

The flowers looked plenty fresh to Hannah. She said as much.

'I'm glad you think so. I'll find a vase to put them in then.' Lili walked off towards the stairs at the back of the shop. She was familiar with the flat above the shop. Very familiar. This was where she'd stayed, invited by the then shopkeeper, Joseph, when her holiday on the Suffolk Coast with Maisie had come to an end and she'd had to vacate her hotel. She'd split up from her last boyfriend and had found she had nowhere else to go. The kindly old gentleman had taken her in – and the rest was history. Oh, how Hannah had to force herself not to be envious of how far Lili had come in the months since she'd made the Suffolk Coast her home; of her thriving business, beautiful home and instant family.

Instant family. Hannah raised her eyebrows, thinking of Nate, William and Maisie.

Lili stomped up the stairs.

Hannah raised her eyes, hearing Lili's footsteps on the ceiling. She looked at the flowers that Lili had deposited in her arms and suddenly remembered something. She had hardly any food in the cupboard or in the fridge.

'Shall I make a cup of tea while I'm here?' Lili called down.

That reminded Hannah that she had no milk either. 'Er ... no, no – that won't be necessary. I'm very busy, you know.' She was just frowning at her outright lie when the bell above the shop door suddenly tinkled, making her jump in surprise.

Hannah turned around to find that the people she was sure had just been in Lili's flower shop were now in hers. One was carrying a bouquet, the other a small potted plant. She overheard one of them say to the other, 'I need some notepaper, but I was going to leave it until we stopped off at the big supermarket in Ipswich.'

'What made you change your mind?'

Hannah tried to melt into the background, pretending she wasn't earwigging on their conversation. 'That painting caught my attention.'

'Mine too.'

'So, I decided to pop in for that notepaper, and see what else caught my eye.'

'Are you interested in the painting?' her companion asked.

'Who wouldn't be? It's just so vivid, isn't it? With those orange and golden hues. I could stare at it all day. I can just imagine the price tag, though. I couldn't afford such a beautiful painting.'

'No, me neither.'

'Well, I'm sure in a place like Aldeburgh there will be plenty of people with deep pockets who can.'

'It's not for sale,' Hannah blurted, immediately wishing the ground could swallow her up for revealing she was listening in on their conversation. She expected them to ask her why she had it displayed in her window if it wasn't for sale. Instead, her new customer said, 'Well, if it was mine, I wouldn't sell it either, dear. It does make for a very lovely window display.'

'I'm hoping it will draw people in,' Hannah said honestly.

'Well, we're here, so that's a good sign. How long has it been in your window?'

'For about half an hour.'

'Well, there you go,' said her friend. 'I think you're on to something.'

Hannah smiled at them. 'So, you need some notepaper?'

'Oh, yes, but first we're going to have a browse. You know, every time we visit the yard, my friend and I have been meaning to pop in here, but we've just never got round to it.'

'Until today,' Hannah said brightly, her eyes drifting to her good-luck charm on its easel in the window. She felt like jumping up and down and punching the air. It was working.

'I see we haven't been the only ones visiting Lili's flower shop.'

'Oh, I didn't—'

'You should put those in water.'

Lili appeared at the back of the shop with a vase of water. Hannah's two new customers spotted her immediately and waved. Hannah could just imagine the three of them greeting each other like old friends when they visited Lili's shop. Hannah supposed Lili's regular customers *were* on friendly terms with her. If only she could build up a clientele like this who visited week in, week out.

'Oh, Lili, we missed you today.'

'Shhh! I'm not meant to be here,' she said to her customers. 'It's my day off. I'm just visiting my friend.'

They both turned to look at Hannah, studying her.

Hannah could feel her face growing red under their scrutiny.

'We didn't know you were Lili's friend.'

'Oh, yes – we go way back.'

One of the friends turned to the other, and said, 'See, I told you we should have popped in and browsed this shop sooner,' as though being Lili's friend was a recommendation.

Hannah sidled up to Lili with the flowers, watching her first customers of the day – in fact, of the whole week – browsing her shop. As she gave Lili the flowers to snip and arrange in the vase – Lili had brought down a pair of scissors too – she whispered, 'It sounds as though my new customers are pleased that we know each other.'

'Yes, it's surprising how much business can come our way through word of mouth,' said Lili, smiling as she took the flowers, snipping the ends into a carrier bag before arranging them in the vase she'd placed on the counter.

'Is it?' Hannah asked.

'You have no idea. I didn't like to say when I handed you the keys to this shop. It seemed like a good idea at the time, but I can't lie – I was worried.'

'About me?'

'About the business, especially in this location. Building it up and getting customers is quite a feat, I can tell you. It's all about friends telling friends and building it up through word of mouth in the community. After all, very few tourists and people unfamiliar with the area are going to show up in the yard – you'll be lucky if they even know where it is.'

'So, that's what you've been doing – checking up on the shop?'

'No, checking up on you, really, and hoping you're not getting disillusioned when things don't take off immediately.

'But your shop is successful. It's been making me feel—'

'Disillusioned. Yes, I get that.' Lili furrowed her brow and followed Hannah's gaze.

'You don't think I'm cut out to be a businesswoman.'

'No, no – that's not it at all,' said Lili still keeping her voice down so that the customers didn't hear their conversation. 'Look, I just think anyone starting a business in a small town such as this starts with a huge disadvantage.'

Hannah didn't see how that was the case for Lili. 'But your shop doesn't appear to have started that way.'

'Only because I took it on with loads of customers that were shopping there already. I'm no businesswoman, if that's what you're thinking. I owe its success to my predecessor, Sarah.'

Lili finished arranging the flowers and took both of Hannah's hands in hers. 'I didn't mean to set you up to fail. Can you forgive me?'

Hannah was about to say something when the bell tinkled again. She turned to see more customers trooping in. Each took a little basket by the door for their purchases and glanced in the window as they nodded at Hannah.

Hannah turned back to Lili, and said, 'I don't think you have. In fact, I'm starting to feel lucky. Thanks, Lili.'

Lili glanced at the customers browsing the shop and adding lots of things to their little wicker baskets. 'Don't thank me. You make your own luck.'

'Yes, but sometimes you need a bit of help.' Hannah grinned. She had a feeling that Lili hadn't spotted the new addition to her window display. She wasn't sure how that had happened. After all, Lili must have crossed the yard. However, she'd had the bouquet in her arms and was probably keeping an eye on the petals, making sure the arrangement was just so before she walked into the shop.

Hannah left her customers to browse and hopefully heap their baskets full of purchases. 'Follow me,' she said to Lili. 'I've got something to show you.' She took Lili outside the shop.

7

'How did I miss that?' Lili turned to Hannah, wide-eyed. 'Did Maisie paint that?'

'No, it's old. There's a date on the painting – 1962. It's called *Sunrise Over Seashell Bay*.'

'Hmm, *Sunrise Over Seashell Bay*.'

'Do you know it?' Hannah asked eagerly.

'The painter?'

'No! Seashell Bay.'

'I don't think there is a Seashell Bay in Suffolk.'

'That's just what Mabel and Marjorie said.'

'They've seen it too?'

'Oh, I bought it this morning from the charity shop. They think – well, Mabel thinks – this beach is somewhere in Suffolk, and the painter just made up the name. I'd love to find it.'

'Why don't you get in touch with whoever handed it in – the painting – and ask?'

'Well, that's the thing. It was left outside last night wrapped in an old sack. No note, nothing.'

'Curiouser and curiouser,' commented Lili.

'What do you mean?'

'Well, it's a gorgeous painting. And the painter is clearly in love with their subject. And presumably the woman was in love with the painter, so why give it up?'

'Unless it's been inherited, and both of them are dead, and their relatives really couldn't care less about it.'

'That is possible. Then again, why leave it here anonymously in the dead of night, and early, before the shop opened? Surely if it was inherited, there would be a lot of other stuff they wanted to get rid of too. Why just the painting? It's a bit strange.'

Hannah stared at Lili. She did have a point. Hannah glanced around the yard. 'It's a shame there's no CCTV here.'

'We don't need that. We're a trusting lot, us shopkeepers in Cobblers Yard.'

Hannah felt her face grow red hot at that comment – if they weren't so trusting, she couldn't have broken into Joseph's antiques shop.

'Oh, Hannah, I didn't mean to bring up …'

'It's all right. It was just a figure of speech.'

'Exactly.'

Hannah still wished Lili hadn't made the comment. Betraying Lili's trust the way she had, and ending up in prison, still haunted her. She cast that thought aside, really not wanting to revisit that horrible, humiliating episode in her life. If it wasn't for Lili stepping in and looking after Maisie, she'd have lost her to the care system, foster parents, and may not have got her back. She shuddered at the thought.

'Why don't you ask around. If the beach exists, surely someone will recognise it?'

'Will you ask Nate to stop by and take a look at it?'

'Of course I will. He grew up here, didn't he?'

Hannah nodded.

'You know what? Let me take a photo on my phone. Then I can show him and text you if he knows anything about the painting or the painter.'

'Thanks, Lili.' She watched Lili get out her mobile from the back pocket of her jeans and take a photo.

'Actually, I'll send it to him,' Lili said.

'Oh, you don't have to.'

It was too late – she had. Disappointingly, Nate texted back almost immediately. He'd never seen the painting before and didn't recognise the beach.

Hannah shrugged. 'Ah, well. It was worth a try.'

'Look, I'm just nipping back to the flower shop before I go and meet up with Nate. I'll let my assistant know to mention the painting in your window. Who knows, someone might stop by and give you the answers you're looking for.'

'Oh, I hope so.'

Lili turned her attention on Hannah. 'It means that much to you?'

'Yes. Don't ask me why. It just does. I love this painting.'

'I never thought I'd hear you say that.'

'I always say that about Maisie's paintings.'

'But she's your daughter. You'd say that if she just drew stick men.'

Hannah smiled. 'I know her artwork is exceptional, but I was never really a lover of art. I had no idea about the art world until I met Ray and Sarah. I have to be honest, though. I've now been to a lot of art galleries, and seen a ton of artworks, but this painting is different. It really resonates with me. I would love to find that beach, and the artist who painted it.'

Lili turned to the window. 'Well, it's displayed prominently in your window, and I'll be sure to ask everyone in Cobblers Yard to tell their partners and friends about it. Perhaps they might mention it to their customers in conversation – have you seen that wonderful painting in the art shop window?'

'It's not for sale, though. I don't want people thinking that.'

'You could put *Sold* by the painting.'

'But I haven't sold it.'

'Technically, it has been sold – by the charity shop to you.'

'Ah, yes. That's true.'

'Perhaps you'll be lucky, and someone will happen along who recognises it.'

Hannah hoped so. In the meantime, she thought she might search online and see if any similar paintings popped up. Maybe the painter had painted others. She shared her thoughts.

'Good idea, Hannah.' Lili peered in the shop window. 'Oh, look! You've got quite a queue forming at the checkout. I think you'd better get back inside.'

For a split second, Hannah thought Lili was having her on, but when she looked through the window, she was shocked to see a queue snaking through the shop. Other customers had walked into the shop while they were standing outside.

Lili looked at her mobile. 'Ah … Nate says William, Maisie and her friend are occupied at the trestle table on the beach painting stones.'

Hannah knew what she was talking about. Near the RNLI station, beside the old hut on the beach, there was a trestle table with a selection of paints and paintbrushes, and loads of different-sized stones collected from the beach that children could paint with little motifs and even messages before leaving their stones around the town. 'They're going to be a while, I bet. Why don't I help you for a bit? You could take payment for their purchases while I bag them up. How about it?'

Hannah looked at her doubtfully as she opened the shop door. 'Are you sure? It is your day off, and you do love spending time with Maisie when she's staying.'

'It's fine. She's with her friend, so she doesn't care about Auntie Lili.'

Lili was affectionately called Maisie's auntie even though they weren't related. Although Hannah was aware they soon would be, by marriage. She'd become Maisie's stepmum.

Lili rolled up her shirt sleeves. 'Come on – at this rate, it looks as though there's going to be quite a lot of stock to reorder by the end of the day.'

Hannah couldn't believe she'd started her day staring out of the shop window, imagining the shop would be dead and she'd be closing early. 'I think I might keep the shop open for longer than usual.'

More people were crossing the yard from the bookshop and glancing in the shop window before stepping inside. Hannah had never thought she'd utter the words *rushed off my feet*, but when Lili invited her to join them for lunch – fish and chips on the beach – although Hannah was grateful for the offer, and she was tempted, she had to decline. The sunny day had already clouded over, and it looked like rain, which meant they would be eating in the fish and chip restaurant, but that wasn't Hannah's reason; she wouldn't mind that. What she didn't want to do was lose any potential customers because the shop had closed at lunchtime.

'I'm going to stay open all day.'

'In that case, I'll stay and help.'

'No, Lili. I appreciate you helping me with this queue, but afterwards go and spend time with Nate and the children. You're going to see a movie – remember?'

'Oh, yes. I forgot. All right. But before I go, I'm going to pop upstairs to your flat and make you a sandwich.'

Hannah could feel her face glowing red hot with embarrassment at the thought of Lili discovering her sparse kitchen cupboards and virtually empty fridge. There was a box of cereal and some milk left, but no bread or sandwich fillings. Hannah caught her arm. 'No, please don't do that. I'll nip to the Co-op around the corner and grab a sandwich.'

'All right. As long as you're sure.'

'Yes, positive.'

'I think it will probably do you good to have a break for lunch – don't you?' Lili motioned to the window.

Hannah raised her eyebrows. She turned to Lili. 'Where did they all come from?' There was a group of people gathered around her window, looking at the painting.

'I guess I didn't need to pop into the other shops to ask them if they'd drop your shop into conversation after all.'

Hannah grinned. 'I guess not.' It seemed that everybody who ventured into the yard was stopping by her window display.

The two ladies who had been first in the shop walked up to the counter, their little wicker baskets brimming with purchases. Hannah thought, *I'm going to need bigger baskets* as she took the items one by one, cashing them up on her register and passing them to Lili, who bagged them up.

'Who's next?' Hannah called out, smiling at the queue of customers that had suddenly appeared. The next customer stepped up to the counter. In conversation, Hannah asked each one whether they'd noticed the painting in the window. Of course, they had. But not one of them could give her any information about it, apart from letting her know how much they loved it, and in some cases asking if it was for sale.

An hour later, when there was a lull at the till, Hannah saw Lili texting. She looked at her watch; the morning was flying by. It wasn't long until lunch time. 'Lili, I can take it from here.'

Lili looked up from her phone. 'Are you sure? Sorry, Nate keeps texting, asking where I am. I told him I'd just stopped by your shop. He's been asking me what's taking so long, so I told him I was just helping you out for a bit.'

Hannah frowned. She expected that hadn't gone down well. Nate was aware of how much Lili had helped her out over the years, and she could just imagine him getting annoyed with her helping in Hannah's shop when it was her day off.

Hannah waved her off at the door. Lili turned around before leaving. 'I can pop in after lunch, check you don't need a hand before we head off to the cinema?'

It was all Hannah could do not to tell her off. 'I'll get cross if I see you here again today, Lili. Go spend time with your—' The word *family* caught in her throat. When they married, Nate and William would be her new family – and that did include Maisie. Her best friend seemed to have fallen into this wonderful life, with a good man in Nate, and an instant family, all the things that Hannah – who had come close to marrying many times before – just never seemed to achieve.

As if reading her mind, Lili put a gentle hand on Hannah's shoulder. She leaned down, gave her a goodbye peck on the cheek, and whispered, 'Things will work out for you in the end, I promise.'

Hannah imagined she'd guessed what she was thinking and was just being kind. Nobody could make that sort of promise.

At the door, Lili turned around. 'You've got the painting. It's brought you luck already. Who knows …' she said lowering her voice so the customers browsing in the shop didn't overhear. 'Perhaps you'll look through the window one of these days and a handsome young man, the man of your dreams, pausing to look at your beautiful painting, will be staring right back at you.'

Hannah's eyes darted over to The Bookshop of Memories. She rolled her eyes. She knew where Lili had got that idea – Thea. The man of Thea's dreams had turned up at the bookshop, and although he'd kept his real identity under wraps for some time, and it had nearly spelled disaster for both of them – Hannah had heard all about it from Lili – they'd patched things up, started a relationship and never looked back.

They ran the bookshop together, although she understood that Thea's dad, who sadly had dementia, still lived there and thought he ran the bookshop. Keeping herself to herself, Hannah hadn't visited the bookshop and introduced herself. After having met Mabel and Marjorie, who were lovely, she resolved to walk across the yard and introduce herself.

Hannah glanced over her shoulder at her shop, which was brimming with customers. At this rate, she didn't know when she'd find the time to make social calls.

Still, Hannah scoffed at Lili's absurd idea of her finding love right there in Cobblers Yard. 'That will never happen.'

'Why ever not?'

'Because I always end up with the wrong sort of guy – you know that. And besides, I'm not that lucky.'

'Really? I have an idea that stumbling upon that painting this morning has turned your luck around.'

Hannah couldn't argue with that.

Lili smiled encouragingly. 'And long may it continue.'

'Excuse me.'

'Oh, no – excuse *me*!' Lili said, stepping aside for another customer to enter the shop – two, in fact.

'Such a gorgeous painting in the window,' the young man commented as he stood in the doorway.

'You don't like art,' the young woman with him commented. 'You're always dragging me away from coming into this shop whenever we come into the yard for you to visit the bookshop.'

'Well, today I changed my mind. What do you need?' he asked her.

'Really – you're going to buy me whatever I want?'

'If you can paint me something like that, then yeah, go for it.' The young man turned around and looked at Lili and Hannah. 'Sorry, do you work here?'

'I do,' said Hannah.

Lili mouthed something that Hannah ignored – she knew what she was getting at; the guy was cute. But he had a girlfriend already – most did. And she imagined most wouldn't be interested in a young woman with a very gifted and rather precocious nine-year-old who had a mind of her own, and a very loud, argumentative voice when she felt like it.

Hannah smiled at Lili as she waved goodbye and headed off. She followed the customers into the shop. 'How can I help?'

'Is the painting for sale?'

'You want to buy a piece of art?' His girlfriend looked positively stunned. She turned to Hannah. 'I'm sorry, just ignore him. He won't set foot in a gallery, says he doesn't get the whole art thing.' She turned to him. 'And now you want to *buy* a painting?'

'Don't worry, I used to be just like that. Didn't get the whole art thing really,' said Hannah. She felt guilty for saying it when she had such a gifted artist-in-residence. But it was true. 'Until I saw this.'

The young woman turned to the guy she was with. 'Anyway, you're wasting your time. I bet we couldn't afford that painting.'

'We might, if you didn't need to purchase that list of stuff.'

'But it's for college, and I need it.'

'You're at college studying art?' Hannah asked.

'Yes. Fine art. I'm starting my second year in the autumn term, just a couple of weeks away when the first year finishes their freshers' week.'

Hannah stared at her. She was imagining Maisie all grown-up at art school. She knew that it was years away, but then again, her first nine years had gone by in a flash.

The young man walked over to the painting to look at it more closely.

The young woman said, 'I'm a student, so money is tight, but my boyfriend is in work so I could really do with him treating me to some supplies before I return in September.'

'Well, lucky for you and me, the painting isn't for—'

A loud thud interrupted Hannah.

'Oh, no!' exclaimed the young woman, looking over Hannah's shoulder at the window. 'What did you do?'

Hannah closed her eyes and slowly turned. She could barely bring herself to look.

'You were going to say it isn't for sale, weren't you?' the student said through gritted teeth. 'I suppose you'll be wanting us to buy it now we've broken the frame.'

'The frame?' Hannah's eyes shot open. She rushed over to her precious painting with a huge sigh of relief. While she was extremely fond of everything about the painting, at least it was only the frame that was broken – that could be repaired or replaced.

Hannah was about to say yes, the boyfriend should pay towards repairing the frame, when she saw that all the customers in the shop had stopped shopping and were looking her way.

Hannah pursed her lips and thought better of asking the young man for money.

He said, 'It was an accident. I hardly breathed on it.'

'You idiot!' The young woman folded her arms. 'You touched it – I saw you.'

Hannah stared at her. She did not want an argument over the broken frame in the middle of her shop. That was a sure way to empty the shop of her customers. They might not come back.

Hannah diffused the situation. 'It's fine, honestly. It was an old frame.' At least that was true. 'It's my fault, really.' Hannah did blame herself. 'I should have secured the painting on the easel. It's quite large. It could have slipped off any time.' A gust of wind from the front door, or even someone slamming it shut, might have dislodged the painting. When she had propped it up there, she had known the easel wasn't the same size as the one that had been in Mabel and Marjorie's shop window. She knew she should have listened to her instincts and waited until she'd ordered something more appropriate. But she hadn't. And there she was with a broken frame.

'Here – let me help you.' The young man helped her prop the painting back up in the window, using a chair from behind the counter. It wasn't ideal, but at least it could still be seen from the street, and it wouldn't fall off the easel again.

Hannah managed to prise the broken frame edge temporarily back in place, although she'd seen the state of the back of the painting. The old brown tape had given way, and the backing was bulging out. She'd need to get that fixed too, along with the frame.

The young man got out his wallet, still offering to pay for the damage.

'No, please, it's fine. Why don't you continue to shop, and I'll throw in an item for free just for the inconvenience.' Hannah had no idea why she'd blurted that. Then again, the young woman was probably going to buy a lot of supplies, and if she was happy, and so was her boyfriend, they'd be back. *As long as he doesn't go near my window display again*, she thought.

She stared at her painting, feeling relieved. It could have been worse; he could have damaged the painting. She heard him ask his girlfriend, 'Is it for sale, though?'

'Are you seriously asking that question after you damaged it?' She held up her hand. 'Don't answer that. Lucky for us it isn't for sale, otherwise she might have insisted you buy it.'

Hannah overheard him say, 'Shame.'

He got a punch in the arm for that. 'Now, hold this basket. Actually, I'll need at least four.' Armed with two baskets in each of her boyfriend's hands, her new customer started shopping.

8

Hannah slipped behind the counter and spent the rest of Saturday afternoon serving customers, packing up their items, and hearing the beautiful ring of her old-fashioned cash register as she rang up purchases. Her eye drifted to the painting propped up on the chair, and she found herself wondering where she could go to get the frame repaired. In the worst-case scenario, she'd have to get it reframed.

She was sure she had some superglue somewhere at home. She shook her head. What was she thinking? She could damage the painting if she spilled the glue. She'd need a professional. She'd have to use some of the takings from that day, which she wasn't happy about, but then again, without the painting she'd have spent the morning alone in the shop and would probably have shut up early and joined Lili for fish and chips on the beach and the cinema in the afternoon.

Whilst that would have been fun if the shop had still been quiet, Hannah preferred having the shop as it was, buzzing – even though she now had a damaged picture frame along with an unexpected bill. The thing she didn't want was to have to send the painting away to be mended.

She looked at all the art and craft materials in her shop. It was a shame she couldn't fix it herself. She wondered if Maisie's grandfather, Ray, might be able to, or might know someone with that sort of expertise locally.

Hannah was still thinking about that when she closed the door on her last customer at five to five on Saturday afternoon. She was about to turn the sign in the window to *Closed* but thought better of it. There were still five minutes to go. Time enough for a last-minute shopper.

She was tempted to keep the shop open longer but decided against it. Cobblers Yard now looked deserted; the last of the shoppers and the visitors to Joss's office next door were drifting out of the yard, and she needed time that evening to reorder stock. Besides, she'd worked hard, her takings were through the roof, and she felt exhausted.

As she was about to pull the blind down at the front window, looking out for anybody else in Cobblers Yard, she caught sight of a tall, slim gentleman who looked to be around retirement age stepping out of the bookshop. He had a head of silvery grey hair and a moustache that made him look quite distinguished, and he was wearing a long black coat. Hannah spotted Thea in the doorway, closing the door and turning the sign around to *Closed*.

The older gentleman, who was carrying a book in his hand, passed by her shop, glancing in the window as he strode purposefully by.

Hannah was just about to pull the blind, deciding to call it a day five minutes early after all. Cobblers Yard was now deserted, and the other shops were closing too. Then she spotted the tall, slim gentleman suddenly stop on his way out of the yard and turn around.

She thought nothing of it, apart from wondering if he'd accidentally left something in the bookshop. Then his face appeared in the window, startling her. She was standing to one side of the window, so the man hadn't spotted her. His pale blue eyes stared fixedly in the window.

She knew what he was staring at – the painting. He must have glanced at it as he passed her shop. The expression on his kindly face was one of surprise or disbelief; Hannah wasn't quite sure which. But what she was sure of was that he was not someone who had been drawn to her shop window just because he *liked* the painting. He obviously recognised it.

Hannah stood stock still, staring at him. He got out a white handkerchief and nervously wiped his brow, where beads of sweat had suddenly formed. She thought for a moment that he might faint. The colour had suddenly drained from his cheeks.

She turned from the window, thanking her lucky stars that she hadn't turned the door sign to *Closed*, expecting he'd walk into her shop and ask after the painting. But he did not appear. She walked to the door and opened it, hoping to catch him. He had gone.

She ran outside and spotted him on the small lane between the shops which led out into the high street. She chased after him, unsure what she'd say if she caught up with him. She wanted to know who he was and what connection he had to her painting.

Without locking her shop, she raced across the cobbled yard and down the lane, coming to an abrupt halt in the high street. It always surprised her how busy it was, with cars going by and people looking in the pretty boutique-style shop fronts. She looked left and right, trying to see the old gentleman – he shouldn't be that hard to spot, she thought, with his old-fashioned, long black coat. She spotted him getting into a car parked along the street. 'Damn!' Hannah exclaimed, catching the attention of a couple of passers-by, who raised their eyebrows.

Hannah didn't know whether she'd catch him, but she ran all the same, wondering what she'd say if she did manage to get to his car and bang on his window for him to stop. But she was too late anyway. She stopped in the middle of the street when she saw the car pull away from the kerb. It was just as distinguished as the old gentleman. Hannah had no idea what the make and model of the old car was, but she knew it was very old, maybe from the sixties – although from what she could see there wasn't a speck of rust. Its blue paintwork and little chrome wing mirrors gleamed. She imagined that the old car was regularly and lovingly polished.

Hannah was disappointed that she hadn't managed to catch the man, but at least she'd recognise the large vintage car if she saw it again. She was convinced that the old man could tell her something about the painting. Would he return to Cobblers Yard? She had no way of knowing, although she was aware that the yard was more frequented by people local to the area who were aware of its existence.

She was just walking back to her shop when she noticed that the lights were still on in the bookshop. That wasn't unusual. She and Maisie weren't the only ones who lived in a flat above their shop. Thea's dad lived above his shop too, but not on his own; she'd heard there were carers who stayed overnight. He couldn't live on his own, but at least he could still stay in his own home. Hannah knew that he never ventured outside of Cobblers Yard. It sounded to her that if he was amongst familiar things – the same routines, and people and places – he could still function without his condition robbing him of the life he loved just yet.

She wondered how advanced his dementia was, and whether he would remember the gentleman who had just visited his shop and bought a book. Had he been in there before? Was he a regular customer? Did they know his name?

For the second time that day, Hannah decided to venture out of her shop and introduce herself to one of her shop neighbours in the yard.

She returned to her shop and paused for a moment in front of the painting in the window. She had a thought: why close the blind in the shop window? Obviously, she didn't want to encourage a break-in by leaving the gorgeous painting in the window for all to see when the shop was closed. She cringed at the thought of a break-in, remembering her own past and what she'd done right there in Cobblers Yard.

She didn't want to think about that. Her life was on a new trajectory now; she had a flourishing business, albeit one that had only really taken off that day. Who knew how long it would last? Whatever the future held, just then, Hannah wanted to enjoy it – although she did still want to know more about the painting that had changed her luck and brought her so many new customers that day.

She couldn't imagine that anybody would really venture into the yard after closing time, so there was little point leaving the blinds up and the painting on display. Why tempt fate? Why attract unwanted attention? She went inside and drew the blinds, and then made sure the door was locked before heading for the bookshop. She knew the bookshop was now closed, but she didn't want to wait until Monday to ask about their last customer of the day. They might not remember by then whom she was talking about.

Hannah got there just in time. Thea was in the window, rearranging a display. Hannah tapped on the window. She knew Thea would recognise her; she had waved from time to time, and Hannah had waved back but had not gone to the door to say hello. She regretted that now, especially as it would seem as though she only wanted to meet Thea because there was something she wanted – information.

Thea looked up, surprised to see her. She left the window display and unlocked the bookshop door. 'Hello.'

'Hello. I'm Hannah from the art and craft shop.'

'Oh, yes of course. I'm Thea. It's lovely to meet you. Would you like to come in and browse? Or did you have something particular you're after? We're closed, but I'm just putting out some more stock, so you're welcome to come in.' Thea opened the door wide.

9

Hannah stepped inside. It wasn't like other bookshops, with their table displays showcasing newly released books, and books of the same genre grouped together on clearly labelled, modern bookshelves.

'Goodness! You have a lot of books.'

'Ah, yes, customers new to the bookshop can be a little overwhelmed.'

Hannah stared around the cluttered shop, which was rammed full of floor-to-ceiling bookshelves. There were boxes full of books on tables, and even on the floor.

'It's mainly a second-hand bookshop, although I display new releases in the window to get people's attention and draw people in.'

Hannah thought of her painting and understood.

'My father has collected so many books over the years and won't hear of de-cluttering. However, you'd be surprised how many people come to us looking for an old book that is out of print and find that we have a copy.'

Hannah nodded. She glanced around and saw that one corner of the bookshop had an old sofa, a coffee table, a lamp, and a coffee machine. It made her think of setting up a corner of her shop with a table and art and craft materials that could occupy children while the adults browsed. 'That's a lovely idea, having a little space to sit with a book,' Hannah remarked.

Thea followed Hannah's gaze and smiled. 'Yes, I thought so. Mabel donated her old coffee machine that she said she'd hardly used, although I did live to regret that a little … at first.'

'Oh dear,' said Hannah, pulling a face. 'You felt obligated to keep it even though it makes terrible coffee?'

Thea shook her head. 'Oh, no, it wasn't that. The machine makes the best cup of coffee I've ever tasted. Would you like to try one? They come in pods – we have …'

Before she knew what she was doing, Hannah had taken a seat on the rather comfy old leather sofa while Thea reeled off the names of the different coffee pods. Hannah had never heard of most of coffee choices. She opted for Puerto Rican at Thea's suggestion.

A few moments later, after much gurgling and puffing of steam from the coffee maker, Thea handed her a mug of frothy coffee. Hannah gingerly tasted it. She looked at Thea. 'Wow, that old machine does makes an amazing cup of coffee.' She paused. 'So, how come you regretted taking the coffee maker? I don't see what's not to like.'

Thea looked about her and lowered her voice. 'Well, you know the saying, nothing in life is free …'

Hannah listened, trying to curtail a smile when Thea told her that every day since Mabel had gifted her the coffee machine, Mabel had come into the bookshop for a cup of coffee, elevenses, and a natter. Thea did smile, though.

'Don't get me wrong; I do love my neighbours in Cobblers

Yard. We're quite the little community.'

Hannah's heart sank at hearing that comment. She felt guilty for keeping herself to herself, although she did have her reasons. But now, in the space of a day, with her shop suddenly thriving, Hannah had quite forgotten all her cares and was enjoying sitting on the sofa in The Bookshop of Memories, enjoying the coffee and Thea's company.

'It's not that I don't like my shop neighbours coming in for coffee,' Thea quickly added. 'It's just that most times, Mabel sits here for so long over her coffee that Marjorie has to come and fetch her, and then I've got both The Gossip Girls on my sofa. I wouldn't mind if on occasion they bought a book!'

Hannah smiled. She could just imagine the two of them rather enjoying their free coffee.

Thea grimaced. 'I shouldn't have called them The Gossip Girls.'

Hannah was still smiling. 'Why not?'

'Ah, you've heard their reputation as the town's gossips.'

Hannah nodded, remembering why she was there. She told Thea about the painting she'd bought in the charity shop that morning and placed in her shop window. 'To be honest, Thea, my shop hasn't been doing well at all. I've been spending my days worried about it, and it hasn't helped seeing the influx of customers to your shop, and Lili's flower shop, even the charity shop, when hardly anybody has been coming into mine.'

Thea sat down on the sofa next to Hannah. 'Oh, Hannah, I wished you'd come in for a coffee and a chat. I'm not sure how I can help, but even so, you know what they say – a problem shared is a problem halved.'

Hannah wasn't sure how she could help either – until that

evening. 'Actually, there is a way you might be able to help,' she said.

'Oh, I'd love to – just tell me how.'

'I put this painting in the window, and suddenly it's turned my fortunes around. Today my takings have been amazing.'

'Really? That's wonderful – sounds like the painting has turned out to be a good-luck charm.'

Hannah thought so too.

'It doesn't sound as though you need my help.'

'Well, actually, I'd really like to know some background on the painting. Mabel told me they found it this morning. It had been left outside the charity shop.'

'Ah, people leave boxes of trinkets and bags of clothes outside the charity shop when it's closed a lot. I think it's easier for people to get a parking space just outside the entrance to Cobblers Yard to offload things when all the shops are shut.'

'Yes, but a painting … although Mabel said it was wrapped in some sacking. Even so, what if it had rained?'

'Yes, I see what you mean. I've never heard of a painting being left outside the charity shop.'

'It's such a lovely painting – I just had to have it.' Hannah was too embarrassed to tell Thea that her impulse buy had cost her the last twenty pounds in her purse, which had been intended for grocery shopping. Worse still, that she'd discovered, on her way out of the charity shop, that the real price tag was ten times the amount she'd paid for it. Hannah had put by some of her takings, aiming to do that each day until she had the full amount she should have paid for the painting, so that she could donate the money to the charity. If Mabel and Marjorie wouldn't take the money, which she had a feeling they would not, then she intended to donate it to their charity anonymously.

Thea shook her head. 'I'm so sorry, but I doubt I'd know anything about the painting. Can you tell me more about it?'

'It's called *Sunrise Over Seashell Bay*.'

'Doesn't ring any bells.'

'I think the place in the painting exists somewhere in Suffolk,' Hannah said. It was what she was choosing to believe until she was proved wrong. 'I think the painter made up the name.'

'I can nip out across the yard to your shop and have a look.'

'Thank you,' Hannah said, 'you don't have to do that now, though. I was hoping that someone might happen by and recognise it.'

'That's definitely a possibility. I would assume that someone local donated it.'

'Yes, yes, I think you're right. So anyway, I was just closing the shop today, when a gentleman glanced in my shop window as he passed by. I thought nothing of it, obviously, until he suddenly stopped, did an about-turn and walked up to my shop window. Now, I've had a lot of people today drawn to that painting, but I saw the expression on his face.'

'He recognised it?' Thea asked.

'Yes, I think so.'

'What did he tell you about it?'

'Nothing. Even though I hadn't turned the sign to *Closed* in the shop door, he still didn't come in. Didn't even attempt to. Just hurried away.' Hannah decided not to mention that she had followed him down the little lane and emerged into the high street only to see him get into a car and drive away. 'That's where I was hoping you could help.'

'Perhaps he'll visit again. After all, it was nearly closing time. Perhaps he had somewhere to be.'

Hannah remembered him speeding off in the old vintage car. It had certainly appeared that he had somewhere to be; he had seemed in quite a hurry.

'He visited your bookshop and bought a book. So rather than wait and see if he returns, I was rather hoping …' she trailed off.

'He bought a book just before closing time?'

Hannah nodded. 'I was just going to close the blind when I saw him step out of your shop with a book. He must have been your last customer.'

'Can you describe him?'

Hannah had thought Thea would remember her last customer, who had only left the shop fifteen or twenty minutes earlier, but she described him anyway. 'He was tall, slim, around retirement age. He was wearing a long coat, kind of old-fashioned, like a man would wear to work with a suit, I guess. He had silvery grey hair and a moustache.' She still thought he had looked quite distinguished, and shared her thoughts with Thea.

Thea looked at her with interest. 'All right – come with me. Let's go and ask my dad.'

'Your dad?'

'Yes. I'm afraid I was sorting some stock at the back of the shop, so I didn't see him.'

'Does he sound familiar?' Thea asked as they stood up from the sofa.

'He does, actually. Although I'm afraid I wouldn't know him by name. Dad serves all the customers who buy books.'

'Oh, I see.' Hannah tried to hide her disappointment. She

expected Thea's dad would struggle to remember, although she did wonder whether he might have written down the sale in an old-fashioned ledger.

'Dad!'

'Yes, Thea?' An older man, small in stature, with thin, greying hair, spectacles, and a kindly round face appeared from behind a bookcase with a book in his hand. Sparkling blue eyes settled on Hannah. 'Oh dear, I thought we were closed. I'll go back to the counter so I can serve our customer.'

'No, it's fine, Dad. This is Hannah. She's popped in to say hello. She has a shop in the yard.'

'Really?' Thea's dad peered at her. 'You're new – aren't you?'

Hannah hadn't only just moved in, if that was what he meant, but she didn't want to confuse him, so she just said, 'Yes.'

'Welcome to Cobblers Yard, Hannah.' He put the book down and enthusiastically shook her hand. 'Welcome, welcome. We're all friends here. We're always in and out of each other's shops.'

Hannah knew this wasn't quite true; he was probably just remembering something from years earlier. She guessed that if Thea's dad ever ventured outside, he would get confused and frightened – his condition quickly manifesting itself the moment he left the yard. She didn't know what his short-term memory was like. Would he even remember the last customer who'd been there minutes earlier? Would he even remember her once she'd left the shop?

'So, Dad, what can you tell me about the last customer you served before we closed the shop today?' Thea said.

Hannah described the well-dressed gentleman with silvery grey hair, providing the same details she had to Thea. She wanted to know if the man had been in before. Was he a regular customer? Did Thea's dad know his name?

Thea was standing there with her forefinger on her chin. 'I do know who you mean – he's a regular customer. I just don't know his name. He always insists on being served by my father. Apparently, they go way back, but he won't say how they know each other.'

Both young women turned to look at Thea's dad.

'Dad? That man who comes in regularly, the one Hannah just described. He says you two go way back. Is he your friend?'

Thea's dad stood there, eyes wide behind his glasses.

Hannah whispered, 'Perhaps he doesn't remember.' She was trying to be tactful by at least not specifically mentioning his dementia. She hoped he didn't overhear her.

Thea whispered back while her dad stood there scratching his chin. 'When it comes to the past, I swear his memories are pretty much all there.'

Hannah raised her eyebrows at that, extremely pleased to hear it.

Suddenly, Thea's dad shook his head and picked up a few books out of a box that he had been placing on bookshelves. 'Oh, dear me. No,' he said.

'You don't remember him, Dad?'

'Of course I do, but …'

Hannah's shoulders sagged. She'd known there would be a *but*.

'But what, Dad?'

'I am sworn to secrecy.'

Hannah thought this was unlikely. The old man had only been there to buy a book. What could he possibly be hiding?

'Why were you sworn to secrecy?' Thea persisted.

'Percy and I go way back. And I made a promise that I would never tell.'

Hannah stared at Thea's dad. Was it her imagination, or had he just told them the old guy's name? *Percy.*

'Never tell? Dad – what are you talking about?'

'Sworn to secrecy,' he said, tapping his nose. 'Now, I must get on with stacking the shelves before your friends arrive. Just make sure you keep it down when you get in from the party as I shall be in bed.'

'You've got friends visiting?'

Thea shook her head and grabbed Hannah's arm. 'Sorry, I didn't mean to grab your arm quite so harshly,' she said, letting go when they were behind a bookshelf out of earshot of her father. 'It's the carers. We tried to explain why they come during the night, but we just can't seem to make him understand. He thinks I'm like a teenager having friends round.'

'Oh, I see. I am sorry. It's just so sad.'

Thea's face crumpled, but she didn't cry. Instead, she swallowed and moved on. 'Sorry, I … we can't be of any help.'

'Oh, but he has helped. He said his name – Percy.'

Thea frowned. 'That's not much to go on, is it? Hold on, let me check the ledger.'

'You have a ledger?' Hannah said in surprise. Although it had crossed her mind that they might have one, she'd quickly dismissed the idea. It was very old-fashioned. But then again, so was Thea's dad. She guessed that Thea's dad had become a father later in life.

Thea motioned for Hannah to join her at the counter. She opened the ledger and ran her finger down the page to the last entry. 'I'm afraid it just says *Percy*.'

Hannah rolled her eyes.

Thea said in a low voice, 'I guess if they are friends who go way back, why would he put his surname?'

'There's no address either.' Thea added, 'Look, next time Percy comes into the shop, I'll nip across the yard and let you know.'

'Oh, Thea that is so kind of you.' Hannah had not expected her to do that.

'Not at all. I'll have a look at your painting too. Who knows, maybe I'll recognise the beach.'

Hannah was about to ask if she'd come and look straight away when there was a knock on the bookshop door.

'Ah, that will be the carers. They are a lovely couple. We always have a little catch-up and chat about how Henry – that's my dad – is getting on, even though they only saw him last night.'

'I'd better be off then.'

'It's been lovely chatting,' said Thea. 'You must stop by again, have a coffee.' Thea surprised Hannah by stepping forward and giving her a hug. She said, 'If you need anything, anything at all, just pop in.'

Hannah thanked her. She was just turning for the door when she had a thought. 'Thea, there's just one more thing …'

'Yes?'

Hannah glanced at the ledger. 'What book did Percy buy?'

❖

'Percy,' Hannah said to herself as she crossed the yard. She stood outside her shop, staring at the painting in the window. Her eyes drifted to the corner of the frame, which she'd fitted back together. It had come loose again – she could see the small gap between the painting and the frame.

She glanced over at the bookshop and wondered if Thea might happen to know someone. The trouble was that Hannah didn't want her painting gone for long. Thea had been right when she had said it had brought Hannah luck. She didn't want to part with it, even for a short time. It occurred to her that as it was only standing in the window, as long as no one touched it, it should be okay left where it was. She decided it wasn't going anywhere. In the meantime, she'd try and look for a picture-framing service that could send someone to her shop to fix the frame, or even re-frame it if necessary.

Hannah yawned. It had been a very busy day. At least the next day was Sunday. After a lie-in, she was going to do a stock-take and put an order in for more stock before she drove over to Lili and Nate's house for a Sunday roast. She didn't feel like doing the order that evening as she'd originally planned. She just wanted a long, hot soak in a bath. She was looking forward to the next day now that she no longer had to face a difficult conversation with Lili about her financial situation.

She still couldn't believe that in the space of one day, her fortunes had turned around. Hannah had counted her day's takings, and she knew that if the situation continued, she could eventually put down a deposit and take on another rental. Although she and Maisie could live quite adequately in the little flat above the shop, it didn't feel like a home.

The cottage they'd been renting had felt like home, with its beamed ceilings, woodburning stove and cottage garden – Maisie had enjoyed sitting out in the sunshine with her easel, and Hannah had loved sitting on a bench under the kitchen window with a book, enjoying the summer sunshine peeking through the trees of the wild garden.

Hannah didn't know if the estate agent had rented the cottage again since they'd left. She hoped not, but even if it were still available, she knew she'd have to wait at least that month to get the deposit money together. But that wouldn't stop her finding out if it was still empty and starting to look for another suitable place if not.

It was only early September, but she did not want to spend Christmas in the flat. That was why her good-luck charm had to stay in the window.

She stepped into the shop, turned the sign to *Closed*, and thought of Percy. She still had no way of finding him. The book he'd bought hadn't given her any clues – she didn't know why she had bothered asking. It was a second-hand non-fiction book on auctions.

Thea had said there were some small auction houses in Suffolk where you could send your furniture and other items. Perhaps he had some connection to those auction places, Thea had suggested.

Then there was his distinctive car. She hadn't brought that up when she'd chatted to Thea. Perhaps someone who worked in the local Co-op, which he'd parked outside, would know of the car and its owner.

Hannah turned to look at the painting in the window. She smiled, thinking she wouldn't bother visiting those auction houses or questioning the shop assistants in the Co-op. Percy was a regular visitor at the bookshop, by the sound of it. Percy would be back.

10

'I've got something to show you, Maisie,' said Hannah as they walked down the lane between the shops to Cobblers Yard.

'What is it?' Maisie asked, her hand in Hannah's. They swung their arms back and forth.

Hannah had Maisie's school backpack with her pyjamas, toothbrush and toothpaste, reading book and favourite teddy slung over her shoulder. They'd just returned from Sunday lunch at Lili and Nate's house, where Hannah had picked up her daughter after her sleepover. As expected, Maisie had had a fantastic time with her dad, soon-to-be stepmum, and her half-brother, William. However, Hannah had felt very different when picking her daughter up compared to when she'd dropped her off just the previous morning.

What a difference a day makes, thought Hannah. Now her fortunes had turned around, and she didn't have to tell Lili that things weren't working with the shop. After Maisie had already mentioned their move back to the flat, she had told Lili that the move was just temporary while she looked for something better. That had taken Lili by surprise. 'I thought you loved it there,' she'd said.

It was just as well Maisie hadn't been able to keep a secret because Hannah had realised that she couldn't keep where they were living from Lili. What if Lili popped round to the cottage for some reason, and she wasn't there? She just didn't want to tell Lili she'd had to move out for financial reasons. Hannah had been trying to think up a reason for the move, when Lili had said, 'I'm not surprised you moved back to the flat.'

Hannah had said, 'How so?', wondering if Lili had known all along that she'd been struggling to make a living out of the shop.

'You want your own home. You can't pay a rent *and* save up a deposit, can you? It makes perfect sense to move back to the flat temporarily.'

Hannah had stared at her best friend. *My own home.* She didn't know why it hadn't crossed her mind that if the shop continued to do really well, rather than save up a deposit and hand it all over, along with rent money, to another landlord, she could get a mortgage and buy something instead.

Hannah had hugged Lili, who'd asked, 'What did I say?' Hannah had just shaken her head, and said, 'Can't I give my best friend a hug?' Lili had helped her out in so many ways over the years, putting her own life on hold to help Hannah with childcare, and now she'd given her the best idea. It would mean they'd be living in the flat for longer while she saved for a deposit to buy something, and it most likely would not be in Aldeburgh, which was very expensive. It would have to be somewhere in the countryside, which would be cheaper. It would mean she couldn't walk to work, but that was a small price to pay for a place to call her own.

Hannah had enjoyed eating a Sunday roast with Lili and Nate in their large farmhouse-style kitchen overlooking the extensive garden. She'd been thinking of her plans to move out of the flat and back into a cottage, if she could find something suitable. Better still was Lili's idea to save up for a place of her own. It would not be on the grand scale of Nate and Lili's house, but then again, there was only her and Maisie – how much space did two people need?

Unless two people became a family of three – or four. Hannah smiled at such a silly thought. She knew that she was young and pretty and could attract all sorts of guys. But therein was the problem. She did tend to attract all sorts of guys – normally the wrong sort, who invariably led her into trouble, or didn't want her child around. And the thought of meeting a guy with a child too, as Lili had with Nate … well, she supposed that might make them father material for Maisie, but she wasn't sure, unlike her best friend Lili, that she had it in her to be a mother to someone else's child – it was enough with her own.

They stopped in Cobblers Yard, Hannah exchanging a smile with Maisie before she looked over at the little art and craft shop. Her smile faltered when she had a thought – perhaps she shouldn't get ahead of herself and make plans just yet. What if the successful day had been a blip, and the novelty of that painting in the shop window, and the shoppers beating a seemingly endless path to her door, subsided? Or more worryingly, just fell off a cliff?

'What is it?' Maisie asked, looking up at her mother.

Hannah swept her blonde bob behind her ears. 'Oh, it's nothing. I was just thinking about the flat. I'm not sure how long we'll be living there exactly.'

Maisie just shrugged.

'But we will find somewhere – I promise.'

Don't make promises you can't keep, said a little voice in her head.

But I'm going to keep this one, she silently replied. There was no reason she wouldn't, unless the shop's takings nose-dived.

'I wasn't talking about living in the flat, Mummy.'

'Oh, right.' Hannah looked down at Maisie, wishing she hadn't said anything, although she did have to remind herself that Maisie was nine – a big girl, as Maisie kept telling her. She'd said recently, 'You can tell me things, Mum. I'm not a baby anymore.'

Hannah had managed not to shed a tear at that comment. She'd wanted to say, *But you'll always be my baby.*

'You said you had something to show me, Mummy.'

'Oh, yes, that's right.' Hannah brightened when she thought of her good-luck charm. She led Maisie to the shop and stopped outside. Maisie looked up at her mum. 'It's in the yard?' she asked, looking about her.

'Well, yes, sort of.'

Maisie raised her eyebrows.

She gently took her daughter's shoulders and turned her round to face the shop window. 'Just wait right there.' Hannah whipped into the shop and pulled up the blind. A moment later she joined Maisie outside. 'What do you think?'

In that moment, Hannah just realised she was asking an artist, and a prodigy, about the painting. Hannah wanted her to love it just like she did, not critique the brush strokes, or the style, or the use of colour, or whatever else she might be about to notice. She unlocked the shop door and pushed it open.

'Oh, Mummy, I just love it.' Maisie ran straight past her and into the shop.

'Maisie – wait!' As Hannah rushed into the shop, she had

visions of Maisie touching the painting and knocking it over from where she'd propped it up carefully. This time, the whole frame might come apart.

To her relief, Maisie did no such thing. She was standing in front of it in the window display, transfixed. 'Where is this beach?'

Hannah smiled at her reaction. 'That's what I want to find out.'

'I'll look for Seashell Bay online.'

'I tried that. I'm afraid the painter made the name up. But I think the place is real, and it's right here on the Sunrise Coast. That's what Mabel and Marjorie think too.'

Maisie turned around. 'They've seen the painting too?'

'Well, actually …' Hannah told her all about her first visit to the charity shop. She'd enjoyed meeting the sisters and having a cuppa and a chocolate biscuit with them. A thought occurred to her. 'Do you get chocolate biscuits every time you go there?' she asked.

Maisie avoided eye contact, probably thinking she was in trouble. She said in a small voice, 'Yes.'

'Well, I've been missing out by not coming with you, haven't I?'

'See! I told you you'd love it there. Mabel and Marjorie are *so* nice.'

I'll say, thought Hannah. Not only had they let Maisie 'buy' things with her measly pocket money – Hannah intended to up her weekly pocket money if the shop continued doing okay – but they had let Hannah buy a painting that was worth a lot of money.

Maisie turned around, frowning when Hannah told her

where the painting had come from. 'You bought this in the charity shop?'

'Um, yes,' Hannah replied, wondering what was wrong with that.

'But why would someone give up such an amazing painting? I don't understand.'

Hannah did. Or at least she thought she did. The more she studied the painting, with its cared-for old VW campervan parked in the sand dunes, and the beautiful sunrise, and the equally stunning woman collecting seashells on the beach, the more she believed it was a love letter to the woman the painter loved. *She's dead*, Hannah thought with a start. The love of the painter's life is gone, and he couldn't bear to look at this painting anymore, and although he wanted to be rid of it, either the painter or the family couldn't bring themselves to destroy it, so they left it anonymously at a charity shop.

'But if they wanted to sell it, why didn't they put it in an art auction, or advertise it online, or approach an art gallery?'

Approach an art gallery. Hannah smiled at her young daughter. Anyone listening in to that question would wonder how a nine-year-old could articulate so well. But when it came to art and the art world, she didn't just paint beyond her years, producing striking and sophisticated paintings – she was also wise beyond her years.

'I think they are grieving, sweetheart, and although they loved their painting, they needed to let go, like I'm guessing they had to let go of the woman they loved. I think you're right – they could have made a lot more money, but that wasn't the point. They could well have just thrown it away …'

Maisie looked at her mother, clearly aghast at the thought.

'But,' Hannah continued, 'they chose not to, and gave it to a charity shop instead where someone ordinary, someone like me, might happened upon it, and love and cherish it just like they once did.'

'The painter?'

'Yes, the painter.'

Maisie turned to look at the painting. 'Can we find the beach in the painting, Mummy?'

Hannah grinned. 'That's the plan.'

'Do you think the campervan will still be there?'

Hannah frowned at a sudden thought. What if she was just reading way too much into the painting, and seeing what she wanted to see? What if it was just a work of imagination? It was one thing being disappointed herself, but the last thing she wanted to do was disappoint her daughter.

'Mummy?'

'Oh … yes!' Hannah slapped a smile on her face. 'Well, we'll have to find the beach first and then see if the campervan is there.' It looked new in the painting; if it did still exist, then it would have to be lovingly maintained to still look so pristine. That was, if it had ever existed. Hannah was back to thinking she'd read too much into the painting – even the existence of the beach.

She glanced around the shop. Rather than focus on things that might not exist, she knew that she had to focus on the things that did – her shop, and the money she needed to earn. But it was Sunday, and the afternoon was free to focus on Maisie.

'I'd like to find out about the painter too,' said Maisie.

Hannah decided to steer the conversation away from the painting. 'Now, what are we going to do this afternoon?'

11

'I want to find the painter,' Maisie said excitedly. 'I know how, Mummy. We just look for the campervan then we've found the beach – and the painter.'

Hannah sighed. If only things were that simple. She didn't want to burst Maisie's bubble, but she didn't want to lie to her either.

'Maisie, this painting – it was painted decades ago, sweetheart.'

'How do you know?'

'Mabel found an inscription.' Hannah decided not to mention the significance of the date – the Cold War or the nuclear threat at that time. She'd rather not give Maisie nightmares.

'If the campervan did exist, and the painting wasn't a figment of the painter's imagination, then I don't think the painter or the van will still be there, decades later, I'm afraid.'

'It wasn't painted from imagination,' said Maisie.

'Why do you say that?'

'I don't paint from imagination.'

Hannah thought of the outline of Cobblers Yard Maisie had

drawn on a canvas. It was sitting on an easel in front of the window in the flat upstairs. She was going to paint the yard outside. 'I know that's how you paint, but other artists have a different approach – look at the expressionists.'

Hannah resisted a smile. She wasn't arty in the least, which was kind of funny given that she ran an art and craft shop, but thanks to Maisie's grandparents, at least she knew enough to have a conversation with Maisie about art.

'You can't know that for sure,' said Maisie, following her mum up the back stairs to their little flat above the shop.

Hannah stopped at the top of the stairs, watching Maisie head up too. 'Know what for sure?' she asked. She crossed the small landing, carrying a bag of groceries from the local Co-op, to the old-fashioned kitchen with its eighties-style light oak kitchen cabinets and brown linoleum floor. She had been so busy the previous day that she hadn't had time to shop, but on the way home from Nate and Lili's they had visited the Co-op and bought all Maisie's favourite things – her favourite cereal, which Hannah hadn't been able to afford to buy for a while, and peanut butter, which was also pricey, and chocolate croissants for breakfast, which were a treat they'd had when living in the cottage before she'd realised that paying for everything using credit cards on the assumption that the shop business would take off was a big mistake.

'That the painting isn't real,' Maisie replied. She suddenly ran up to the kitchen counter. 'Is that Nutella?'

Hannah grinned. When they'd arrived back in the high street after their Sunday meal at Nate and Lili's, Hannah had told Maisie she wanted to pop into the Co-op to grab some groceries she hadn't had time to shop for. Maisie had looked at her crossly and asked for the shop key so she could go home while Hannah nipped into the Co-op; it was just a walk down the little lane into Cobblers Yards. Unexpectedly for Maisie, Hannah had said no.

'But you can watch me walk down the lane, and Thea's dad is always in the bookshop if anything happens.'

Hannah hadn't told Maisie that Thea's dad wasn't a well man. But that wasn't the point. She knew Maisie would be perfectly okay. There was no one in Cobblers Yard on a Sunday – no customers, at any rate; just Thea's dad and his carers once Thea had gone home. The shops were closed, and all Maisie would do was unlock the shop and go straight upstairs to her painting. She would not get up to any mischief.

Hannah had wanted her to wait so she could surprise her with the painting in the window. So, a grumpy nine-year-old had insisted on waiting in the car, not realising that the shop window wasn't the only surprise she was in for that Sunday.

'Chocolate croissants!' Maisie exclaimed. 'And peanut butter!' She watched Hannah take out one surprise after another. She turned to her mum. 'But I thought we were on a budget and couldn't afford these things?' Maisie looked worried. 'You didn't …'

Hannah stopped unpacking. 'I didn't … what?'

Maisie started to pack the shopping back in the plastic bags. 'We need to take them back.'

'Why – don't you like them?'

'I don't want you to get into trouble.'

'Why would I get into trouble?'

Maisie was still furiously packing the shop back in the bags.

'Maisie – stop! What's got into you? I thought these were all your favourite things?'

Hannah felt very guilty that she'd had to deny her daughter some of life's little luxuries. It was totally unnecessary; all Hannah had to do was tell the world about her daughter – the art prodigy. She knew she could open a TikTok account and introduce strangers to Maisie the nine-year-old artist. Despite all her faults – and Hannah thought she had many, especially when it came to being a mum – she knew she'd never use her daughter for money. Although it had sometimes seriously crossed her mind.

Hannah had started to think about the thousands that some TikTok families made posting videos. She could buy Maisie new things – even a house if she was really successful. Why deny Maisie all the good things in life just because she wouldn't get off her high horse about posting videos of her daughter painting?

That niggle hadn't lasted long when she'd read of families breaking up, and parents and kids falling out over social media because the children were no longer having normal childhoods; everything revolved around TikTok shorts and making money. She could just imagine that the pressure to keep that going was immense.

Despite the fact that she imagined using Maisie's gift would give them both a materially much more comfortable life in the short term, she knew there would be a cost down the road. Hannah didn't even allow Maisie to have a mobile phone.

She'd had a wobble when she'd thought the shop wasn't going to pay off her debts and they'd had to let go of the cottage rental and move back to the flat. She'd taken a video of Maisie sitting at her easel, painting, and had even opened a TikTok account. On the morning she'd found the painting, despite her strong views over using Maisie and her gift to get her out of her financial hole, Hannah had been seriously considering posting the video online and ruining all her good intentions to protect Maisie from the public domain and keep her gift private so she could lead a normal life.

She was so thankful that she'd walked across the yard to the charity shop before she'd made such a huge mistake. Once Maisie was in the public eye, Hannah knew the genie would be out of the bottle and she would never be able to put it back in.

She'd already closed down the TikTok account first thing that morning before heading over to Nate and Lili's.

'You didn't steal them – did you?'

'What was that, sweetheart?'

'The shopping. You're not going back to prison, are you?'

Hannah swallowed. She knelt down and took Maisie's little face in her hands. 'Look at me, Maisie. I made you a promise. I will never, ever steal anything ever again. It was a stupid mistake. I didn't have a very nice boyfriend, and he found out about this shop when it was an antiques shop, and had lots of things worth a lot of money, and I … I was very, very foolish, and helped him steal from Joseph. That was a very bad thing to do. But that's all behind us … me. It is never going to happen again. All this has come from a very good day at the shop. It's been so busy, and Mummy has made a lot of money today. So we are all good. Okay?'

Maisie's little face broke into a grin. 'Can I have some Nutella, Mummy?'

Hannah smiled and kissed her. 'You can have anything you want, sweetheart. Well, anything from the shopping bag!'

Hannah got out a slice of bread and opened the jar of Nutella.

'When I've finished my painting of Cobblers Yard, can I put it in the window with *Sunrise Over Seashell Bay*?'

Hannah was just spreading some Nutella on the slice of bread when she stopped, surprised by the question. She looked at Maisie, catching her dipping her finger in the Nutella.

Maisie looked at her sheepishly. She licked her finger. 'Sorry.'

Hannah wasn't bothered about the finger in the jar of Nutella. Maisie had never asked to display one of her paintings in the shop window before. 'But what if someone wants to buy it?'

Maisie shrugged. 'That's fine. Lots of painters sell their paintings.'

Hannah regarded her for a long moment. Would it hurt to sell the paintings locally? It didn't mean anybody had to know that a nine-year-old had painted them. 'I could open a savings account for you at the local bank, and if it sells, then I will put the money in your account.' Hannah had no doubt that it *would* sell.

'But don't you need the money, Mummy?'

'What do you mean?' Hannah wondered why she was surprised by the question. Although she thought she'd protected Maisie from her financial worries, she was a single parent and Maisie was very bright.

Hannah could feel her cheeks going red. She stopped spreading the Nutella on the bread and turned to Maisie. 'I hope you're not thinking of selling your paintings for me.'

Maisie bit her bottom lip. 'I thought it might help us get the cottage back.'

Hannah's heart sank. It was not what she had wanted to hear. 'Look, everything is fine. I just told you the shop is doing well. In fact, it's for the best that we've moved back here for a little while.

You see, I'm going to save up to buy our own place.' Hannah gave her a confident smile. It had by no means been the original plan, but it was now.

'Our very own home, that's all ours and nobody can ask us to leave?'

'That's right, sweetheart. And I don't need the money you earn from your paintings.' She had her very own good-luck charm in the window.

'All right. But what about *Sunrise Over Seashell Bay*?'

'What about it?'

'What happens when you sell it? Then what will we put in the window?'

'Oh, that painting is not for sale.' Hannah was glad she'd brought that up. She'd forgotten to tell her. 'So, if you're in the shop and someone asks if it's for sale, you know what to say.'

Maisie grinned. 'Good, because that will mean they'll buy my painting instead.'

Hannah frowned, although she'd had a thought. She knew that Maisie could paint an excellent copy of the painting if someone was desperate for it, but she was not giving up the original, even if it did have a broken frame that she still needed to fix.

'I want to finish my painting so it can go in the shop window too.'

'We'll see.' That meant *no*, but Hannah didn't want to cause an argument when Maisie found out she wasn't putting her paintings up for sale. Not that evening, anyway, after she'd had a fantastic day in the shop. Hannah wanted to celebrate with peanut butter and Nutella sandwiches. She suggested the combo to Maisie.

Hannah put the plate with the peanut butter and Nutella sandwich on a little coffee table beside the easel. She returned with a glass of orange juice but knew not to disturb her daughter once she was in *the zone* as Maisie called her mental state when she was in the middle of painting.

Hannah hovered for a moment behind her, taking in the painting that she was starting from the outline she'd drawn. She expected it would be finished by bedtime. Hannah frowned at the thought. There would be an argument the next morning when Maisie found out it was not going in the shop window.

Hannah made herself a cup of tea and sat down on the little sofa under the eaves, watching Maisie sitting at the window and painting a wonderful street scene of Cobblers Yard.

She sipped her tea, thinking – not for the first time – what a difference a day had made; and all because of *Sunrise Over Seashell Bay*. She had the most wonderful feeling that her life was going to finally come together.

For everyone else she knew who'd arrived on the Suffolk Coast to make a fresh start, things had worked out. They'd got good jobs or started business, or in the case of Thea, had reopened a business that had been closed for years, and made a success of it – and along the way, they'd all met the loves of their lives.

She was thinking of Thea, along with Lili, and Joss next door. He'd met a lovely young woman, a vet. They lived in her parents' former guesthouse on Shingle Cove.

Hannah had no expectations of meeting the love of her life. She was far too busy running the shop and trying to make up for her past mistakes. For just a few minutes, though, she sat with her tea, staring at Maisie's painting, daydreaming about meeting someone she'd spend the rest of her life with. Then she cast that thought aside and focused on her good-luck charm sitting in the window downstairs. The broken frame was still bothering her.

Hannah didn't want to wait for it to be repaired. What if something happened and the frame, and the backing, came away completely. Could she do it herself? How difficult could it be? Hannah put her mug down on the little coffee table in front of the sofa and picked up her old laptop. A few minutes later, she had her answer – despite her earlier misgivings about attempting it herself, it was doable. And she had the materials she needed in her shop – a special glue. She'd just have to take her time with no distractions.

Hannah glanced at her biggest distraction, who was busy painting and wouldn't disturb her while she attempted to fix the frame.

She was about to tell Maisie what she was going downstairs to do but thought the better of it. Hannah didn't want to break Maisie's concentration and be told off for it.

She washed up her mug and Maisie's plate before heading downstairs. She was looking forward to mending the frame and placing it back in the window in readiness for the shop opening first thing on Monday morning.

12

In the back room of Hannah's shop, late afternoon light filtered through the dust-covered windowpanes, casting golden shadows across the cluttered space. Hannah looked around the room she used as a stock room. She'd already put a stock order through online and was hoping that Maisie wouldn't mind helping her out with restocking the shelves one evening after the order arrived. But for the time being, Hannah's focus was on the painting.

Hannah placed the painting gently on the worn wooden table, the image of *Sunrise Over Seashell Bay* catching the last of the sunlight. She'd taken it into the back room for a closer look. The frame was very loose at one corner, with the canvas pulling away slightly from the wood. She'd had to very carefully lift it out of the shop window and carry it through the shop, hoping to goodness she didn't drop it. She could have asked for Maisie's help, but then she'd want to get involved in fixing the frame. Hannah didn't want a chatty nine-year-old putting her off what she imagined would be a delicate job.

Once the painting was safely on the table, Hannah rolled up her sleeves and leaned in.

With careful fingers, she pressed along the back panel. It

shifted beneath her touch. 'Strange,' she murmured.

Using a small flathead screwdriver from a nearby drawer, she gently prised the edge of the frame. She frowned. She was meant to be fixing the frame, not disturbing it more, but there was a slight bulge in the backing that she'd half-noticed earlier.

Hannah winced when the back gave way with a faint creak, revealing a slim, dust-filled compartment tucked behind the canvas. It explained why the backing appeared bulky – the painting was hiding something.

There was something inside. Wrapped in brittle brown paper and tied with a once-red ribbon, there appeared to be a bundle of letters.

Hannah's breath caught. If the frame hadn't been damaged, she wouldn't have made this discovery. She lifted them with care, her fingertips tingling. Perhaps this was a clue to who the painter was?

The paper was soft with age; the ink faded to a gentle sepia. On the topmost envelope, written in elegant looping handwriting, were the words:

Miss Kitty, Somersby Hall, Suffolk 1943

The room seemed to fall still around her as she slowly untied the ribbon and unfolded the first letter.

My dearest Kitty,

The days grow longer without you. Each sunrise brings a longing I cannot shake. The war rages on, but thoughts of you are my only peace. I see you in the curve of the coastline, in the shifting light over Seashell Bay, in my memories of that place. I ache to return to you, to stand with you once more in the orchard behind the hall, where the apple blossoms fell like snow ...

The words blurred as Hannah blinked quickly. There was

something achingly real, devastatingly tender about the language. The writer – Owen, signed at the bottom – clearly loved Kitty with a depth that transcended wartime circumstance.

'Mum?'

Startled, Hannah turned around. Maisie stood in the doorway, her plaits slightly crooked, holding a half-eaten biscuit.

'What are you doing?' Maisie asked, stepping into the room. She peered down at the painting. 'The picture frame is broken.' She looked at her mum wide-eyed. 'What happened?'

Hannah explained that one of her customers the previous day had knocked into the painting and it had fallen off the easel, damaging the corner of the frame. 'I Googled how to fix it, and thought I'd attempt it while you were busy with your painting. But I found these.' Hannah showed her the small bundle of letters. 'These letters ... they're from someone called Owen. He wrote them to a woman named Kitty, a long time ago – during the Second World War.'

Maisie touched the paper delicately. 'Why were they in the painting?'

'I don't know,' Hannah said. 'But it must have meant something. Someone must have hidden them for a reason.'

Maisie's eyes lit up. 'Like a secret?'

Hannah smiled faintly. 'Yes. A very old secret.'

As she looked back at the letter, a chill ran down her spine. There was something there – something worth pursuing. The painting. The letters. Somersby Hall.

She felt it in her bones: it was the beginning of something.

❖

Hannah spent the next hour fixing the frame, trying not to let her attention stray to the bundle of letters from Owen to Kitty at Somersby Hall, which she'd carefully placed in a box file. She'd taken the file upstairs to the flat to look at the other letters once she knew she'd fixed the picture frame and the painting was back safely in the window.

'There, it's all done.' Hannah smiled at Maisie. It turned out she'd needed an extra pair of hands to hold the frame in place while she taped up the edge of the backing. 'Thank you for your help, Maisie. I couldn't have done it without you.'

Maisie said, 'Can we look at the letters now? I want to find out about the secret.'

'The secret?'

'Yes, why someone hid them in the back of the painting.'

Hannah knitted her brow. 'Don't you mean Kitty – why Kitty hid them?'

Maisie shrugged. 'I guess.'

Hannah assumed it was Kitty who had, for some reason, hidden the letters she'd received from Owen. Perhaps they were having an affair. She wasn't about to tell Maisie that, but even so, it did make her think that her assumption about Kitty hiding the letters might have been wrong. And it might not have been for the reasons she thought. Perhaps they'd just been put there for safekeeping.

It struck her that whoever had left the painting outside the charity shop perhaps had no idea about what was hidden in the picture frame.

She smiled at Maisie. 'I think you'd make a very good detective.'

Maisie's eyes lit up. 'Like Grandpa! Maybe I'll be an art cop.'

Maisie's paternal grandfather, Ray, had also been an amateur artist. Hannah imagined he'd gone into the police because he couldn't earn a living from his paintings. She looked at her daughter. She'd prefer it if Maisie used her gift and became an artist. She knew that Maisie's talent meant she'd earn a good living. She was sure of it. But mostly she just wanted Maisie to be happy. She said, 'Whatever makes you happy, sweetheart.'

'I'm happy when I paint.'

Good answer, Hannah felt like saying. 'Then that's what you should do, Maisie.'

Hannah carefully carried the painting through the shop and placed it on the easel in the window. She gave a relieved sigh. The painting was back where it belonged.

But was it? Hannah frowned at the thought of the old man looking surprised when he'd caught sight of the painting in the window. He'd recognised it. She'd wanted someone to appear who might tell her about the painting, the painter, and whether the bay depicted in the painting actually existed – although she now felt sure that it was real.

But now, finding the letters … she was concerned someone might happen along and claim it, even though she had bought it from the charity shop fair and square. What if someone had cleared out a house and taken it to the charity shop by mistake, and the owner or their descendants wanted it back?

'Mummy?'

Hannah turned around. She realised she'd been standing there for some time, lost in thought.

'Can we go upstairs now to look at the letters?'

'Yes, of course. I was just wondering whether to take the painting upstairs and hang it in our flat.'

'Yes, then I can put *my* painting on the easel in the window when I've finished painting it.'

Hannah did love Maisie's paintings, and although Cobblers Yard was a very attractive cobbled yard with cute little shops with leaded windows, she just didn't see how a painting of the yard would attract customers in like the painting of Seashell Bay with its brilliant, vibrant orange and yellow hues capturing the beautiful Suffolk sunrise.

'Perhaps I'll think on it a bit.'

Maisie knitted her brow. 'Don't you like my painting?'

'Oh, sweetie, I love it. You know I love all your paintings.'

'You're just saying that because you're my mum.'

'No, I mean it, Maisie. I love them all. I didn't mean I'd think about putting yours in the window, I meant I might leave this one in the window for a little bit.'

'Why?'

Hannah fixed a smile on her face. She felt awkward. She didn't want to lie, but she couldn't tell Maisie that she knew the painting she'd bought at the charity shop would attract more customers. She didn't want to hurt her nine-year-old's feelings and risk her turning her back on her art just because of something her mum – or someone else – had said.

So, leaving aside Maisie's rather lovely painting of Cobblers Yard, Hannah told her about the man she'd seen. 'There was a gentleman who happened by last thing yesterday as I was closing the shop. He'd just left Thea's bookshop – he was their last customer of the day – with a book. I saw the bag he was carrying, and knew he'd walked from the direction of the bookshop.'

Hannah caught the look of disinterest on her daughter's face.

'I think he knows something about the painting. He looked

as though he recognised it.'

'What did he say?' Maisie asked, her interest piqued.

'Oh, he didn't say anything. I was closing up, you see, but when I went to the door, he was gone.'

'Oh.'

Hannah told her she'd run out of Cobblers Yard to find him. 'He'd got into an old car and sped off.'

'He might come back tomorrow, when you're open.'

Hannah hoped so, although she wasn't so sure he'd be back. Something in his demeanour had said that he not only knew the painting, but that he wasn't happy to see it in the shop window.

'Was he Owen – do you think? The one who wrote these letters?'

'Ah, that is a good question, but I don't think so, Maisie.'

'How come?'

'Well, for one thing, Thea's dad mentioned his name was Percy. In any case, I'm guessing that Owen must be in his nineties. I think the man was not as old as that.'

A look of disappointment crossed Maisie's features. Hannah knew she'd be disappointed too if the old man didn't return. She got her mobile phone out of her back pocket. 'Here – look.' She handed Maisie her phone.

'It's a blue car,' said Maisie.

'Yes, a very, very old blue car. I think it's a classic. I'm going to keep an eye out for it.'

'I will too. He might know something about the letters.'

'Talking of which, I think it's time to go upstairs and have another look at those letters,' said Hannah. She smiled at the painting in the window. She was looking forward to Monday morning, and her good-luck charm bringing a steady flow of customers through her door. Although she was starting to have a change of heart about finding Percy despite what she'd just said to Maisie. She was still concerned that someone might happen along and claim it. Percy seemed surprised to see the painting in her window. What if someone *had* taken it to the charity shop by mistake, and the owner or their descendants wanted it back?

13

'Is it okay reading someone else's letters?' Maisie asked, stopping Hannah in her tracks as she was reaching inside the box where she'd placed the old bundle of letters for safekeeping.

Hannah stared at Maisie. 'I see what you mean, sweetheart. But the letters are very old, and I imagine that Kitty and Owen won't mind.'

'How do you know?'

'I think they're most likely gone, sweetheart.'

'Gone? Gone where?'

'To heaven.'

'Oh.'

'Reading the old letters might give us a clue as to who Kitty and Owen were.'

'Then we can return them.'

That had been Hannah's initial idea, although she worried that if she found Kitty and Owen's descendants, if the couple in love had had children, then she might feel duty-bound to hand over the painting too. She did not want to do that.

'Why don't we start with reading the letters.' Hannah handed Maisie one. 'Do you want to read one?'

Maisie took an envelope. 'What's an airgraph?'

Hannah had started reading another heartfelt love letter from Owen, who it appeared had been stationed in Cairo during the Second World War. 'I'm sorry, what did you say, sweetie?'

'Look, on the front of the envelope – there's a strange word.'

Hannah hadn't taken a lot of notice of the yellowed envelopes apart from whom they were addressed to – Kitty at Somersby Hall.

But Maisie was right: there was a strange word stamped in faded blue on the top right of the small envelope with a winged arrow symbol below. On hers there was the same word but a cloud symbol and an oval window for the recipient's name and address, rather than a rectangular window. Hannah thought they must be variations of the same thing.

She looked at Maisie. 'I have no idea.' She reached for her laptop and tried Googling, but the internet was slow and went down. They had that a lot in the shop. It wasn't ideal, and she knew she should get somebody in to sort out the problem, but she had enough money problems without a large bill for that too.

It was something she'd definitely have to look into if the shop took off, and she knew she'd need decent internet if she was considering selling online too. She hadn't minded not having reliable internet for herself, though. She thought it was a time drain, and preferred reading a book after work and avoiding social media.

She preferred Maisie to paint rather than sitting looking at screens too. They had terrestrial television or DVDs, and that was how they'd lived in the cottage they'd been renting – without internet.

Hannah sighed. Now that she actually wanted to use it for

once, the internet had gone down completely. Her gaze travelled across the room to the window. 'But I know someone who I'm sure would know about these sorts of letters.'

'Who?'

'Thea in the bookshop.'

'Do you think she's got a book on airgraphs?'

'She might, but I was thinking about what she used to do in London before she moved here and reopened the bookshop. Lili told me she was an archivist in a London museum, so I imagine she might know about things from the past.'

'Can we go and see her now?'

Hannah shook her head. 'It's Sunday evening. She won't be in the bookshop.'

'But there's a light on.'

'Thea's father lives in the flat above the bookshop, remember?'

'Oh, yes. Will he know what an airgraph is? Can we see him instead?'

Hannah said, 'Thea's dad's memory isn't what it was. I think it's best to ask Thea, and besides, she'll probably be the most knowledgeable one, with her background working for a museum.'

'Where does Thea live? Can we go and see her now?'

Hannah didn't know. She wasn't exactly good friends with Thea like she was with Lili. That was her own fault for keeping herself to herself. She wished she hadn't, but knew it was all because she was worried about people finding out about her past. Thea seemed lovely, and she'd like to be good friends with her.

'First thing in the morning, before the shop opens, I'll go and see Thea.' Hannah knew she'd arrive at her shop before opening time too. 'And I'll tell you what I find out after school.'

Maisie brightened. 'All right. I could ask one of my teachers too. They might know what an airgraph is. I could take in one of the letters to show and tell—'

'No!'

Maisie looked at her mother sharply. 'Why not?'

Hannah didn't mean to sound so abrupt, but she still had the painting on her mind. She felt as though she could trust Thea with the secret letters, and where she'd found them, but until she knew a bit more herself, she'd rather word about the letters didn't get out. She didn't know Maisie's teacher all that well. She was probably being paranoid, but what if someone in the school had a connection to Somersby Hall?

The irony wasn't lost on Hannah that one of the reasons she'd put the painting in the shop window was that she wanted someone to come forward who might know about it. Now she wanted to keep what she'd discovered under wraps.

Hannah reminded herself that she wanted to find out about Kitty, Owen and the painting. Even so, she wasn't happy at the thought of word getting out about the letters just yet.

'It's very sweet of you to offer to help, Maisie. But the thing is, these letters are quite old and precious—'

Maisie's bottom lip quivered. 'You don't trust me to look after one.'

'No, it's not that at all. But what if it got accidentally torn, or someone else spilled something on it?' Although that wasn't Hannah's primary concern, in a classroom full of thirty children, it wouldn't surprise her.

Maisie said, 'You're right,' sounding quite grown-up. 'Things happen, don't they? I'd be so upset if the letter got ruined.'

'Me too.' Hannah leaned over and gave Maisie, sitting beside her on the old worn sofa, a hug. 'Now, how about we read these letters and see if we can find a clue about Kitty and Owen, and the painting, apart from what we already know – they were in love, and Kitty lived at a place called Somersby Hall.'

'They're not letters, Mummy. They're called airgraphs.'

They looked like letters to Hannah, although they weren't written on blank sheets of paper. They looked a bit like forms that were filled in. There were the same instructions on each sheet of paper, beginning with a sentence above a rectangular square, or in some cases an oblong: *Write the address in large BLOCK letters in the panel below. The address must NOT be typewritten.*

There was a date stamp and then a further sentence followed below the address: *Write the message very clearly below this line.*

Just below the line were two words: *Sender's Address.*

Below the sender's address was the handwritten message, and then a further line with an instruction to leave the area below the line blank, and a final typewritten message reminding the sender to complete the address in the panel.

'Oh, look at this one.'

Hannah looked up from the beautifully written love letter she'd been reading. 'What is it?'

Maisie passed over the one she'd opened. 'There are drawings on this one.'

'So there are. It looks a bit like a greeting card but on a sheet of paper.' They both peered at it closely.

'That looks like a Christmas tree!'

'So it does,' Hannah said, smiling. The date said it had been sent on Christmas Eve. She couldn't tell if it was hand-drawn or if it came printed on the paper. She asked Maisie for her expert opinion. Hannah always did that in all things related to art.

Maisie scrutinised the drawings. 'It's hard to tell without seeing others.' She cast a glance at the box.

'Let's work our way through them.'

Hannah read every single one and discovered little drawings on others – a beach, a sunrise, and most telling of all, a seashell. Maisie had found that one.

'Hold on!' Maisie said. She jumped off the sofa.

'Where are you going?' Hannah asked, but Maisie was already out of the door and running down the stairs.

Hannah had just stood up, about to follow, wondering if she'd heard somebody knocking at the shop door downstairs. Hannah had been too engrossed in the letters.

She was just crossing the lounge when she heard Maisie running back up the stairs. 'It's him!' she said.

'Who – him? Was someone at the door?'

Maisie looked at her as though she'd asked a very silly question. 'No.' She held up the airgraph in her hand – the one with the drawing of a seashell. 'I compared it to the seashells on the beach in the painting. It's Owen who painted *Seashell Bay*.'

Even though Hannah had been pretty sure that was the case – after all the letters *had* been found hidden in the painting – it was still just guesswork. Now her little genius artist had confirmed it.

'So, what do we know about Kitty and Owen so far?'

Maisie joined her mum on the sofa. 'They loved each other,' said Maisie.

'Oh yes.'

'And Owen was a painter.'

'We don't know if he was a professional painter yet, sweetheart. But we do know he could paint, and he was in the

RAF stationed in Cairo in 1944, according to the date stamp on these letters.'

'Airgraphs,' Maisie corrected her.

'Airgraphs.' Hannah nodded.

'The letters don't tell us much more,' said Hannah, disappointed that there was no mention of what he might have done in civvy street, or anything about Kitty, apart from the fact that with each letter he loved her more – which were his exact words.

'There's still one left at the bottom of the box,' said Maisie.

'Oh, we missed one.'

Maisie picked it out of the box. 'It's addressed to Owen at RAF—'

'Wait – what?'

Maisie opened the envelope and handed it to her mum. 'What does it mean – the different address?'

'It's the only one addressed to Owen, unlike the others he sent to Kitty.'

'In Cairo?'

'Yes, Maisie, when he was in Cairo.' Hannah scanned the letter. She knew who had written it before she saw the scrawled name at the bottom. 'It's another love letter, this time written to Owen from—' Hannah halted.

'What is it, Mummy?'

'Jemima.' Hannah creased her brow. She turned to Maisie. 'Here, I'm not imagining things – am I?'

Maisie read the letter, and then who it was from. 'Who's Jemima?'

'Good question.' Hannah wondered if Owen had been having an affair with Kitty. Maybe Jemima was his wife. Her first thought had been that Jemima might be a relative – his sister, his mother – but it was definitely a romantic love letter too.

Maisie was studying the envelope. 'There's no round post mark or date on this – what does that mean?'

'The letter was never posted.' The fact that it had been kept with the other letters suggested this, but she had been assuming it was Kitty who had hidden the letters in the backing of the picture frame. Why would she have a love letter to Owen from another woman? It didn't make any sense.

'Is it a secret?' Maisie asked.

Hannah had been staring at the envelope, wondering at this anomaly, when she heard Maisie ask that question. 'I think it's certainly intriguing, and I bet someone was keeping secrets.' Hannah was thinking of Owen; whether he was married or not, it appeared he was involved with two women.

But did they know each other? It didn't make sense why Kitty would have hidden her letters in this painting, along with the one that hadn't been sent from Jemima – whoever she was. Hannah reminded herself that she didn't know who either of them were, and she couldn't make head or tail of any of it.

'I think I should visit Somersby Hall,' Hannah announced.

'Do you think Kitty is still there, at Somersby Hall?'

Hannah scratched her head. 'I don't think so, sweetheart. Like I explained about Owen, we are talking about a very, very long time ago. I doubt very much either of them, or this Jemima, are still alive. And even if they are, I imagine they'll be in care homes.'

Maisie looked at her blankly.

'They are homes where people who can't live on their own anymore are looked after.'

Hannah put the letter from Jemima that Owen had never received back into the box.

'But what if their relatives live at Somersby Hall?'

'Their descendants?' Hannah smiled at her bright daughter. 'Now that might be a possibility.'

'Do you think they'll want them back – the airgraphs?'

Hannah's smile slipped. That was a possibility too. She was thinking again about the painting that she did not want to give back. 'Perhaps I'll go and visit Thea tomorrow first and see what she says about these lett— I mean airgraphs.'

14

A little bell jingled as Hannah pushed open the door of Thea's bookshop, and the familiar scent of old pages and freshly brewed coffee from Mabel's coffee machine brought back a fond memory of her visit there just the day before yesterday. It was early Monday morning, and although it wasn't yet nine, and the bookshop hadn't officially opened, the door was unlocked.

Hannah had ventured across Cobblers Yard as soon as she had spotted that the blinds in the bookshop window were open. Although she'd been trying to keep a lookout for Thea's arrival, hoping to catch her before the shop opened, she'd had other things to do before opening time, namely making sure Maisie was ready for school.

She'd seen Maisie off to school – she didn't have to take her to the school gate. They always waited in the high street, outside the Co-op, for Maisie's friend whom she walked to school with along with her friend's mum. Hannah had kissed her goodbye, whispering in her ear that she'd find out as much as she could from Thea about the airgraphs while she was at school.

Hannah had walked very briskly back to Cobblers Yard, aiming straight for the bookshop. She stood awkwardly just inside the shop, aware that it hadn't officially opened and she'd had the gall to walk straight in. Thea could be busy.

Thea glanced up from behind the counter, her reading glasses perched halfway down her nose, a cup of coffee beside her.

'Hannah,' she said, smiling. 'I thought you'd be back sooner rather than later.'

'You did?'

'Oh yes. The trouble is that once you've tasted the amazing coffee from that machine …'

Hannah smiled. She wondered in passing if she should get a coffee machine too, to encourage people to stop in her shop a while and browse. She'd already thought of setting up an area in the shop for young and old to try their hand at painting. Perhaps at the weekends, Maisie might lend a hand and cast her expert eye over people's creations, even giving them a few pointers. It wouldn't be the first time.

She was thinking of Sarah's bright, airy studio on the top floor of her house, overlooking the sea, where she ran art classes. Sometimes, when Maisie popped round, and Sarah was running a class, Maisie would look in on them. Sarah's regulars were used to her nine-year-old granddaughter walking around the class, studying their paintings and giving them invaluable tips and constructive criticism.

Sarah lived in a house on the seafront just a street away from Cobblers Yard. A beautiful townhouse with amazing light that flooded through the long Georgian windows, it was the perfect spot overlooking the beach and the sea for Sarah and her students to draw inspiration for their paintings. Her students were mainly locals of her generation who, from what Hannah gathered, were not offended at all by Sarah's grandchild popping in from time to time and giving advice. They looked forward to it.

From what Hannah had heard, Sarah also had students, some international, who came for artists' retreats in the summer. They stayed at her house, and she took them out on day trips to charming Suffolk coves and the countryside to gain inspiration.

Hannah knew that Sarah always took her budding artists to Flatford, a National Trust property where they could discover the views that John Constable had painted in the small hamlet in the Dedham Vale countryside in Suffolk.

That reminded Hannah to show Sarah *Sunrise Over Seashell Bay*. Hannah took Maisie to Sarah's once a week for dinner after school and also popped in for a cup of tea whenever they passed by out on a walk along the beach promenade. Sarah also often popped into Hannah's shop – it was where she bought all her painting supplies.

She didn't have to do that. It would be easier and cheaper to source all her materials online. Hannah told her this, but Sarah wouldn't hear of it. Hannah knew what she was doing – supporting her endeavour to turn over a new leaf. Sarah was Hannah's biggest customer. If it wasn't for her, the shop would have folded months earlier.

Sarah was the only person she'd confided in about the move back to the flat – apart from giving Maisie's school her new home address. Sarah had immediately offered for them to go and live with her. It had been tempting. She had spare bedrooms, although that was where her retreat students stayed.

Sarah thought she'd declined the invitation because of the people who were booked to stay with her on the retreats.

However, Sarah always kept one of her spare bedrooms free in case Maisie or William wanted to go to Granny's for a sleepover, which meant that although Hannah would have had to share with Maisie for the summer, there would still have been room for them to move in with Sarah while Hannah sorted herself out.

Hannah had thanked Sarah for the invitation, but it would have felt like a step backwards; she needed to prove she could support herself and Maisie. And besides, it worried her that once she'd moved into Sarah's beautiful home overlooking the sea, she wouldn't want to leave – and neither would Maisie.

It had crossed Hannah's mind to let Maisie go and live with her granny for a bit in her lovely home on the seafront. She'd only be a street away. And Hannah knew she could meet her for breakfast, and still have her stick to her school routine, walking to the Co-op to meet her school friend. She had asked Maisie if she would like to stop at Granny's instead of moving back to the little flat above the shop. Maisie had brought a tear to her eye when she'd said, 'I want to be with you, Mummy.'

Sarah had inevitably shared the fact of Hannah and Maisie's new temporary living arrangements back at the flat with her husband, Ray, who had offered to put them up on his houseboat, moored in a village called Walberswick, across the river from the grand Victorian seaside resort of Southwold. That had been a lovely gesture too, but Hannah thought she might feel a little seasick living on a boat, even though Ray had said it was quite stable.

But that hadn't been her primary concern – it had been the thirty-minute journey getting from his place to Aldeburgh every day for Maisie's school and Hannah's shop. It didn't sound a long journey, but Maisie was used to the short walk to her local school, and Hannah imagined it would prove a long day for her.

Sarah and Ray's living arrangements were certainly unusual. They'd split up and had been in the throes of a divorce when they'd moved from London to Suffolk, retiring from their full-time jobs. But they'd fallen in love with each other all over again and had torn up the divorce papers. But what they hadn't changed were their separate living arrangements – they were together but living apart.

It hadn't really made sense to Hannah, but it obviously worked for them. It made her wonder if their unusual living arrangements had actually saved their marriage. Hannah wasn't sure that she could live apart from someone she was in love with. Perhaps it was unique to their generation, although she had read about middle-aged couples, and even young couples, living apart in a committed relationship.

'Penny for your thoughts?' Thea asked. 'You were miles away.'

Hannah turned around and smiled at Thea. She'd been closing the shop door behind her when she'd caught sight of Lili's flower shop, and it had reminded her of Sarah, who had run The Potting Shed before Lili took it over.

'I'm sorry for disturbing you, Thea, when I'm sure you're busy.'

'Not at all,' Thea replied, taking off her glasses. 'Is everything okay?'

'Yes, perfect. I just wanted to catch you first thing this morning before you opened the shop.'

'Is it about the painting? Did you find out who the man was?'

'Yes … no.' Hannah rephrased. 'Yes, it's about the painting, but no I still don't know who the man is – apart from his name.'

Thea said, 'I tried asking my dad again, but he got irritated, and told me what he'd said before, that it was a secret, and he was sworn not to tell. Shame you didn't manage to catch the man before he got in his car.'

'Actually, I think I already have some idea where the painting comes from.'

Thea put her calculator down. She had various sheets of paper – they looked like bills – spread out on the counter. 'Wait just one second – I want to hear this.'

Hannah hoped she wanted to see more too – the love letters and the painting. She guessed there would be no happy-ever-after ending, because Somersby Hall would have to give up its secrets.

Hannah told Thea all this.

Thea surprised her by bursting out laughing. 'Sorry, I didn't mean to be rude, but that just sounded so melodramatic.'

Hannah smiled too. 'It did, didn't it?'

Hannah stepped forward and carefully laid the bundle of letters – yellowed, delicate, and tied with a faded red ribbon – on the counter. 'I found these hidden in the back of the painting's frame.'

Thea's eyes widened. She set her glasses down properly and leaned in, untying the ribbon with gentle fingers. 'Letters?'

'From someone called Owen to a woman named Kitty. Sent during the war – from Cairo, I think. And they're all addressed to Somersby Hall.'

Thea ran a fingertip across the envelope's upper corner. 'Airgraph,' she read aloud. 'Haven't seen one of these in years.'

'Airgraph,' Hannah echoed. 'I meant to ask – what is that? It's on every envelope.'

'They were a form of wartime communication,' Thea explained, already moving toward the shop's back room. 'A way to get letters to and from soldiers quickly without weighing down the mail planes. You'd write your letter, and it would be photographed, then the negatives shipped and printed at the destination. Saved tons of space and time.'

Hannah followed her into the snug room behind the shop where boxes of vintage books were stacked high, leaning like curious scholars peering over each other's shoulders. Thea flicked on a lamp, the warm amber light casting an inviting glow as she reached for a leather-bound volume from one of the lower shelves.

'I've got a couple of history books on British military correspondence during the war,' she murmured, setting the book on the table. 'And … somewhere in here … some records on Somersby Hall. I came across them years ago while archiving local estates.'

As Thea searched, Hannah sifted through the letters, re-reading a particularly moving passage where Owen wrote about sketching the sun over Cairo rooftops and dreaming of Seashell Bay. She swallowed down the lump in her throat. 'Whoever Kitty was … Owen adored her.' Hannah didn't mention Jemima. That was a mystery she doubted Thea could solve.

Thea found a book she was looking for. 'Here – this mentions Somersby. Mostly about it being used as a convalescent home for returning officers for a time. No Kitty, though.'

Hannah looked disappointed, but Thea kept scanning. 'Wait. Here – this is interesting. There's a brief mention of an artist, O. Hartley, who was known for a style similar to the *Sunrise Over Seashell Bay* painting you found. He painted a series of landscapes during the fifties and sixties that were exhibited locally, then vanished from public record.'

'O. Hartley,' Hannah murmured. 'Owen Hartley?'

'Could be,' Thea said. 'If it's the same man, and he was in Cairo during the war, it fits.'

Hannah's mind raced, threads weaving faster than she could untangle them. Kitty. Somersby Hall. Owen Hartley. The paintings. The hidden letters. 'I need to visit the hall,' she said, more to herself than to Thea. 'There's something more to this.'

Thea closed the book and looked at her kindly. 'Just be careful. Old houses keep their secrets for a reason.'

Hannah smiled faintly. 'I just want to know the truth.'

'I don't know what your intentions are if you find Kitty, which obviously would be very doubtful – she'd be extremely old now.'

'I know.'

'But she might have descendants.'

'I've thought about that. They might want the airgraphs.'

'Here's the thing, Hannah. These are collectibles. Airgraph documents are very rare and prized by collectors. And you've got a whole set here, in immaculate condition, which tell a love story too.'

'Are you saying these could be worth some money?'

'A lot of money, Hannah.'

Hannah wanted to know what she meant by a lot of money.

'You could sell them to a museum or a private collector. The sort of money we're talking about is … well, anyone's guess.'

Hannah stared at them. A while earlier, she'd been handling them with a nine-year-old; Hannah had been drinking a mug of tea, and Maisie a glass of orange. Either one of them could have spilled their drinks all over these precious airgraphs.

'Life-changing money, Hannah.'

Hannah fell silent, thinking, *my painting wasn't a good-luck charm, it was the goose that laid the golden egg.*

'Hannah?'

'Sorry, I'm speechless.'

'I'll bet. I would be too.'

Hannah inwardly cringed at the thought of what they'd been doing when they'd handled the airgraphs. She hoped Maisie hadn't put sticky fingers on any of them.

Hannah decided to explain to Thea that Mabel and Marjorie had let her buy the painting for twenty pounds. 'It was the last bit of money I had in my purse. I was going to spend it on grocery shopping, but I irresponsibly bought a painting instead.' Hannah didn't think it was irresponsible now that she had more customers and felt even better now she had the airgraphs.

The painting had certainly brought her luck, and she intended to repay that gift. 'It wasn't for sale for twenty pounds, but two hundred! I saw the price ticket as they took it out of their window and gave it to me in return for a fraction of the price. But here's the thing – they still let me have it. So, I'd already planned to put some money aside to pay them back, and if I sell the airgraphs for a lot of money, I'm going to give them a percentage too.'

Hannah thought they might be interested to read the airgraphs she'd found in the painting. 'I wonder if they'd know Kitty, Jemima and Owen?'

'I think they are in their eighties, so it's possible they might have known them or known of them decades ago. What they'll remember from all those years ago, who knows. But you know about their reputation as the town's gossips. And even if you do want to share any profits with the charity shop if you sell, in the meantime, you need to keep the letters safe.'

'I haven't got a safe or lockbox in the shop.'

'Oh, I don't mean that – I meant protecting them from light, moisture, and humidity – or our damp, cold climate as the case may be. Although you do have a point, Hannah. But I can't see anyone breaking into one of the shops – can you? Unless they're desperate for a second-hand book, a bunch of flowers – she nodded in the direction of The Potting Shed – or want to be first in line for some legal advice in the morning.'

Hannah could feel the colour rising in her cheeks. Fortunately, Thea had no idea about her past. That was a story for another time, if she got to know Thea well enough to share it with her one day. Just then, she was focused on the future, and how to keep the airgraphs safe, storage-wise.

'Can you store them for me?'

Thea immediately shook her head. 'I wouldn't dare.'

'I don't understand …'

'As I said, they're very valuable. What if something happened to them? I couldn't leave them in the shop with my dad. I'm afraid he's a bit of a liability, and if he came across them …'

'What about your house?'

'Oh, I live out in the sticks. Don't get me wrong, Pettistree is a lovely little village, but there are no shops where I am, just a spattering of country houses, and … well, crime is pretty rare in our sleepy Suffolk towns, but burglaries are not unknown.'

Hannah's face coloured in embarrassment again. She looked away.

'If someone burgled me, and they came upon the airgraphs,

they'd probably have no idea of their value. But even so, I just wouldn't want the responsibility.'

'What do you suggest I do?'

'You need to store them in an airtight container away from moisture and light.'

Hannah stared at her. The only containers she had were A4 box folders or some plastic cereal pots.

'I take it you don't have anything suitable?'

Hannah shook her head. She'd have to go shopping – but where? She couldn't imagine she'd find anything suitable locally.

'I can look online, but in the meantime, can I make a suggestion? It's going to sound a bit … strange.'

'What is it?' Hannah asked, intrigued.

'Seal them back up in the backing of the painting.'

'What?'

'They've survived there very well indeed for all these years …'

'It means I'll have to take the frame apart again. I've only just fixed it.'

Thea looked nonplussed. 'Small price to pay to keep your letters safe.' She joked, 'Just don't sell that painting!'

'Oh, I've got no intention of doing that.'

'Or lose it!'

'I wouldn't let it out of my sight.'

'I thought not. I'll see what I can come up with in terms of storage.' Thea looked at her thoughtfully before walking out of the back room. 'I'd better open up the shop now.'

Hannah had to return to her own shop and do that too, but she paused by the counter, waiting for Thea to return from putting the *Open* sign in the bookshop window.

Thea's father appeared at the foot of the stairs, looking at his pocket-watch. 'Ah! Well done, Thea, for getting up early and coming down before me to open up.'

Hannah exchanged a glance with Thea. She didn't live there. He'd already forgotten the carers had left and his daughter had arrived for work.

'Dad, do you mind serving any customers? I just need to have a word with my friend, Hannah.'

'All right.'

'Thanks, Dad.'

Thea took Hannah by the arm and led her over to the cosy corner, with the old leather sofa, reading lamp, coffee table and the coffee machine that made the most delicious coffee.

Hannah eyed the coffee machine, and said, 'I'd really love to stop and chat, but I need to open my shop.'

Thea grinned. 'That's what I want to talk to you about. Now, are you sure I can't tempt you with a cup of coffee?'

15

The bell above the door to the art and craft shop jingled as Hannah shoved her hair out of her eyes and glanced up from the half-emptied box of paintbrushes. She'd been at it since dawn, unpacking stock and wondering if her idea of creating a try-before-you-buy corner was wildly impractical. The space in the back was bare but for a faded rug she'd rescued from the charity shop and the promise of what it could become.

It was Thea's fault for tempting her with that cup of coffee on Monday. Hannah had nipped across to her shop before she opened to ask her opinion about the airgraphs. Thea had suggested while she was there that Hannah could make some space in her shop to create a cosy corner, just like in Thea's shop.

While Hannah's shop was doing well, and she was drawing in customers, Thea suggested she could encourage people to stop a while longer over a cup of tea or coffee and a biscuit. Then they could take more time browsing too. Perhaps, like Thea's bookshop, it might become a bit of a meeting place.

It had been something Hannah had already considered after the first time she had ventured into Thea's shop and had discovered the small cosy corner set up with a sofa, rug, floor lamp, coffee table and coffee machine.

After Thea's suggestion, Hannah had said, 'But aren't you worried that I'll take your customers away from sitting around and browsing in your shop?'

'Not at all,' Thea had replied. 'There's plenty of customers to go around, and besides, we're all of a mind that any one of us attracting customers into our little yard is going to benefit the others, as people often have a browse around the yard, looking in the other shops before they go.'

Hannah had noticed quite a few window shoppers, although few had ventured into her shop until she'd put her painting in the window.

And less than a fortnight after that conversation, there she was on Sunday, still wondering if it would all turn out to be a big mistake and a huge waste of time and money. What if it didn't help at all? She was worried about Lili and Nate coming to help. It was Maisie's sleepover weekend again, but instead of going to collect her and having a Sunday roast at their house, Hannah was thinking of inviting them to a local pub – her treat. She actually had the money to take them out, which was something.

She hoped they still didn't mind helping in the shop beforehand. Maisie had been excited about going there after her sleepover and getting stuck in, making some suggestions for what materials to put out for budding artists to try. Hannah had thought that Maisie might enjoy sitting with both younger and older people, giving them some pointers, although she imagined not everyone would appreciate tips from a nine-year-old. And besides, Hannah was trying to keep her daughter's talent under wraps. Maisie giving free art classes might be a step too far. The cosy corner was meant to be a place to have a bit of fun and try materials before buying.

'Permission to barge in?' a warm voice asked.

Hannah straightened up to see Thea balancing a stack of second-hand paperbacks in her arms, along with some comics and old colouring books. 'I thought these might be useful for little ones or for adults to read while they're waiting for their kids to finish colouring or waiting for a friend or relation to finish shopping.'

Behind her, two women squeezed through the door together, arms laden with bags. Mabel and Marjorie from the charity shop were already bickering.

'Don't you drop that lamp, Mabel, it'll shatter.'

'Oh hush, it was your idea to bring the thing in the first place.'

Hannah blinked. 'Wait – you all came to help?'

'Not all. I'm afraid Callum couldn't come or Henry. They send their apologies.'

Hannah knew why that was. Henry couldn't really venture out of the bookshop; he'd only get very confused, so Thea's partner, Callum, had stayed behind in the bookshop with Henry.

'Oh, don't be silly, Thea.' She glanced around at the other shopkeepers. 'I still can't believe you all came.'

Thea smiled, setting her books down. 'That's what we do here in Cobblers Yard, Hannah. We pitch in when someone's starting out.'

Hannah wasn't exactly starting out. She felt guilty for avoiding the other shopkeepers in Cobblers Yard, but she'd had good reason. She put to the back of her mind the thought that they might find out about her past and what had happened there in that very shop when it had been an antiques shop run by

Nate's grandfather. It had made her cringe when Thea had talked over where to safely store the valuable airgraphs, and Hannah had said in conversation, 'But I can't see anyone breaking into one of the shops – can you?'

Thea hadn't been there when the shop had been Joseph's antiques shop – thank god. But The Gossip Girls had. They knew all about her past. At first, she had wondered why they hadn't gossiped about it to the other shopkeepers who didn't know – Joss, Thea and Reggie.

'Everyone deserves a second chance,' Mabel had said. That was why.

Thea said, 'I hope you don't mind that I've left the books and magazines on your countertop by the till.'

Hannah shook her head. Of course she didn't mind. 'I could do with some bookshelves,' she said, thinking of Lili and Nate, who were donating a two-seater sofa and a couple of easy chairs. They didn't match, but Hannah didn't mind in the least. They were redecorating their house and were in the midst of ordering a new three-piece suite. The sofa would go in the cosy corner with the lamp that Mabel and Marjorie were donating from their charity shop, along with the old rug. Hannah was investing some money in quality books on art. Maisie and Sarah had helped her choose titles suitable for different age ranges and abilities.

The two chairs would be positioned near the try-before-you-buy area so that mums, dads, grandparents and carers could sit and keep an eye. Effectively, Hannah was creating two different seating areas to cater for different needs. *And why not*, she thought. Shopping could be quite tiring, so she hoped people would be tempted to Cobblers Yard for a friendly, laid-back shopping experience.

The bell tinkled above the shop door as a young man in paint-splattered overalls ducked in, carrying a shelving unit over one shoulder as though it weighed nothing. He had blond hair with a streak of sawdust caught in it and a crooked smile.

'You must be Hannah.' He extended a hand. 'Joss. Joss Harper. I've got this spare shelving unit from my office next door. Heard you needed a hand.'

'Thank you,' she said in surprise, shaking his hand and looking him up and down.

'Oh, this?' he said flicking a finger at his overalls. 'Used to do some odd jobs when I left my old corporate law job before I moved here. I dug out the overalls as I thought you might need a hand with odd jobs. If you do, I'm definitely your man.'

Hannah smiled at him shyly. Unfortunately, he was somebody else's man.

She turned to Thea, wondering if she'd told the whole yard about the work that was going on in the art and craft shop.

'I think these cosy corners are really going to catch on,' commented Joss.

Thea said, 'I think it's you who started it with your laid-back, cosy office next door.'

Joss set the shelving unit down with a grunt of satisfaction. 'Perfect spot for this, right by the wall in front of the rug.'

Hannah stared at Joss, wondering why she couldn't find a lovely man like him to settle down with.

'Thinking of which …' said Thea.

Hannah glanced at her. Had Thea just read her mind? She hoped her friend didn't say anything about cute men.

Thea continued, 'Hannah was going to come in and see you.'

Hannah caught Mabel and Marjorie raising two very

interested eyebrows as one of them put the lamp, the base of which was a plastic elephant, on top of the bookshelf.

'Ah, not just my muscle you're after then,' he said playfully.

'Beauty and brains,' said Thea, winking at him.

'Brains indeed,' another voice piped up, this one rich and melodic. An older man with a silver earring and a tweed waistcoat sauntered in carrying a box that rattled like maracas.

Hannah recognised him from the music shop across the yard, next door to the charity shop. She'd never been in his shop, although she had caught him waving at her when he was sitting in his shop window mending an instrument. She'd always waved back. Perhaps he was wondering why she'd never ventured across the yard to say hello.

'Reggie!' Joss crossed the room and shook his hand enthusiastically. 'How's things?'

'Oh, you know me, jogging along. I needn't ask how you are. Rushed off your feet, I bet.'

Hannah felt guilty that Joss was there, helping her out on one of his precious days off. It sounded as though he needed them.

'And when you aren't working there, you're at home helping Emily with *her* business.'

'No rest for the wicked,' said Joss, laughing.

'I'll say. But then we business owners know all about that – don't we?' Reggie said, walking up to Hannah with a smile. 'Reggie. Music shop, other end of the yard,' he said, although he didn't need an introduction. He glanced at the box in his hands. 'I've brought you some old records – no charge.'

'Records?' Hannah asked, smiling despite herself.

'Trust me, darling. Nothing inspires creativity like a little Ella Fitzgerald in the background.'

She didn't realise Reggie sold records too. She hoped they weren't from his own private collection. She didn't have the heart to tell him she didn't have a record player – but who did, these days?

She made a mental note to ask Mabel and Marjorie if they had one. She hadn't spotted one in their shop the last time she'd visited, when she'd bought her painting, but then again, it was so full of clutter there might have been one right under her nose and she wouldn't have seen it.

'We have one in the charity shop, if you're in need of a record player,' said Mabel.

'Really?' Hannah didn't know why she was surprised.

Reggie glanced at The Gossip Girls and frowned. 'I have one I was going to lend Hannah.'

'Why loan her one when we can give her one to keep?'

Hannah looked from Mabel and Marjorie to Reggie, and got the feeling there was a little bit of friendly rivalry between them, possibly stemming from being next-door shop neighbours. She'd heard that, like the widowed sisters, Reggie had been running his shop for years, with a bit of a wobble recently when the landlord had thought he'd hike the rent on the shop, which Reggie leased.

Lili had told her this at the dinner table one Sunday when they'd been chatting about the businesses in Cobblers Yard. It had all worked out in the end, and the rent hike hadn't happened, otherwise Reggie would have had no option but to leave. His shop wasn't super-profitable, but he had a steady flow of customers over many years who bought the string instruments he sold and then had them repaired. He also tuned pianos and – as Hannah had only just found out – offered music lessons.

Hannah thought of Maisie. A lot of her spare time was

spent painting. Hannah wanted her to have other creative outlets too, if for no other reason than to broaden her horizons and make new friends. She had been meaning to nip across the yard and ask Reggie if he knew of someone who offered music lessons. One of Lili's friends had a maternal grandmother who offered piano lessons, but what if Maisie didn't want to learn the piano? What if she didn't want to learn any musical instruments?

I must ask her, thought Hannah.

'How about it?' Marjorie asked.

Hannah looked at the jazz records Reggie had passed to her. 'Oh, the record player. Well, I couldn't possibly accept something like that as a gift.'

'But you must, darling,' said Mabel. 'We want to help you out.'

'But you've already given me a lamp.'

'A lamp!' Reggie exclaimed, 'Pah!' he said dismissively.

Marjorie put her hands on her hips. 'And what is wrong with a lamp? It gives a room, or a cosy corner in this case, more atmosphere. It's got an elephant base, you know.'

'And that makes all the difference,' Hannah heard Reggie mutter under his breath.

Lili arrived, thankfully interrupting the disagreement between Reggie and The Gossip Girls, brushing soil from her hands and lugging in a trailing ivy in a clay pot.

'What's this?' Hannah asked. She wasn't actually asking about the clay pot with the trailing ivy, although she was used to her best friend bringing her bunches of fresh flowers. She was wondering why Lili looked as though she'd been gardening. It was Sunday. She normally dressed up for Sunday lunch.

Lili looked at her dirty dungarees. 'We stopped at The

Potting Shed first so I could bring you something a bit different to decorate your cosy corner.'

Maisie and William ran in behind Lili and straight up to Hannah, offering her a potted plant each.

'Hello, you two. What's this?' she said taking the pots out of their hands.

Maisie said, 'I planted the pot from the flowers in The Potting Shed.'

'Me too!' William chimed in.

'That's lovely. I shall put them …' She turned around and saw the bookcase, the perfect spot for a very pretty potted plant or two. After she'd placed them, she turned to find spindly arms around her waist. She bent over them and gave them each a kiss on the forehead.

William said, 'Urgh!'

Maisie said, 'Love you, Mummy.'

'And I love you too, sweetheart. Both of you,' she added, ruffling William's dark hair and casting her gaze at the door, expecting Nate to walk in any minute.

Lili said, 'Sorry, but of all the days, he got paged by the hospital. They wanted to see if he could come in for a last-minute shift.' She shrugged apologetically. 'You know Nate – he's married to the job.'

'He'll be married to you, soon, so he'd better remember that.' Hannah hoped she didn't sound bitter. She wasn't, but it was a reminder that Lili was moving on with her life. *So am I, though*, she told herself. With her business taking off, soon they'd be moving out of the flat and back into a cottage. That was the plan, anyway.

Glancing about her at her new friends in Cobblers Yard, she

had a feeling she'd be sorry to go. *But I won't be going. I'll still be here, like the rest of them, running their shops. I just won't be living here, like Reggie. I will have my own home like Thea, Joss, and Lili.*

Hannah said to Lili, 'I bet Nate's glad he got out of helping out at the shop this afternoon.'

'Not at all.'

Hannah threw her best friend an expression that said, *yeah right!*

'Well, perhaps a little. Not that he doesn't want to see you, and help out, it's just getting stuck into practical things like this … he's rather hopeless at DIY.'

'Just as well he's at work instead,' said Mabel.

'Hear, hear,' said Reggie.

'Finally, something we agree on,' quipped Mabel, smiling at Reggie.

16

The last people to arrive were Maisie's grandparents, Ray and Sarah, who were struggling to get something through the door. They gave up and walked inside.

'What's this?' Hannah asked, walking over to the door.

'It's the sofa, Mummy.'

Ray handed Hannah a bottle of bubbly. 'We noticed the sofa outside. Wondered what it was doing here. Then realised it must be for your cosy corner.'

Sarah added, 'Going to be fun getting it inside the shop.'

'How on earth did you guys get it *outside* the shop?' Hannah asked in surprise, turning around to look at Lili.

Maisie, who had been helping Thea arrange her books on the bookshelves while William arranged some little paints on one of the easels, said, 'Daddy brought it on the roof of the car.'

Maisie said, giggling, 'You should have heard his language when he was trying to get it up there.'

William's head shot up. 'Oh, yes. Daddy said the words, *for chrissakes*—'

'William!' Lili exclaimed, cutting him off before he came out with any more expletives. 'What did we say about repeating that?'

Maisie mimed something, grinning at her brother.

William sniggered into his hand.

Hannah watched the interaction between the two of them; a private joke between siblings. She had been an only child herself, and it meant a lot to her that she'd moved there for a fresh start and reconnected with Maisie's father and Maisie's younger half-sibling. Even though she hadn't got her happy-ever-after like Lili had with Nate, seeing the two children together reassured her that she'd done the right thing by moving.

Lili said, 'Fortunately, it's on wheels, so we just trundled it from the car, through the yard and up to your door. Well, Maisie and I trundled. William had a ride on the sofa. Then we nipped into The Potting Shed.'

Maisie said, 'After Daddy helped us get it down from the car roof, he had to shoot off.'

Hannah smiled at her expression. She was clearly parroting what Nate had said.

In the background, Joss had opened a paint pot. 'When we get that sofa in here, you guys can finish off organising things.'

Hannah looked at the paint pot. 'Oh, you don't have to do that, Joss.'

'I rather think I do.' He held up a paintbrush. 'You've got peeling paint, I'm afraid. It would be such a shame if the exterior lets it down. I've got metal paint, so it will be fine for touching up the old metal frames.'

Hannah didn't know how to thank him. She glanced at the overalls he was wearing ready to do the painting.

Joss said, 'I'll give you a hand with the sofa. Nice plant, by the way, Lili.'

'Greenery makes everything homelier,' Lili declared, already shifting Hannah's paint racks to make room.

What followed was chaos of the best kind. Once the sofa was in the shop – the handy wheels eventually had to come off to get it in – everyone wrestled to get the wheels back on and then get the sofa into place while Mabel fussed with a knitted throw that she insisted made it look inviting.

Marjorie set up the lamp in a different place, grumbling about the dodgy plug. Reggie unearthed a record player from somewhere – Hannah wondered if he'd nipped into the charity shop and pinched the one Mabel and Marjorie had planned to bring over – and filled the shop with the first brassy notes of a swing tune. Thea arranged colouring books in a basket, while Lili trailed the ivy so that it curled around the edge of the window as if it had always belonged there.

Hannah stood in the middle of it all, dazed and a little overwhelmed. The corner she'd only half-imagined that morning had come to life before her eyes: easels standing ready with blank sheets, jars of pencils and brushes glinting in the lamplight, the sofa nearby softened by mismatched cushions, and the scent of fresh coffee percolating from the machine that Mabel had somehow produced. 'Turns out I had two of my famous old coffee machines, so you now have one too.'

Hannah couldn't believe her luck. 'Now we really will be in competition,' she said to Thea lightheartedly.

Thea whispered, 'You know what this means – don't you?'

Hannah shook her head.

'Now you're going to find The Gossip Girls gracing *your* door.'

Hannah looked at her.

Thea added, 'I think Mabel had an ulterior motive in helping to create another cosy corner in one of the shops and finding that other coffee machine. Another place to hang out and hear all the gossip.'

'Hey, don't look so pleased,' Hannah said, half-jokingly. She had a feeling that Thea had just realised an unexpected perk of all the hard work.

'There,' Ray said, straightening with a grin. 'Cosy corner and try-before-you-buy area complete, although I rather think Sarah and I haven't been much help.'

Hannah disagreed. 'You bought some bubbly to celebrate!'

'Looks like it's all been here for years,' said Lili, slipping an arm around Hannah's shoulders and admiring the set-up.

Reggie lifted a paintbrush as if it were a conductor's baton. 'All it needs now is someone to christen it. Any volunteers?'

The shop erupted in laughter just as Joss walked in. He had quickly gone next door to wash his hands and change out of his overalls. He was back in ripped jeans and a t-shirt. 'Did I miss something?' he asked.

Hannah felt her throat tighten, tears pricking unexpectedly. She hadn't expected this friendship, this warmth, this feeling of belonging.

'Thank you,' she managed, her voice thick. 'I … I don't know what to say.'

'Say you'll let us come back and use the coffee machine,' Mabel quipped, and the group chuckled again.

Hannah laughed too, the sound bubbling up like relief. For the first time since taking the leap of turning the shop into an art and craft shop there in Cobblers Yard, she didn't feel alone.

Thea said, 'I've come up with another idea to help promote your shop.'

Hannah turned to her. 'Oh, Thea, you've done enough already.' She caught Thea looking at Mabel and Marjorie, who were smiling. So were Reggie, Joss and Lili.

Hannah stopped, getting a feeling they were all in on it. She said as much. 'Hey, what's going on?' she asked suspiciously.

While Ray and Sarah went to the flat upstairs and brought down some glasses and juice for Maisie and William, Thea sat down on the sofa, patting the seat next to her for Hannah to join her.

Hannah tentatively took a seat, getting the feeling that she was the last to know about Thea's idea.

Mabel and Marjorie took seats in the armchairs, which Reggie had turned around to face the sofa before they sat down. Joss perched on the arm of the sofa. The two children sat cross-legged on the rug, drinking juice. Lili had brought over the stools from behind the counter, one each for Ray and Sarah. She found a spare chair for Reggie and joined the children, kneeling behind them, arms around their shoulders, as Ray handed around glasses of sparkling wine.

Hannah leaned forward in anticipation. 'Well, aren't you going to tell me your idea?'

'First, a toast!' said Reggie, raising his glass.

They toasted the new cosy corner, everyone raising their glasses to Hannah's continued good fortune in turning the shop around and making it successful.

Hannah raised her own toast to her new friends in Cobblers Yard and to their continued success, and she said a silent thank you to her good-luck charm in the window, reminding herself that she must pop next door and see Joss in a professional capacity about what she'd found hidden in the painting. If one of her customers hadn't knocked over the painting and damaged the frame, she'd never have known about the valuable items in her possession.

She looked towards the window as she drank the wine, hoping that Percy, the man who'd visited Thea's bookshop and had paused outside her own shop window on his way out of the yard, didn't return and try to claim the painting. That was why she needed to see Joss. As much as she wanted to find the location of Seashell Bay, if it existed, she also wanted to keep her painting and the precious airgraphs.

'Now, on to my next idea,' said Thea.

17

The evening sunlight slanted across Cobblers Yard, catching the worn cobbles and the hanging baskets that trailed bright geraniums outside The Potting Shed. Hannah stood at the doorway of her shop, arms folded, watching with something that felt dangerously like pride as her neighbours transformed the yard into a festival of colour.

'Up a bit higher, Callum!' Thea called, one hand shading her eyes as Callum balanced on a small stepladder beside the old-fashioned lamp post in the centre of the yard. He was looping strings of bunting – striped, spotted, and floral – from the lamp post across to Thea's bookshop on one side and to Reggie's music shop on the other. A string of bunting already ran from the lamp post to Hannah's shop, to Joss's next door, and to the charity shop across the yard next door to Reggie's music shop.

'You mean this high?' Callum teased, stretching it just out of her reach.

Thea swatted the air. 'Stop showing off, or I'll think you're not concentrating and will fall off, and I'll have to fetch Marjorie to hold the ladder steady.'

'Don't you dare,' Marjorie retorted from the other side of

the yard, where she and Mabel were stringing fairy lights along the charity shop window. 'I've enough on with these tangles without having to rescue him.'

Hannah stepped out of her shop, leaving the door wide open. 'I'll hold the ladder,' she said.

It was Friday evening, and the shops were closed to customers. All this activity after hours reminded her of the previous Sunday, when they'd created the cosy corner in her shop, all mucking in to get it prepared for Monday morning. It had gone down a storm. The shop had been buzzing all week – so much so that Hannah wondered whether she might need a part-time shop assistant like Lili had in The Potting Shed. Zoe was amazing, but she was balancing her part-time job with a university course, so she wouldn't have time to work for Hannah too.

The cosy corner meant mums and dads could leave little ones drawing and reading books while they shopped, and adults could try different paints and different canvases before buying, and anyone could help themselves to free tea, coffee and cake. Hannah had discovered that Emily, who was Joss's fiancée, had a talented mum – she baked the most delicious cakes. Wendy, who was retired, volunteered next door in Joss's legal practice, offering people tea and homemade cake and directing them to the little ticket machine to take a ticket and then a seat to wait their turn.

During the week she had popped into Hannah's shop with homemade cakes and treats. Hannah had felt rather overwhelmed that the people of the yard cared so much for each other and the success of their neighbours' businesses. Wendy was baking more homemade cakes, scones, tiffin, and all sorts of other sweet treats, just like the ones she brought in every day for Hannah's customers, who enjoyed coffee and cake, and taking a seat on the sofa when it wasn't occupied by Mabel or Marjorie.

The two sisters particularly enjoyed Wendy's homemade cakes, giving them another excuse to enjoy Hannah's cosy corner. As Thea had predicted, they'd both cross the yard several times during the week; they saw it as their duty to test the coffee machine and make sure it was in perfect working order. How many times they had to do this, Hannah had no clue. It seemed to be a regular occurrence. And where one sister appeared, inevitably the other followed. She smiled at them affectionately, hearing them still bickering, their voices growing louder, still trying to untangle the fairy lights.

'All right down there?' Callum asked, glancing down at her holding the ladder, an easy grin lighting his face.

Hannah nodded, holding each side of the ladder firm. She returned his smile, wishing again that she could meet someone. She'd promised herself she wouldn't get involved in any relationships until Maisie was eighteen. She'd told Lili, who'd scoffed at the idea. Lili said she deserved to find her happy-ever-after with someone too.

All the women Hannah knew who'd moved to Suffolk seemed to have found their soulmates. Hannah was afraid that if she did meet someone, she'd make the same mistakes as before. All Hannah wanted to do was put Maisie first. If that meant waiting, then so be it. But her best friend was right: she did deserve to find happiness too, like Lili with Nate, and Thea with Callum. And Emily with Joss.

Thea and Callum had met when they'd both returned to Suffolk and both taken and an interest in the bookshop, working together to successfully reopen her father's business, which had been closed for years. Hannah still didn't know the story behind Thea's father's disappearance years ago, and his reappearance, but she hoped that as their friendship grew, Thea might confide in her about what had happened in her family's past. Perhaps she'd confide in Thea about her own past. But for now, Hannah's focus was on the preparations being made for Thea's fantastic idea.

Hannah glanced across the yard. Reggie, meanwhile, was setting up his pride and joy, an old-fashioned gramophone horn, with a crate of vinyl records stacked beside him. He placed the needle on a record and a burst of mellow trumpet and Ella Fitzgerald's velvet voice spilled into the yard.

'Now *that's* the spirit,' he announced, doffing his cap. 'Nothing says party like a little jazz music.'

Hannah threw him a smile. Everyone was contributing in their own way.

Lili emerged from her shop with Zoe, both carrying an arm full of potted herbs and trailing sweet peas to put on the trestle table outside their shop. There were trestle tables outside each shop; the idea was to place a few odds and ends for people to browse, which would entice them into the shops. Lili and Zoe had already added vases of blooming flowers on each table. 'People linger longer when there are flowers,' she said firmly.

'And chocolate digestive biscuits,' Marjorie added, emerging with a tin under her arm. 'Don't forget cake,' said Mabel, who had a tin too. 'I know Wendy has made fairy cakes and various tray bake cakes, but …' she lifted the lid with a flourish, releasing the buttery scent of Victoria sponge. 'I baked three of these. Marjorie burned the fourth.'

'I did not burn it. I *experimented*,' Marjorie huffed, but her eyes twinkled. 'We wanted to show you what we'll be laying out on the trestle tables tomorrow morning.'

Maisie darted between them all, arms full of more flyers she'd drawn – a charming sketch of the yard with its crooked old slate rooftops and bowed window shop fronts, with neat hand-lettering announcing: *Cobblers Yard Party – Saturday, 2pm.* She had a streak of ink on her cheek and a determined grin. They'd spent all week putting flyers around town, in as many places as they could think off, including stuck to lamp posts.

'Clarissa said she's putting one in the newspaper office's front window too,' Maisie reported proudly, sticking one up on Hannah's own door. 'She took a really nice photo of you, Mum.'

At the mention of Clarissa, Hannah's stomach tightened, as it had all week. She could still feel the click of the camera, the forced smile. What if the journalist had dug deeper, found out about her past, her secret?

Lili sidled up to her and touched her arm gently, guessing what was on her mind. 'She's only written about the shop, Hannah. About your cosy corner, about how you're bringing something fresh to the yard. That's all anyone's interested in. Trust me.'

Hannah swallowed hard, the knot in her throat loosening. Around her, fairy lights were being tested – little warm sparks blinking in the daylight. Reggie's record spun, and the yard filled with laughter as Callum pretended to nearly topple from the ladder, sending Thea squealing and Maisie into fits of giggles.

Hannah no longer felt like an outsider waiting for someone to whisper her secret. She felt part of something – messy, noisy, wonderful.

'Come on, Mum,' Maisie tugged her hand. 'Let's put out the pencils and paints for the kids' table.'

Hannah looked up. 'Have you finished, Callum?'

'Yes, I think we're all done.' He started down the ladder, the bunting wrapped around the lamp post now in place, stretching across the yard to each shop, making a colourful display.

Hannah nodded, letting her daughter pull her toward the trestle they'd set up outside the shop. She smoothed the paper over the boards, set out jars of coloured pencils, and arranged watercolour sets alongside them. Children would be able to sit and paint while their parents browsed. Hannah still wasn't sure about putting all this outside that evening instead of first thing in the morning, but she'd checked the weather forecast, and it would be a clear night with no rain.

Hannah had bought some face paints, and Maisie had spent all week practising on whoever she could find so that she could do face painting on the day of the Cobblers Yards party. It had been quite amusing to see Marjorie and Mabel face-painted as a cat and dog, Reggie as a lion, and Thea as a leopard. Of course, Hannah hadn't got out of being used as a guinea pig to test Maisie's creative skills. Maisie had painted an exceptional likeness of a dalmatian, spots and all, on her face.

Two chairs had been positioned next to the trestle table where Maisie could offer the children free face painting.

The yard was beginning to look magical: bunting strung from shop to shop like a patchwork sky, fairy lights draped along the windows ready for dusk, tables and chairs clustered invitingly, ready for tea, coffee and Mabel's sponge cakes, Marjorie's chocolate biscuits, and the gorgeous, sweet treats Wendy was baking.

Hannah looked around, her heart unexpectedly full. The next day was Saturday and would be a day at the yard like no other – she hoped, if the article in the newspaper had got around, and the local community had seen the flyers. Maisie had made lots, and each evening after school they'd walked into shops, the museum, the local cinema and the library, as many places as they could think of that might be prepared to display their flyers.

But the yard party wasn't just about customers or footfall – for Hannah, watching all her fellow shopkeepers and friends getting involved, it was about belonging.

Once again, Hannah had a feeling she was going to miss living in Cobblers Yard when she found another cottage to rent, but she'd promised Maisie a garden – and a pet.

She decided not to think about that for the time being. She was just enjoying the moment, and thinking about the next day, hoping the yard party would be buzzing with people.

18

By the time the church clock chimed two in the afternoon, Cobblers Yard was buzzing. The bunting fluttered overhead, fairy lights twinkled in the afternoon sunshine, and the air was thick with the scent of sponge cake, freshly brewed coffee, and the faint salt tang drifting from the sea. A seagull's cry could be heard faintly over the noise of friendly chatter. The yard was brimming with people, young and old.

Reggie's gramophone spilled out the lilting tones of a jazz trumpet, the notes curling around the cobbles and drawing people in from the high street. Locals wandered through the archway into the hidden yard, blinking as if they'd stumbled upon a secret fair. Children tugged their parents towards Hannah's table, where Maisie was carefully painting butterflies and tigers onto eager little faces. Hannah hoped she'd thought of everything: she glanced at the prominent sign they'd remembered to put out that morning regarding face paint allergies. Nearby, jars of brushes and pencils sat ready for any child who fancied colouring.

At the trestle tables, Thea displayed a selection of signed first editions, smiling proudly as she introduced the guest of honour,

Margot Dorey, the local writer who lived not far from Aldeburgh. Margot lived at Willow Tree Cottage in a lovely little seaside village, Walberswick, and her children's books always topped the summer reading lists. Margot perched on a stool in front of Thea's shop, reading a passage from her latest book. A hush fell over the yard as her voice carried, only broken by the clink of teacups and the occasional flutter of bunting overhead. When she finished, she signed copies for delighted fans, giving them away with a wink.

'Best yard party yet,' Lili declared, setting another jug of lemonade down by the cake stall. Her herb pots decorated the tables, filling the air with mint and rosemary.

'How many yard parties have you had?' Hannah asked, handing more glasses of lemonade to two children passing by with their parents as they browsed the tables.

Lili grinned. 'This is the very first one. But I can tell you – it won't be the last. What a fantastic idea of Thea's.'

Hannah agreed. 'Totally.'

'I don't know why we didn't think of this before.' Lili smiled. 'Actually, this was all your doing.'

Hannah looked at her, bemused. 'Not at all. Like you said, it was Thea's idea.'

'No, I meant if it wasn't for you taking over Joseph's old shop, and turning it into an art and craft shop, and Thea thinking up ways to keep your shop going with more customers – which I have to say has helped all of us tremendously too – I don't think we'd be out in the yard on a Saturday afternoon hosting this little party.'

Hannah frowned.

Lili looked at her, catching her expression. 'You don't agree?'

'Well, yes, but actually, all this is because of my good-luck charm.'

'Ah!' Lili's eyes went wide. They both turned to look in the window of Hannah's shop. 'You're talking about *Sunrise Over Seashell Bay*.'

'Yes.' If it hadn't been for the painting, Hannah would never have ventured into Thea's bookshop to ask after the man who'd stopped in front of her window on his way out of Cobblers Yard.

Percy. Would he turn up at the party? It was something she hadn't previously considered. She wasn't sure she wanted to meet someone who might have a connection to the painting; the same unease pervaded her thoughts about the painting and the airgraphs. She didn't want anybody appearing out of the blue who might take them all away from her.

She felt like having a word with Joss about it there and then, but although Wendy was there, helping out by serving cakes and drinks, and Joss was handing out leaflets, advertising his legal drop-in centre in Cobblers Yard, it wasn't the time or place to discuss it. Besides, Joss was having a rare Saturday afternoon off. He normally opened all day Saturday, because many people worked during the week, and for some the weekend was the only time they could drop in to see him.

The morning session had finished, but the afternoon session had been suspended. Quite rightly. It didn't seem appropriate for people to be trying to discuss their problems with Joss while there was a party, and music, chatter, and children running around outside. Instead, he was handing out free leaflets, and Hannah was pretty sure there were one or two people who Joss had taken aside to have a quiet word with in his office.

'You do know that your painting is still in the window.'

'Yes.' Hannah wasn't sure what Lili was getting at. 'It's always in the window.'

'But what about the raffle?'

The raffle was for charity, with the proceeds going towards local causes. Each shop had chosen a charity, and the proceeds would be split equally between them. Hannah had chosen a charity supporting ex-prisoners with their physical and mental wellbeing and providing advice on housing and jobs. Hannah didn't know what she would have done without Lili and Nate's help. Without them, she wouldn't be there, with a business and friends – and, most importantly, her daughter. She was just so grateful. But not everybody had that sort of support. 'I've been so stupid, Lili,' Hannah said, lowering her voice. 'I wish I'd got to know the others in the yard much sooner.'

Hannah nodded. 'I wish you had too. Then maybe we would have had one of these yard parties ages ago!'

Hannah slapped her arm playfully. 'But seriously, what were you getting at when you were talking about my painting and the raffle?'

'Oh, yes. We're all donating something from our shops, aren't we, for the raffle …' They both turned to look across the yard.

Mabel and Marjorie were running the raffle, waving tickets like auctioneers. 'Only a pound a strip!' Marjorie bellowed. The prize list stretched from potted plants, to jumping the queue for an hour of Joss's free legal advice, to a bundle of books, an item from the charity shop, or a free music lesson from Reggie, along with a basic musical instrument.

'Win anything you like from one of our shops – anything at all!'

'Oh!' Hannah's eyes went wide. She was thinking of a basket of art supplies from her shop, not … 'Not my painting!'

'You did remember to put a note on your painting saying *Not for sale?*'

'Oh, yes – yes I did.' Hannah breathed a sigh of relief. 'I think I'll just go check it's still stuck to the frame.'

Hannah drifted across the yard, dodging children running around, their faces painted, carrying balloons. People were at the trestle tables, and some were taking selfies by the old lamp post, trying to absorb the laughter and chatter that filled every corner of the yard. Parents carried shopping bags, children darted between tables, and couples lingered over slices of sponge cake at the bistro-style tables set up outside the bookshop. It was everything she'd once been afraid to hope for – finding the place she felt she belonged.

Then, for the briefest moment, she froze.

Across the yard, half-hidden behind the crowd, she saw him: tall, broad-shouldered, with a familiar tilt of the head. The world seemed to narrow to that single figure. Her heart thudded painfully.

But as she blinked, he was gone.

'Hannah?' Lili's hand was on her arm. 'What's the matter?'

Hannah swallowed hard, her throat suddenly dry. 'Nothing … I just thought I saw someone from my past.'

Before Lili could respond, Mabel bustled up, cheeks pink with gossip. 'Oh, did you see that tall, good-looking young man just now? Who is he?' Her eyes narrowed shrewdly.

'I … I'm not sure,' Hannah managed.

'Shame,' Mabel said, pursing her lips. 'He went to walk in, then left. Perhaps he thought it was some private party he was stumbling into.' She eyed Hannah a moment longer before turning back to the raffle to call out the winning numbers.

The rest of the afternoon was a whirl of laughter, clapping, jazz music and the glow of fairy lights as dusk began to fall. By the time the last raffle prize was claimed and the final crumbs of cake were devoured, lanterns and strings of lights bathed the cobbles in golden warmth.

When the trestle tables were folded away and the yard had finally quietened, the shopkeepers gravitated naturally into Hannah's shop. The cosy corner glowed with lamplight, and the old sofa was surrounded by mugs of coffee and the chatter of friends winding down.

'That was marvellous,' Thea sighed, tucking her legs beneath her on the sofa. 'I've not seen the yard so busy in quite some time.'

'Nor have I,' Reggie agreed. 'I wish we'd had this idea a long time ago. We'll have to do it again some time.'

Hannah glanced at Lili, who was sitting on Nate's knee. Lili offered her a knowing smile as they both remembered their conversation earlier about the yard party.

Reggie tipped his mug in a toast.

'Here's to Hannah, the newest recruit to our little gang.'

A chorus of cheers and laughter followed, and Hannah felt her cheeks heat. She looked around the cosy corner – Thea's books stacked on the bookshelves, Lili's ivy trailing down the window, Reggie humming along to himself, Mabel and Marjorie bickering fondly, Joss leaning back in the old armchair with a contented grin – and joined in their laughter.

Later, after Maisie had been tucked into bed with her face still faintly painted like a tiger – Nate had had a go and had managed a surprisingly good face painting job on his daughter – Hannah returned to the shop to tidy up. The yard outside was silent, lit only by the faint twinkle of fairy lights, the bunting gently swaying from the lamp post to the shopfronts.

She stacked mugs and gathered pencils back into jars. When she looked up, she froze.

At the front door, there was a shadow. Tall. Broad-shouldered. Just as she had thought she'd seen earlier.

Her breath caught as he lifted a hand and tapped gently on the glass pane.

'Kyle?' she whispered, the name tumbling out before she could stop it.

He looked just as Mabel had described – a tall, good-looking man, his face both achingly familiar and impossibly out of place in the warm glow of Cobblers Yard. She had thought she would never see him again.

And he was waiting at her door.

19

The fairy lights still twinkled across Cobblers Yard, their glow softened by the night air. The cobbles were damp from the evening mist rolling in off the sea, and the scent of cake and coffee lingered faintly, like a memory of the party just hours before.

Hannah froze at the sound of him gently tapping to be let in.

Kyle.

He stood framed in the lamplight outside her shop door – his hair a little longer than she remembered, his jaw sharper. For a heartbeat she thought she might be imagining him, but then he lifted his hand again, and the faintest smile curved across his lips.

Her hands shook as she unlatched the door. 'Kyle?'

'Hello, Hannah.' His voice carried the same gravelly warmth that had once been able to melt her heart.

She swallowed hard, stepping back in surprise. 'I thought I saw you at the yard party.'

'You did.' He slipped inside, glancing around the tidy shopfront, the art supplies stacked neatly, the cosy corner still glowing with lamplight. 'I didn't think it was the right time to meet again. Too many people. Lili. Nate. I didn't reckon they'd want to see me again.'

Of course they wouldn't want to see you again, thought Hannah. Her eyes darted across the yard before she closed the door. Although it was late, and she couldn't imagine anyone else would have spotted her evening visitor, she still quickly scanned the shops. Mabel and Marjorie had gone home. Their shop was locked, the blinds drawn. Thea and Callum had gone home too, returning to their house in the village of Pettistree, leaving Henry and his carers settling in for the evening. Joss and his mother-in-law had left hours earlier. Reggie's light was on in the flat where he lived above his shop, but he had his curtains drawn. She could hear his record player, the faint sound of jazz carrying on the evening breeze.

Hannah closed the door against the chill breeze and the soft music. She turned to Kyle. Her chest tightened. 'Why are you here, Kyle?' *And more to the point,* she thought, *how did you find me?*

He looked at her with a softness that unsettled her. 'I've been looking for you. For months. I wanted to apologise. In person. But I didn't know where you were. You'd left London …'

'I was in prison.'

'Yeah, I know – but you didn't return to London when you were released. When I went round to Lili's place, where she used to live with a guy … what was his name?'

'Lili's previous boyfriend, Alex …'

'I thought they could tell me where you were, but he'd gone, and so had Lili. The forwarding address was Washington DC!'

'They split up, and Lili moved to Suffolk permanently,' said Hannah.

'That's what the neighbours said. That's where I knew I'd

find you – after all, who would you have turned to when you got out? Your best friend, of course. But where in Suffolk? There was no way I thought I'd find you right here.'

Hannah frowned. She knew what he was referring to – finding her right there at the scene of the crime.

'I know things didn't end well for both of us, but when I read that article in the local paper, all about you taking over the antiques shop, and saw your photo … I couldn't believe you ended up with the very shop that we—'

Hannah held up her hand for him to stop. 'That's all in the past now.'

'Of course it is.' He paused. 'I bet you thought you'd never see me again,' he said. 'Imagine my luck when I saw that article in the paper, and then the flyers about the yard party all round town.'

'I saw you, but then you disappeared.'

'I wanted to talk to you alone. About what happened … can you forgive me? I just want to start over.'

Memories battered at her – late nights spent alone in that enormous modern house where they had lived together, which she'd had no idea how he had afforded, the constant whir of unanswered questions about where he'd been, the tension in his shoulders, the way he'd persuaded her to do the unthinkable.

'You've got a nerve,' she whispered. 'After everything.'

'I know,' he said quickly. 'I know, Hannah. I was no good for you. I dragged you down with me. But I've changed. Prison changes a man.'

She blinked. 'Prison?'

His mouth twisted. 'Out in Thailand. Got mixed up with the wrong people again. Paid for it this time.'

Hannah stared at him. This was all news to her – not the part where he'd got mixed up with the wrong people; he always did. But paying for it. She'd committed a crime because of him. And she'd served time because of him. They'd planned to go to Thailand together, to get away from people he owed money to, but she'd assumed he'd still gone on his own and that while she'd been languishing in prison, he'd been enjoying himself living it up in Thailand.

'But when I got out, I swore I'd go legit,' he continued. I've got a shop now. Antiques. All above board.'

She let out a sharp laugh. 'Antiques? Are you for real? After what you made me do?'

'I know what you're thinking.' He raised his hands, palms out. 'Mad idea, right? Antiques. But I knew I could make it work. And I couldn't stop thinking about you. About us. I wanted to make something of myself – properly, this time. For you. For Maisie.'

At the mention of her daughter, Hannah's spine stiffened. She remembered them making plans. He'd wanted Maisie to go to boarding school so that it was just the two of them and her daughter was out of the picture.

She heard the creak of a floorboard upstairs, light footsteps. Then Maisie's sleepy voice floated down the stairs.

'Mum? Who is it?'

Hannah turned, her heart pounding. Maisie stood on the staircase, hair rumpled, face still faintly striped with the remnants of her tiger face paint. Her eyes narrowed the moment she saw Kyle. 'You,' she whispered.

Kyle's expression faltered. 'Maisie … you've grown.'

Maisie's lips pressed into a thin line. 'What's he doing here?'

'Back to bed, sweetheart,' Hannah said gently, though her own voice trembled. 'It's … it's nothing. Kyle just came to the yard party and popped in to congratulate me on my new business.'

'Yeah – Joseph's old antiques shop has certainly changed. Wouldn't recognise the place.'

Maisie lingered another moment, glaring at Kyle. Then she turned and padded back upstairs, her door clicking shut.

Silence stretched in her wake.

Kyle rubbed the back of his neck. 'She's not pleased to see me.'

'What did you expect?' Hannah snapped, her voice low. 'You left me to face prison. You knew what you'd asked me to do, and you didn't show up at the trial. I thought you'd run.'

'I didn't know,' he said urgently. 'Not until later. I thought you'd changed your mind, that you didn't want to come with me to Thailand when you didn't show up at the airport. Then when I saw that article online – *Antiques burglar confesses to theft to save her best friend* – I realised what you'd done. That you'd turned yourself in to protect Lili.'

'Stupidly, I wore her coat when I went to Joseph's shop to steal the antiques and took that blasted ghost orchid.' It was the ghost orchid that had caused all the trouble. She'd only taken it to give to Lili as a surprise. Lili, who had gone to stay temporarily with Hannah and Maisie in Kyle's house, had previously been living in the flat above what was then Joseph's antiques shop. She'd sent Hannah on an errand to fetch a box of her things from the flat. Kyle had seen an opportunity. Although Lili had given Hannah a key, he'd worked out that if she stole some of the antiques, and staged a break-in, it would absolve her of any responsibility for the burglary – after all, why would she break in if she had a key?

Hannah didn't feel comfortable staging a break-in, although she did do Kyle's bidding and steal some antiques. Joseph's old shop had been full to the brim with them, but they were not, Hannah guessed, worth much money. She'd warned Kyle of that fact, but still he insisted she went through with it, holding the threat of losing it all – the roof over their head – if she didn't.

Hannah hadn't had a job or any way of supporting herself. She'd felt trapped, so she'd done as he said, only taking a few odds and ends that she hoped Joseph wouldn't miss. And that was the reason she didn't stage a robbery either. But her downfall had been wearing Lili's coat – Reggie had seen her leave the shop, mistaking her for Lili because of the distinctive coat.

Perhaps some of the things she'd stolen wouldn't have been missed. She'd never know. But it was the missing ghost orchid that had brought it all to a head and had led to Lili's arrest. Of course, Hannah couldn't leave her languishing in jail for a crime she hadn't committed. So, Hannah had owned up, knowing she stood to lose everything – Maisie, Kyle and her home. She knew she'd done the right thing by Lili and Maisie. She couldn't have taken Maisie on the run, living in Thailand, evading the police. That was no life for a child.

She'd been so lucky that Lili had known a fantastic social worker who had stepped in and stopped Maisie from being taken into care, allowing Lili to look after Maisie until Hannah had served her time. The ghost orchid. If only she hadn't taken it, not realising its rarity and value. Kyle had taken one look at the plant and had somehow known immediately. She had turned up with a lot of worthless items that weren't going to fetch anywhere near the money he needed to pay back the money he owed, but the ghost orchid – that was another matter entirely.

Hannah stared at Kyle. She didn't bother asking what had happened to the rare, valuable plant when she'd handed it over.

He shook his head. 'I admired you for doing that – owning up to save your best friend from prison. I still do.'

Her chest ached. 'You admired me, but you didn't come back and explain to the courts that I wasn't the mastermind behind it, and that you made me do it.'

'I couldn't,' he admitted, voice raw. 'I told you – I was in prison myself. Believe me, I've paid for what I did. More than once over. But I'm not that man anymore. I swear to you, I'm clean. My business is legit.'

Hannah stared at him, her heart tugging against her better judgement. He was no good. He'd broken her once, nearly ruined her life. And yet here he was, flesh and blood, looking at her as though she was the only person who'd ever mattered.

'You never told them about me,' Kyle said, eyeing her keenly. 'All that time you went through the trial, you didn't bring my name into it. They could have stopped me boarding that plane, you know, if you'd spilled the beans about my involvement, in fact, about everything you knew about my life – which, granted, wasn't much. I didn't involve you in my shady deals and business affairs, but I know you suspected I wasn't above board.'

Hannah had her reasons. She said, 'I'm not a snitch.' Like her, he hadn't had the best start in life, and he had tried to give her everything she wanted – a nice house, a fancy car, nice clothes – none of which she'd worked for. And she had been afraid that the nasty people would come after him if he didn't pay his debts.

He paused, looking her up and down and smiling. 'You look good, Hannah. Really well. Haven't aged a day.'

She felt her cheeks grow hot under his gaze.

'When I saw that article in the paper. About your shop. About the yard party.' His voice dropped, almost pleading. 'I thought it was fate. I've been looking for you, Hannah. I wanted to say sorry. To see if … if we could be friends again. Maybe more, in time.'

Her thoughts spun. Lili had given her a second chance, Nate had trusted her, and the shopkeepers had welcomed her into their fold. Everything in her life was finally going right. And yet, some fragile part of her wondered if this – if he – was the final piece of the jigsaw. The icing on the cake.

But Maisie's face, wary and angry, flashed in her mind.

'I don't know,' Hannah whispered.

'Let me prove it,' Kyle said softly. 'Just give me a chance. That's all I'm asking.'

Hannah drew a shaky breath, the fairy lights casting shifting shadows across the cosy corner. She had everything to lose, and yet, the tiniest spark inside her whispered: *what if?*

20

The morning after the yard party dawned pale and damp, a mist creeping in off the sea and curling against the shopfront windows of Cobblers Yard. Hannah was standing at the kitchen counter, spooning coffee into the cafetière, when she heard Maisie padding in behind her. It was Sunday, the shops were closed, and Cobblers Yard felt eerily quiet, deserted, after all the festivities of the party.

Maisie sat down at the table with her arms folded, a frown already darkening her face. 'Mum, we need to talk.'

Hannah looked at her daughter. She could almost have laughed at how grown-up she sounded. But she didn't. Instead, her heart sank. She set the spoon down carefully. 'About last night?'

'About him.' Maisie's voice was sharp, older than her years. 'Why was Kyle here? Why did you let him in?'

Hannah turned, her throat tightening. 'Because he wanted to talk. I told you, he came to the yard party yesterday, but there were just too many people, and we wouldn't have had a chance for a catch-up.'

Maisie's jaw clenched. 'I don't like Kyle. I hope he doesn't come back. He's not coming back – is he?'

Hannah sighed. She wasn't surprised in the least by Maisie's reaction. She wondered if her daughter could get past what had happened. Hannah couldn't deny that it was a huge deal for someone so young, being separated from their mum because of a prison sentence.

But things are different now, Hannah thought. I'm not dependent on Kyle, on any man. I've got a successful business, and most importantly I can take care of myself and Maisie. Their relationship, if that was where it led if she resumed their friendship, would be on a completely different footing than before. She wouldn't feel compelled to do anything she didn't want to do this time.

Hannah wasn't about to explain all that to a nine-year-old. She poured some breakfast cereal for Maisie and got two warmed croissants out of the oven. 'Look – your favourite,' she said, putting the croissant on a plate beside Maisie's cereal. The smell of warm, buttery croissants filled the little kitchen in the flat, eliciting a smile from Maisie, who poured some milk over her cereal and began to eat.

Hannah sat opposite her with her coffee and croissant, wishing that it had been Maisie's sleepover weekend with Nate and Lili. Then she wouldn't have been there when Kyle had called. She raised her eyebrows. Hannah had never once, on the weekends she spent with Maisie, wished that her daughter was away with her father instead. In fact, it had always been the reverse; she selfishly resented each weekend that she couldn't have Maisie.

She knew she was lucky after her prison stint to have her at all, let alone have her most of the time. The original plan had been for shared custody, but she had Maisie most of the time.

Hannah admonished herself for being so selfish as to wish for a moment that it had been Nate's weekend so that she could have avoided this awkward breakfast conversation with Maisie. Then again, if Kyle were to come back into her life permanently, Maisie would have to find out some time.

Hannah drew a breath. 'I know he's not your favourite person.' She winced, aware that was an understatement. 'But doesn't everyone deserve a second chance?'

Maisie frowned again. '*He* doesn't deserve a second chance.'

Hannah hadn't thought the conversation was going to be easy. She picked up her strong cup of coffee and took two large gulps. Maisie was strong-willed and independent-minded. It was everything Hannah wanted her daughter to be – basically the opposite of herself, with her habit of forming relationships with men like Kyle and being beholden to them because she hadn't been strong-willed or independent. Hannah knew many would ask why she would even consider letting a man like that back into her life. But she wasn't that same person; she'd grown and changed. If she were to give Kyle a second chance, this time would be different.

'Don't you remember what he did, Mummy? What he made you do?'

Of course she remembered. She remembered every sleepless night in that prison cell, every letter she couldn't bring herself to write to Lili who, after everything she'd done, had miraculously stood by her. She remembered the humiliation of facing Lili, knowing her best friend had taken the fall for her, however briefly, because of that stupid mistake. And she remembered the ache of believing Kyle had vanished, leaving her to pick up the pieces alone. 'I haven't forgotten,' Hannah said quietly. 'But people change.'

Maisie shook her head. 'Not him. He's no good, Mum.'

Hannah put her coffee down, watching her daughter finish her breakfast cereal, get up and put her cereal bowl and spoon in the sink before resuming her seat and picking up a knife to spread some butter on her warm croissant. How had she ended up with a daughter who had such a mature head on her shoulders? Hannah felt like she was having this conversation with a nineteen-year-old, not a nine-year-old.

'You told me that you had to leave the past behind. Why would you bring him back now?'

Hannah swallowed hard, the weight of her daughter's words pressing against the fragile flicker of hope she'd felt the previous night. *He's no good. But what if?*

Everything else in her life was going so well; the shop thriving, friends rallying around her, the yard party a success. Lili had given her a second chance. Nate had trusted her enough to share custody of Maisie. Didn't Kyle deserve the same grace?

They could start slowly. Just friends. See if he really had changed. And if he hadn't, well – then no one needed to know. Not even Maisie.

Maisie's eyes were shining, fierce. 'Promise me you won't see him again.'

Hannah forced a smile she didn't feel. 'We'll see, sweetheart. Don't worry about it.'

Maisie's frown deepened.

Hannah avoided her gaze. Maisie knew when her mum was being evasive. Hannah had made the classic mistake of using those two words – *we'll see.*

Maisie finished her croissant in silence. When she'd finished, she scraped back her chair and left the kitchen, muttering under her breath.

When the door closed behind her, Hannah sank into the chair. Her chest twisted with guilt. If Lili found out that Kyle was back, she'd tell Hannah she was making the biggest mistake of her life. Maisie clearly wanted nothing to do with him.

But Hannah wanted to find out for herself. She would have to keep it secret. Just for now. She realised it was the only way.

Hannah called out, 'Maisie?' as she rose from her chair with her empty coffee mug and plate, walking over to the kitchen sink to wash up.

Maisie appeared at the door, still frowning at her.

Hannah really didn't want to tell fibs, but sometimes she believed that what someone didn't know couldn't hurt them. She smiled sweetly at her daughter. 'Look, I've been thinking …'

'About Kyle?'

'Yes.'

Maisie frowned some more.

'You have a point. So …' Hannah said a silent prayer hoping she was doing the right thing, and crossed her fingers behind her back, 'I won't see Kyle again.' *Not while you're here*, she thought, but she didn't tell Maisie that.

Maisie's face broke into the biggest grin. She ran over and hugged her mum. 'Mummy, you're the best.'

Am I? Hannah's smile faltered. *What she doesn't know can't hurt her,* she said to herself. If things worked out with Kyle, and he proved to her that he had changed, then she'd reintroduce him to Maisie.

She had a plan. Every other weekend, when Maisie went to

stay with Nate, Hannah could meet Kyle. No one would need to know. If it didn't work out, then it would vanish like a dream. If it did – if Kyle truly had changed – then maybe, in time, she could prove to Maisie and Lili that this wasn't just a repeat of old mistakes. For the time being, Kyle was her secret.

'Maisie, can you do something for me?'

Maisie nodded enthusiastically.

Guilt gnawed at her, sharp as salt on a wound as she looked at her daughter's trusting face smiling up at her.

'Will you promise me not to mention Kyle's visit to … anyone?' Hannah was thinking of Nate and Lili – Lili especially. 'Can we just forget Kyle's visit yesterday ever happened?' While Hannah was saying this, a little part of her thought, *Should I do that too in case they find out I've seen him again?*

She pressed her palms flat against the table, steadying herself. Why should they find out? she told herself firmly. This is my choice, my life. And for once, I want to decide for myself.

But even as she thought it, a chill ran through her. Because secrets had a way of surfacing – especially in a small town like Aldeburgh, and especially in Cobblers Yard, where nothing stayed hidden for long. Hannah was thinking about what she'd done there. Kyle reappearing had brought all that flooding back. What if the shopkeepers in Cobblers Yard found out her secret? It was still something she was afraid of – that her new friends would look at her differently, would no longer be her friends, and all the camaraderie would vanish.

That's not going to happen, Hannah convinced herself. All she was going to do was to see if she had a future with Kyle.

21

The following Saturday, the flat felt too quiet without Maisie. Hannah watched from the shop window as Nate walked out of Cobblers Yard with Maisie. Her daughter glanced behind her, hand lifted in a half-hearted wave.

Maisie hadn't said it outright, but Hannah could feel her disapproval lingering, unspoken, as she'd got her bag together for her weekend with Nate and Lili. Unfortunately, she knew about Hannah's meeting with Kyle that day. Hannah had still sworn her to secrecy, saying it was absolutely a one-off. Kyle wanted to see her, and until he had, he'd probably be back and forward to the shop. Which was true.

Kyle had called into the shop again during the week, which had surprised Hannah, as she'd thought Kyle had his own antiques shop to run and would be far too busy to call in. He'd told her that his shop was on the Norfolk Suffolk border, which was miles away.

Kyle had mentioned he had an assistant who manned the antiques shop while Kyle attended trade fairs, auction houses, and people's homes when they called on him for valuations. It sounded as though he'd offer to put those items he'd valued up for auction to secure the best price possible and take a commission, or he'd buy them himself and resell them in his shop for a small profit, that being his commission.

To Hannah's relief, his business did sound all above board, and the mention of his assistant got her back to thinking about hiring someone part-time; she could then go to trade fairs and also have Saturdays off, so she wasn't working six days a week. Hannah had discovered that running a business, and a successful one at that, had its down sides.

She knew she had no right to complain now the shop seemed to have turned a corner financially, but the demands on her time were greater than ever. However, Kyle had persuaded her to shut the shop early on Saturday, at lunchtime, and take the afternoon off. 'Your business is not going to suffer if you take one afternoon off,' he'd assured her.

She'd agreed to the weekend meet-up when she'd seen him in the middle of the week. Now, with Maisie gone, but her daughter's disapproving glare still pervading her thoughts, Hannah told herself she wouldn't go. She'd keep the half day for herself – well not entirely for herself; there were things to catch up on for the business, such as stocktaking and accounts. But then maybe she could take a long walk by the sea, along the promenade in Aldeburgh to Thorpeness, and sit by the boating lake on her own with a book and an ice cream. But as the clock hands edged toward noon, her phone buzzed with a message.

I'll be at The Green Man in Snape. No pressure. Just a coffee. K.

Her heart leapt. She sat staring at the screen for a full minute before her fingers typed back: *I'll be there in half an hour.*

❖

The Green Man was one of those pubs that tourists stumbled

into after a walk along the banks of the river Alde – all low beams, crooked windows, and the faint smell of woodsmoke even in summer. It was far enough from Aldeburgh that she wouldn't risk bumping into anyone from Cobblers Yard. It wasn't as though they'd pop there in their lunch break. It was a drive away, and you could forget parking at Snape Maltings on a Saturday afternoon in lovely weather unless you got there early. Hannah was going to park in the little pub car park on the outskirts of the town.

Hannah checked her hair and makeup in the bathroom mirror, finding a red lipstick in her makeup bag that she didn't normally use. She was wearing a dress for a change, a pretty floral knee length summery dress along with a jean jacket – fortunately the warm summer weather had extended well into late September.

She stared at her reflection in the mirror and felt as though she was going on a date, not meeting her ex just for a coffee and a chat.

Hannah walked back into the shop downstairs. She'd already turned the door sign to *Closed*. She saw a couple with children looking in her window, their expressions one of disappointment at finding her shop closed. Hannah watched them leave and felt a pang of guilt, and regret, that Kyle had persuaded her to take the afternoon off rather than meeting him after work. She understood – he had a bit of a journey, travelling over this way to meet her, so it was give and take. And only one afternoon.

She tried not to think of the money she was losing that afternoon. 'They'll be back,' she said under her breath, standing in the window, watching her potential customers cross the yard to the bookshop.

Hannah returned to the counter for her handbag and took a deep breath before opening the shop door. She wasn't sure what she'd say to the other shopkeepers when they discovered her shop was closed on Saturday afternoon. *I've been so busy, I just needed a break, some time to myself.* They'd understand. She glanced at her phone. Time was getting on. She didn't want to bump into any of them and have to explain why her shop was closed. She did consider that the other shops might be so busy – everyone's footfall had picked up since the yard party a week ago – that they wouldn't even notice she was closed. By the time they closed up too, and left, they might think she'd just closed at five too.

Hannah nipped outside, locked her door and quickly crossed the yard, hoping no one saw her.

❖

'Marjorie – did you know that Hannah was only working half a day today, and closing her shop early?'

Mabel had been rearranging the shop window to add some new donations – since the yard party, they'd had so many customers that the sisters had to constantly put out new donations from their storage room in the back. She'd spotted Hannah locking her door and leaving the shop – rather furtively, Mabel thought.

'Perhaps she's gone out to grab a sandwich, or have lunch at one of the cafés.' Marjorie had joined her sister in the window, carrying some more clothes to arrange in the window display.

'She didn't look as though she was just going to lunch,' Mabel remarked.

Marjorie turned to Mabel. 'I think you're right. She's closed the shop for the afternoon. Look, she's pulled the blinds.'

Mabel, whose eyesight wasn't as sharp as her sister's, peered through the shop window. 'So she has.'

'That is odd. She never closes early.'

'My thoughts exactly,' agreed Mabel. 'And she didn't even tell us.'

Marjorie raised her eyebrows. 'Does she have to?'

'Well, no, of course not, but we all look out for one another here in Cobblers Yard, and we all know each other's business.'

'You mean we *like* to know everyone's business. And you're not just talking about shop business, are you?'

They exchanged a knowing smile before Mabel said, 'Do you know something even stranger?'

'No.' Marjorie shook her head. 'But I have a feeling you're about to enlighten me.'

'I think she's going on a date.'

'A date? How marvellous. She deserves to meet someone nice. She must feel that everyone she knows who has come to make a new life for themselves in Suffolk has met their Mr Right. It's about time she met hers.' Marjorie caught her sister's expression. 'What's so strange about that?'

'I don't know … it's just the way she left, as though she was …'

'She was …?' Marjorie prompted.

'Hiding something.'

'Hiding something? Oh Mabel, you read too much into things. She's going on a date, most likely a first date, and she probably just wants to keep it under wraps because it's early days. She wants to see if, you know, things progress, and he's a keeper.'

'I'll ask Maisie when she pops in next time.'

'You'll do no such thing, Mabel. Honestly, you really are

incorrigible sometimes. That's her private life. I'm sure she'll introduce us if things go that far and they become an item.'

'It was just odd the way she snuck out.'

Marjorie heaved a deep sigh, shook her head at her sister, and said, 'I'm going to put the kettle on.' She left Mabel staring out of the window at the closed shop across the yard.

'I'll tell you what, though,' Marjorie called out from the back of the shop, 'for someone she's just met, he must have made quite an impression for her to choose to close up her shop on a Saturday afternoon and spend the afternoon with him – assuming, of course, that you're right and it is a date!'

Mabel raised her eyebrows and thought of that tall, handsome broad-shouldered young man who she'd seen enter the yard during the party last weekend, then swiftly do an about-turn and leave. 'Someone she's just met …' Mabel mused, repeating Marjorie's last words. She remembered catching Hannah going ashen during the party, as though something – or someone – had surprised her.

'Or a face from her past …'

'What was that?' Marjorie asked, carrying a tea tray into the shop, a plate of chocolate digestives balanced precariously on the edge.

'I'd like to meet him.'

'And you will, in time,' replied Marjorie, 'if she has started dating again.'

'I worry for her. She's fallen in with the wrong sort in the past.'

Marjorie sighed. 'I know what, or rather who, you're thinking about, her ex – can't remember his name – who led her into a life a crime.'

'It wasn't a life of crime,' Mabel said indignantly. 'She made a mistake, stealing from the antiques shop to get him out of a spot of bother. I just don't want her making the same mistakes.'

'You are not her keeper, Mabel.'

'But she's my friend, and I worry … for her and Maisie.'

'I'm her friend too.' Marjorie placed a comforting hand on her sister's arm. 'Don't worry. She's got a life now, here in Cobblers Yard, and she's not stupid enough to repeat the same mistake and risk it all. Not now. Not when it's all going so well. I'm sure she knows what she's doing,' she said confidently. 'Now, how about a cup of tea and a biscuit?'

22

Hannah walked into the pub, unsure if she knew what she was doing. On the drive there, she'd probably had too much time to think. She knew her friends would warn her about getting involved with Kyle again, but she kept reminding herself that everyone deserved a second chance – even him. And besides, she was only meeting him for a coffee, not committing to a full-blown relationship.

But you are here, she also reminded herself. *And anything could happen.*

She spotted Kyle instantly. He was at a corner table, jacket slung over the back of his chair, a pint untouched in front of him. He stood when she entered, and for a moment, time fell away. He had the same crooked smile, the same confident tilt of his head.

'Hannah.' His voice warmed, rich with relief. 'You came.'

She forced a small smile, slipping into the seat opposite him. Their table was in a private alcove with no other people sitting near them, to Hannah's relief. The pub was also quieter than she'd expected. She was relieved about that too; she was afraid she might bump into someone she knew.

She looked across the table at him. 'Just for a coffee. Don't read anything into it.'

'Fair enough.' He signalled to the bar, and a young waitress brought over the drinks menu. They both ordered a cappuccino.

'So. How've you been?' he asked.

Hannah arched a brow. 'You really want me to answer that?' Even though life was treating her very well now the shop was profitable, and she felt she was finally settling into life on she Suffolk Coast, she wasn't going to let him off the hook that easily. She'd worked hard to find a life, and some semblance of stability and normality for Maisie after what had happened – all she was looking for now was to move out of the flat and find a place to call home.

His grin faltered. 'All right. I deserved that. I know I don't have the right to ask about your life after what happened. But … I've thought about you every day.'

Her stomach twisted. The sincerity in his eyes unnerved her, even as suspicion prickled at the back of her mind. He'd said things like that before – words that sounded like promises until they dissolved in the cold light of morning.

'I'm not the same woman I was,' she said firmly. 'I don't need anyone to look after me anymore. I've built a business, and I'm raising Maisie on my own. I don't want …' She paused, being careful. 'I don't want to slip back into old mistakes.'

Kyle leaned forward. 'I don't want that either. I've changed, Hannah. I swear. After prison, I knew I had to.'

She thought about what he'd told her that evening after the yard party, when he'd turned up that first time unannounced at her shop. 'Antiques.' She was still wrapping her head around that. She lowered her voice, leaning towards him, and said in hushed tones, 'You sell antiques, after persuading me to steal them?'

He winced but didn't look away. 'Yeah. It's ironic. But I wanted to prove I could do it right this time. No dodgy deals, no back room bargains. Just honest work.'

She sipped her coffee to give herself time, the foam bitter on her tongue. Could she believe him? He looked older, wearier, the cockiness she remembered replaced with something quieter. Yet she couldn't shake the thought that Kyle always had a story ready, always knew how to spin things to make himself sound repentant.

'I don't trust easily anymore,' she said finally.

'I know. And I don't expect you to.' His voice dropped. 'That's why I asked for this. Just coffee. Just a start. Let me show you I'm not the same man.'

The fire crackled in the grate. Around them, the pub started to fill up with walkers and families, nobody paying them the slightest attention. Hannah's heart tugged in two directions – the voice of reason warning her he was no good, and another voice, quieter but insistent, whispering, *What if he really has changed?*

She set her cup down, her fingers trembling. 'This has to stay between us. Maisie doesn't want you in her life. And Lili – she wouldn't forgive me if she knew I was seeing you again.' *Not until I can prove to her that you really, truly have changed.*

Kyle nodded slowly. 'Understood. No one needs to know. Not until you're ready.'

Hannah met his gaze, steady but wary. 'Every other weekend when Maisie's staying with her dad. That's the only time I'll see you. And if I think for a second that you haven't changed …'

'You won't,' he said softly. 'Not this time.'

Hannah leaned back, her heart pounding with both fear and

something she hadn't felt in a long time – possibility.

She wasn't ready to forgive. She wasn't ready to trust.

But she was ready to find out.

'So, what can I do to prove to you that I've changed?'

Hannah thought about it. In the past, when they'd been together, he had never talked to her about his business deals. Of course, she knew why – because they were shady at best. And for her part, for that reason, she didn't want to know. But now … Hannah narrowed her eyes. 'I'd like you to tell me all about your new business.'

Kyle smiled a disarming smile. 'I can do better than that. I can show you.'

23

Hannah had told Kyle, quite clearly, not to visit Cobblers Yard again. Not yet. Not until she was sure she wanted the others to know he was back in her life.

So when the knock rattled her shop door mid-morning, she almost dropped the stack of sketchbooks she'd been arranging. She turned, already knowing who it would be. Nobody else would knock on a shop door that said *Open* – only someone who knew they shouldn't be there.

The last time she'd seen him, when they'd met for coffee at the pub in Snape, had been a week earlier. They'd chatted long into the afternoon and early evening, eventually having a meal together. He hadn't wanted to go home, and neither had she, but she'd held steadfast to her guiding principle – until she was sure he'd changed, she wasn't getting romantically involved. She knew that was what he wanted – his body language spoke volumes. He had reached out to hold her hand across the pub table, and as they had stepped outside the pub late in the evening, still chatting, the wind had whipped around her, and he had reached out a gentle hand to brush her hair away from her face.

He had risked a goodbye kiss before they'd got into their

cars and left, and much to her annoyance, her resolve had crumbled, and it had been all she could do not to fall into his arms. She hadn't done that, not quite, but she had let him hold her and kiss her, long and lingering, making her realise what she'd been missing, and longing for – love.

Kyle stood outside her shop, grinning as though he'd never left, hands shoved in the pockets of his leather jacket. For a moment, Hannah froze, torn between irritation and that unsettling rush of familiarity that still stole through her whenever she saw him.

She opened the door and hissed, 'I told you not to come here!' There was a reason she'd told him they could only see each other every two weeks when Maisie was on her sleepover weekends. But as luck would have it, William was at a birthday party with his schoolmates, and Nate had wanted the opportunity to spend some time with Maisie, just the two of them – something he hardly ever got a chance to do.

Nate knew that meant he'd have had Maisie two weekends on the trot, but he'd said it was an absolute one-off, and it went without saying that the following weekend would be Hannah's to spend with Maisie instead.

Hannah had readily agreed, quite excited that it had turned out she didn't have to wait a fortnight to see Kyle again. Even so, she still didn't want him turning up at her shop on the day they were meeting again.

He had the grace to look sheepish, though the sparkle in his eyes softened the effect. 'I know, I know. I'm sorry. I just … couldn't wait to see you again.'

Her pulse quickened; with anger, or with something else, she couldn't say. People in the yard were busying themselves, shop doors propped open, bunting still faintly fluttering from the party three weeks earlier. They'd left the bunting and twinkling lights up in the old-fashioned yard, knowing they brightened up the place and made it more welcoming – especially the twinkling lights, which would bring warmth to the shop fronts when the clocks changed and the evenings started drawing in.

They'd been talk of holding another yard party. It was the first weekend in October, and Lili had come up with a brilliant idea – a Halloween party. Halloween fell perfectly on a Friday at the end of the month during the school half-term holiday. The party could go on into the evening, with children playing trick-or-treat in the yard. Maisie adored the idea, and so did Hannah.

Just then, though, Hannah had other things on her mind than another yard party. She grabbed Kyle's arm and pulled him inside, worried that at any moment one of her neighbours could step out and see them. 'You didn't have to stand outside knocking, you know. The sign on the shop door does say *Open*.'

'Oh, I hadn't noticed.'

'I told you I would be open until lunchtime.' Hannah poked her head outside and had a quick look around the yard. Thankfully she didn't see anybody in their shop windows, from where they might have spotted Kyle. 'You can't do this, Kyle. Come here. Not yet. I thought you were going to wait in the car outside, like we arranged?'

'Sorry. I arrived early. I promise, no more doorstep surprises.' His voice lowered, almost contrite. 'I'll behave. I just … I just wanted to make sure you hadn't changed your mind.'

She rolled her eyes. 'You could have just texted me from your car. I would have shut the shop early and come now.'

Hannah raised her eyebrows, surprised at what she'd said.

Before she knew it, she'd be closing her shop every other weekend just to spend time with him. That wouldn't do her end-of-month figures any good. She realised that she couldn't continue with these secretive meetings for long; someone in the yard would soon wonder what was going on – why she kept closing early or, at this rate, not opening at all on a Saturday.

She hesitated. Her better judgement told her to chuck him out, slam the door and remind him that her life now was steady, ordinary, good, and he couldn't just turn up when and how he wanted. She hoped he wasn't already slipping into his old ways, doing just what he wanted. But her curiosity gnawed at her. She'd said she wanted to see his business, to know where his money came from. This was her chance.

He gently lifted her chin, his disarming smile catching. 'I said I was sorry. Now let me take you out and impress you with my new antiques business.' His disarming smile was catching.

'Fine,' she muttered, but the smile on her face betrayed her. She couldn't stay mad with him for long. 'But we leave now. Before anyone notices.'

His grin widened. 'Deal. I'll turn the sign to *Closed* in the window.'

Hannah was just putting her coat on, glancing at the clock on the wall, realising it was barely eleven, when she heard Kyle say, 'We're closed! Can't you read?'

Hannah rushed over, catching a group standing outside her door. 'Kyle!' She was about to admonish him when she heard quite distinctly her potential customers say, 'How rude. I'm not going to shop there anymore, and I'm going to tell my friends too.'

Hannah stood there with her hands on her hips as Kyle

slowly turned around. 'Sorry, sorry. I'm just so desperate for you to come with me today, and show off my shop, and what a success I'm making of myself. I stupidly got a little antsy thinking you might let them all in, and then we'd be here for god knows how long.' He looked at her contritely. 'Sorry. I'll go after them if you want and apologise.' Kyle started opening the door.

Hannah shot a look across the yard and saw Mabel in the window of the charity shop. She quickly closed the blind on the door and the blinds in the shop window, forgetting she hadn't intended to do that. She'd closed the blinds the weekend before last when she'd gone to meet with Kyle at lunchtime in Snape and had thought in hindsight that she was more likely to draw attention to the shop being closed by drawing the blinds rather than simply turning the sign on the door.

It was possible that the other shopkeepers might not have even noticed she was closed; it wasn't as though they could see the sign from their shop windows, unless they were staring into the yard, watching her movements – like Mabel was at that moment from across the yard.

Hannah knew she was being paranoid. Mabel was probably just putting more odds and ends in the window. She'd noticed that the number of customers had increased for all of them, especially the charity shop. But if Mabel hadn't been watching her shop, she'd certainly have a reason to watch her movements now the blinds had been drawn.

Kyle took her in his arms. 'Finally, we have some privacy from prying eyes in the yard. Honestly, I don't know how you work here, putting up with all those other shopkeepers looking in at what you're doing.'

'Why would that bother me?' Hannah asked, surprised.

'They're lovely people.'

'Yes, they are, very helpful – especially Thea in the bookshop and the old guy in the music shop.'

'What?' Hannah wrestled herself out of his arms. 'You've been in the other shops?'

'I told you I got here early, so I had a wander before I knocked on your door.'

'Oh, god, don't tell me you went into the charity shop!'

His smiled slipped. 'Er, no … why would I go in a charity shop?' He said the words *charity shop* as though she'd just asked if he'd gone into a slaughterhouse.

'Oh, thank god!' Hannah said in relief. 'But why did you go into the other shops?'

'I told you, I arrived here early. I was just curious.'

'Did you tell them who you were?'

'I told them I was Kyle and all about our history, and how we're carrying on this secret liaison …'

Hannah stared at him agog.

His face creased into the biggest grin. 'Of course I didn't! What do you take me for – stupid? I get that you're protecting your past. After all, god knows what they'd think if they found out.'

'Thanks,' Hannah said sarcastically. She did not appreciate the comment and did not need to be reminded of her secrets. 'Mabel and Marjorie know,' she blurted, cursing herself for saying that.

'Who are Mabel and Marjorie?'

'The octogenarian sisters who run the charity shop.'

'Ah, now I get why you were so concerned that I'd been in their shop. But they wouldn't recognise me, would they, as the guy who got you into so much trouble?'

Hannah shook her head. 'No, why would they? They've never seen a photo of you.' Hannah didn't have a photo of the two of them. She'd deleted them all off her old phone and bought herself a new phone.

'What are you so worried for, then?'

Hannah couldn't answer that. 'I guess if they found out who you were, they might try and put a stop to this.'

Kyle burst out laughing. 'What could two women in their eighties possibly do?' Before Hannah could get a word in, Kyle added, 'And how would they find out who I am anyway?'

'Lili, I guess.'

'Or Maisie,' said Kyle, frowning. He brightened. 'Look, all the more reason for me to prove to you that I've gone straight, for real, I'm on the up-and-up, and then nothing, and nobody, can come between us – right?'

Hannah smiled. 'Right.'

On the way out, Hannah surreptitiously glanced across the yard, breathing a sigh of relief when she realised that neither of The Gossip Girls were in the charity shop window. She'd sent Kyle ahead so that they didn't walk out together and hoped that if anybody had spotted him walking out of her shop, they'd think he was just the last customer that morning before she closed the shop.

The fact that he had been browsing in the other shops and hadn't mentioned that he'd been hanging around waiting for Hannah actually worked in her favour. Hannah turned around, locked the shop door and hurried out of Cobblers Yard. Although she was looking forward to her day out with Kyle, seeing his business and having him prove that he had definitely turned over a new leaf, she couldn't wait for this to be over – keeping secrets from her friends.

But I'm already keeping one big secret from Thea, Joss and Reggie – my past, she thought. She tried to brush the thought aside.

As Hannah left the yard, she glanced back as Mabel appeared at the window, her gaze settling on Hannah's closed shop.

24

The drive took them along winding lanes, the fields spilling gold and green to either side, the trees starting to shed their golden leaves. Kyle chatted easily, telling her stories about the antiques fairs he'd been frequenting, about the auctions he'd managed to win. Hannah listened, half believing, half weighing every word. He sounded … proud. Honest, even. But Kyle always had been a good talker.

They crossed into Norfolk, with its flatter landscape, before pulling into a small market town with cobbled streets and a central square. The Saturday bustle was in full swing. Stalls selling flowers, cheeses, amateur artists' landscape paintings and books crowded the pavements, and the air smelled faintly of roasted coffee and fresh bread from the small cafés, which had tables and chairs outside, lining the pavements.

Kyle parked just off the square and gestured toward a narrow-fronted shop with a painted sign above the window: *Stanford & Co. Antiques.*

Her breath caught. 'Stanford?'

He smiled faintly. 'My mum's maiden name. Thought it sounded respectable.'

Hannah looked at him. What it sounded like was that Kyle was purposely not using his own name, going incognito in case his past caught up with him.

Kyle was about to get out of the car when he caught her expression. 'I know what you're thinking, Hannah. I am not hiding behind the name. I thought it just sounds—'

'Respectable – yeah, I heard.'

Hannah kept her thoughts to herself. If anybody did find out about his past, it didn't matter what name he used – they'd think his business was far from respectable. She actually felt sorry for him, and she did understand. It was just what she was afraid of for herself – putting all that hard work into a business only for it to fold because people found out about her past and couldn't put it behind them. She reminded herself how difficult it was to start over – and that was with help. What help had Kyle been given?

As they got out of the car, Hannah asked, 'Your assistant – has he worked here long?'

'She.'

'Oh, right.' Hannah couldn't hide her surprise. For some reason she'd just assumed that his assistant was a man. Some antique furniture was quite cumbersome and heavy, and she imagined a couple of guys would be needed to shift things in and out, and around the shop floor.

Hannah wondered how old the assistant was. As they walked towards the shop, she asked, 'So, how long has your assistant been in the antiques business?'

'She's been happily married for thirty-odd years.'

Hannah looked at him. 'That's not what I asked.'

He grinned at her. 'Isn't it?'

Hannah wished he couldn't read her like an open book.

'And to answer your faux question – longer than me. A lot longer. Her father ran an antiques business for years. Then she stepped in to work with him, but he obviously wanted to retire, so she was looking for a new business partner.'

'And that person was you?'

'Oh … yes.'

'So, she's not really an assistant.'

'Um no. Sorry, I shouldn't have called her that. She's my business partner.'

'Why didn't you just say she was your business partner in the first place?'

He lowered his eyes. 'I guess I just wanted to impress you. Didn't want you to think less of me because I didn't go into business on my own, like you, Hannah.'

'I didn't go it alone. I had help, Kyle, from Maisie's father, Nate, and from Lili. So no, I do not think any less of you going into business with someone else. Sometimes two heads are better than one.'

He grinned at her, exhaling in relief.

'But …' Hannah had to ask. 'Does she know about your past?'

'Yes. Everything. She decided to give me a chance to prove myself. Like you're doing for me now.'

Like Lili and Nate did for me. Hannah decided she'd like her.

'You'll like her.'

Hannah took Kyle's arm. 'I can't wait to meet her.'

Inside, the shop was neat and well-lit, with the scent of beeswax polish mingling with old wood. Glass cabinets displayed silverware, shelves held china teacups and gilt-framed mirrors, and the window featured a handsome oak writing desk. Nothing about it whispered of shady back room deals or menacing creditors.

A young assistant – barely out of his teens – looked up from behind the counter and smiled. 'Morning, Kyle.'

Kyle gave him a friendly nod. 'Morning, Tom. This is Hannah, a friend of mine.'

Hannah's eyebrows rose at *friend*, but she said nothing. They were just friends at the moment, although that wasn't strictly true – they had kissed. But Kyle knew she was taking things slowly; they were getting to know each other in their new lives.

She whispered, 'Sorry, I'm confused. I thought you said your assistant, I mean business partner, was a woman?'

'This is her son.' He looked at Tom. 'Where's Diana?'

'She's nipped out to do a valuation.'

'Ah, I see.' He turned to Hannah. 'Ah, well – there'll always be next time.'

Next time. Hannah liked the sound of that. From what she'd seen, it was the sort of shop she wouldn't mind having a wander around to see if she could find an item or two she'd like to buy. Not for the flat above her shop, but for a place she was going to find to call home.

An old gentleman walked in, looking at the oak writing desk in the window. 'Excuse me, do you work here?' he asked Tom.

Kyle said to Hannah, 'Do you mind if I speak with this customer? Tom is a whizz with the order books – he's doing an accountancy course – but I have a feeling he might be out of his depth with the customers.' Kyle said all this, whispering in her ear, his hot breath making her ear tickle and her thoughts turn to their kiss.

'Okay.' Hannah wasn't really listening now. Had it really been a fortnight since they'd seen each other?

'So, you don't mind if I see to this customer?'

'It's fine,' Hannah said, smiling. 'I'd quite like to browse myself.'

'Great. Back in a tick.'

Hannah wandered slowly around the shop, listening to Kyle with the customer. Kyle was a salesperson; there was a saying that was quite apt for Kyle: he could talk the hind leg off a donkey. But from what she was overhearing, he was very knowledgeable about antiques, certainly the ones for sale in the shop. He was also very professional, not overselling, just giving the customer whatever information he asked for and then stepping back, letting the customer decide.

He glanced her way, and they exchanged a smile. Hannah continued to browse. The stock was genuine. She could tell that much even with her untrained eye; pieces with small histories, catalogued and priced with care. Not the sort of thing you sold to pay off gangsters in dimly lit pubs.

Kyle joined her by a shelf of porcelain figurines while the customer took a good look at the desk. 'Well? What do you think?'

Hannah traced a finger along the smooth edge of a blue-and-white plate. 'It all looks … respectable.'

He laughed softly. 'That's high praise from you.'

She turned, meeting his gaze. 'You're telling me everything here is above board? No strings, no debts, no hidden backers?'

'Not a one,' he whispered back. His expression was earnest, almost boyish. 'I've worked hard for this. I've built this up with Diana and Tom's help, Hannah. Fairs, auctions, saving every penny. I wanted you to see it for yourself.'

Hannah thought of the help she'd received from her friends and fellow shopkeepers in Cobblers Yard. She understood completely.

'Honestly, I don't know what I would have done without Diana and her family.'

For the first time in a long time, she saw something in him that wasn't slick charm or desperate bravado. Pride, yes. And a desire for her approval that unsettled her more than she wanted to admit. She folded her arms, torn. 'It's a start. But one shop doesn't erase the past.'

'I know.' His smile dimmed, but he didn't look away. 'I'm not asking you to forget. Just … let me keep proving it.'

'I'll buy it, by jove!' the older gentleman announced, slapping his knee.

'Fantastic!' Kyle beamed. 'Let me take you over to my colleague, Tom, and we can sort out the paperwork and arrange delivery.'

Hannah watched him guide the older gentleman over to Tom. She glanced around again, the neat displays, the assistant drawing up the paperwork with methodical care. A shop, legitimate and open to the street. If Kyle was lying, he'd gone to a lot of effort to make it look convincing. Still, a whisper of doubt lingered.

As they stepped back out into the sunlight, she let the cool breeze clear her head. How could she possibly doubt him now?

A moment later, Kyle joined her. 'Now, in the spirit of still proving myself, would you like to see just what all my hard work has achieved?'

'I thought you showed me already – the lovely antiques shop.'

'Yes, but my home in the countryside is even lovelier.'

'You've bought a new home?' It hadn't occurred to Hannah where he lived. She guessed she was under the impression that, like herself, he had a flat above the shop, or maybe a rental.

'Well, it's not *new*. Nothing like my last house where we used to live. I'm afraid I couldn't afford something that size. One of the downsides of going legit.'

She gave him a sideways glance and caught him smiling at his own joke. She was actually relieved to hear he couldn't afford a big house. She didn't quite know how lucrative the antiques trade was, but if she'd turned up to some sort of mansion, she'd just know he was back to his old self and doing shady deals.

'Do you want to see the place I call home?'

Hannah hadn't been expecting this, but she was curious. 'Actually, yes I do.'

'Oh, thank goodness. You see, I've arranged dinner at my place, kind of hoping you'd say yes. I've already pre-prepared the meal.'

Hannah had been wondering if he was going to take her out for dinner. She said, 'Ah, I was hoping for a candlelit dinner for two.' She was only half joking.

'Well, you won't be disappointed. I do have candles.'

They both laughed as they headed back down the street towards the car. That's when Hannah felt his hand in hers. They walked along, hand in hand. Hannah looked at him. She hadn't wanted to get her hopes up that this could work. In fact, she was still looking for something that told her this was a mistake, the two of them, reconnecting after all that had happened in their past. But she couldn't deny what she was feeling – that this was only the beginning – in a good way.

25

The bell above the door tinkled softly as Hannah stepped back into her shop late that evening. The golden light of dusk fell across the shelves of sketchpads and paint sets, casting long shadows that made the cosy corner glow with warmth. Normally, that glow made her feel safe, at home. Tonight, it made her uneasy.

She closed the door, slid the bolt, and leaned against it for a moment, her heart still unsettled from the day. Kyle's shop, his pride, his eager eyes watching for her approval – she hadn't expected it to look so real. So ordinary. For the first time, she'd seen him not as the reckless charmer from her past, but as a man who'd built something steady.

And yet the guilt pressed down on her like a weight she couldn't shake.

Maisie.

She thought of her daughter, bright and perceptive, already suspicious. If Maisie ever found out she'd gone to Norfolk to see Kyle, she would feel betrayed. Nate would be no better – he'd throw it in her face that she was reckless, unreliable, still trusting the wrong man. And Lili – Hannah's chest tightened – Lili would never forgive her. Not after the coat, the arrest, and her time in prison after being falsely accused. All these thoughts had put a damper on her lovely evening with Kyle in his new home – a sweet little semi-detached cottage he'd bought in the Norfolk countryside with two bedrooms, a small lounge with a wood burner, a dining kitchen which overlooked a patio and a wild cottage garden beyond. She tried not to imagine herself in that cottage, curled up with Kyle in the evenings in the coming winter months with a glass of wine in front of the log fire, or to picture herself outside, taming that wild garden.

She'd said to him over dinner by candlelight in the small dining kitchen, 'I want a place like this to call home.' His reply had surprised her. 'You could call this place home.'

How could she? It was miles away from her home in Suffolk. Maisie would have to change schools, and what about her shop in Cobblers Yard?

Kyle had suggested that Maisie could change schools and that Hannah could sell her business and join him working in his antiques business. He seemed to have all the answers, including what to do about Lili, Nate and Maisie putting a stop to their relationship. 'It's your life. Perhaps it's time to make a fresh start, move away. I think it's a bit suffocating – living and working with the people in the yard, don't you?'

'They're just looking out for me,' Hannah had responded.

She crossed to the counter, dropping her keys in the little ceramic dish Maisie had made years ago, which she still kept there. Her eyes lingered on it and the guilt intensified. What would Maisie say if she knew about these dates with Kyle, let alone that she was considering packing in their lives there and moving in with him?

But we're not doing that, thought Hannah. *Not yet, anyway.*

Hannah busied herself with tidying, folding the knitted throw on the sofa and straightening the cushions, then putting away pencils left out from the try-before-you-buy table. But her thoughts refused to become still. Every time she picked up a sketchpad, she saw Kyle's grin. Every time she stacked a tin of paints, she heard his voice – *Let me prove it.*

The truth was, she had really enjoyed her day with Kyle. The drive, the easy conversation, the way he'd looked at her across the table when they were having dinner together. For a few hours, she'd felt … lighter. Younger. Like she wasn't just Hannah-the-ex-con, Hannah-the-mother, Hannah-the-cautious-shopkeeper, but Hannah who could still be wanted. Her cheeks warmed at the thought even as guilt pricked her conscience.

She flicked on the lamp by the sofa in the cosy corner, sinking down into its cushions. The fairy lights she'd strung up for the yard party still twinkled faintly in the shop window, a reminder of how the others had welcomed her in, how they'd rallied round to help her: Joss giving her a handy bookcase, Thea bringing along books and handing her mugs of tea. And Reggie, dear, sweet Reggie, providing jazz music she'd never known she loved until he'd introduced her to it with an old record player. But they had no idea what she was hiding.

And she *was* hiding.

For the first time since Kyle had reappeared, Hannah let herself say it aloud, a whisper into the empty shop.

'I liked it. Being with him again.'

The words hung in the air, fragile as glass.

She covered her face with her hands, groaning softly. What was she doing? Lying to her daughter, to her best friend, to the very people who had given her a second chance. She was building her life on secrets again, the very thing that had destroyed her before.

And yet, when she closed her eyes, she didn't see prison bars. She saw the glint of pride in Kyle's eyes as he'd showed her around his shop, the gentle way he'd said, *I'm not asking you to forget. Just … let me keep proving it.*

Hannah drew a long breath and sat up straighter, pressing her palms against her knees.

Maybe she was a fool. Maybe she was gambling with everything. But until Kyle showed her otherwise, she wasn't ready to let go of the possibility that he really had changed.

And so she would keep her secret.

For now.

26

Maisie sprawled on the new sofa in her dad's house, legs tucked under her as the smell of shepherd's pie drifted in from the kitchen. Normally, weekends there felt like a treat – a chance to be spoiled a little, to walk along the beach with Dad, Lili and William, and to have fish and chips, and to stay up too late watching movies. But that night she felt restless, her stomach knotting in a way that even her favourite dinner couldn't ease.

Nate glanced round the doorframe, tea towel slung over his shoulder. 'You've been awfully quiet, love. Everything all right?'

Maisie shrugged, fiddling with the hem of her jumper. 'Yeah. Just tired.'

It wasn't a lie, but it wasn't the truth either. She *was* tired – tired of pretending nothing was wrong, tired of carrying the sharp, uneasy feeling that her mum was keeping something from her.

The evening of the party, when Maisie had woken to voices downstairs, muffled but tense, she had started down the stairs, and that's when she had seen him.

Kyle.

She hoped Kyle didn't come back. Her mum had said he

wouldn't. She remembered her exact words, 'I won't see Kyle again.' So why was it still bothering her?

Nate came in with two steaming plates, setting one down in front of her. He ruffled her hair, trying to make her smile. 'There we go – your favourite.'

Maisie picked up her fork. 'What about William and Lili?'

'I've left some in the oven for them, although I doubt William will want any after eating so much party food. Sorry you couldn't go to William's classmate's birthday party today, but his classmate had only invited boys.'

'It's all right. I don't mind.'

'Well, we get some one-to-one time, you and me, for a change. That's why I asked your mum if you could come this weekend as well.'

Maisie offered her dad a smile. The house felt warm, safe – the opposite of the unsettled coil twisting inside her. She stared at the pie for a long moment before blurting, 'Dad, do you think Mum would keep a secret from me?'

Nate paused, fork halfway to his mouth. 'That's a big question.' He studied her carefully. 'Why do you ask?'

Maisie hesitated. She didn't want to betray her mum, not really. But she also couldn't shake the feeling that something was going on. Just the other day, after school, she'd visited the charity shop with her pocket money, and Mabel had asked if her mum was seeing someone, like going out on a date.

Mabel said she'd noticed her mum closing the shop early one Saturday and going out looking all dressed up during Maisie's weekend away at her dad's. And then Mabel talked about the young man she'd seen briefly at the yard party, wondering if her mum was going to meet him. When she described the man she'd seen, Maisie knew exactly who it was.

Maisie stared at her food, miserable thoughts going round in her head. *She promised she wouldn't see Kyle again. She promised.* It made her wonder what her mum had been doing while she was away on this next sleepover weekend. Had she closed the shop early again and gone out? And if she had – was she seeing Kyle?

'Sweetheart, you haven't touched your food. What is it?'

She picked at the crust of her pie. 'After the yard party, this man visited. It was Kyle.'

The air between them seemed to thicken. Nate set down his fork slowly, his jaw tightening. 'Kyle.' He said it as though the name itself was a bitter taste. 'Are you sure?'

Maisie nodded, her throat dry. 'I saw him.'

Nate leaned back in his chair, eyes narrowing as though he was looking miles away, somewhere into the past. 'I hoped he'd never show his face again.'

Maisie's heart thudded.

Nate sighed, dragging a hand through his hair. 'You're right to be wary.'

'I know. I made Mummy promise me she'd never see him again.'

'And did she?'

'Yes.' Maisie's lip quivered when she thought of what Mabel had said to her about her mum shutting the shop early on Saturday and going out. She didn't tell her dad. She'd said too much and didn't want to get her mum into trouble.

He leaned forward, his voice low, steady. 'Listen to me. If you see him again, or if your mum mentions him, I want you to tell me. Straight away. All right?'

Maisie swallowed hard and nodded. Relief mingled with

dread – relief that she'd told her dad, but dread because now her dad was involved.

'And I want you to promise me something else – we can't tell Lili about this conversation just yet.' He stopped to look at her. 'You definitely haven't seen him again – have you?'

Maisie shook her head, biting her bottom lip and thinking of Mabel. Her eyesight wasn't the best, but she wouldn't have been mistaken about her mum closing the shop early on a Saturday. It was bothering Maisie a lot. It wasn't something she expected her mum to do now her shop had lots of customers.

And beneath it all, there was a simmering fear: if Kyle was back in their lives, what would that mean for her mum?

For all of them?

27

By Friday mid-morning, Hannah was already second-guessing herself. Closing the shop on a Friday felt wrong, reckless, as though she were hanging a sign in the middle of Cobblers Yard that said: *I'm hiding something.*

She could almost feel Joss's curious glance from next door when she pulled down the blind, could hear Mabel's whispers ready to start up as soon as she disappeared down the lane. But she ignored them. She had a plan. Everyone thought she was going to an art and craft fair. It was technically true – there was a fair in Norfolk. Only that wasn't the real reason for her trip.

The real reason was Kyle.

It was barely a week after her trip with Kyle to see his shop the previous weekend, and she was desperate to see him again. The problem was Maisie. It wasn't her sleepover weekend with her dad – it would have been, but he'd swapped the previous weekend, so Maisie was meant to be spending the weekend with her mum. Hannah had other plans. So Hannah had asked Sarah to have her for the entire weekend instead, including Friday night. She tried not to feel guilty at the thought. That would be the third consecutive weekend she hadn't spent with her daughter. When Hannah had arrived outside Stanford & Co. later on Friday afternoon, she hadn't told Kyle she was coming. She wanted to surprise him. He knew Maisie only stayed with her father every other weekend, so thinking that she had Maisie that weekend, he would be very surprised to see her.

Inside, she spotted her immediately: Diana, the older business partner Kyle had mentioned, her silver hair pulled into a bun, half-moon glasses perched low on her nose. Relief rippled through Hannah – at least that part was true.

Diana was at the desk at the back of the shop, phone pressed to her ear. Hannah drifted toward a cabinet of jewellery, pretending to browse.

'Yes, sir, I understand,' Diana's voice sharpened. 'But what we paid you was fair at the time. Markets fluctuate. If the piece sold at auction for more, that's hardly our fault … No, we didn't fleece you, and I won't be offering you more money. The price you were paid is final. That's not how this works.' She slammed the receiver down, muttering under her breath.

Hannah's stomach tightened. Re-sold at a higher price? Fleeced? She was about to move closer when a voice startled her.

'What are you doing here?'

Kyle.

She spun around. He stood in the doorway to the back office, his expression taut with surprise that bordered on irritation.

'I couldn't wait until next weekend to see you,' Hannah said quickly, forcing a smile. 'Don't worry, I arranged everything – Maisie's with her grandmother for two nights. I thought we could have a whole weekend together.'

For a beat, silence stretched. Then Kyle's eyes flicked to

Diana. Something unspoken passed between them. Hannah thought he'd at least introduce her to his business partner.

'I had something on this weekend,' he said.

Hannah's heart sank. 'Can't you change your plans? Please?'

His jaw tightened, then he exhaled. 'All right. We'll make it work.' He shot Diana another look, one Hannah couldn't quite decipher.

❖

Later on Friday afternoon, they were cruising along the Norfolk Broads, the slow putter of the canal boat a soothing counterpoint to the uneasy encounter at the antiques shop. Kyle kept up a steady stream of chatter, pointing out herons on the reeds, telling stories of boyhood fishing trips. Hannah had not known that Kyle had spent his childhood there in Norfolk. She let herself relax, the wind tangling her hair, the sunlight glittering on the water. It was a beautiful autumn day. The exceptionally bright, unseasonably warm weather they'd had in September was stretching into mid-October too.

For a while, the weekend was almost perfect. Dinners in little pubs, walks through market towns, Kyle's hand brushing hers as if no time had passed at all since they'd been living together, before it all went horribly wrong. Hannah brushed that thought aside. She was having a wonderful time, and although she knew she'd be staying with Kyle in his cottage, he had offered her the spare bedroom. That first night, she'd slept fitfully next door to him, willing herself to take things slowly.

Her resolve had crumbled on Saturday evening after a lovely meal in a local pub, late-night drinks – they had both been drunk when they'd arrived back at the cottage, and Kyle had fumbled with the key for ages. Luckily the pub had been walkable distance from his cottage. And that was when it had happened. They'd managed somehow to get upstairs and had fallen in a heap, fully clothed, on his bed – and kissed.

She'd woken up Sunday morning lying next to Kyle. For a moment, she couldn't remember what had happened the previous night. Then she'd thrown off the duvet and found her answer: nothing. She'd discovered they were both still fully dressed from the night before.

Hannah was relieved. She still wanted to take things slowly, and before she ended up back in bed with him – without being drunk and fully clothed – she wanted to be sure. So far, any doubts she'd had that maybe he hadn't changed had been proved wrong.

She'd propped herself up on an elbow to watch him sleeping and had smiled. She had a feeling that quite soon things would come to a head, and she'd have to tell Maisie.

It was Sunday afternoon, and she was having the best time with Kyle, better than she could ever have imagined, considering her plans for the weekend hadn't exactly got off to a good start with Kyle's reaction to her turning up. But all that was behind her. She couldn't have asked for a nicer weekend away.

And yet – Diana's sharp voice on the phone still echoed in Hannah's mind. *Fleeced.* Kyle had brushed off her questions that evening. 'Just business. You can't please everyone.' He'd smiled, poured her another glass of wine, and she'd let herself believe it. Or half believe it.

❖

By the time she pulled into Aldeburgh on Sunday evening, her contentment had curdled into unease. She was later than she'd meant to be; the streetlamps were already glowing. When she unlocked the shop, glancing furtively around her, worried someone would see her arrive home, she didn't have to worry; the yard was dark. The twinkly lights were all off, and there were no lights on in Reggie's or Henry's flats above their shop. Or in her shop. She'd expected that Sarah would bring Maisie home. Maisie had a door key.

'God – how late is it?' Hannah said to herself. She got out her phone to check the time as she unlocked the shop door and discovered five missed calls.

Her stomach lurched. They were all from Sarah.

She rang back immediately, her hands clammy.

'Finally,' Sarah's voice bristled down the line. 'Where on earth have you been? It's Sunday night, Hannah. A school night! When I couldn't reach you, I put Maisie to bed here. She was asking for you.'

'I – my phone was on mute. I didn't realise—'

'You never put it on mute,' Sarah cut in. 'Maisie needed you home.'

Hannah closed her eyes. She hadn't put it on mute. She never did. A chill crept down her spine. Had Kyle?

'I'm sorry,' she whispered. 'I'll come round straight away.'

'No, she's asleep now. Leave her. But really, Hannah – you need to get your priorities straight.'

The line went dead.

Hannah sank onto the sofa in the cosy corner, her guilt a knot in her chest. Nate would know by now – Sarah would have called him too. Lili, probably. Everyone would think she'd slipped again, putting herself first, palming Maisie off onto other people.

And wasn't that exactly what she had done?

Her phone buzzed with a text.

Had the best weekend. Can't wait till next time. Still on for next week? K x

She stared at it, torn in two.

Maisie had barely seen her over the weekend for the past two weeks. For two weekends on the trot she had been round at someone else's – Nate's, now Sarah.

A horrible thought struck her: maybe she hadn't changed as much as she liked to think. Maybe she was sliding back into her old ways, chasing the wrong man at the expense of the one person who mattered most – Maisie.

Hannah resolved, right there and then, that the weekend after next would be Maisie's. Just hers. No Kyle. And no secrets – she'd have to tell her she was back with Kyle.

But it would be the last weekend in October and the start of the October half-term holiday, so there would be plenty of time to spend together, and for Hannah to break the news about Kyle. She thought of Lili's idea of a Halloween party in the yard on the Friday at the end of the half-term holiday and promised herself she'd spend the time with Maisie preparing another yard party – Maisie would love that, carving out pumpkins, buying treats for the trick-or-treat, and shopping for a Halloween costume.

But even as she made the promise, she already felt her resolve slipping.

Kyle would have other plans.

28

Sarah banged the teapot down on the kitchen counter harder than she meant to. The china lid rattled. She pressed her lips together, fighting to keep her temper in check. She spooned sugar into her tea with brisk, irritated movements. The clink of the spoon against porcelain was sharp, echoing through her neat little kitchen on the Aldeburgh seafront.

Lili sat at the table, cradling her own cup, watching her with quiet patience. It was early on Monday morning, and Lili had popped into Sarah's house on the seafront on her way to work in The Potting Shed.

'I don't know what's got into her,' Sarah said at last. 'I assumed she'd be back Sunday afternoon or thereabouts. Do you know what time it was when I finally got Maisie to bed? Nearly nine o'clock! On a school night! Hannah didn't even notice I'd rung her half a dozen times trying to find out where she was. And poor Maisie – asking for her mum, looking at the clock, getting more anxious by the minute.'

Sarah shook her head as she took a breath. 'Maisie's unsettled,' she went on. 'I can see it. She's restless, clingy. When she was here this weekend, she couldn't sit still. Kept saying she missed her mum. I've been around long enough to know when someone's keeping secrets,' Sarah said. 'Hannah has something going on, and I don't like the way it's affecting Maisie.'

Lili stared into her tea. Hannah had been so determined these last few months to change her life, so hopeful. And yet …

'You think she's slipping back?' Lili asked quietly.

Sarah's expression softened just a fraction. 'I don't want to, but yes. All the signs are there. And if she is … well, Maisie's the one who'll pay the price.'

A heavy silence settled in the room, broken only by the faint crash of waves on to the pebble beach. A storm was brewing.

'She said her phone was on mute, didn't she?'

Sarah gave a short, humourless laugh. 'Hannah has never put that thing on mute. Not once in all the time I've known her. She lives with it glued to her hand. No – someone else muted it, or she didn't want to hear me ringing.'

There was a pause. The only sound was the kettle ticking as it cooled.

'Where did she say she'd been?' Lili asked carefully, aware that Hannah had meant to spend the weekend with Maisie after the last two weekends Maisie had spent with her dad.

'Some fair in Norfolk. Craft thing.' Sarah shook her head in dismay. 'But she left Maisie with me for the *entire* weekend. *Entire* weekend, Lili, since Friday. Closed her shop Friday afternoon, apparently, according to Mabel. I knew I was picking her up after school. Maisie wanted to stop by the yard, say goodbye to her mum, but she was already gone. We found out what time she'd left her shop when we stopped by the charity shop so Maisie could spend some of her pocket money.'

Sarah stared into space. 'I can't believe she just upped and left the shop on Friday afternoon with no word, no plan for exactly when she'd be back. And then she's late – on a school night.'

Lili bit back her instinct to defend her friend. She'd thought Hannah had turned a corner and left all her past behaviour behind. Lili stirred her tea, eyes thoughtful. 'It's not like her. Not lately, anyway. Since she moved into Cobblers Yard, she's been steady. Hard-working. I thought she'd turned a corner.'

'That's just it,' Sarah said, lowering herself into a chair with a sigh. 'I thought so too. But this …' she heaved a sigh.

Lili stared at Sarah. 'I do agree that it feels like old times. When Maisie was small, and Hannah was chasing trouble instead of being at home. The thing is, Sarah, it was only this once. Perhaps it's just a one-off.'

'Ah, I'm not so sure this isn't just the start of it.'

'Why do you say that?'

'Because Mabel told me that she's closed the shop on Saturday twice on the trot when Maisie was over at yours on her Daddy weekends.'

'Really – on a Saturday?'

'Yes.'

'That is odd.'

'Mabel seems to think she's seeing someone.'

'Oh, really?' Lili said in surprise. 'She never mentioned she's dating again. I'd have thought if she'd met someone, she'd have told me.'

Sarah stared at her. 'My sentiments exactly. Something doesn't smell right about all this. She was so focused on her shop being a success, and now it appears she's closing earlier and earlier on the weekends, and now not opening at all, on the busiest day of the week. It does not make sense.'

Lili set her spoon down. 'You think she's hiding something?'

Sarah met her gaze. 'Don't you?'

Lili hesitated, but the silence between them filled with unspoken truths. Hannah avoiding questions. Closing the shop unexpectedly. That flustered look in her eyes whenever Lili had popped in with fresh flowers. She just wasn't herself. She was definitely hiding something.

'Funny thing …' mused Lili. 'Last weekend, when I took William to a birthday party, and Nate spent some time on his own that evening with Maisie, I got the feeling something was going on, but Nate said he didn't want to bother me with it. I wonder if Maisie confided in her dad that things were going on at home with her mum.' Lili sighed heavily. 'I feel so guilty if that's the case, Sarah.'

'What on earth have you got to feel guilty for?' she said indignantly.

'I've been so busy with work, and things going on planning my wedding, and redecorating our home, that in hindsight I missed the signs that something was going on with Hannah and with Maisie.' She paused for a long moment. 'She *is* hiding something,' Lili said at last, her voice firm. 'And if we don't find out what it is, you're right: Maisie is the one who'll pay the price.'

Sarah leaned forward, tapping her finger against the table. 'We keep an eye out. For Maisie's sake. If Hannah is slipping back into her old ways, she won't admit it – not until it's too late. But if we're watching, maybe we can stop her before the damage is done.'

Lili nodded, though her stomach churned. She'd given Hannah her trust once already when no one else had. If Hannah was gambling with it now – gambling with Maisie's stability, their new lives in Cobblers Yard – then Lili wasn't sure how much longer she could stand by quietly.

And in the pit of her stomach, a cold unease settled. This felt just like before, when she was in relationships with guys who were no good. She hoped she'd got it wrong, that they both had, and that Hannah had just spent a weekend away at a craft fair for her business. But something told her there was more to it than that.

Whatever Hannah was hiding – whomever she was hiding – Lili knew she'd have to do more than sit back and *keep an eye out* as Sarah had suggested. That wasn't Lili's style. She'd have to confront Hannah – for Hannah's own sake, and for Maisie's. But first, she was going to find out everything she could. And she knew exactly who she would be speaking to first – The Gossip Girls.

29

Hannah padded softly into Maisie's room on Monday morning, guilt still thick in her throat from the night before. Sarah had dropped her off early that morning so that Maisie could have breakfast with her mum and get dressed in her uniform ready for school. Sarah hadn't lingered, her raised eyebrows making it clear she still wasn't impressed with Hannah's behaviour. Hannah gleaned that perhaps there was a bit of suspicion too about where she had really been all weekend.

Maisie was already dressed in her uniform, lying on her stomach on her bed with her sketchbook open, though her pencil lay untouched.

'Alright, sweetheart?' Hannah said gently. Maisie had been very quiet over breakfast, Hannah noticed. Not her normal, chatty self. Hannah had had an idea. 'I thought maybe next weekend you could stay here with me instead of going to your dad's. Just us two, eh? A girls' weekend. We'll do whatever you want – fish and chips on the beach, a movie night, ice cream for breakfast if you fancy.' She was sure Nate wouldn't mind. After all, she'd let him have Maisie the weekend before last when she should have been with Hannah.

Maisie turned, her eyes searching. 'But I'm meant to go to Daddy's.'

'I know.' Hannah perched on the edge of the bed, smoothing Maisie's hair back from her forehead. 'I'm sure he won't mind, as you've been away from home the last three weekends. I've hardly seen you.'

Hannah cringed. That wasn't Maisie's or Nate's fault. She could have spent all weekend with her daughter, but she had chosen to spend the weekend with Kyle instead.

Maisie sat up, hugging her knees. 'You were late last night. Really late. Granny was worried. I was worried. And now you want me *not* to go to Dad's next weekend?' Her voice trembled with suspicion. 'Mummy … are you hiding something?'

Hannah's heart gave a painful squeeze. 'Sweetheart. I just … I want some special time with you, that's all. I promise.'

Maisie didn't look convinced. She only muttered, 'I want to go to Daddy's at the weekend like normal,' before climbing off her bed to go and clean her teeth.

All that day, Hannah wrestled with herself. Maybe Maisie was right. Maybe keeping the routine with Nate was best. That way Maisie had certainty, and Hannah – well, Hannah could keep her own secrets safely tucked away for one last weekend. When Kyle texted later, suggesting plans for the weekend, she almost said no. Almost. But his words were a tug on her heart she couldn't resist.

So, Maisie was going to Nate's next weekend after all. Hannah told her they'd plan their 'special weekend' the following weekend instead – the start of the half-term holiday. She meant it, she truly did. But even as she kissed Maisie goodbye at the door, she couldn't escape the guilty feeling.

And when Maisie arrived home to the shop after school, she barely said a hello. As soon as she'd dumped her bag at the door, she whipped across the yard to the charity shop with her pocket money and barely a backward glance, leaving Hannah standing at the door. Maisie was still making her feel guilty for leaving her at her grandmother's the previous weekend. Hannah wished she'd change her mind and not go to Nate's at the weekend, but she knew her daughter wouldn't change her mind, and neither would Kyle. He had plans.

❖

Mabel adjusted her glasses, watching Hannah close her shop door. How many times had she seen her hurry out of the yard these past weeks, her coat flapping and her eyes darting like she was late for something? Marjorie, sorting through a box of donated books, caught her sister's frown.

'She's been up to something,' Mabel murmured. 'Secret liaisons, if you ask me. I've seen that dreamy look before. She's sneaking about with someone, and not the sort she'd want to parade in front of us.'

'Someone locally, from the town perhaps?' Marjorie said.

'No,' Mabel replied firmly. 'Someone else. Someone from her past, I'll wager.'

The bell above the door tinkled then, and Maisie stepped in, cheeks pink from running at full pelt across the yard.

'Hello, Maisie love,' Marjorie said warmly. 'Come to see what treasures you might find today? We've had new storybooks in.'

Mabel and Marjorie exchanged a glance, both thinking the same thing – what was Maisie doing there on a school night? She normally had homework, and once that was done, she spent her evenings painting. She usually visited at the weekend, although the last time she'd visited had been Friday after school with her grandmother. Mabel would never forget the sad look on the poor child's face when she discovered she couldn't say goodbye to her mum before the sleepover with Sarah; her mum had already closed the shop and left.

Maisie wandered over to the children's section. Mabel watched her a moment, whispering to Marjorie, 'She's not her usual chatty self,' before deciding to press gently. 'Maisie,' she said, 'your mum's been very busy lately. We noticed she closed the shop early again. Is she seeing someone, do you know?'

Maisie, who was kneeling in front of a box of books, rifling through, stiffened. 'Why do you want to know?'

'Because,' Mabel said softly, 'we're worried about her. We know she's been going off to Norfolk. And we've heard she's been seen with a man there. An antiques dealer. Kyle.'

Mabel and Marjorie had discussed this between them, whether to talk to Maisie about what they knew. It had been terribly, terribly nosy of them, but they'd enlisted help to find out why Hannah had been closing her shop early and where she was going. They'd decided to pop into Hannah's shop and have a coffee in her cosy corner, and get chatting; perhaps Hannah would then reveal what was going on. But every time Mabel had ventured across the yard during the week, Hannah had virtually refused her entry, coming up with excuses – she was tidying the cosy corner, or the coffee machine was on the blink – until Mabel had given up. That was when Mabel had resorted to her other idea.

They didn't have a car, so it would have been impossible to follow her.

But Reggie did.

And so, the previous weekend, they'd enlisted Reggie's help. They'd debated whether they were in the wrong to even consider having her followed, but their octogenarian hunch, along with their nose for gossip, told them that something was going on.

At first, Reggie had looked at the sisters as if they were mad. 'I am not following Hannah. Whatever is going on is her personal business, and we shouldn't interfere.'

He'd climbed off his high horse when the sisters had said that they were worried about her, and that as her friends, and members of the yard, they felt a duty to look out for her.

Reggie had not disagreed. So, it had all been planned that Reggie would follow Hannah on the Saturday afternoon during Maisie's sleepover the next weekend, only for them to be caught out when she closed her shop early on the Friday. They'd had no idea that Maisie would be staying with her grandmother for the entire weekend. It had turned out that Maisie would be spending three consecutive weekends away from home, which was highly unusual.

So, as soon as Mabel saw Hannah leave her shop on Friday, she'd phoned Reggie next door. He was out like a shot, having shut up his shop, and followed Hannah in his car all the way to a small market town just across the Suffolk border in Norfolk, where she met a man in an antiques shop. A quick Google on his phone, and the man in question popped up as one of the owners – Kyle.

And that, much to the chagrin of the sisters, was where Reggie had left his spying for one weekend.

Kyle.

Mabel said gently, 'I think your mum has been meeting a

man called Kyle.'

The name hung in the air. Maisie's lip trembled. 'She promised she wouldn't see him again!' Maisie looked at Mabel and Marjorie. 'You know about him?'

'Not enough,' said Marjorie gently. 'But we'd like to.'

Maisie sank onto a stool at the shop counter, joining Mabel and Marjorie, eyes huge. 'He's my mum's ex. He made her … he made her steal things. From the old antiques shop. She went to prison.'

'We know about that, sweetheart.'

'It was his fault. But she never told on him.'

Marjorie offered her a chocolate digestive biscuit.

Maisie took one and nibbled the end while Mabel and Marjorie exchanged a sharp look. They were both thinking the same thing – that was one piece of information they had not known.

'Will you help me?' Maisie whispered. 'Will you help me stop my mum seeing Kyle?'

Mabel leaned towards her. 'Have you told your dad?'

Maisie nodded. 'Yes, I told him I saw Kyle in the shop after the yard party. He said I was to tell him if I see Kyle again, or Mummy talks about him. I don't want to get Mummy into trouble.'

Marjorie reached over and squeezed Maisie's hand. 'Darling, it's not trouble you're getting her into – it's trouble you're keeping her out of.'

Maisie swallowed hard. 'Daddy says we shouldn't bother Lili with this, because she'll worry. But … maybe he's wrong?'

Mabel's jaw set. 'Of course he's wrong. Hannah is Lili's best friend. She'll want to know.'

Before Maisie could protest further, Marjorie had already slipped next door to The Potting Shed. Moments later, Lili came in, wiping her hands on her apron, her brow furrowed. 'I'm glad you popped in, Marjorie. I've been meaning to speak to you and Mabel.' She stopped when she spotted Maisie, tears rolling down her cheeks. 'What's going on?' she asked.

Once Lili had given Maisie a hug and dried her tears, and Maisie was feeling a little better, Lili and the sisters left her at a little table in the back room with juice and chocolate digestives, and the box of books, saying that they just wanted a word together. They closed the door firmly behind her. Then they told Lili everything.

When they'd finished, Lili pressed her hand to her mouth. 'Oh, my god. I knew something was going on with her. How did this happen? How did he even find her?'

Mabel sniffed. 'The yard party. If he had even a whiff she was in Suffolk, well – her face was in the paper, and the flyers were everywhere. I saw him myself that day, just for a moment. It was too busy for him to get close, but he was there.'

'You recognised him?' Lili said, not understanding. 'You've seen him before?'

'No, not at all. But I saw him again, going into Hannah's shop, and Reggie described him to us.' They'd both told Lili about Reggie following Hannah to the antiques shop in Norfolk on Friday.

Marjorie's eyes narrowed. 'But why? If she knows he's a bad-un, why would she take him back?'

Lili's expression was bleak. 'Because Kyle's a charmer. I've seen it. I bet he's convinced her he's changed, that he's gone straight.'

'But you don't believe that,' Mabel said flatly.

'No, I don't.'

Marjorie gave a little gasp. 'Poor Maisie suspected something's being going on, worrying about this all on her own. She wasn't sure her mum had been meeting Kyle, but she obviously had a feeling that something was wrong. And she knows now that her mum *has* been meeting Kyle.'

'Oh, Maisie, sweetheart,' Lili murmured, glancing toward the back-room door. 'She must have been so scared. Keeping this to herself, seeing Kyle again and bringing back all those bad memories of her mum going to prison.' Lili looked at them wide-eyed, a hand over her mouth.

Mabel and Marjorie exchanged a glance. Marjorie said, 'It's alright. We know about Hannah's past. But obviously, we didn't know about this Kyle, until now.'

Mabel folded her arms. 'Maisie told her dad that she saw Kyle.'

Lili looked at them, stunned. 'Really? Why didn't he tell me?'

Mabel put a hand on her arm. 'He didn't want to worry you. Nate told Maisie to tell him if Kyle returned or her mum mentioned him again, but neither of those things happened – not when Maisie's been around. Hannah has obviously been seeing him, though, but he's been keeping a low profile.'

Marjorie leaned in, her voice low. 'And there's more. I've been doing some digging. His antiques business, Stanford & Co. – it's not what it seems. They're fleecing people. I think they're targeting older people, perhaps property-rich, cash-poor people, preying on the vulnerable by offering cash for their antiques well below market value and then reselling them at auction for double, sometimes triple. Customers are furious.'

'And his business partner,' Mabel added darkly. 'Diana. Reggie saw her in the shop and thought her recognised her from somewhere. Then he remembered a newspaper article from some years ago. Her husband is in prison. Some kind of kingpin. Though rumour has it she's the one really running things.'

Lili's eyes widened. 'Oh god.' She rubbed her temples. 'This is worse than I thought.'

'What are we going to do?' Marjorie whispered.

'For starters,' Mabel said firmly, taking charge in the way she always did, 'we tell Hannah. We tell her everything we know. And this time, she'll have to listen.'

'But when is the right time?' Lili asked.

'The right time for what?' Maisie asked.

They all turned around to see Maisie standing there. How much had she heard?

Lili said, 'We're discussing the right time to catch your mum and tell her she has to stop seeing Kyle.'

'Now!' Maisie said.

Lili shook her head. 'You've got school tomorrow. I think we should leave it until the weekend.'

'But it's my weekend with you and Daddy which means Mummy is going to go out with Kyle again.'

'No, Maisie. We are not going to let that happen,' Lili reassured her, looking to Mabel and Marjorie to back her up. 'We will catch her before then. You can count on us, I promise. But for now, we keep things as normal as we can.' Lili didn't want to voice a horrible thought – that if Kyle got wind of the fact that they all wanted rid of him, he might persuade Hannah to take Maisie and flee, leaving Cobblers Yard and going to live with him.

'Do you promise?' Maisie said, trusting eyes searching her face.

Lili took her hands in hers. 'You are going to go to Daddy's at the weekend as planned, but I'm going to pop into The Potting Shed on Saturday before lunchtime, when she's taken to closing up the shop for half a day, so I'm here before she leaves to confront her and tell her …'

'That she can't see Kyle anymore.'

Lili wasn't exactly going to put it like that. She couldn't tell Hannah how to lead her life, and with whom. Sarah was right: she wasn't her keeper – but she could tell her everything they'd found out about Kyle and the business, and the people he was really associated with, before she found out the hard way for herself, and possibly got dragged into it, along with Maisie.

Lili said, 'Yes, exactly.' She was thinking that Saturday couldn't come around soon enough.

Mabel said, 'We could go to Norfolk and visit him in his shop, warn him off.'

Lili laughed despite herself. 'Do you think he's really going to back off when confronted by me – a horticulturist – and two octogenarians? No offence, ladies.'

Marjorie turned to her sister and spoke. 'I rather think she has a valid point.'

Mabel considered for a moment. 'We need reinforcements.'

Lili looked at the sisters. 'Just what did you have in mind?'

30

On Saturday morning, Hannah was putting away a new delivery of stock when a sharp knock startled her. She frowned and glanced up with a feeling of déjà vu. Her stomach plunged when she saw him. *What the hell? Not again!*

He was leaning against her shop window, grinning at her through the glass as though he owned the place. She'd told him the last time he'd done this not return to the shop.

She opened the door, frowning. 'Kyle, what are you doing here? We were supposed to meet in Thorpeness.' They had planned to have a walk around the mere and some lunch before they set off for the weekend to his place in Norfolk.

'I know,' he said easily, slipping inside. 'But I've got something important to ask you.'

Her pulse quickened. Important? The way he was looking at her – too intense, too certain – set her mind racing. She prayed he wasn't about to drop down on one knee.

Instead, he took her hands. 'Move in with me. To the cottage. With Maisie. Properly. Start over, the three of us.'

Hannah's breath caught. 'Move in? Kyle, I have my shop. My friends in Cobblers Yard. My life here.'

He scoffed, waving a dismissive hand toward the window. 'This place? I'd find it stifling, to be honest. Everyone watching, everyone knowing your business. Look at us – sneaking about, hiding. It's ridiculous. When are you going to tell people about us?'

'I told you,' she said, voice tight. 'I'll tell Maisie next weekend. It's the start of the October half-term holiday, and I've thought of some nice things to do with her for Halloween.'

'Perfect,' Kyle said with a smile. 'Then you can tell her about the move too.'

Hannah pulled her hands back, her heart beating hard. 'I haven't made up my mind yet. You've only just sprung this on me.'

'Sprung it on you? I thought you loved the cottage. I thought it was obvious.' He leaned closer, earnest now. 'Look, it's not like I'm asking you to send Maisie off to boarding school, is it? I want her with us this time. Maisie deserves more, you know she does, and we'll make a good team, the three of us.'

Hannah blinked, startled. The way he said *this time* – and the fact he had included Maisie – softened her resistance. He had changed. Hadn't he? And he'd said, *the three of us,* although it was a little odd referring to the three of them as a team, rather than a family. *But it's just a turn of phrase*, Hannah thought. *It's no big deal.*

Still, unease tugged at her. She thought of Lili, of Reggie and Thea, of cosy evenings in the shop's little corner with Maisie drawing beside her. Could she really walk away from all of that?

Kyle's eyes searched hers. 'Come on, Hannah. Maisie deserves more than this flat above a shop. She deserves a proper home. And you deserve me.'

Hannah felt heat rise to her cheeks, torn between doubt and

longing. She leaned forward, almost ready to put her arms around him – until she saw their reflection in the shop window. Anyone could see.

Wordlessly, she tugged the blind down.

'Good idea,' Kyle murmured. He reached for the door, flipping the *Open* sign to *Closed.*

'I wasn't going to close this early,' Hannah said, though her voice had lost conviction.

'You'll be closing the shop for good soon,' Kyle said with a smile that didn't quite reach his eyes. 'Doesn't matter if you lose a few customers now. And I, for one, will be glad when this charade is over and I never have to set foot in Cobblers Yard again.'

Hannah swallowed hard, a nagging question playing on her mind: was she really about to give up everything she had worked for – her shop, her friends, Maisie's life there in Suffolk – for him?

And if she did … what would that mean for her? It would mean giving up her independence, giving up running her own business, returning to a life dependant on Kyle. Hannah frowned. Her eyes drifted to her cosy corner. She didn't want to give him up, but she couldn't give up all this either. She stood in his embrace. *What on earth am I going to do?* she wondered.

Kyle drew back, releasing her from their embrace. 'Hey, I never got a chance to tell you how much I love that painting in the window – what's it called?'

'*Sunrise Over Seashell Bay.*'

'Did Maisie paint it?'

Hannah looked at him. That was a peculiar thing to ask. Hannah had never shared her daughter's secret with Kyle. 'No, I bought it in the charity shop across the yard.'

'You found that in the charity shop?' he said, surprised. 'Wow. I should have a look around in there. Perhaps I'll come up with something for a few quid that's worth a fortune.'

Hannah recalled the episode she'd overheard in his shop when Diana was on the phone, irritated by a customer who was clearly complaining that they'd undervalued an antique.

Hannah said, 'That painting is not worth a fortune.'

Actually, it was, if you counted the airgraphs hidden inside the frame, but Hannah didn't want to tell him about those. *I don't trust you*, she thought.

Kyle said, 'I bet it's worth more than you paid for it.'

Hannah didn't see the point denying it. 'Look, it is worth a lot more than I paid for it, probably about two hundred pounds, but I only paid twenty.'

Kyle smirked. 'That's my girl. Nothing like turning a profit. How much have you got it up for sale for?'

'It's not for sale.'

He whirled around. 'What do you mean – it's not for sale?'

'It's my good-luck charm. Its sentimental value is worth far more to me than money.'

'Sentimental value?' Kyle scoffed. 'I'd take a profit any day.'

'And by the sounds of things you do,' Hannah blurted, still thinking of the conversation she'd overheard Diana having.

Kyle went to say something but clammed up.

Looking at her painting, Hannah said, 'I don't suppose you know where Seashell Bay is?'

Kyle knitted his brow. 'What do you mean?'

'The bay in the painting. I'd like to find it.'

Kyle rolled his eyes. 'It's a painting, Hannah. It's not real.'

'But it might be.'

'It's just a figment of the painter's imagination – that's all. You'll never find it because it doesn't exist.'

'But I think it does because—'

'Because …?'

Hannah stared at him, swallowing the word *airgraphs*, the story of the love letters she'd discovered. *Don't tell him*, a voice in her head said, the distrust resurfacing again.

Hannah had a question. 'Why did you ask me if Maisie painted that?'

He grinned. 'Now, I'm really pleased you asked me that question because I've got a little favour to ask you. Can we go upstairs, talk in private?'

Hannah didn't understand. 'But it's private down here. The blinds are closed, the door is locked, nobody is coming in.'

'Yes, but I want to go up to your flat.'

'Why? What's wrong with the sofa in the cosy corner?'

'Because we're in Cobblers Yard and god knows if one your neighbours will knock and interrupt our conversation.'

Hannah looked towards the door. He did have a point. Hannah was thinking of The Gossip Girls. She'd been avoiding them, coming up with excuses when they'd popped over, knowing they wanted to sit in her cosy corner, with a long, drawn-out cup of coffee, and ask her what was going on – why she kept closing early on Saturdays. The last thing Hannah wanted was to answer that question.

He took her hand, curling his fingers in hers, his smiling eyes roving over her. 'I want you all to myself.'

She grinned at him. He was flirting with her. 'Oh, alright. Let's go upstairs and sit in my lounge instead. Then you can tell me this little favour you're after.'

They were on their way upstairs, when Kyle stopped halfway and said, 'Can I have a cup of coffee?'

'Of course. Let's go on up and I'll make you one in the kitchen while you tell me what's on your mind.'

'Actually, I bet that coffee machine in your shop does a decent cup of coffee.'

Hannah grinned. 'Oh, you have no idea. I'll nip downstairs and make one.'

'Yes, why don't you do that.'

Hannah shrugged. 'All right.' She felt a little guilty for telling The Gossip Girls that her coffee machine was on the blink.

A few minutes later, Hannah called up the stairs, 'You might as well come down for it, rather than me carrying two mugs upstairs.'

When he didn't respond, Hannah left the coffee on the table and walked upstairs, expecting to find him lounging on the sofa in her lounge.

He wasn't in the lounger, the kitchen, or her bedroom. She'd half expected to find him there, sitting on the end of her bed, hoping she'd join him.

'What are you doing?' Hannah raised her eyebrows when she discovered him in Maisie's bedroom. He was standing in front of the easel, staring at one of Maisie's paintings. He turned around.

Hannah saw what was in his hand. She patted her back pocket and discovered her phone was missing. 'Hey, that's my phone!' She frowned. 'It was you, wasn't it, who muted my phone last weekend?' When he didn't admit it, she looked at him staring at the painting, and said, 'This is Maisie's room. You shouldn't be in here.'

He looked at her. 'Yes, I get that. And I know why.' He held up her phone. 'I knew it wasn't a deepfake.'

'What are you talking about? Give me my phone back.'

'Not before I play this again.' He scrolled through her phone and held up the video she'd taken ages ago of Maisie painting an Old Master – the one she'd briefly considered uploading to TikTok in a moment of desperation to earn money.

'She's as real as you and I,' Kyle said, forcing her to watch the video.

'How did you find that?'

'I switched your phone to mute last weekend, so there wasn't any chance you'd get a call because your kid was sick or something, and that was when this came up on your phone – *look back at your memories* – and this video was playing. I couldn't believe my eyes.'

'So, that's why you turned up at my shop today, to see for yourself. Give it back!'

Kyle handed her the phone. With trembling hands, she quickly deleted the video.

'There's no use deleting it,' said Kyle.

'Why?' She looked at him wide-eyed, afraid he'd posted it to social media. She said as much.

'Do you really think I'd do that?'

'You're protecting her secret too?'

'Yeah, of course. Why would I let anybody else know what I've discovered? Your secret is safe with me.'

'Oh, thank god.' Hannah breathed the biggest sigh of relief.

'But you've got to do something for me in return …'

Hannah's relief, she realised was short-lived. 'What do you want?' she said slowly.

'Look, I'm in a spot of bother.'

Hannah stared at him.

'And I need your help.'

She couldn't believe it. This was like history repeating itself. 'How is that possible? Your business is thriving.'

'Yes, it is. But this time it's a personal matter.'

'What do you mean?'

'I like a little flutter, Hannah. It's my only vice. And my gambling debts have got a bit out of hand …'

Hannah stared at him. She looked at Maisie's easel and knew what was coming.

If she just paints me an Old Master, I can flog it as the real deal. It could be a great money spinner.'

'Oh, my god. Are you for real?'

'Just this one time, I swear. And then we can pretend like it never happened.'

Hannah grimaced. 'You'd involve my nine-year-old daughter in crime?'

'No one will know it was her.'

'But *I'll* know!' And she knew something else – it wouldn't stop at one painting. She remembered what he'd said when he'd asked her to move out of Cobblers Yard, away from all her friends, away from Maisie's father, Nate – *the three of us, we'd make a good team*. Not a family. He'd said *team*.

Hannah narrowed her eyes. She knew what he saw in Maisie – the big score. He was still looking for that, and if it couldn't be done legit, then he didn't care. After all, what had he said? He'd take the profit any time. His business was a front. It was legit, but she bet they'd scammed loads of people, probably elderly people living in East Anglia and beyond – property-rich, cash-poor people. He worked under a veneer of respectability, valuing their old antiques at well below market value to make a quick, easy profit. But he had no qualms in going further and passing off a copy of a painting as genuine to make a lot of money.

Hannah's eyes darted to the corner of Maisie's room.

Kyle followed her gaze.

'What's this?'

Hannah stepped forward. 'No!'

He lifted a sheet under which were various framed paintings. He lifted one up. 'Well, well, what have we here?' He smiled. 'And here's one she painted earlier …'

'Give that back!'

Kyle whirled around, holding the picture frame tightly. 'Do you want me to tell the whole world your daughter's secret?'

Hannah looked at the painting in his hands.

'Do you want me to tell all your friends in Cobblers Yard who you really are – a thief who stole from Joseph, a vulnerable old man?'

Kyle started walking towards her. 'Do you want me to tell your best friend, Lili, all about what you've been up to these past few weeks, neglecting your daughter, neglecting your business, to come out with me?' He stopped in front of her. 'Don't get me wrong. I love you, I really do. As I said, we'll make a good team. I won't give up her secret, Hannah, but you need to pack up your life here and come to live with me in my cottage. Diana will make you really welcome in the shop. Hey, you could even carry on your art and craft shop if you really want to. We'll find a vacant shop in the village.'

Hannah swallowed. 'You'll want her to paint.'

Kyle glanced over his shoulder. 'I think there's enough here to get started – don't you? Then we'll take it from there.'

Hannah followed him down the stairs to the front door, the painting covered with the sheet in his hands.

'Kyle – don't do this.'

He stopped at the door. 'Everything is going to be fine. I suggest you talk to Maisie when she returns, tell her about us and our new life together. You won't regret it.'

Hannah was already regretting it. Everything. She felt like such a fool. She didn't doubt he was in love with her, but he was in love with money, and his next big score, more, and she'd fallen right back into the life with him she swore she'd never live again.

'I'll be back for the rest. In the meantime, I suggest you start thinking about packing. You're going to be starting a new life in Norfolk, and it's going to be amazing. Just you wait and see.'

He looked at the door. 'Well, aren't you going to open it?'

Hannah slowly unlocked the door. She stood there watching him carrying the painting out of Cobblers Yard. 'What have I done?' She stared across the yard and caught Mabel in the window. Mabel walked out of the shop, and called across the yard, 'Hannah – is everything alright?'

Hannah turned her back, and slammed the door shut, locking it. She slid down to the floor, pulled her knees up to her chest and looked around her shop. Her gaze settled on the cosy corner, her eyes filling with tears. 'What. Have. I. Done.'

31

Someone knocked on Hannah's shop door and then tried the handle. She was still sitting behind her door, knees drawn up, wondering what she was going to do. She frowned when whoever it was knocked again. She couldn't imagine it was Kyle. He'd be long gone, driving back to Norfolk with his prize sitting on the back seat – Maisie's painting.

Hannah frowned at the *rat-a-tat-tat*. Didn't anyone read signs anymore? Her shop was closed. She couldn't imagine how she'd reopen the shop today. Besides, she had something urgent she needed to do. Hannah stood up, the blinds still drawn on the shop door and the window. She imagined that whoever had been trying her shop door had gone. Her hands shook as she slid the bolt across, intending to go outside and call on her shop neighbours. Outside, she knew the yard was quiet. It was still early on Saturday morning. There would be few customers, which meant that hopefully there would be time to speak to her friends.

When she opened the door, she stepped back in surprise. The doorway was crowded with faces – Mabel and Marjorie at the front, their lips pursed with grim determination, Thea just behind them, arms folded. Lili's eyes searched Hannah's, soft but worried. Reggie stood awkwardly, his gnarly hands clasped, and Joss lingered near the back, tall and steady, his briefcase in hand like a shield.

Hannah stared at them standing there outside her shop, thinking back to the last time they'd all gathered in her cosy corner, when it had been for celebration. That warm afterglow of the yard party, cups of coffee in hand, laughter bouncing off the shelves. Hannah's heart ached with the memory. Now, weeks later, because she had let Kyle back into her life, she was about to lose everything – her friends, her second chance, her daughter's trust.

She swallowed hard. She knew why they were there. They'd all noticed she had been closing earlier and earlier, sometimes for a whole weekend – and she'd been avoiding them. They wanted to know what was going on.

Hannah sighed. 'You'd better come in.' Little did they know that she'd been about to call on her neighbours and gather them right there in her shop.

They filed into the cosy corner, filling every chair. Reggie dragged over an upturned sturdy box. The little lamp flickered, throwing golden light on their faces.

It was Lili who spoke first. 'Hannah … we know about Kyle.'

Hannah's throat closed. She'd imagined this moment countless times, dreaded it. Still, hearing it said aloud made her knees weaken. She sank onto the sofa. 'How?'

Mabel adjusted her spectacles. 'Maisie.'

'Oh god.' Hannah pressed her hands over her face.

'She only told us because she was frightened for you,' Marjorie added gently.

'We didn't want to get involved in your personal life,' Thea said, her voice firmer, 'but then again … we could all see it wasn't leading anywhere good. So we met. Behind your back. To figure out what to do.'

Hannah let out a ragged laugh. 'You had a yard committee about my disaster of a love life?'

'Call it … crisis management,' Reggie said, giving her a small smile. 'Sorry.'

Hannah knew she should be very cross with them indeed for talking about her, and her personal life, behind her back. But she wasn't. It just made her love them all the more for being such concerned friends. And she wasn't cross with Maisie either for confiding in Mabel and Marjorie. Hannah inwardly groaned at how naïve she'd been to think that she could lie to Maisie about Kyle and that her bright, perceptive daughter wouldn't sense that her mum was hiding things from her.

Joss leaned forward, clasping his hands. 'Now, it turns out that Kyle visited the bookshop and Reggie's music shop, asking questions.'

Hannah recalled that Kyle had told her he'd visited some of the shops in the yard. She didn't see why that was relevant. But she listened.

Joss continued, 'Thea says he wanted to know if she had any rare books. Reggie says he asked after valuable violins. He's been sniffing around, Hannah. It doesn't feel right.'

Hannah's chest tightened. She looked at each of them – their concerned faces, their quiet solidarity – and realised she couldn't hide anymore. She took a shaky breath.

'You're right, it's not,' she whispered. 'I should have told you from the beginning. Kyle is my ex. He talked me into stealing from this very shop when it was still an antiques shop. I wore Lili's coat, and she got arrested instead. I confessed, went to prison. And Kyle …' her voice faltered, '… he disappeared. I've been such a fool, I know that now. I was on my way out to invite you all here and … and tell you about my past.'

Mabel and Marjorie exchanged a glance and looked at her sheepishly. 'I'm afraid we've already apprised the others of the situation.'

Hannah went bright red. She stole a glance around the room, afraid what their reaction would be.

Reggie reached over and patted her hand. 'You've done your time. You've made good. None of us are judging you.'

Hannah blinked back tears. 'There's something else …' Hannah looked at her friends. She didn't want any more secrets. She knew they could be trusted. 'It's about Maisie …' Hannah stood up and paced, tears rolling down her cheeks as she recounted what had just happened – Kyle discovering Maisie's gift and taking her painting.

'You mean *stealing* it,' said Mabel. 'I saw him walking out of your shop with something. Although it was covered up, I guessed it was a painting, but you don't sell paintings, and it wasn't large enough to be *Sunrise Over Seashell Bay*.'

Hannah nodded. 'He said just the one to pay off his gambling debts, but I don't believe him. It's not going to stop there, and now my daughter is going to be dragged into criminal activity all because of me.' Hannah sat back down and burst into tears.

Lili came over and perched on the arm of the sofa chair, putting her arms around Hannah.

Hannah looked up at her. 'Oh, Lili, I want him out of my

life. I do. But I don't know how.'

'That's where we come in,' Joss said. His voice was calm; almost matter of fact. 'Men like Kyle don't change. He's gone back to his old ways – it was only a matter of time. But if we want to stop him, we need to catch him in the act.'

Hannah wiped the tears from her eyes. 'You mean catch him in the act of stealing something?'

'Yes, but the problem is …' He spread his hands. 'None of us has anything valuable enough to tempt him.'

Hannah hesitated, then met Thea's gaze. 'Actually … that's not true.' Hannah stood and walked over to the window display. She lifted the painting down with reverent care and carried it back to her circle of friends.

Lili shook her head. 'Hannah, I know you love that painting. It's a treasure to you, but I don't think it's going to be worth enough to tempt him.'

'No. Not the painting.' Hannah set it down on the coffee table and knelt. With trembling fingers, she began tearing at the backing.

Several of them shot to their feet. 'Oh my god, Hannah! Have you gone mad?' Lili cried.

'Sit down – all of you,' Thea said sharply.

The paper gave way. Hannah reached inside and drew out the neat, delicate bundle she had kept hidden. She set it on the table.

The airgraphs.

Thea explained what they were, and how much they were potentially worth, and the plan Hannah had discussed with her about giving some of the proceeds to the charity shop if they were sold.

Reggie gave a low whistle, then chuckled. 'I think that will do it.' He leaned back, the corners of his mouth twitching with grim amusement. 'Now we just have to set the stage …'

Hannah's pulse thundered in her ears. She looked around at the people she'd once feared would cast her out. Instead, they were there, plotting with her, protecting her. Family, Reggie had called them.

And for the first time since Kyle had made off with Maisie's painting, and her secret, Hannah felt a glimmer of hope.

32

The bundle of airgraphs lay in the middle of the table, their fragile paper whispering of secrets long hidden. No one spoke at first. The weight of what they were considering seemed to hover in the air like smoke.

It was Joss who finally broke the silence. 'If we're going to do this, it has to be carefully thought out. We can't confront him directly – he'll charm his way out of it, or worse, turn nasty. We need evidence. Something that proves his intent to steal.'

Reggie rubbed the back of his neck. 'So what – you're saying we dangle these as bait? Leave them lying around, let him find out they're worth a fortune, and see what he does?'

'Exactly.' Joss nodded. 'But it needs to look natural. We can't shove them under his nose.'

Thea tilted her head, arms folded. 'He's already been sniffing around for rare books. If he comes into my shop again, I could mention the painting, how it's a 'family heirloom' with something hidden inside. Make it sound casual. If he thinks he's overheard something rather than being told directly, he'll be more likely to believe it rather than being suspicious.'

Mabel leaned forward, frowning. 'That sounds dangerous,

Thea. What if he thinks you're hiding the airgraphs in your shop and decides to break in?'

'That's the point, isn't it?' Thea replied. 'We need to lure him into trying.'

'No.' Hannah shook her head sharply. 'I won't have any of you at risk. It's my mess, my past. I'll be the one to bait him.'

'Sweetheart, you can't do this alone,' Lili said, her voice firm but gentle. 'That's how he got to you before – isolated you, made you feel like it was just the two of you against the world.'

Hannah shook her head. 'I shouldn't have sneaked around and hidden my relationship.'

Lili said, 'Well this time it's different. You've got us in your corner.'

Marjorie cleared her throat. 'We'll all play our part. That's the only way it will work. Safety in numbers.'

Reggie grinned faintly. 'Besides, I've always wanted to be in a sting operation. Makes me feel like I'm in some detective drama.'

Even Hannah smiled at that, though her heart still thumped nervously.

Joss leaned forward, tapping the table for attention. 'Right, let's be practical. First – we need Kyle to believe the airgraphs are valuable. Hannah, you let something slip to him, maybe mention an old wartime collection you came upon in the charity shop. Thea can back it up if he fishes in her shop again.'

Hannah nodded. 'Yes, that would work. I already told him about the painting, and that I bought it from the charity shop well below its true value. He loved hearing that and actually said that he was intending to visit the charity shop, see what else he might find along those lines.' Hannah looked apologetically at Mabel and Marjorie. 'Sorry.'

'Don't be, Hannah. We're just pleased we can help stop him fleecing more people out of their money.'

Hannah shook her head sadly. 'I've been so blind.'

'Once a con artist, always a con artist,' said Lili, reaching over and squeezing her hand.

'So, where do we keep the airgraphs?' Mabel asked, returning to the business at hand.

'In here,' Joss said, gesturing around Hannah's shop. 'Somewhere he thinks he can get at them. We stage it so he has the chance to take them.'

'And then what?' Hannah whispered.

'Then,' Joss said, his voice calm and measured, 'we catch him in the act. Phones at the ready. Record everything. If he tries to lift them, that's attempted theft. Enough to go to the police with.'

Lili pursed her lips. 'We'll need to be discreet. He's clever. If he smells a trap, he'll vanish.'

'I'm afraid he'll try and take some more of Maisie's paintings too,' said Hannah.

Lili reached across and took Hannah's hand. 'We'll make sure you're never alone with him. Not again.'

The group murmured their agreement.

Reggie leaned back, thoughtful. 'So, who does what? Thea plants the seed. Hannah tempts him further. Joss covers the legal end. I can hang around the yard, keep an eye out if he shows up at odd hours.'

'And we,' Mabel said, gesturing between herself and Marjorie, 'will do what we do best. Keep watch. We notice everything that goes on in this yard. If Kyle so much as breathes suspiciously, we'll know.'

Marjorie nodded gravely. 'We've got eyes everywhere.'

Despite her fear, Hannah laughed softly. They were The Gossip Girls; they always had their eyes open.

Joss's expression sobered the group again. 'There is a risk. If Kyle feels cornered, he could lash out. I need to know you're all certain about this.'

One by one, the shopkeepers nodded.

Hannah pressed her palms together, looking at each of them. 'I don't know what I did to deserve you all. But thank you. If this works … maybe I can finally put Kyle behind me. For good.'

Lili squeezed her hand again, her eyes shining. 'Then let's make it work. Together.'

The airgraphs lay between them. The trap was set.

33

The Saturday afternoon sun slanted across Cobblers Yard, throwing long shadows against the brick walls and warming the air with a golden glow. Hannah sat behind the counter of her shop, her hands busy sorting through a box of paints, though her eyes kept flicking to the window. Every sound – the distant sound of cars passing in the high street, the echo of footsteps – sent her stomach lurching.

She'd told herself he might not come, but when the bell above the door chimed, her heart knew before her head did.

Kyle stepped inside, his smile all easy charm. 'Afternoon, Hannah.'

She forced her own smile, though her fingers clenched around the tube of paint. 'I didn't think you'd return today.'

'I was surprised you called, saying you wanted to see me again so soon, and here in Cobblers Yard,' he said, glancing around the shop as if he owned the place. His eyes swept over the shelves, the cosy corner with its old sofa and lamp, the neat display of paints and sketchbooks. 'I've never really taken all this in, you know, not properly. You've made the place lovely. Very … homely.'

It was meant as a compliment, but Hannah heard the faint note of disdain behind it. She didn't respond.

Kyle's gaze drifted to the ceiling. She knew what was on his mind – Maisie's paintings. Hannah said, 'Help yourself to a cup of coffee from the coffee machine,' distracting him.

'Yeah – good idea.'

She watched him walk over to the cosy corner and pick up a mug, placing it in the machine and pressing the button.

'This is a pleasant surprise, you know. Not sneaking around. You've certainly changed your tune.'

Hannah pursed her lips. She hadn't thought of that – would he start getting suspicious over what she was up to, texting him to come round in the middle of the day while the shop was open?

He turned around with his cup of coffee and glanced over at the shop window, the blinds up, the door wide open.

'Now, I know why you've called me here, rather than meeting in secret like we normally do.'

Hannah could feel her heart beating in her chest. *Oh, god – he knows what I've got planned.* She took deep breaths, trying to slow her heart rate. After all, how *could* he know?

'You've finally decided to tell that lot,' he gestured at the window, presumably talking about her fellow shopkeepers, 'about us. Are you still going to tell Maisie when she returns tomorrow?'

'She knows.'

'That's fantastic. So now we can get the ball rolling with the move to Norfolk. I was thinking we should start by taking all Maisie's paintings. I think we should store them in my shop.'

Hannah didn't respond. She eyed the airgraphs, which were spread out on the coffee table. He hadn't spotted them yet. She said, 'Why don't you take a seat? I'll be with you in a moment.' She made to look busy, arranging the tube of paints on the shelf to one side of the counter. Her back was to him, when she heard him exclaim, 'What have we here?'

She smiled to herself before turning around. 'Oh, those?' she said casually. 'It was another find in the charity shop. Well, not exactly. I discovered them hidden in the backing of the painting. Thea advised me to store them back in the painting for now while I decide what to do with them.'

They'd all discussed this when they were planning the trap for Kyle and had decided it was best to stick close to the truth because then it was less likely that Hannah would catch herself out.

His eyes sharpened, peering at them. 'These letters … they look old. Valuable.'

'Not really,' Hannah lied, her voice deliberately dismissive. 'They're love letters. Just sentimental.'

Kyle gave her a sidelong glance, the corner of his mouth curling. 'You've always been a terrible liar, Han.'

The words cut like a knife, but before she could answer, the bell rang again. Thea breezed in, carrying a stack of books.

'Oh, Hannah, I nearly forgot – here's that catalogue I promised you.' She set the books down on the counter, her eyes flicking briefly to Kyle. 'Oh. Hello.'

Kyle's smile shifted into charm mode. 'Kyle. Old friend of Hannah's. Well, more than old friends. Hannah and I are seeing each other.'

'Thea,' she said crisply, her hand barely brushing his before she turned to Hannah. 'You'll find the section on wartime memorabilia particularly interesting.' She tapped the catalogue and lowered her voice just enough for Kyle to overhear. 'Especially for those … letters. I have a feeling they could be quite valuable.'

Hannah's pulse leapt. Thea slipped her a look that said, *your turn.*

'Thanks,' Hannah said, playing along. 'I'll take a look later.'

Kyle leaned forward in his seat, feigning nonchalance. 'Didn't know you had an interest in wartime history.'

'I dabble,' Hannah said quickly, tucking the catalogue aside.

Thea said, 'Now, remember Hannah, you must seal them back up in the painting when you've finished looking at them, so you keep them safe.'

Hannah nodded. 'Will do.'

Thea was about to go when she said, 'Have you got any plans this evening? All the shopkeepers were thinking of going out, having a meal together. I expect we'll be out quite late at the pub. But Maisie is on her sleepover with her dad, so maybe you can make it?'

Hannah kept her expression in check, listening to Thea's rehearsed lines. This was all for Kyle's benefit, hoping he took the bait. She was taking a risk inviting Kyle there. There was no way she wanted to go out with him again, but if he found out they would all be out of Cobblers Yard that evening, hopefully he'd go home and come back later.

She cast a glance at Kyle. 'I think we might have had plans.'

His eyes lingered on her, measuring, weighing. Then he stood up, brushing imaginary dust from his sleeve. 'Actually, something has come up. I'll leave you ladies to it. Go out for your meal, Hannah.'

'Are you sure?'

'Yeah – definitely.' He walked over to the counter and leaned in to kiss her. Fortunately, the counter was between them, so he couldn't kiss her properly. 'Besides, I think it will be good for you to go out with them, say your goodbyes.'

'Goodbyes?' Thea said.

'Ah, she hasn't told you yet. She's closing down the shop and moving to Norfolk with me.'

Thea feigned surprise. Hannah had already apprised them all of Kyle's plan for her and Maisie's future – but it was never going to happen; not now she had all her friends helping her extricate herself from Kyle.

At the door, Kyle turned around. 'Unusual markings on those letters – what the hell is an airgraph?'

'That's what I've got these books for – to find out.'

On his way out, Hannah saw him on his phone. She knew what he was doing – Googling to find out.

The bell jingled as he left.

Thea exhaled sharply. 'He was sniffing around, no doubt about it.'

Hannah nodded, her knees weak. 'He knows about the airgraphs, and I imagine he's already found out just how valuable they are.'

Thea's eyes hardened. 'Good. That's exactly what we wanted. Now we just have to be ready when he decides to strike.'

Through the shop window, Hannah watched Kyle cross the yard, his figure tall and sure, his smile already turned toward Reggie, who was pretending to sweep his doorway. He was weaving himself into the yard's rhythm, testing the waters.

And every step he took brought him closer to the trap.

34

Cobblers Yard was quiet – the kind of quiet that carried every creak of a shutter and whisper of the sea breeze across the cobbles. But that Saturday night, there was a new hum beneath the silence – the discreet CCTV cameras Ray had helped install, their tiny red lights blinking like watchful eyes.

Reggie was the one keeping vigil, seated in his music shop with his record player switched off for once, the computer monitor glowing on the counter before him.

Hannah couldn't sleep, though Ray had assured her she must rest, so she'd forced herself into bed. Maisie was tucked in safely at Nate's.

Hannah's mind reeled with nerves. When – *if* – Kyle turned up to steal the airgraphs, he'd think the shopkeepers, including her, were out for the evening, having a meal and late-night drinks at the pub.

❖

It was gone eleven when Kyle arrived, slipping into the yard with a thief's grace. He moved like he belonged to the shadows, head turning once, twice, before he produced a key.

A key that wasn't his.

Inside the shop, he paused, listening. No sound. No movement. Satisfied, he padded to the painting in the window. His fingers were sure as he lifted it down, the weight more than he'd expected because of what lay hidden inside: the airgraphs.

He grinned to himself, whispering, 'Perfect.' Kyle had a plan. His car was outside, along with the materials he needed. He was going to undo the backing, take the airgraphs, and seal the backing again before carefully putting the painting back on the easel in the shop window. Hannah would be none the wiser that he'd return to her shop and that the airgraphs were no longer hidden in the painting. Then, during her house move, the removal company, for a generous backhander, would conveniently mislay the painting. Kyle would sell the airgraphs to the highest bidder, without her knowledge, and she'd never know that her painting, which had gone missing during the move, no longer had the airgraphs sealed inside.

He knew Hannah; she was the sentimental type. He had a feeling that, as with her stupid painting, she'd start getting sentimental over the airgraphs too if he suggested selling them. She'd called them love letters. He wouldn't be at all surprised if her idea was to try to find the lovers who'd written the letters.

Kyle quietly walked out of the shop, carrying the painting. As he walked across the yard with the painting under his arm, headlights cut across the cobbles from the entrance to the yard. Two police cars rolled up in the high street, doors opening with swift, practised movements.

Kyle heard the cars. *Oh, god – they're back*, was his first thought. He'd assumed that the shopkeepers were all still having drinks in the pub after dinner and would be out until very late.

He looked towards the shop door in a moment of indecision. But it was too late to put the painting back, lock up the door, and disappear. There was only one way in and out of the yard. He was trapped. Standing there in the middle of the yard, he was trying to think up a plausible excuse for what he was doing there in the middle of the night with the painting tucked under his arm. Hannah had always been so gullible, trusting. He was just thinking that whatever bullshit he came out with, she was sure to believe him, when two men in uniform emerged from the shadows.

'Mr Kyle Turner?' the officer called. 'Put the painting down. Now.'

Kyle froze in shock. 'How the hell—?'

The officers advanced, one holding handcuffs.

Kyle glanced back toward Hannah's shop, confusion written all over his face. He'd been so careful. She was out. How could the police have possibly—

Reggie flicked his light in his shop on, stepping outside his door. Joss, who had been monitoring the CCTV with Reggie, joined him.

The outside light of the bookshop flicked on too, along with the lights in the window as Thea opened her door. Callum had been waiting too with Thea.

Mabel and Marjorie were next. Lights appeared in their shop window before they too stepped outside.

Kyle looked at the two old women. 'Oh, you have got to be kidding me.'

The police took the painting, handing it carefully to Ray, who had followed them in from the street. There was grim satisfaction in his eyes. 'Thought you'd get away with it, did you?'

Lili stepped out of the shadows, her face pale but resolute.

'We look after our own in the yard,' Reggie called out, his voice steady.

Kyle's gaze darted from one face to another, realisation dawning. He laughed, though it sounded thin. 'This is a set-up.' Kyle's expression changed. He snarled, 'You've no idea who you're dealing with. I run a legitimate business. Stanford & Co.!'

'Your business affairs and Stanford & Co. are exactly what we'll be looking into next,' one of the officers cut in.

❖

Cobblers Yard buzzed with camera crews and reporters on Sunday morning. But in Hannah's shop, the cosy corner was filled with quiet voices. The shopkeepers were gathered around mugs of coffee, and the only sound was the rustle of the newspaper.

Clarissa's headline stretched across the page: they'd got an advance copy of the paper that would be hitting the shops on Monday morning – *Antiques Dealer Arrested in Cobblers Yard Sting – Police Investigate Wider Plot.* There was even a grainy still from the CCTV: Kyle caught red-handed with *Sunrise Over Seashell Bay* tucked under his arm.

'Looks good in print,' Reggie said, taking a self-satisfied sip.

'Yes, he is very photogenic. Quite the charmer,' Mabel agreed, though her eyes twinkled. 'A charmer, but certainly not *charming*.'

Hannah stared at the article, her chest a tangle of relief, sorrow, and something else. She knew what it was: she'd thought she was in love. She'd been so happy until it had all come crashing down. Kyle hadn't changed – not one bit.

The article described Stanford & Co.'s little antiques shop swarming with investigators. Behind its polished counters and polite smiles, they uncovered far more than dusty curiosities. A painting – a near-perfect forgery – stood waiting. Alongside it were meticulous plans for a museum heist, with the original to be switched for the fake and sold on the black market.

When pressed about the forgery, Kyle gave his most outrageous answer yet. 'It wasn't me. It was my girlfriend's nine-year-old kid. She's the one who painted the forgery.'

His desperate claim only sank him deeper. If he'd lie about something so ludicrous, what else was he concealing?

Thea set down her cup and turned to her. 'What now, Hannah?'

Hannah lifted her gaze, steady at last. She knew exactly what now. 'I'm going to do what I meant to do before Kyle came back,' she said quietly. 'I'm going to visit Somersby Hall.'

And with those words, the air in the cosy corner shifted – away from secrets and shadows and towards something new.

35

Cobblers Yard had a different feel on Monday morning. Not tense, not suspicious, but lighter, as though the shadows had finally lifted. The bunting from the yard party weeks earlier was long gone, yet the little square seemed to sparkle with the same brightness.

Hannah still couldn't quite believe Kyle was gone – not just gone but *arrested*. The news had spread like wildfire. She'd overheard townsfolk already; some sympathetic, some tutting, some with their own embellishments to the tale. But inside the yard, the atmosphere was one of relief and of quiet triumph.

Maisie appeared on the shop floor, her schoolbag slung over her shoulder ready for school. 'Mum?'

Hannah looked up from straightening a display of paintbrushes. 'Are you sure you don't want a day off school, sweetheart? I can ring the school.'

Maisie shook her head. 'I want to see my friends.'

Hannah smiled, thinking it was for the best that Maisie stayed in her normal routine.

Maisie came closer, her eyes searching her mum's face. 'It's really over, isn't it? He's not coming back?'

Hannah knelt down so they were eye to eye. 'No, Maisie. He's not coming back. I should've told you sooner, about everything, but I wanted to believe—' She broke off, swallowing the guilt that threatened to rise. 'I promise you, it's just us now. No more secrets.'

Maisie studied her, lips pursed. Then, slowly, she leaned forward and wrapped her arms around Hannah's neck. 'Good. I don't like secrets. I just want my mum back.'

Hannah held her daughter tightly, breathing in the scent of her hair, the warmth of her little body.

A knock on the door interrupted them. It was Lili, with a smile soft enough not to intrude. 'Thought I'd check in. How are my favourite girls this morning?'

Maisie pulled back, grinning. 'Better. Lots better.'

It wasn't long before everyone in the yard had gathered in Hannah's shop again. They were all stopping by before they opened their shops that morning. Reggie had brought a record with him. 'What this place needs is a bit of music. Nothing says the bad times are over like Duke Ellington.'

Lili brought flowers from The Potting Shed, filling the room with the scent of lavender and rosemary. Marjorie arrived with a tin of biscuits under her arm, muttering, 'No family meeting should ever be without sustenance.' Mabel bustled in last, straight up to the coffee machine to make herself a cuppa and settle in her favourite spot. She said, 'Joss sends his regards. He'll pop in later to say hi, but he's up to his eyes with clients already this morning. Wendy sent in these cakes, though.' Mabel set the cake tin down on the coffee table.

Hannah smiled. She wasn't surprised that Joss couldn't be there, although it did remind her that she still had to speak to him and get his advice about the valuable airgraphs.

'Did you see the paper today?' Marjorie asked, producing a folded copy. 'Clarissa wrote another article. She did us proud. Says we were heroes, taking the likes of him out of business. Not by name, mind,' she added, with a wink. 'But *we* know.'

Maisie beamed. 'I think Grandpa Ray was the real hero.'

Reggie chuckled. 'Well, he certainly played his part. But you know what? So did you, Maisie. You spoke up and told the truth, and that was brave.'

Maisie blushed and ducked her head. 'I just didn't want my mum to get hurt again.'

The cosy corner filled with chatter and the clink of mugs. The air was warm with coffee, cake, and the kind of laughter that comes after a storm has passed. For the first time in weeks, Hannah let herself relax fully into the moment.

When the others drifted back to their shops, and Hannah had seen Maisie off to school, Hannah returned to her shop to find Lili and Thea lingering inside by the door. 'We wanted to make sure you were okay,' said Lili. Thea nodded her head.

'I feel like I've let everyone down,' Hannah confessed, crossing the shop floor and slumping down on the sofa. 'Maisie most of all.'

Lili and Thea exchanged a glance and followed her back to the cosy corner, Thea sitting down next to her on the sofa, Lili perching on the sofa chair she'd positioned next to Hannah.

'I promised Maisie that I'd never drag her back into that old life, and the first chance I had, I let Kyle in. What kind of mum does that make me?'

Lili leaned forward, her gaze steady. 'It makes you human, Hannah. Just human. We've all wanted to believe the best of someone we loved. You're not the first and you won't be the last.'

Hannah shook her head. 'But it feels like I haven't changed. Like all the work I did to build a new life here meant nothing, because I slipped straight back into my old ways.'

Thea turned to Hannah, covering her hand with her own. 'That's not true. Look at what you've built here. Your shop, your home, the way you're raising Maisie – she's bright and kind and strong because of you. That's change. That's growth. Kyle can't take that away.'

'But you both found love when you moved here,' Hannah murmured, glancing between them. 'It's hard not to look at you and feel like I've failed, like I'm destined to end up alone – or worse, to keep making the same mistakes.'

Lili's smile was small, almost wry. 'It wasn't as simple as it looks from the outside. We made mistakes too, we doubted ourselves, we questioned whether we were ready. Love doesn't just fall into your lap – it takes time, and trust. Don't punish yourself for wanting it. Of course you want someone to cherish you. That's natural.'

Thea nodded. 'But the thing is, it won't come because you're searching desperately for it. It'll come when you least expect it, with the right person. And in the meantime, you've got us. All of us. Your family in Cobblers Yard.'

Hannah's throat tightened, her eyes stinging. For the first time since Kyle's arrest, she allowed herself to breathe. Maybe she had stumbled. Maybe she had let her guard slip. But she wasn't alone anymore.

'You've got good people around you here,' Lili said gently. She touched Hannah's arm. 'Just promise me, no more men like Kyle. You don't need them.'

Hannah nodded, her throat tight. 'I know.'

Lili frowned. 'Now, don't go thinking you should be a nun. You'll meet someone. I agree with Thea. The right person is waiting out there for you, and you know what they say?'

Hannah shook her head waiting for her best friend to enlighten her.

'You'll find love where you least expect it, just like Thea said.'

Hannah felt tears in her eyes. 'I don't deserve such wonderful friends.'

'Yes, you do,' Lili and Thea said in unison. They all stood and hugged before Hannah walked with them to the shop door. She glanced outside and smiled as Thea and Lili walked over to their shops. The first customers of the day had arrived in the yard – more than she expected at that time in the morning. She had a feeling that what had happened there, with all the newspaper coverage over Kyle attempting to steal her painting, had really put Cobblers Yard on the map.

As she turned the sign in her window to *Open*, her gaze settled on her painting, *Sunrise Over Seashell Bay*. Her thoughts turned to Somersby Hall and her promise to herself to visit the hall and find out more about the love letters. Kyle had almost derailed her, but now she was free to go where her heart had been pointing all along.

36

Hannah visited Thea at the bookshop during her lunch break the following day. This was her new normal, popping into the other shops, enjoying the camaraderie of her friends in the yard.

Thea said, 'Remember you mentioned you were going to visit Somersby Hall when you came in to ask my advice about the airgraphs?'

They were sitting in *her* cosy corner for a change, drinking coffee.

Hannah nodded. After all that had happened when she'd met Kyle again, that conversation almost seemed like a lifetime ago. She'd managed to get online that morning and had Googled the place. The stately home was an imposing Edwardian house with large windows, tall chimney stacks, and a rather grand front door. The once vibrant red brickwork and white painted windows had faded over time.

The property was an impressive three storeys. She imagined there were deep window seats and high ceilings inside, letting in plenty of light. There were smaller windows in the gabled roof, which she imagined in years gone by had been the servants' quarters on the top floor. She could just imagine what the grounds fronting the house might have looked like when neatly manicured. Now the front lawn was overgrown, and the pond was full of weeds. The grounds matched the hall's weathered appearance.

Despite its worn façade, Hannah felt an immediate connection to the place. It was hidden away along a secluded private road, nestled in such a way that you could easily overlook it if you weren't specifically searching for it.

'You've been already?'

'No. I saw a photo online.' Hannah had come across a recent photo of the hall in a small article on an auction house website which was advertising the auction that was being held there.

'Ah. May I suggest that you don't go there?'

Hannah was taken aback. 'I want to find out about the painting and the airgraphs, and the links to Somersby Hall.'

'I know you do, but …'

'But …?'

'The airgraphs are very valuable, and you love that painting. What if …' Thea trailed off.

'The descendants of Kitty and Owen want them back?'

'Yes.'

'I was going to give them the love letters, if I found Kitty and Owen, which I know is really doubtful.'

'And now …?' Thea asked.

Hannah hesitated.

'They're yours too,' Thea said. 'I wouldn't blame you for keeping them and selling them on for a profit. If I was in your position, I'd do exactly the same.'

'You would?'

'Of course I would. If you want to be sure, check it out with Joss next door.'

Hannah knew that was a good idea. Even so, she said, 'But it's not like I bought them in the charity shop, is it? I only bought the painting.'

'The painting came framed, so I presume anything that was part of the frame, including the hidden airgraphs, is now rightfully yours – although I know you plan to share any profits with the charity shop anyway. But like I said, check it out with Joss. He might be able to clarify your position, legally. In the meantime, I'd steer clear of Somersby Hall.'

'But what about that guy who visits the bookshop, the old man who bought a book and passed by my shop? Your dad's friend, Percy. I just know he recognised the painting.'

'Well, if he returns, take it upstairs and tell him it's sold, gone.'

'I can't do that!'

'I know it's telling a fib—'

'It's not that. The painting brings me luck, draws in customers. It has to stay in the window. Besides, I still want to find out where the place that the painter called Seashell Bay is on the Suffolk Coast.'

'If it exists,' said Thea.

'Oh, I just know it does now because of the love letters.'

'You're going to visit Somersby Hall, aren't you?'

'Yes. I won't say anything about the painting just yet. Maybe someone there can tell me about Kitty and Owen.'

'Why is it so important to you?' Thea asked.

'I don't know. I just love the painting, I guess, and I want to know more about the couple in love. There was something strange, though.' Hannah told Thea about the last airgraph. 'It was the only one written to Owen in Cairo, but it was never sent.'

'What did Kitty say in that letter?'

'That's the thing, Thea, it wasn't written by Kitty. It was signed *Jemima*.'

'Jemima?'

'Yes.'

'Oh, I wonder if that was his wife, and he was having some sort of illicit affair with Kitty.'

'That's what I wondered – but why is it bundled with the letters from Owen to Kitty?'

Thea scratched her head. 'It's certainly strange. That's another reason not to visit the hall. But if you do, don't mention the airgraphs.'

'I don't understand …'

Thea pointed at the letters. Every family has its secrets, right? I think you've happened upon a family secret from Somersby Hall.'

'But that was years, decades ago. Owen, Kitty and Jemima are most likely dead and gone. What does it matter now?'

'It might not matter at all, but then again …'

'Then again …?'

'Past secrets can ripple down the generations. Who knows what the fallout might be for future generations if a family secret was revealed.'

'You mean for their descendants?'

'Yes.'

Hannah had a feeling that Thea had some personal experience of this.

'I'm sworn to secrecy,' said Henry.

They both turned around and stared at Thea's dad, who was rearranging a bookshelf behind them.

Thea and Hannah exchanged a glance. 'Did you just overhear our conversation about Owen, Kitty and Jemima?'

He continued rearranging the bookshelves.

Hannah recalled what he'd said when he'd mentioned his friend, Percy – the man who had stopped outside her shop window. 'I made a promise that I would never tell. Sworn to secrecy,' Thea's dad had said, tapping his nose.

Hannah looked at the airgraphs in her hand. Did Percy have something to do with these?

'Dad? I thought you were manning the counter, serving customers,' Thea said.

'But there aren't any, sweetheart.'

There was a tinkle of the bell above the shop door – their first customer of the day. 'I must go and see who that is,' said Henry. 'Make me a cup of tea will you, love?'

Hannah bit her bottom lip as her attention drifted to the old, bowed window of the shop. It rather suited the old Dickensian-style interior of old books and the slight musty smell. The tinkle above the door reminded Hannah that it was time she opened her own shop.

Thea sighed. 'I'm afraid you won't get much out of my dad. You're lucky he gave you a name, though.'

'Percy – yes, I know. Like I said, he seemed quite shocked when he caught sight of the painting in my shop window, dabbing his perspiring brow with an old handkerchief. I'm sure the colour drained from his face.'

'Hmm.'

'Your dad said he made a promise that he would never tell. Do you think it was a secret about Kitty, Owen and Jemima? Do you think Percy knew them?'

Thea shrugged. 'Who knows? Perhaps if Percy returns, he'll stop by your shop, Hannah. Then you can ask him.'

'That would be a bit odd, wouldn't it? Asking him out of the blue – hey, did you know Kitty, Owen and Jemima?'

'Yes,' agreed Thea. 'And if he does, he's bound to ask you how *you* know about them.'

'Ah, yes. I hadn't thought of that. I've got to be honest, I won't give up those airgraphs.'

'You want to keep the money for yourself and the charity shop. I don't blame you. But I definitely think you ought to check it out with Joss before you go revealing to anyone else – other than the gang of us who know already – what you've found.'

Hannah had intended to do that, but she'd been so busy in her shop, and she could see how busy Joss had been with the constant visitors next door for legal advice that she just hadn't had the time to go next door and spend time waiting to see him.

It felt as though Thea was badgering her, but Hannah realised she was looking out for her, like good friends do. Hannah said, 'Will you pop into my shop when you have a spare moment? Just for a cuppa and a chat, this time. Nothing dramatic.'

'Of course I will. What are friends for?'

Hannah and Maisie's horizons, because of their new friends in Cobblers Yard, had certainly expanded. Hannah had popped into Reggie's music shop and arranged some music lessons for Maisie who had decided she wanted to learn to play the violin. Maisie also loved visiting the bookshop. It felt at times that she spent more time there than at her mum's shop at the weekend, but Hannah didn't mind. Maisie loved going on a book hunt, as she called it, and had discovered, like in the charity shop, that she found all sorts of treasures in the lovely old bookshop. 'I hope you don't mind that Maisie pops into your bookshop so often.'

'Not at all. My dad loves having her around. I think she reminds him of me when I was little. She loves helping him stack the bookshelves, like I used to do, and she's a bossy little madam, when she wanted to be – just like I used to be.'

'Used to be?' Hannah said with a grin.

'Hey!' Thea exclaimed, smiling – until she looked at the bundle of airgraphs, carefully tied up with ribbon, in Hannah's hands. 'So, you're set on visiting Somersby Hall?'

'I want to see the place where these letters were sent – and where one wasn't posted.' Hannah was thinking of Jemima's letter.

'You can't just turn up there. It's not like a National Trust house. I imagine it's someone's home.'

'I know.' Hannah hadn't really thought it through, although she knew where it was. 'It's not far from Aldeburgh, but it's down little lanes out in the countryside.'

'Sounds lovely.'

'It is – just the sort of place I'd love to live,' blurted Hannah, surprising herself. At first, she'd thought she would find moving from London to the Suffolk Coast hard, being used to the city, but now she couldn't imagine returning to London. She was surprised, though, to find that now she'd even consider moving out of the coastal town to live in the countryside with no shops within walking distance.

'I live in the countryside, and I love it,' said Thea. 'I came from London, you see, just like you, and I thought it would take time to adjust, but oh how I love the peace and quiet. I must be getting old,' she joked.

Hannah smiled. Thea had just voiced what she was thinking.

'Why don't you look for a rental in the countryside? Shame the cottage in Aldeburgh you were renting didn't work out.'

Hannah didn't want to tell her it was for financial reasons that they'd had to leave and return to the flat above the shop. But that was before she'd happened upon *Sunrise Over Seashell Bay* and everything had changed.

Hannah had liked Lili's idea of saving up for a deposit to buy somewhere, but it occurred to her that time wasn't really on her side in that respect. It would take a long time, and Maisie's childhood was now. How long would she have to wait to have a garden again, and a large enough place for her to have a spare room, which she needed as a studio?

A move to the countryside might not be a bad idea at all. If she started looking for another rental, and found somewhere, they might be moving out of the flat within weeks.

After the episode with Kyle, Hannah felt it was just what she needed – a fresh start, just her and Maisie.

Hannah stepped forward and gave Thea a hug when they reached the shop door. 'That's for making up my mind.'

When they parted, Thea said, 'So, you're not going to Somersby Hall?'

Hannah looked at her quizzically.

Thea caught her expression. 'I thought that's what you were talking about when you said you'd made up your mind?'

'I wasn't talking about that – I meant about looking for another rental, this time in the Suffolk countryside, like you suggested.'

'Oh, I see.'

'About these …' Hannah held up the letters.

'You're not going to let it go and just be thankful for your good fortune?'

Hannah shook her head, knowing she couldn't let it go.

'I can make some enquiries about their current value – speak to one of my former colleagues in the museum where I used to work.'

It wasn't that Hannah was uninterested in finding out their value now; it was just that she wanted to find out more about the three people named in the letters.

'You'd better think of a good pretext for your visit.'

'How do you mean?'

'Like I mentioned before, Somersby Hall is a private house. You can't just rock up there and knock on the door.'

Hannah had the impulse to say, *why not?* But she knew Thea had a point.

'Or are you intending to ask whoever lives there now outright about the painting, and what you'd found hidden in the backing?'

The thought had crossed her mind – just cut to the chase and not beat about the bush.

'Look, it sounds like quite a large country house. Perhaps if you looked online, there might be some history buff out there who knows a little bit about the history of the house, and has posted online, or even a member of the family on social media that you can connect with.'

Thea had a point when she added, 'You'd probably get a better reception than just turning up, in person, out of the blue. People are wary, you know, about what people might be after – especially if they're rich.'

'Rich?'

'Well, wouldn't you be if you owned a stately home?'

'Of course, yes – you're right,' Hannah replied. She thought of the size of the place. Although not as big as some, it was still substantial; much bigger than a standard family home. Much bigger than Nate's house. Somersby Hall was not dissimilar to some of the properties owned by the National Trust. 'Very rich,' she added. She wondered who lived there, and whether they were the descendants of Owen and Kitty, or Owen and Jemima. Hannah voiced her thoughts.

'You know, a place that size all those years ago would have had servants. They could have been working there, and after the war all moved on.'

Hannah's shoulders slumped. She hadn't thought of that. 'You mean the three of them might have been servants, and have no connection with the hall other than as their place of work?' She had not considered that before. 'How will I find them, then?'

Thea shrugged. 'Your biggest clue is the painting that was left at the charity shop. If their descendants are not living at the hall, they've got to be somewhere. After all, someone left that painting outside Mabel and Marjorie's shop. They had to be fairly local to know this place or at least have had some connection to Aldeburgh in the past.'

Hannah nodded thoughtfully.

'On the other hand, Hannah, the fact that someone left that painting just says to me that they knew one of them, or of them.'

'A descendant?'

'Most likely. But they must have had no idea of the significance of the painting, and certainly not known about the valuable airgraphs, otherwise they would never have cast it out.'

'That's true.'

'Listen, Hannah, I know all about family secrets.' Thea cast her glance over to her father.

Hannah followed her gaze.

'They can rebound around your life, I can tell you.'

But will she, thought Hannah, *tell me about the family secret that have clearly rebounded around her life?* She didn't know why, but she had a feeling it was all bound up with the bookshop.

'Perhaps one day I'll tell you all about my father's disappearance, and The Bookshop of Memories.'

'I'd like that,' Hannah said, smiling at her friend. She turned to walk out of the shop, so pleased that apart from Henry's story, there were no more secrets between them – secrets like Kyle. Thea caught her arm. 'If you go to Somersby Hall, you don't know what Pandora's box you might open.'

37

The sun was beginning to dip behind the trees as Hannah drove up the long driveway to Somersby Hall, the letters tucked safely in her shoulder bag. It was the following Saturday, and she'd locked up the shop dead on five in order to make the journey along the winding country lanes to the hall.

Despite her daughter's protests that she wanted to accompany her, Maisie had reluctantly agreed to have tea with her granny, Sarah, while Hannah 'ran an errand'. Unfortunately, she couldn't pull the wool over Maisie's eyes, and Maisie soon wheedled it out of her where she was going.

After what had happened with Kyle, Hannah felt ever so guilty for not telling Maisie exactly where she was going. Maisie needed to know she wasn't keeping any more secrets from her.

Hannah felt so relieved that she wouldn't be spending the first day of Maisie's October half-term holiday telling her that she and Kyle were together. Instead, she was off to Somersby Hall with the airgraphs and was looking forward to a blissful week with her daughter preparing for the Halloween yard party at the end of the week.

An argument ensued with Maisie because she really wanted

to visit Somersby Hall too, until Hannah convinced her that it would probably be a wasted trip. But if she did find out something about the painting, of course she'd tell her when she returned.

Hannah parked the car on the large gravel driveway in front of the hall, surprised at the number of cars parked there along with a van. Were they having a function or a family get-together? She suddenly thought – what am I doing here? Thea had pretty much warned her not to visit the hall. And if she did, to be wary of showing anybody the valuable airgraphs, and to at least have an excuse for visiting and arrange the visit beforehand.

Hannah hadn't listened to that advice. She'd Googled the house again, but nothing much had come up online about the hall or its occupants. The family obviously wasn't on social media and guarded their privacy, so there was nothing further she could glean other than from the small article she'd found.

Then something totally unexpected had turned up. She'd been browsing local estate agents online that morning before she'd dropped Maisie at Sarah's house, looking at rentals, when she'd come across Gatekeeper's Cottage. She'd browsed the photos and liked what she saw very much.

It was a small, detached grey stone cottage, with beamed ceilings, and bedrooms upstairs in the eaves with sloping ceilings and dormer windows. The cottage came furnished or unfurnished, and the interior was painted in a warm yellow throughout. It had a wood burner in the small lounge, a dining room, a shaker-style kitchen with wooden worktops and a stable door that opened on to a small cottage garden.

Although the garden looked quite wild and unkempt, as though someone either hadn't lived there for quite some time, or hadn't bothered looking after the garden, that hadn't put Hannah off. It had a small patio outside the back door, and an old, cobbled path that wound through the unkempt garden, and Hannah could just imagine sitting on the patio with a glass of wine, with Maisie at her easel painting the wild garden.

Then the final picture had stunned her. From the main bedroom window, there was a view across a manicured lawn to the house in the grounds of which the cottage was located. She loved the cottage anyway, but the moment she saw its location, she wanted to rent it. Her only niggle, which she didn't want to think about, was that the takings in her shop had started to go down again.

She didn't know why she was so surprised after the way she'd behaved – reducing her opening hours at the weekend, prime shopping time, and one weekend not opening at all. It was little wonder she'd been losing customers and money over the last few weeks. She'd also rather neglected the stock, letting it run down. She thought of all the times she'd said to a customer, *I can order that in for you,* only to be met by the reply, *Thanks, but I'll get it online instead.*

After the bumper weekend when she'd first put the painting in the window, and the yard party that had followed soon after, she didn't want it to turn out that her amazing sales had been just a blip, and then she'd find her profits would slide back to what they had been before – perilously low, despite reopening all weekend, and ordering in lots more stock.

Hannah ignored her head, which was telling her to wait until at least the end of the month and see what her takings were. Instead, she listened to her heart. She rang the estate agents advertising the property on her mobile once she'd dropped

Maisie off at her grandmother's. Hannah wasn't keeping secrets again; she just didn't want Maisie to get her hopes up over the possibility of moving back into a cottage with a garden and lots more space to paint.

They couldn't meet her to show her the property that day. Hannah had told them she didn't need to view the property – she'd take it. She gave them her details and her references. They were going to chase her reference from her previous tenancy – Hannah had given notice and had left the cottage spotless, so she knew she'd get a good reference.

If everything was in order, the lovely lady she'd spoken to at the estate agent said they'd draw up the tenancy agreement. The lady had asked if she still wanted to arrange a viewing. Hannah didn't see the point. It sounded as though the landlord was keen to rent it as soon as possible. If she had any doubts at all that it wasn't for her, she'd seen the outside of the cottage, stopping her car on her way up the drive to Somersby Hall. It looked even better than the photos.

It had to be fate or serendipity that Gatekeeper's Cottage had come on the rental market around the time she was planning to visit Somersby Hall. The estate agent had said they'd been excited to be instructed. It was the first time the cottage had been available to rent. It had always been the home of the head gardener who looked after the grounds of Somersby Hall, but since he'd retired and moved away, they'd decided to rent it out instead.

The lady in the estate agent had said they expected a high level of interest, and that although they wouldn't advise taking on a property unseen, Hannah got the impression they thought she'd done the right thing as far as this property was concerned.

They weren't providing accommodation for whoever was the next gardener. It sounded as though the old gardener had been working for the family who owned the hall for years and years, so he would probably have stayed there in retirement if he'd not moved away.

Even though the family weren't providing Gatekeeper's Cottage as accommodation for a new gardener, that didn't mean they wouldn't employ someone else to look after their grounds. Hannah had immediately thought of Lili. Although she had The Potting Shed in Cobblers Yard, she didn't have to run the shop solely by herself. Her part-time shop assistant, Zoe an eighteen-year-old who had planned to go to university, had stayed on, choosing to remain living with her parents and apply to attend a university within a reasonable driving distance. The cost in university fees alone made Hannah's eyes water when she heard, without the additional money she'd have to find so she could rent in halls of residence or find student digs.

Hannah thought of Maisie and wondered how expensive it would be by the time she reached eighteen – especially if she wanted to follow in the footsteps of her grandparents and do an art degree at one of the London universities.

Hannah didn't want to think about that, or her daughter growing up and leaving home. It would be a huge adjustment, as there was just the two of them.

Lili had been over the moon that her young shop assistant was sticking with her part-time job at The Potting Shed, which she enjoyed and where she could work full-time during the holidays. That left Lili free to take on extra gardening projects – she always had some on the go.

Shame I can't do gardening, thought Hannah. Lili seemed to have no shortage of work. Lili now employed a small team of gardeners, and although Lili enjoyed pitching in with the practical work too, she couldn't work on all the gardening projects herself. Although Hannah knew Lili would offer her a job on her gardening team if she wanted one, Hannah much preferred running her shop. She just didn't know what she'd do if it folded.

Actually, she did – although Hannah's shop assistant would be available for more hours over the long university vacations, she would only be working part-time during term time. Hannah would gladly work in the flower shop. She knew Lili would employ her. But Hannah couldn't live off a part-time income.

Perhaps the next yard party on Halloween would give her a shop a similar boost and make up for her lost profits over the last few weekends. She hoped so. But when she really thought about her customers, they were mainly parents with school-aged children, university students, and Sarah's art students, whom she'd taken along to Cobblers Yard one day to introduce them to the best art and craft shop in town, and encouraged them to buy. Hannah brushed that thought aside, trying to convince herself it was still her good-luck charm that would draw people in.

Her thoughts turning to Gatekeeper's Cottage instead. She'd seen it from the road as she neared the entrance to Somersby Hall's driveway. It sat just inside the gates, which fortunately were open. Two tall majestic wrought iron gates, with the words *Somersby* on one and *Hall* on the other, looked as though they hadn't been closed in decades. There were weeds growing around the bottom of gates, and the gates themselves had faded over time, looking as though they needed whatever you painted ironmongery with to restore them to their black, shiny original appearance.

The gardens were a bit overgrown. She didn't know where the estate agents had got the photos of the manicured lawn from, but Hannah wondered just how long the owners of Somersby Hall had been without a gardener. The problem was, as Lili had told her, that the longer a garden was left, the longer it would take to clear up, and the more it would cost.

When Hannah stopped the car on the drive to Somersby Hall, deciding to have a peek at the inside the cottage through one of the windows, she'd noticed the gate to the wraparound garden was locked with a padlock. It wasn't that high, but Hannah didn't want to be caught climbing over it and trespassing. She was aware that anybody turning into the drive would immediately see her, and besides, she couldn't leave her car unless she parked in the little gravel driveway beside the cottage.

The driveway to the house was a single track, which meant somebody trying to pass her would have to drive on the grass. Not that that would really matter, given the state of the grounds leading up to the house. But further along she could see a passing place. Perhaps she could tuck it in there and walk back to Gatekeeper's Cottage.

Hannah thought better of it. Despite the state of the grounds of the hall, leading her to wonder if the estate agent's photos of the interior of the cottage had not been taken recently either, she didn't want the owners of the hall finding out their potential new tenant couldn't obey a simple rule – viewings of the property were strictly accompanied, and that obviously included the grounds of the cottage too.

Hannah had returned to her car, driving up the long driveaway to the house instead. She sat in her car, looking up at the house. Even though she might be their new tenant, that still wasn't an excuse to visit the house and speak to the owner. That was why they had hired the estate agents. And besides, she was afraid they might not like their new tenant and would ring the estate agent to let them know.

She couldn't volunteer her friend to do their garden either. She could just imagine the reception if she turned up at their door, and said, 'Your garden looks a mess.'

Hannah sighed. There was an alternative – just be honest. All she wanted to know was whether there was anyone by the name of Kitty, Owen or Jemima still living there, and if they knew anything about the painting.

Thea's warning suddenly came to mind about family secrets, and opening Pandora's box.

Hannah looked up at the house. The house stood solemn against the fading light, ivy clinging to its timeworn brickwork like secrets refusing to be shaken loose. She got out of the car, drawing in a deep breath before making her way up to the front door.

Honesty is the best policy, she thought as she reached for the door knocker. She'd tried the bell, but it didn't seem to work – either that or nobody was home. She glanced over her shoulder at the cars and the van in the driveway. Clearly that wasn't the case.

She was about to raise the knocker when the front door swung open and a young man, very good-looking, with slate-grey eyes and light brown wavy hair, wearing pale blue chinos and a white polo shirt, took her by surprise.

38

She didn't know who she had really been expecting to answer the door, but judging by the state of the house – the exterior didn't look far short of Miss Haversham's house in the Dickens novel she'd momentarily forgotten the name of – she'd assumed it was someone old who had been living at the hall for decades.

'Who are you?' the man said rudely.

'Who are you?' Hannah shot back, immediately wishing she hadn't reacted. She could be living at the end of his garden in a matter of weeks; they'd be neighbours, albeit not very friendly neighbours if this was anything to go by.

'You'd better be the auctioneer,' he said, not answering her question.

'And what if I'm not?' said Hannah, folding her arms crossly, raising her eyes to meet his and silently cursing herself for quickly looking away when his gorgeous grey eyes met hers.

What is wrong with me? thought Hannah. *I'm not a teen with a crush – I'm a grown woman, a single parent, a businesswoman.* She knew, though, that she'd love to meet someone and fall in love.

Hannah met his gaze again. She certainly wouldn't fall in love with someone so blasted rude, no matter how good-looking and well-spoken he was. He sounded as though he'd been somewhere like Eton, and then on to Oxford. Well, that should be no surprise if he could afford a place like this, she reasoned. But that did not give him the right to talk down to other people.

He stood there, tapping his foot impatiently. 'Look, I haven't got all day.'

'Well, neither have I,' Hannah replied curtly. She had to get back and collect Maisie. She gave in and answered his question, 'No, I'm not the auctioneer.' Her eyes drifted past his shoulder to the expansive hallway. Lots of people appeared to be coming and going, carrying various things – she spotted vases, chairs, an ornamental clock, and paintings.

'Yeah, well, I should have guessed. You don't look like one.'

'You mean someone fat, middle-aged, and balding, wearing an old waxed jacket?' Hannah had no idea why that picture of an auctioneer had jumped into her mind. She'd never met an auctioneer, apart from those she'd seen on TV programmes about farmers taking their cattle to market. She didn't even know why she'd been watching that programme – she had no interest in animals or farms.

'No, I mean the young woman I'm expecting. I'm expecting someone dressed smartly in a suit, with a briefcase. Not … not …' He looked her up and down and wriggled his index finger, indicating what she was wearing.

Hannah looked herself up and down. She'd been sorting through some boxes she hadn't got around to unpacking after their move back to the flat from the cottage. They'd been stored in the back room of the shop – Hannah hadn't bothered to take them upstairs to the flat; they wouldn't be there long, so she'd decided not to lug them upstairs. The trouble was that they were collecting dust, and now she had some of it down her faded blue dungarees. Hannah was already anticipating her move.

Added to her faded, dusty dungarees, she was also wearing a grey t-shirt, which had once been white but had got mixed up with dark washing, and an oversized checked flannel shirt that she'd found in the charity shop. She'd slipped on the comfortable lined woollen shirt over her t-shirt and dungarees, which meant she didn't have to wear a jacket as the weather became cooler.

Hannah hadn't bothered to change when she'd left the shop. She hadn't even been sure she'd call on the house – she'd thought she'd just drive there and see the place where Owen had sent the letters to Kitty. But then she'd arrived and had felt so captivated by the grounds and the house that she'd felt compelled to find out who lived there.

Now she had, she felt very uncomfortable in her outfit – all because she'd anticipated an elderly couple, not this gorgeous guy looking her up and down. Hannah wished she'd changed. Then she decided she was pleased she hadn't. She shouldn't be looking for another relationship. Lili had told her not to get involved with the wrong guys again. Her best bet to avoid any possibility of that, Hannah decided, was to not get involved in anyone at all. That way, there was no chance she'd repeat her mistake.

'So, who are you? What do you want?'

Hannah did not like his condescending tone, or the way he was looking at her with disdain. She was about to tell him to do one, thinking, *I'm not paying you my hard-earned money even if I'd love to live in your cottage*, when she felt something wet touch her hand.

She flinched and was about to back away from the door when she looked down and saw a greyhound, its brown, soulful eyes looking up her.

'Hey, who are you?'

The dog whined and licked her hand.

The young man frowned at the dog and tried to push it away. 'I thought you were a good guard dog? You growl at everyone else. You growl at me. What's so different about her?'

'The dog likes me,' said Hannah smugly. *Unlike some people*, she thought.

Now the door was wide open, Hannah could see clearly some of the items that were in the auction. She thought of Nate's grandfather, Joseph, who had once run the antiques shop in Cobblers Yard. She imagined Joseph would have loved some of the antique pieces of furniture.

'Such a shame – I'm sure Joseph would have loved some of this stuff for his shop.' She hadn't meant to share her thoughts.

'You work at his shop?'

'Yes, but—'

'Then bring him along.'

'No, he's—'

'Well, if he can't make it, you come. It's in just over a week's time.'

'Oh, I assumed it was today. You said you were waiting on the auctioneer?'

He had his phone to hand. He scrolled on his phone. 'The auction is definitely next Sunday. Oh, damn, I've got the date wrong.'

'Of the auction?' Hannah asked, thinking that it would be good if the auction was the next day, if he hadn't finished getting things organised.

He looked up, beautiful eyes studying her. 'No, the auctioneer. She's not coming until next Saturday to do some valuations before the auction. No wonder she hasn't turned up. I got the wrong day.' He sighed. 'Look, if Joseph, or whatever his name was can't make it, bring a friend to the auction. The more the merrier.'

Hannah caught his tone. Something in his voice told her he wasn't happy about auctioning off some of the things in the house. 'My friend is busy planning her wedding,' said Hannah sulkily, wondering why she'd told him that. Lili was busy doing a lot of other things too, like running a successful business and redecorating her lovely home.

'Would she like to plan mine too? I've got enough to do.'

'You're getting married?' Hannah tried not to sound disappointed, although she wondered why she was surprised. He was far too good-looking to be single, even though, with his attitude, she didn't envy the young woman who was marrying him.

'That's none of your business.'

Hannah frowned at him. 'But you brought it up.' Her initial impression was that he was the cutest guy she'd ever seen, until he opened his mouth and spoiled it. It wasn't his posh accent that annoyed her, but his condescending attitude. 'Why are you selling all this stuff?'

'My grandmother is moving on.'

'Oh, I'm so sorry. Is she going into a care home?'

'No. What makes you say that?'

'But you just said—'

'I meant she's got to move out of the house. She might be bloody ancient, but she's as independent as hell, and wouldn't be caught dead in a care home – her words, by the way. We're auctioning it off too.'

'The house?'

'Yes.'

'Next Sunday?' Hannah wondered what was going to happen to Gatekeeper's Cottage.

'Of course not. I think we should probably consider trying to sell it on the open market first.'

Hannah was relieved, but also disappointed. She knew a six-month tenancy would fly by. She liked the house and the grounds so much she could just envisage herself and Maisie there for a lot longer than a mere few months – that was, unless Gatekeeper's Cottage was being sold too. It was in the grounds, so she imagined that would be the case.

Hannah thought it was such a shame to sell the house. 'Don't you like this house?' Hannah did. It was the most beautiful thing she'd ever seen. It needed work, but there was something about it.

'Everything has to go.'

Hannah thought of the painting. 'Did you leave some things you think won't sell at auction to a charity shop?'

'What are you talking about? Everything is going into auction. We won't make money giving stuff away.'

Hannah pursed her lips, wondering how the painting had ended up at the charity shop. Perhaps it hadn't come from the hall. She was making a big assumption, just because it was the address in the old letters from the forties – that was eighty years ago. 'Who does this house belong to?'

'My grandmother – I think I mentioned that.' He rolled his eyes. 'If you want to buy some stuff then come to the auction next weekend.'

Hannah didn't know the first thing about antiques, and she

wasn't really all that interested in buying anything. She imagined they'd be expensive. But it was the perfect excuse to visit Somersby Hall. And she'd been invited by none other than the owner's grandson. She didn't fancy attending the auction on her own. She hoped Lili could accompany her. Perhaps there would be some pieces of furniture that Lili would be interested in for her new home.

'I'll come, then, and see if I can bring my friend.'

'Good for you,' he said like he couldn't care less one way or the other.

Hannah was just turning to go when she had a thought. She turned on her heel. 'Is her name Kitty?'

The young guy was just closing the door. He threw her an irritated look. 'Who?'

'Your grandmother.'

'Why would you think my grandmother is called Kitty?'

Hannah shrugged, wishing she hadn't brought it up. 'Has your grandmother lived here long?'

'Look, I really haven't got time for this. Our family history is none of your business.'

Hannah frowned. 'But I only wanted to know her name.'

He slammed the door shut.

'How rude!' Hannah frowned at the door and headed back to her car. She realised she could find out his grandmother's name because as the owner of the hall, she must be the person who was renting out Gatekeeper's Cottage.

Before she got in the car, she turned and looked up at the house. She had the impulse to withdraw from the Gatekeeper's Cottage rental and look for something else, but despite the rude young man, she still loved it there – the house, the grounds, everything about it, even though the place had seen better days.

As she stared up at the house, taking in the red brickwork, the tall, elegant windows, and the ivy creeping up the walls, she imagined what it had been like in its heyday – a working household, bustling with staff, the grounds pristine, the water fountain in front of the house working and filled with water.

Hannah was staring at the house, just imagining what it might look like if the old brickwork was sandblasted, when she saw an old lady looking out of a window on the second floor. Hannah had no idea why she waved. Perhaps it was because she felt sorry for the old lady who was having her home, and everything she owned, sold from under her by her mean grandchild.

If she was in the grandson's shoes, she'd try and think of any way that the house did not have to be sold. *Perhaps it's her decision*, thought Hannah. She knew nothing about the family and their reasons for selling, although she imagined it boiled down to one thing – money.

Bizarrely the old lady waved back, surprising Hannah.

'Who are you waving at?'

Hannah's eyes dropped to the young man. He'd opened the door and was marching towards her.

Hannah took a step back in surprise. She quickly dropped her hand, feeling as though she was being told off. 'Nobody.'

When she looked up, Hannah noticed the old lady was gone. Hannah opened her car door. 'I'm going.' For a moment, she thought he was going to have a go at her because she was still there. Instead, he held out a leaflet.

'What's this?' Hannah asked, taking it.

'The details of the auction.'

'Oh, okay.'

'You're still coming – right?'

'Yes, yes of course.' She didn't want to see him again, but she was so interested in the house. It was the only way she could think of to get inside and have a look around.

Perhaps the auction would be a success and the old lady who owned the place would choose not to sell. Or perhaps they still would sell, but they'd spend the money from the auction on sprucing the place up first.

Hannah was about to drop in a good word about Lili's landscaping service, when the young guy, who was about the close the door, said, 'Jemima.'

Hannah looked at him. 'I'm sorry – what?'

'Jemima – you asked my grandmother's name. That's her name – Lady Jemima.'

Lady Jemima, thought Hannah as she got into the car. Her mind was racing, thinking of the letters. Did that mean her husband was Owen, and he had been having an affair before he went off to war? Lady Jemima would be very old now, or an extremely young bride then, if that had been the case. And what of Kitty? Hannah didn't want to read anything into a name, but it did sound like the sort of name a person employed there would have had – maybe a maid or a kitchen hand.

Hannah looked up at the old, ivy-clad house one more time before she reversed the car and headed down the driveway.

39

'Who was that?'

'Who?'

'That woman waving at me? I'm sure plenty of people who visit Somersby Hall see me sitting at the window. Nobody waves.'

Rupert looked at her, confused. 'Should they?'

'Well, no, not necessarily. But she did. She reminded me of …'

'Who?'

'Oh, never mind. I'd like to meet her.'

'I don't know who she is, Grandma, I only answered the door. She was really annoying. I went and invited her to the auction, though, in the hope that she might buy something. Although I'm not sure she looked like the sort of person who could afford an antique, much less one of our antiques.'

'Never judge a book by its cover, Rupert.'

Rupert breathed a sigh. How many times had she told him that. 'All right.'

'So, you don't even know her name?' Jemima rolled her eyes.

Rupert looked sheepishly at his grandmother and shook his head.

'So, find out.'

'Why?'

Jemima narrowed her eyes. 'I have agreed for you to sell some of my furniture to help out your father, who has been a silly boy again, and got himself into another spot of bother. But what happens to the house when I die is still undecided.'

'What do you mean – undecided? You're ninety-five, for god's sake. How many more years is it going to take you to make up your mind?'

Jemima cocked her head to one side. 'Do you want the house or not?'

He nodded and pursed his lips. His father was in more trouble than she knew. He didn't want her to have a heart attack when she discovered just how much debt he'd got himself into this time. Too much debt for Rupert to bail him out. That was why he was there, selling off some of the family heirlooms.

At least that had been the original plan until he'd arrived there for the first time in years – he hadn't been back to the hall since childhood – and discovered the state of the place. He'd always assumed that his grandmother was leaving the house to him. What she didn't know was that he was already putting plans in place to sell it. He was intending to broach the idea with his grandmother, when she was in a good mood. It wasn't what he'd choose to do, and he knew his grandmother wouldn't choose to sell either, but she had to face the fact that the house needed repairs neither he nor she could afford.

Rupert frowned when he thought of the young woman he'd just met. He shouldn't have told her he was selling the house. If she met his grandmother, she was bound to say something. Rupert was going to make sure they didn't meet. Perhaps she wouldn't turn up at the auction after all. He hoped that was the case. He didn't know why he'd invited her.

Rupert frowned some more when he thought of the reason he had – not in the hope she'd buy something, but because stupidly he wanted to see her again – those beautiful blue eyes, her blonde hair, cut into a bob and falling in waves around her face, and her cute dungarees, along with her feisty spirit. She wasn't like anyone he'd met before, and such a contrast to his fiancée.

He didn't know why he'd been so rude to her. Or maybe he did. She'd turned up, a stranger at his grandmother's house, and he'd immediately felt drawn to her. *I've got a fiancée,* he kept reminding himself.

'Rupert – what is it?'

'Nothing,' he said trying to get the young woman out of his mind. He turned his attention to his grandmother, sitting in her favourite chair, her room looking like something out of the 1940s. In fact, the whole house had changed little from that era, as far as he could tell from the family photos he'd seen.

Rupert now regretted staying away from Somersby Hall for so long. Over the years, he'd seen his grandmother from time to time when Percy drove her to Eton or up to Oxford, but that had mostly been around ten years earlier when he was fresh out of university and embarking on his career in London. Since then, he'd been Skyping her, keeping in touch that way, even though it would have taken him no time at all to drive down from London at the weekend – a couple of hours at most. But every weekend, he was either too busy socialising, or just too tired from his ridiculously long working week to get in the car and go to see her.

Until his father had phoned.

Jemima cut across his thoughts. 'I want to meet the young lady who had the courtesy to wave at me and acknowledge my presence.'

'She's coming to the auction next Sunday,' blurted Rupert, scolding himself for telling her that. 'Can't it wait until then?' he added, hoping she didn't turn up. 'Besides, like I said, I don't even know her name.'

Jemima considered. 'All right, but if she calls again, you are to let me know.'

'Of course,' Rupert mumbled, avoiding eye contact, knowing he'd do no such thing.

She leaned forward in her chair. 'Now, did you find that painting I've been looking for?'

He shook his head. 'Are you sure you didn't get rid of it a long time ago? I've looked everywhere, in every bloody—'

'Don't swear! What have I said to you before – manners maketh the man!'

'In every room,' said Rupert, rolling his eyes. She'd been telling him that, along with other pearls of wisdom, all his life – at least that was how it seemed, although they hadn't had contact for a long time during his childhood. After he'd lost his mother to cancer when he was only five years old, it had just been him, his dad and his grandmother. That was, until the awful day his father had woken him in the middle of the night at Somersby Hall, when he was about seven, and told him they were leaving right away. He'd bundled him in his pyjamas and dressing gown – they'd even left their clothes behind – and had left just like that.

He remembered that scary night. His father had been very angry. He'd never seen him so angry. Rupert had been woken by loud voices, his grandmother, father, and a man's voice he didn't recognise, arguing. And that was when they'd left in a hurry, Rupert sitting in the back of the car, in his pyjamas and dressing gown, clutching the teddy he'd had since birth, the one his grandmother had given him, and seeing Somersby Hall disappearing in a cloud of dust, his father in the front seat swearing he'd never darken the hall's doors again – and that neither should Rupert.

His father had made him promise. Rupert never broke his promises. And so, one way or another, he'd avoided the hall – that was, until he grew up and realised his father was just a drunken idiot who shouldn't have any control over his life. Whatever had happened that night had been decades earlier. His father would never speak of it, but that wasn't Rupert's problem – it was his father's.

Nevertheless, he was all Rupert had besides his grandmother, and every time his father had come to him for money, he had bailed him out of the debts he had kept accruing – until suddenly Rupert had a fiancée who'd told him that if they were going to get married and have a life together, he had to stop bailing his father out. It was time his father took responsibility.

Just this one last time, thought Rupert. But he could only give his father so much money before his fiancée noticed. They were meant to be saving for their wedding. Aware that his father would not approach Jemima for money, Rupert had approached her himself, expecting she'd have a tidy sum squirrelled away somewhere. She did not. All her money had gone on the house – the costs of repairing a leak in the roof, a faulty boiler, a burst pipe – the list went on. Somersby Hall needed work. Rupert knew that, but he hadn't factored in the cost of continually having to find the money for repair jobs.

The only way to come up with some cash was to sell stuff. Rupert hadn't been honest at first, and said he needed the money, which he did – to send on to his father. She didn't believe him. His grandmother had said she knew her grandson, and he'd never get himself in a tight fix, financially speaking. And she knew that if he somehow had, he had a fiancée with a good job.

Rupert had no choice but to tell her what had been going on. His father was a wastrel and a drunk, and a dreamer. That wasn't a surprise to Lady Jemima. He'd always been that way. But this time his gambling had got out of hand. Living in a shared house in France with other artistic types, he'd never held down a proper job, always believing he had a novel in him that would be a bestseller and set him up for life. He'd been working on that novel for decades. Rupert had never known his grandfather, but by the sound of the few things he'd heard, he had been just the same. He'd never held down a proper job either and had burned through the cash he'd inherited.

It was Rupert's grandmother who had paid for Rupert to go through private school, and on to Eton, hoping he would get a good job and find a purpose in life, unlike his father and grandfather. She'd once said to him that inheriting money was the worst thing that could happen, and so she'd ensure he wouldn't – she'd spent his inheritance, what money she still had, on his education instead. All that was left was the money-pit called Somersby Hall.

Rupert never knew what had caused the rift, but his grandmother and father had never spoken since that night he'd been bundled into the car – as far as he was aware.

'Well, keep looking.' She interrupted his thoughts. 'I need to find *Sunrise Over Seashell Bay.*'

'What's so important about the painting – is it worth a lot?'

'I'm tired, Rupert. I'll think I'll have a nap now.'

Rupert narrowed his eyes. He knew how old she was, but his grandmother was sprightly for her age, still sharp as a pin, and was not one to take an afternoon nap. She was bluffing.

'Promise me you'll keep looking,' she said as he walked to her bedroom door.

40

'I imagine most people hereabouts have heard of Somersby Hall,' said Lili. 'Their ancestors made a lot of money trading in textiles or something, then the next generation squandered it all. Rumour has it that the grandson is trying to make some money and save the house. That's why they're holding the auction, I guess. It sounds as though he's realised it's a lost cause and persuaded his grandmother to move out and sell.'

Hannah sat behind the counter in her shop, watching Lili arrange fresh flowers in a vase while she chatted. It was Monday morning, and Maisie and William were with their dad. Nate tried his best to take time off work during the school holidays to spend with his children. Lili had popped in, as she always did on the days she was working in her shop and was not out on a landscaping job. She'd brought fresh flowers from her shop across the yard again.

'I'm surprised you hadn't heard about the auction, Hannah. It's the talk of the town, actually. There've been flyers everywhere – didn't you see one?'

Hannah thought she might have, but she had just been too preoccupied to bother reading a flyer. She didn't want to think about who she had been preoccupied with these past weeks – she didn't want to think of him ever again. Hannah was still worrying that the shop would not continue to be profitable, especially now she'd signed the contract for the rental. She was moving in on Sunday, the day of the auction. It couldn't come soon enough. On the one hand that had been a bit unfortunate – auction day on the same day she moved – but on reflection, she thought it was a good thing; hopefully there would be so many people turning up at the auction, and the owner and her grandson would be so preoccupied, that they wouldn't notice their new tenant moving in.

Hannah hoped so because things had not got off to a good start with the grandson. She was worried he might get in touch with the estate agents and withdraw. Not that it was his decision, she imagined, but Hannah had no idea whether his grandmother had all her faculties, or whether he was now acting on her behalf. Luckily, he didn't know Hannah's name, so when they'd received the tenancy agreement to sign, he would have been none the wiser just who would be moving into Gatekeeper's Cottage come auction day.

'Why are you so interested in the auction anyway?'

Before Hannah even had a chance to reply, Lili had come to her own conclusions. She suddenly stopped rearranging the flowers in the vase and turned to face Hannah. 'You like him,' said Lili, wide-eyed but grinning.

'I do not!' Hannah replied brusquely. 'I told you, I don't want to get involved with another guy right now. And besides he was very rude when he answered the door. *Very* rude!' Hannah lowered her eyes. Unfortunately, her best friend knew her too well. Hannah had given herself away – she wasn't being completely truthful. Although it was true – he had been rude – she was still drawn to him.

'I knew it! You *do* like him.'

'All right, yes, he made quite an impression when he first opened the door. He's a very good-looking guy. But—'

'Then he opened his mouth.'

'Exactly. I don't know who he thinks he is. He was just so condescending and miserable. I don't know what he's got to be miserable about – with a grandmother who owns a beautiful house, Somersby Hall.'

Lili continued rearranging the flowers as she said, 'You know, things aren't always what they seem. His name is Rupert, by the way.'

'Rupert,' repeated Hannah, thinking that it was a lovely name. 'But how do you know his name?' Hannah already knew before she'd finished the sentence. 'The Gossip Girls,' they said in unison, sharing a knowing smile.

Lili continued, 'They mentioned something about the grandson, Rupert, and how his father stopped him visiting the hall for years, since he was a child. Sounds as though his father and grandmother are estranged.'

'How do they know that?'

Lili shrugged. 'Local gossip, obviously.'

'Obviously,' said Hannah, realising that it was a silly question.

'We got in conversation about Somersby Hall when they put the flyer in the window for the auction. Mabel and Marjorie do enjoy a good natter over a cuppa and a chocolate digestive biscuit.'

'Tell me about it!' Hannah said with a smile, recalling her first visit, when she'd bought the painting and they had become good friends – not to mention the numerous times since then that both sisters had popped into hers to enjoy her cosy corner. They'd been in even more than normal over the past week, since she had got rid of Kyle from her life.

'Rupert lost his mother when he was a child, so it was just him and his father.'

'That's heartbreaking. Sounds like Nate and William.'

'Yes,' Lili agreed. 'Although Rupert's life took a different turn after his mother died. Apparently, he was sent away to boarding school, and his father lives abroad.'

'Oh, that's so sad.'

'Yes, the family probably thought they were doing their best by him, sending him away for a good education, but I couldn't imagine Nate sending William away like that so young.'

'Oh, me neither,' said Hannah. William was such a sweet little boy. Knowing all this made her rethink her assumptions about Rupert. Her first impression had been that he was spoilt, stuck-up and born with a silver spoon in his mouth – which he had been, until it had all gone wrong when his mother passed.

'Just shows,' said Lili, 'money doesn't buy you happiness.'

Thinking of money, Hannah glanced around her shop. The dwindling number of customers was still bothering her. Even so, she agreed with Lili's sentiments.

Lili placed the vase of flowers in the window and returned to the counter, leaning her elbows on the surface and eyeing Hannah. 'What were you doing at Somersby Hall anyway, and why all the interest in the auction? Do you want to buy some antiques, go back to running an antiques shop here like Joseph used to? I thought your shop was doing well?'

Hannah now felt that had only been thanks to the painting,

and the wonderful cosy corner, and the yard party. She couldn't wait for the next party on Friday – Halloween. Even though the footfall had been dropping, her profits were still up compared to the darkest days before she'd found the painting.

'No, I do not want to buy antiques, and yes, the shop is doing well.' Hannah knew she sounded a lot more confident than she felt. She changed the subject. 'I've taken on a rental – we're moving there soon.'

Lili stared at Hannah. 'When were you going to tell me?'

Hannah's eyes drifted to the painting in the window.

Lili added, 'I thought you were saving to buy a place of your own?' Lili followed her gaze. 'Oh, right. You don't really have to save up for a deposit. You've got a sizeable one right there in that painting if you sell the airgraphs.'

If I sell them, thought Hannah.

She'd forgotten about that conversation with Lili. 'That's going to take time, Lili. If I sell the airgraphs, they'll have to go to auction.' That was a rhetorical question. 'It's quicker to find a rental, and move straight in.'

The flat above the shop was small, with no garden, and Hannah was still afraid that one day Nate would ask Maisie if she wanted to live with them in his large house. 'I didn't want to spend Christmas in the flat,' Hannah said.

'You could spend Christmas with us. We've got the room to put you up.'

That was the last thing Hannah wanted, seeing Maisie wake up on Christmas morning in Nate's house. She wanted her and Masie to have their own Christmas morning in their house – even if it wasn't technically their house, it would still be their home.

'That's very kind of you to offer, but as I said, I've already taken on another rental, so we'll obviously be there at Christmas.'

'Is it in Aldeburgh?'

'No, but it's not far.' Hannah said, 'You'll never guess where.'

'Oh, no … don't tell me you're getting a houseboat like Ray.'

'No, of course not. I think I'd get seasick bobbing up and down all the time.' Hannah had actually been on Ray's houseboat, and it didn't bob up and down at all. Even so, she could tell by Lili's expression that she understood.

'So, don't keep me in suspense – where is it?'

'Somersby Hall.'

'Somersby Hall?' She looked completely taken aback. 'You can't be renting the whole place, surely? Are they renting out a wing or something?'

'Oh, no, it's not in the house. It's in the grounds – there's a little gatehouse at the end of the drive.'

'Ah, that's why you visited the house. To meet your neighbours.'

Hannah frowned. Not exactly, but she didn't want to get into the subject of the airgraphs just then.

'I'm surprised that Rupert didn't put you off.'

'He nearly did, to be honest. But I love Gatekeeper's Cottage so much, I went ahead and signed for it. We move next Sunday.'

'Wow, that's quick.'

'Yes, I'm so happy.'

'So, why the frown?'

Hannah told her what Rupert had said about selling up the house. 'I didn't want just six months. I can envisage being there for … forever!'

Lili shook her head. 'That's the trouble with renting.'

Hannah bit her lower lip, worried she'd done the wrong thing after all, impulsively committing to another rental instead of saving her money to buy somewhere. She knew why she'd done it. She did love the little gatehouse, but it had been the letters and Somersby Hall that had convinced her to do it.

'Look,' said Lili, 'Rupert can't sell the house until his grandmother dies, or she agrees to sell. I wouldn't be surprised if she digs her heels in regarding selling. It's her home, after all, and I bet she's lived there decades. She's one of these old ladies who'll live to … to a hundred!'

Hannah smiled at Lili. She couldn't possibly know that. She was only saying it to make her feel better.

'Although I heard he's preparing to sell the place, it's true,' Lili added.

'How do you know that?'

'Mabel and Marjorie told me. You'd have to ask them. I swear they were spies in their former lives.'

Hannah laughed out loud. 'There are no secrets in this town, obviously.' But there were – secrets even The Gossip Girls didn't know about, to do with the hall, the painting, and what might possibly have been a love triangle involving three people who were connected to Somersby Hall – Kitty, Owen and Jemima. Although everyone in the yard knew about the airgraphs, so far only her, Thea, and Maisie, actually knew the contents of those letters.

'Such a shame if it turns out it's not financially viable to keep Somersby Hall in the family, and it has to be sold. Rumour has it he was set to inherit the hall.'

Lost in thought for a moment, Hannah didn't catch her drift. 'I'm sorry – what?'

'Rupert. Of course it's only hearsay, but that's what Mabel and Marjorie said, and I guess there must be some truth to the rumour that he is set to inherit the place as his father is estranged.'

'Ah. So he's living there?'

'While he's down from London. His grandmother had a health scare, according to Mabel and Marjorie. Sounds as though she had a short stay in hospital, and I rather think he must have thought she was on her way out. But she's not, obviously.'

'Oh dear.'

Lili was grinning. 'I know I shouldn't laugh. But serves him right. What's that saying – counting your chickens?'

'Must be worth a lot of money – the house. I was so disappointed when he mentioned selling up. I guess maybe he's trying to convince his grandmother to sell to release cash to pay off debts. It nearly put me off signing for the rental.'

'I bet a house like that costs a lot to run. But I get the feeling, from what Marjorie and Mabel said, that Rupert's grandmother is so stubborn that she's going to be around for some time yet.'

'Do they know her?'

'I did ask them when we got into that conversation about Somersby Hall over the flyer, but no. Apparently, Lady Jemima has hardly ventured out of the hall over the years, keeps herself to herself. A bit like you used to be.'

Hannah slapped her arm playfully, although she knew it was true. 'That's all in the past now, obviously. I just hope they all know how very grateful I am about them all pitching in to create my cosy corner, and … the other thing.'

Lili knew she was referring to Kyle.

'It was so lovely of Joss especially to volunteer his free time, as I know he's very busy next door.' Hannah's tone turned serious. 'I was really worried in the beginning about people finding out about my past, my stint in prison …'

Lili smiled. 'That's all behind you now.'

'I'm glad it's finally out in the open. I hate secrets.'

'Me too.'

Hannah added, 'Not that I want the world and their mother to know about my past … that's well and truly behind me now.'

'There's no reason that anybody else would find out,' Lili said reassuringly.

Hannah smiled at her best friend, turning her thoughts to her move on Sunday. She thought of the old lady she'd waved at, sitting in the window of Somersby Hall. Lady Jemima. 'I'd love to meet her.'

'Maybe you will. After all, she's your landlord, I mean landlady – not her grandson, Rupert.' She paused. 'It's not put you off, then, the thought that the place will be sold, and most likely you'll have to move again?'

'No. I just wish there was a way the house didn't have to be sold. It's such a lovely place.'

'Yeah, in its heyday,' scoffed Lili. 'The house is in need of a lot of work from the sound of things. Looking after a house that size costs money. I imagine that's why so many stately homes end up being given to the likes of the National Trust – because the families can't afford to keep and maintain them.'

'I don't want that to happen to Somersby Hall. It's just so …' Hannah was having trouble putting into words how she felt about the place. 'The setting is … well, amazing, set in its own grounds, surrounded by trees. It's lovely and secluded down a lane in the middle of stunning countryside.'

'Sounds like it would make a fantastic wedding venue.'

Hannah stared at Lili. She wasn't surprised that weddings were on her mind. She wondered if she'd chosen a venue yet.

Lili noticed. 'What did I say?'

Hannah scratched her head. 'Nothing.'

'Oh, don't do that. I know you. There's something on your mind.'

41

There was something on Hannah's mind – saving Somersby Hall from being sold. She'd just had a crazy thought. Lili was right: it would make a fantastic wedding venue. She wondered if there was a large room in the house big enough to accommodate a lot of people for a sit-down meal, and then a dance or disco afterwards. She imagined with a place that size there was. That wouldn't be the problem – but the grounds would be an issue. They were a bit of a mess, from what she'd seen of the front, anyway.

Every wedding had photos taken outside. The ivy-clad house would make a fantastic backdrop, but the grounds would need a lot of landscaping work to bring them back to their former glory. She knew just the person. Hannah stared at Lili. The problem was that it would cost money – money that Rupert's grandmother clearly didn't have, otherwise they wouldn't be holding an auction and selling stuff off. But Hannah had an idea … it was called bartering.

'No, it was a stupid, stupid thought,' Hannah waved that idea away.

'I want to hear your stupid, stupid thought.'

Hannah pursed her lips, and asked, 'Have you chosen a wedding venue?'

'Yes, actually.'

'Oh.' There went that idea. 'Is it booked yet?

'Ah, we don't need to book it. We're having the wedding at our house.'

'At Nate's house?'

'Well, it will be our house once we're married.'

'Yes, of course.' Hannah tried not to feel jealous. It's not like she wanted Nate for herself. They'd never really been together as a couple. It had only been a silly teenage one-night stand years earlier. However, she still felt envious of how Lili's life, and the lives of all the people she knew, had seemed to come together so easily. All she seemed to do was get involved with the wrong guys – and work. And so far, that Monday morning, she hadn't had one customer.

Hannah was worried. *I've signed a rental agreement*, she thought, praying things would go back to what she'd assumed was the new normal, business-wise.

The only upside of having no customers first thing that morning was that she was having a chance to chat to Lili. Lately, she hardly ever had Lili to herself; just the two of them like things had been before Lili's gardening business had taken off and she'd met Nate.

Across the yard, Lili's assistant, Zoe, would be serving customers. With her dwindling profits, Hannah could only dream of an assistant. Hannah had glanced out of the window from time to time, seeing people walk into the yard, and although they hadn't all ventured into Cobblers Yard for Lili's flower shop, a good few had. She couldn't wait until Friday, and the Halloween party when, hopefully, business would pick up again.

She turned to Lili. 'Don't you want to have your wedding at a proper wedding venue – you know, like you see advertised on billboards outside posh country hotels?' Hannah had assumed that was every woman's idea of a dream wedding.

'Well, yes, of course. But as with most things in life, it boils down to money. We just can't afford it.'

'But your business is doing well, and Nate must be on good money as a doctor. Surely …' Hannah trailed off.

'Surely, we can save up for a wedding?'

Hannah looked away. 'Sorry, it's really none of my business.' She expected Lili to say, *you're right – it isn't.* So what Lili said next surprised her.

'It *is* your business, Hannah.'

'You mean as chief bridesmaid?' Hannah had assumed Lili would ask her.

'No … I mean yes, I do want you to be my chief bridesmaid, but it isn't that.'

'Ah, you mean Maisie. Of course, she'll be a flower girl.'

'Actually, it is about Maisie, but not her role in the wedding.'

'I don't understand …' Were they talking at cross-purposes?

'Nate and I have discussed it, and I'm in complete agreement. The money that we'd spend on a venue, the whole caboodle – I can just imagine how much a wedding can set you back – well it can run into thousands of pounds. We'd rather spend that money on Maisie's future.'

'What do you mean?'

'We've set aside money for Maisie to go to university.'

Hannah hadn't done that – she could barely scrape together that year's new school uniform. *Perhaps she should use the airgraphs to see Maisie through university. Hannah hadn't thought of that.*

'We thought the money was better spent on Maisie and William. But especially Maisie, with her gift.'

'I know she's a gifted painter, but how do you know she'll go on to university? Perhaps she won't.' Hannah said this despite the fact that, just like Lili, she had assumed Maisie would.

'Oh, she's definitely going to university.'

Hannah sighed. 'Just because that's what Nate wants—'

'No, that's what Maisie wants. She said so.'

Hannah didn't know what to say. Maisie hadn't discussed any of this with her. Then again, she had been busy since Maisie returned to school in September.

'And going to university is expensive enough without going abroad.'

'Abroad?'

'Yes, Paris, Rome, we're not sure where, but she's starting French lessons at school this year and seems really taken with the idea of going to study art in France.'

Hannah didn't know she'd started French lessons. She hadn't mentioned that either.

'We said to her, why not see what you think of France first on your school trip before you settle on living there for three or four years.'

'School trip?'

'Yes – to France. She's put her name down.'

'Oh, right. Thanks for mentioning it. I must find out when it needs to be paid.'

'Ah, don't worry about that. We've already paid for it.'

'You didn't have to do that.'

Lili cast her gaze about the shop. There were still no

customers. 'Look, we don't mind helping out. You see, Maisie said things were a bit … tight, and she wasn't sure you could afford it, so she didn't like to ask you.'

Hannah stared at Lili.

'Did I say something wrong?'

Everything she had said was wrong. She had thought Maisie was just spending time with her father and Lili every other weekend – not planning her future and having them pay for things at school. She was Maisie's mother, and she was responsible for her. It was the way things had always been until she'd bumped into Nate on the Suffolk Coast – she hadn't sought him out before then, thinking he had probably married and had another family.

In another life, perhaps they would have reconnected, fallen in love, and lived happily ever after, but in Hannah's experience she was never that lucky in love, or life. And now she felt Nate and Lili were taking over the decision-making with regard to her daughter because they had money.

They're just helping her out, a voice in her head said. *Be reasonable. Nate is her father. Of course he wants to pay for things.*

'Nate asked me to tell you that he's still willing to pay monthly maintenance, rather than the one-off payments he gives on her birthday and Christmas. I know you want to support her yourself, but if things are tight …' Lili trailed off.

'Everything is fine,' said Hannah. She caught Lili glancing around her empty shop.

'The shop is doing just fine,' she added.

At that moment, several people walked into her shop. Hannah almost sighed in relief. 'Why would I be taking on another rental if I couldn't afford it?'

Lili said, 'You will tell me if you need anything, won't you?'

What I need is for you and Nate to butt out of Maisie's life, she thought. She knew she was being unfair; they had her best interests at heart. She was lucky that Maisie's father was in her life, both emotionally and financially. But Hannah wasn't part of a couple, with their income and their beautiful house. How could she compete with them?

It's not a competition, she reminded herself – but that didn't stop her feeling inadequate. She just wanted Maisie to have what they had.

'Hannah? Did you hear what I said? If you need anything, anything at all – just ask.'

'Yeah, of course,' Hannah said, smiling tightly.

A customer stood behind Lili, her basket full of purchases she wanted to make. Hannah reached for the basket in the lady's hand.

The young lady looked at Lili. 'I'm not jumping the queue, am I?'

Lili stepped to one side. 'No, no. I was just leaving.' She whispered, 'Remember what I said, Hannah. Anything you need – just ask.'

Hannah was just cashing up the items when Lili stopped at the shop door, and said, 'I really love *Sunrise Over Seashell Bay*.'

Hannah smiled. Most people did. She turned to her customer, who paid by card as Hannah packed her purchases in a bag.

Lili stepped aside as the customer left the shop. 'I'd like to buy the painting,' she said.

Hannah frowned. 'It's not for sale.' Lili knew that. Maybe Lili thought she might change her mind.

'That's a shame. Well, if you change your mind and need the money, I'll pay whatever you want. It would look amazing over our fireplace in the lounge. It looks lovely in the shop window, but a gorgeous painting like that deserves a home.'

Hannah stared at her. She was right. 'I might take it home with me when we move to Gatekeeper's Cottage,' she said, knowing she probably wouldn't actually do that – not straight away while it was still drawing in customers.

'I meant a *permanent* home, Hannah.'

Hannah bit back a smart retort. *We can't all meet a gorgeous guy with a nice house and have everything fall into our laps*, she thought.

Fortunately, another customer arrived at her counter with items to be cashed up and Lili took that as her cue to leave.

Hannah's eyes drifted to the painting in the window. She hoped she wasn't forced to let go of the painting. There were no other customers milling around her shop. She still had the airgraphs, she reminded herself. It was a shame she couldn't sell those at the auction in Somersby Hall. She didn't want to let them go until she'd found out more about Kitty, Owen and Jemima.

Lady Jemima. Hannah sat behind the counter of her empty shop, resting her face in the palms of her hands. She couldn't wait to move into their new home.

42

'After the Halloween party we'll be going straight back to our new home.'

'Gatekeeper's Cottage?' said Maisie.

'That's right.' Hannah was standing behind Maisie, tying up her hair in a pink hairband.

'I thought we were moving on Sunday?'

'We were, but remember I told you that the estate agent phoned me and said we could move in on Friday instead.'

When Hannah had received that call two days earlier, she'd been so excited that she was getting the keys. The estate agent had said her landlady thought it better if her new tenant could move in before the auction weekend, otherwise there might be a lot of people coming and going up the drive, making her house move tricky. That made sense, although Friday was also the day of the Halloween yard party. Hannah would miss the preparations in the yard in the morning, but she'd be back for the party in the afternoon before she returned with Maisie for their first night in their new home.

It worked out much better for another reason too – Hannah could do the house move while Maisie spent the morning with

Lili and William in her shop, carving pumpkins and helping in the yard.

'I want to help you on moving day,' said Maisie, turning around to face her mum.

Hannah knelt down in front of her. 'I know, sweetheart, but Lili and all our friends in the yard need your help preparing the yard for the Halloween party.'

Maisie didn't look convinced.

'Look, your grandfather is coming over in his car this morning to help me with the boxes, so I will be all right.'

They both cast a glance around the flat. There were a lot of packing boxes, some still open where Hannah was still packing up. Hannah was so excited that moving day had arrived – and sooner than expected. She'd hoped to do the move herself, like the move from the flat to the little cottage in Aldeburgh, and then the move back to the flat, but the difference those times had been that the cottage in Aldeburgh had been only a short distance away, meaning the trips back and forward in her little car had taken no time at all.

This time it was different. Somersby Hall was deep in the Suffolk countryside, and although it was only ten miles away, the twisty lanes, some of them single track, made the going slow. Two cars, especially Ray's large car, would mean they could do it in two trips, three tops, whereas she imagined she'd be back and forward all day without his help, and that would mean closing the shop all day, and missing the Halloween party. It was just fortunate that she hadn't had to book a removal van. The furniture in the flat was remaining where it was. Hannah had opted to take the cottage furnished, saving her the cost of a van. It was also on her mind that it might only be for six months if it turned out that Somersby Hall was to be sold.

Hannah cast an eye over all the boxes, many of which contained Maisie's art materials along with her paintings. Maisie wanted to take them with her rather than leave them in the flat. Hannah agreed. After what had happened with Kyle, although she couldn't imagine anyone else breaking into her shop, it wasn't worth the risk that someone else might happen upon Maisie's paintings. And besides, she fancied hanging Maisie's paintings around their new home to make it feel more like their own home rather than a rental.

She was just grateful for Ray's help. Lili and Nate would have helped, but Lili was looking after Maisie and William, preparing for the party. Nate was at work. Hannah had to close up the shop on Friday morning in order to move. Thea had been kind and offered to mind her shop, but they would be in and out moving boxes so it wouldn't be practical to have customers in the shop too.

Thea had been surprised when she'd stopped by Hannah's shop earlier in the week and asked whether she'd visited Somersby Hall yet, not realising that things had moved on a lot since the week before when Hannah had nipped across the yard to Thea's shop for a catch-up and Thea had surprised her by warning her off visiting Somersby Hall.

'I'm not just going to visit Somersby Hall again,' Hannah had said sheepishly, 'I'm going to live there.'

She remembered the surprised look on Thea's face as she'd said, 'What on earth do you mean?'

When she'd told Thea that Gatekeeper's Cottage had come up for rent in the grounds of Somersby Hall, and she'd immediately snapped it up, she'd thought Thea would be pleased and excited for her. Thea wasn't. On the contrary, she had seemed to do her best to put a damper on her move.

'Why would you do that?' Thea had asked.

'Because I fell in love with Gatekeeper's Cottage. It's got a lovely feel, and the surroundings – the house and grounds are gorgeous.' Hannah knew she seemed to be using that word a lot when it came to Somersby Hall – gorgeous. But what else could she say?

'Don't you mean you fell in love with Somersby Hall?'

Hannah had not replied.

'You're obsessed with that painting and those love letters from Owen to Kitty.'

'I am not.'

Thea had folded her arms and cocked her head to one side, eyeing her knowingly.

'Oh, all right, maybe a little,' Hannah remembered conceding.

'How about maybe *a lot*,' Thea had replied. 'Is it at all possible for you to just keep the airgraphs, and their contents, to yourself, and auction them off to the highest bidder?'

'But I found Jemima already. You know, the woman who wrote the letter to Owen that was never posted.'

Thea had sighed heavily at that point, warning her again about opening Pandora's box. 'You know, if you open up old wounds, or discover some long-lost buried secret that they don't want anyone, let alone their tenant at the end of their drive, to find out about, you might find yourself out on your ear.'

Hannah hadn't understood what she'd meant until Thea had spelled it out. 'If you go poking your nose where it doesn't belong, into their family affairs, and they find out, you're liable to find yourself given notice to quit your lovely rental.'

Hannah hadn't thought about that. Her mouth had formed into a great bit *oh*.

'Oh, is right,' Thea had said. 'In any case, you're not going to give the airgraphs back, are you?' It wasn't really a question. 'So, why even try and find out who Kitty and Owen were? I'd sell them, if I were you. Just let me know, and I'll put you in touch with an auction house in London.'

Hannah was thinking about that conversation with Thea as she walked Maisie across the yard to The Potting Shed where Lili had the pumpkins ready to carve on a table at the back of the shop. William was already there. After Hannah gave her a kiss, and told her to have fun, her brother took her hand, and they both ran up to the table.

Hannah left The Potting Shed and stopped in the middle of the yard, looking up at the flat above her shop. She hadn't wanted to move back there after she'd given up the rental cottage in Aldeburgh, but after all that had happened, and getting to know all the lovely people in Cobblers Yard, and seeing how they'd rallied around and helped her in so many unexpected ways – with her cosy corner, and the first yard party, and Kyle – she felt a twinge of regret that it had been their last night in the yard.

Of course she'd still be there running her shop, but she'd miss looking out on the yard in the evenings, the glow of the lamplight on the cobbles, and hearing the faint sound of jazz from Reggie's flat across the yard, and seeing Henry's light on, imagining him tucked up in bed reading a good book before his carers turned off the lights.

She suddenly noticed someone standing beside her. Lili. She was looking up at the flat too. 'I know what you're thinking.

You're going to miss living here.'

Hannah turned to her with tears in her eyes. 'I really didn't think I would, but now …'

Hannah smiled empathetically. 'I know. But you're moving on, and you're going to love your new home.'

'I know.'

'And we're all still going to be here in our shops in the yard – you included.'

Hannah nodded, although Maisie wouldn't be visiting Mabel and Marjorie after school and spend time helping Henry and Thea in the bookshop anymore.

As if reading her mind, Lili said, 'Maisie can still pop into the charity shop when she's here with you on Saturdays and buy her little odds and ends with her pocket money. And she can still help Henry in the bookshop. And she's starting music lessons with Reggie one evening a week, so you'll be staying late in the yard for that.'

Hannah brightened. 'Actually, she can still do those things after school like she usually does.' Hannah realised that their lives in Cobblers Yard weren't going to change as much as she'd thought.

Hannah pictured the next Monday, Maisie's first day back at school after the half-term holiday. Living in Cobblers Yard, she normally walked with her through the little alleyway out into the high street where she would meet her friend and her friend's mum who lived locally, and with whom she walked to school.

Despite their house move, it wouldn't be the last time Maisie would be walking to school. Hannah had it all figured out. In the morning, she'd drive Maisie to Aldeburgh, and they'd stop by the shop so Maisie could still walk to school with her friend. Hannah had offered to drive her straight to school. But this was better. She could still open the shop by nine, knowing Maisie was off to school with her friend – along with her friend's mum, little sister, and labrador. Hannah didn't have to do the school run. Nothing was going to change. And after school, the shops would still be open in the yard when she returned, so while Hannah waited for closing time, Maisie would have time to visit the charity shop and spend time in the bookshop.

But everything would change if she went digging into the history of Somersby Hall, and potentially opened a Pandora's box full of secrets, according to Thea. She knew Thea was right. She should keep her nose out and just sell the airgraphs.

Lili gave Hannah a hug, wished her luck with the move that morning, and said, 'I can't wait to see your new home when you're settled in.'

Hannah watched Lili return to The Potting Shed before she stopped in front of her shop window and stared at the painting. Thea had been right. *You're obsessed with that painting, and those love letters from Owen to Kitty*, she'd said. Silly as it sounded – and Hannah wouldn't ever say it out loud – but she felt the painting had come into her possession for a reason. She wished they had been simple love letters rather than rare and valuable airgraphs – especially the one that hadn't been sent.

When Thea had offered to mind the shop, she'd said she'd done a further bit of digging – researching airgraphs and picking a former colleague's brain back in London. She'd discovered that the airgraph written by Jemima was the most valuable of the lot.

Hannah sighed. If they had been simple love letters, she could have just handed them back without thinking about the difference a bit of money falling into her lap would make. She'd said that to Thea, who had then reminded her that it wouldn't be as simple as that in any case. First, she'd have to establish just who Owen was. Was he O. Hartley, the painter Thea had found a reference to?

'But I know who Jemima is,' Hannah had blurted, 'Lady Jemima – she owns Somersby Hall.'

What had followed felt like another lecture, with Thea telling her to leave well alone and saying that perhaps it was fortunate they weren't simple love letters that she could just hand back without a second thought. Thea had mirrored her own thoughts when she'd said, 'Sounds like a love triangle to me, but were Kitty and Jemima, oh sorry – *Lady* Jemima – each aware of the other woman. I doubt it. Do you know if Owen is … was … Lady Jemima's husband?'

Hannah had no idea. But she was determined to find out. Not that she revealed her thoughts to Thea. She didn't know why she had this strange feeling that there must be a reason the letters had revealed themselves to her after all these years. Someone had given away the painting, and she imagined had no idea what was hidden in the frame. Was it a relative, a descendant? And if it was, did they have any idea that they might have a connection to Somersby Hall?

Hannah felt she had a responsibility to find out the truth. She frowned. *Am I just nosy, like The Gossip Girls?* she wondered. Either way, Thea was right: she couldn't let it go.

'Penny for your thoughts?'

Hannah whirled around. 'Oh, Ray! You startled me.'

'Sorry.'

Ray bent down and gave her a hug, then stood back, smiling at her warmly. 'Am I forgiven? I think I'm late.'

Hannah could forgive him anything. She loved Nate's parents – Ray especially. If he had been forty years younger, she could have fallen in love with him. That wouldn't have worked, though, because Ray was already taken, and always had been. He was deeply in love with Sarah. Theirs was the sort of love story Hannah craved.

She caught him glancing across Cobblers Yard at The Potting Shed. She'd heard the funny story from Lili about Ray and Sarah. It hadn't started off funny – they'd been in the middle of getting divorced. Sarah had moved from London to retire, although she wasn't the retiring type, so she'd taken on The Potting Shed. Just to be near her, and see her every day, Ray had taken on the lease of the shop across the yard – an art and craft shop next door to Hannah's shop, which was now Joss's office. Apparently, Ray would visit Sarah's shop every day, buying the most expensive bouquet for his wife, including a little note.

This had gone on for some time, until eventually they'd ripped up the divorce papers and got back together – sort of, living apart together.

Lili had told her a little about their background. Hannah had never known Nate's parents previously and had only met them since she'd moved to the area. After meeting at university, both studying art, they'd fallen in love and spent many happy years together raising their son, Nate. Then they'd retired – neither had become artists like Maisie, but they'd had fascinating careers. Ray had been a police officer investigating art theft, and Sarah had worked for the art loss register, tracking down the rightful owners of artworks that had been stolen by the Nazis during the Second World War.

Hannah was still staring at her painting. It occurred to her that with Sarah's background, she might be able to help track down who owned the painting.

Behind her, Ray clapped his hands together and turned back to her shop, interrupting her thoughts. 'So, are you all set for moving day?'

'I think so …'

'Great – let's get this show on the road!'

'Before we do that, Ray, I've been meaning to ask your opinion about my painting,' Hannah said. 'I haven't had a chance, what with everything that's happened.'

43

Ray entered the shop and headed straight for the window display. He put on his glasses, bent his tall frame and studied the painting. 'The way the painter has captured the sunrise, the yellows and oranges, is just exquisite. I love the VW camper van parked on the beach between the sand dunes. Always wanted one of those. Sarah didn't, though.'

'You could get one now.'

Ray shook his head. 'I've got my houseboat, and besides, where would I go in it? It's not like I want to travel around. My life is right here, on the Suffolk Coast, with my family.' He reached out and affectionately brushed Hannah's arm.

Hannah smiled. She turned to the painting. 'I think the painter captured a moment in time, his love on the beach collecting seashells. Have you seen this beach, by any chance?'

Ray shook his head. 'You know, this could be a figment of …' Ray took a closer look at the painting, 'O. Hartley's imagination.'

'I'm sorry – what did you just say?'

Ray straightened. 'The painter – O. Hartley. Look, he's signed his name.'

'Where?' Hannah said in surprise. She hadn't seen a name on the painting, other than what the painting's title, and the date.

'Ah, signatures are not always obvious, unless you know where to look.'

Hannah smiled affectionately at Ray. If anyone knew where to look it was her very own retired art cop.

'Look here …' He pointed in the bottom right-hand corner of the painting where the surf was coming in across the beach, and the seashells. In the frothy white surf, Hannah spotted it. 'Oh, it's almost imperceptible. The painter's name seemed to fade in and out with the ripples of the water.

'Clever – eh?' Ray said, admiring the painting.

Hannah grinned. Maisie hadn't spotted the signature either, but she'd already confirmed from the seashells in the painting and in the letters that they had been the work of the same Owen. And now Hannah knew that he was indeed O. Hartley. And intriguingly, Hannah also now knew Lady Jemima's surname was not Hartley. She'd seen her name when she'd signed the rental agreement – Lady Jemima Davenport.

Hannah turned on her heel and walked over to the counter, under which was a locked drawer. Ray followed. She unlocked it and got out the box containing the airgraphs. Although she'd told Kyle she was sealing the valuable letters back in the painting, that had been a fib. They'd been locked in the drawer the whole time. It had been a risk, knowing Kyle had stolen the spare key to the shop and that he'd be back to take her painting. If things had gone wrong, and he'd got away with it, although she didn't want to lose her painting, she couldn't afford to lose the airgraphs as well.

Ray already knew about the airgraphs from the sting

operation, but he didn't know about their contents.

'These are love letters from Owen Hartley to a woman called Kitty,' Hannah explained. 'One of them mentions collecting seashells on Seashell Bay – that's why I think the painting is a real place, and the woman in the painting is Kitty.'

Hannah had a sudden thought – was it Kitty or Lady Jemima?

'Seashell Bay on the Suffolk Coast doesn't exist – as far as I'm aware,' said Ray, 'but that doesn't mean it's not a real place.'

Hannah beamed at Ray. 'Exactly.'

'And of course the house rather gives it away, on the cliff there overlooking the bay.'

'What house?'

'Didn't you notice it – in the painting? Granted it's very small, and I know you're immediately drawn to the beautiful sunrise, and the colours, and of course the beach and campervan, but see here in the top left-hand of the picture is a house.'

Hannah followed Ray back to the painting and pointed to the top left-hand corner of the painting.

Hannah stepped forward, bent down and squinted at the painting. She looked up at Ray, surprised. 'Why did I not notice that before?'

'As I said, the beautiful beach scene draws you in.'

The ivy-clad house seemed to fade into the distance. Hannah stared at the house. It was Somersby Hall.

'I guess if you find the house, you'll find the beach.'

Hannah slowly shook her head. 'I don't think so.'

'What do you mean?'

Hannah straightened and turned around to face Ray. 'That

house is deep in the Suffolk countryside.'

'How on earth do you know that?'

'Because I've been there.'

'You've seen that house?'

'Oh, yes. In fact, we're going there today.'

'We are? But I thought you were moving house today.'

Hannah raised her eyebrows.

'You mean, you're renting that house?'

'Oh, no. I couldn't afford that, but I can afford the little gatehouse that came up to rent in the grounds.'

'Well, what a coincidence,' Ray exclaimed.

'Yes … and no. You see, the letters are addressed from Owen to Kitty at Somersby Hall …' Hannah trailed off.

'Hannah! Don't tell me because of the painting by O. Hartley you've decided to live there.'

'That and the mystery of the letters.'

'Thinking of those love letters, it does explain why he added Somersby Hall, a place that resonated with him, in the painting even though it's not located near a beach,' mused Ray. He smiled at Hannah. 'You want to find out more about the painter and his love, Kitty.'

'Yes – and Lady Jemima Davenport, the old lady who owns the hall.'

'What's she got to do with the painting and the letters?'

Hannah returned to the counter and found the most important letter of all. She passed it to Ray.

'What's this?'

'It's another airgraph, quite valuable according to Thea because it was never sent. Read it.'

Ray glanced at her before pushing his glasses up to the

bridge of his nose. He carefully unfolded the letter and read.

Hannah watched with interest as his eyebrows shot up. 'Oh, it's a letter to Owen – a love letter from Jemima.'

'Yes. What do you think it means?' said Hannah, interested in his opinion.

'It means your painter has been a very naughty boy. It sounds to me as though he had two lovers.'

'A love triangle,' said Hannah.

'I would hazard a guess that Jemima had no idea that Owen was writing love letters to Kitty from Cairo. But the question is, did Kitty know about Jemima? Presumably Kitty kept all the letters, and I'll hazard a guess that Owen gave her this painting, and that's where she hid the letters, clearly. But how did she come by Jemima's letter – and why was it never sent?' Ray mused.

Hannah was enjoying the conversation immensely. Rather than tell her to drop it, like Thea, Ray was just as immersed in the history, and mystery, of these lovers as she was. She could sense his detective nose smelling something fishy, for sure.

He held up a finger, 'I just had a thought. The mystery here is who exactly was Owen Hartley? Now, he wasn't a famous painter, otherwise I would have heard of him. So, he was an amateur painter, like me and Sarah, which is a shame because judging by this painting he had a remarkable talent. But I digress …'

Hannah smiled. She loved his old-fashioned turn of phrases.

'I do have a theory …'

Hannah couldn't wait to hear it. 'Yes, yes, what is it?'

'We don't know who Owen Hartley is or probably was, but we do know that Kitty and Jemima were in love with him. And judging by these letters, he was in love with Kitty.'

Hannah nodded enthusiastically. 'Yes …'

'Now, the letters were sent from Cairo to Kitty at Somersby Hall, so Kitty was living there at this time.'

Hannah nodded, even though he was stating the obvious.

'And Jemima – we'll assume for a moment it is Lady Jemima, but we really mustn't make assumptions, we need facts.'

Hannah listened with interest. Ray's detective hat was definitely on.

'But a woman by the name of Jemima was sending her letter from the hall. So, they both lived there at that time. Now, if Lady Jemima Davenport was the Jemima who wrote this letter, then who is Kitty?'

Hannah shrugged.

'Now, this is another assumption, but they would no doubt have had staff at that time.'

'You mean servants, like in those period dramas.'

'Ah, I think you're thinking of a famous English period drama in particular, although I believe that was set around the First World War.'

Hannah hadn't actually watched *Downton Abbey*, although she imagined everybody had heard of the famous television programme.

'Yes, but in any case, I'd rather not call them that.'

'Of course not,' Hannah agreed. 'You think Kitty was a serv … staff at the hall?' Hannah had thought the same thing.

'Again, it's an assumption, and this may be very bigoted of me to assume that a name like Kitty would belong to a member of staff rather than the wealthy family who lived at Somersby Hall.'

Hannah could see where he was going with this. 'So, Lady

Jemima may have given the letter to Kitty to post.'

'Yes, it's a possibility.'

'But if she didn't post it, why keep it? She could have put it on the fire.'

'Yes, she kept the evidence that may have got her into trouble or even caused her to be dismissed.'

'Do you think she felt guilty for not posting it and kept it in case it weighed so heavily on her conscience that she still had the option to post it in the end?'

'Yes, that's certainly a possibility.'

'So, why keep it with her letters?'

'That's a good question, Hannah. I assume it was guilt again, and the fact that she might have considered handing it to Owen on his return.'

Hannah hadn't thought of that. 'But that's dumb. Why would she do that? If Lady Jemima asked if he'd received her letter, and he hadn't, they could have presumed it had just got lost or mislaid in the post. It would just make her look bad if Owen discovered she hadn't posted it.'

'That is a point, but of course this is all merely conjecture. We could be completely barking up the wrong tree.'

There it was again – Ray's funny turn of phrase. But Hannah didn't smile this time. 'What do you mean?' She'd assumed they were making headway, and all she had to do now was find out who Owen was, and what had happened to Kitty after she left the hall. She imagined the hall didn't have staff anymore, and even if it did, Kitty wouldn't work there any longer – she'd be far too old, assuming she was even still alive.

'What I mean, Hannah, is that in my experience nothing is ever quite what it seems.'

'Are you talking about all those cases you worked on when you were in the police?'

'Yes, I am. Just when you thought you had a handle on what had happened, or who the perp was, or why they'd done what they'd done, something comes along and throws you a curve ball.'

'A curve ball?' Hannah didn't understand.

'Something you least expect.'

'Oh, right.'

She'd thought they had it all figured out. But then again, Ray was right: they were making some big assumptions – huge leaps over who these people were. Even so, Hannah asked, 'Who do you think Owen might have been?'

Ray put Jemima's letter down and took off his glasses. 'It's impossible to say. He could have been from the circles Lady Jemima and her family mixed with, a suitor who she might have been engaged to be married.'

'Before he fell for Kitty.'

'Yes. On the other hand, he might have been a member of staff, whom Lady Jemima had fallen in love with, but he was in love with Kitty.'

'Oh, I hadn't thought of that. Jemima must not have known about Owen and Kitty, otherwise she wouldn't have given her the letter to post.

'There, you see – nothing is ever quite what it seems. Maybe if Owen worked at the hall, and Lady Jemima's family found out she had a fondness for Owen, they saw to it that he was conscripted.'

'Could they do that?'

'You'd be surprised the influence and connections that

wealthy landed family could have. Her parents would not have approved of the match between their daughter and one of the staff, that's for sure.'

'Do you think that's the curve ball, then?'

'Honestly, I wouldn't know, Hannah. The only person who can give you answers to all this,' he glanced at the letters, 'is Lady Jemima, if she is the same Jemima who wrote the letter to Owen.'

'I think she must be. She sounds as though she's very old and has owned the house for years.'

'How do you know that?'

'Oh, I met her grandson – Rupert.' Hannah knitted her brow.

'I take it from your expression that he didn't make a good first impression?'

'Not. At. All. He was *so* rude.'

'Sounds like Sarah and me. I did not make a good impression either, the first time we met, but you know, sometimes frenemies make the best relationships.'

'Frenemies?'

'Enemies, to friends, to lovers. Oh, never mind. I read far too many romance novels when I was trying to win her back.'

Hannah laughed out loud. 'I didn't know that.'

'No, nobody does. You're the only person I've told besides Sarah. Please keep it under your hat.'

Hannah liked that he'd confided in her.

'Stupid – eh?'

'No, not if you thought you might learn a thing or two from the pages of a good book and win your wife back.'

'Now that's what I like, when great minds think alike.'

Hannah grinned, her smile faltering when she thought, *Why*

can't I meet someone like Ray – someone I can talk to so easily, and that I have such a rapport with?

'Anyhoo,' said Ray, looking at his watch. 'We can't dawdle all day. We'd better get cracking, otherwise the Halloween party will be getting underway and we'll still be here nattering!'

44

'Right – I see you've already brought some boxes down from upstairs. Great, I'll start loading those in the car.' He paused. 'Does it matter what goes in my car or yours?'

Hannah shook her head. 'Not at all. I just hope it won't take too many trips.'

'Well, my car is bigger, so if we start with the one trip, then if another one or two are needed, you could hang back, start unpacking while I get the rest.'

'Oh, Ray, that's so kind of you.'

'Don't mention it, Hannah. What are friends for?'

Hannah had been relieved that Ray was free to help her out. Hannah couldn't ask anybody else. Lili was busy preparing for the yard party with Maisie and William, and besides, Hannah got the feeling that although Lili was happy for her, she wasn't too impressed with her choice of rental – if they sold Somersby Hall, she might well be on the move again.

Hannah imagined what Lili must have been thinking; it wasn't fair on Maisie to go through another house move all because of Hannah's obsession with the painting and Somersby Hall, so maybe her best friend was still putting her own needs first, before those of her daughter. That couldn't be further from the truth – Hannah was taking on the rental for Maise, for both of them to have a fresh start.

Hannah pursed her lips as she passed Ray another box to run out to his car. She followed him with one herself. She cast her glance towards The Bookshop of Memories. She caught Thea standing at the bookshop window, shaking her head. She hadn't exactly been enthusiastic when she'd told her where she was moving either. Hannah hadn't bothered to ask Thea for help on her moving day.

She expected her shop neighbour next door, Joss, would have helped. He was the sort who would gladly lend a hand. But Hannah didn't want him shutting up his shop and turning away people who needed his help in order to help her out instead. If it came to it, Hannah would have done the move on her own, no matter how many trips that entailed.

But Ray, bless him, had stepped in and phoned her to ask when she was moving and whether she needed a hand. He'd heard about her impending move on the family grapevine, meaning Lili and Nate had told Sarah, who had told Ray.

Sarah had an art class that morning, so she'd sent her apologies that she couldn't lend a hand, although she was going to bring along a moving-in present for Hannah and Maisie once they were settled in their new home.

Hannah wondered what it was. Perhaps it would be one of Sarah's artworks that she could hang in Gatekeeper's Cottage – not that she didn't have enough of Maisie's paintings to hang on the wall and make the rental more homely.

She walked with Ray, each carrying a box, to their cars parked in the high street.

'I'm surprised Lili isn't helping. You two are thick as thieves.'

Hannah knew what he meant. They were best friends, and Lili was always helping her out. 'I didn't like to ask. Besides, she's busy preparing for the Halloween party.'

'And …?'

Hannah pursed her lips. Ray had caught her frown. 'I don't think she agrees with my house move to another rental.' Hannah admitted, 'I'm obsessed with the painting which kind of influenced me in my choice of rental – Gatekeeper's Cottage.'

'So, what's wrong with that?'

Hannah offered him a wisp of a smile. He didn't know the whole story. 'Rupert is after selling his grandmother's house. I don't think they can afford the repairs.'

'Ah, so they might sell Gatekeeper's Cottage with it, and then you'd have to move again.'

'Yes. I was thinking of backing out, but I didn't.'

'I don't suppose you have any ideas as to how they could make some money other than by selling Somersby Hall?'

Ray left her with that thought as they returned in silence to the flat to collect more boxes.

The airgraphs suddenly came to mind. She didn't know exactly how much they'd be worth until she had them valued, but if she handed them to Lady Jemima, they might help her financially. But that money could be for Maisie's future. And besides, whilst they might help Lady Jemima out financially, what of Pandora's box? Would Lady Jemima really want to find out the truth about Owen and Kitty, and what had happened to her letter? Assuming it was true that Owen had been involved with both Kitty and Lady Jemima, and Kitty had hidden her letter rather than sending it.

Perhaps Owen had been secretly in love with Lady Jemima, and if he'd received her letter, he would have returned to her rather than Kitty?

Ray returned to collect the next box while Hannah stared at the painting. He commented, 'You know, it would be quicker if we both loaded up the boxes.'

'Oh, yes – of course.' Hannah stopped daydreaming about Jemima, Owen and Kitty, and grabbed a box. She walked with Ray to their cars. On their way out of the yard, Hannah said, 'I did have a thought, but I'm not sure if Lady Jemima would entertain it at her age.'

'What is it?' Ray asked as he opened the boot and placed the box inside his car.

'A wedding.'

'A wedding?'

'At Somersby Hall. The grounds need some work.'

'Lili could do that, I'm sure.'

'Yeah, I thought of that, but I don't think they've got the money to pay for the sort of landscaping job that would be required to bring it up to scratch for wedding photos.'

'Ah, that's a shame. Sounded like a good idea.'

Hannah put the box in her boot. She left the boot open. As they returned to the yard, Hannah said, 'I'm sure the hall would make a fantastic wedding venue, but they'd need a wedding to get them started, with photos and advertising, and reviews from the guests.'

'I see. One of those cart and horse scenarios,' mused Ray as he picked up another box in the shop.

'Yes. But you see, I had this brilliant idea. If Lili did their garden for free—'

'For free?' Ray scoffed. 'Do you know how long it takes to landscape a garden, and the cost of planting etc?'

Hannah didn't – not really, but she guessed Lili had talked about her burgeoning career with Nate's parents at some point.

'It wouldn't technically be free. It could be a barter. She could landscape their grounds in return for holding her wedding at Somersby Hall. And if she wouldn't mind some of her wedding photos being used for publicity, Lady Jemima might just have a lucrative business on her hands.'

They'd been walking across Cobblers Yard carrying another box each as Hannah told Ray her idea to save Somersby Hall from being sold. He stopped mid-stride.

Hannah noticed, paused, and turned to look at him.

'You know, you might just be on to something …' Ray said. 'You have quite the entrepreneurial streak – do you know that?'

'Me?'

'I've heard the art and craft shop has really taken off. I don't know how you managed it, because my takings were pretty lousy when I ran an art and craft shop in the yard. I ended up subsidising it with my pension, more often than not, and in the end I just couldn't afford to keep doing that.'

Hannah was aware that Ray's shop hadn't been profitable. He'd obviously kept it open just so he could be near his wife across the yard. Hannah didn't know why she thought she could do better running an art and craft shop in Cobblers Yard.

'I must say, I was rather taken aback when I found out you were taking over Joseph's shop and changing it from an antiques shop to selling art and craft materials. I mean, I understood it, because Maisie is an artist, but I wouldn't have recommended it. I knew that apart from the beginning of the school academic year, and the beginning of term times when there's a spike in sales, it's pretty much downhill from then on, until the likes of Sarah and other budding artists pop in for some materials.'

Hannah tried to keep up her cheery disposition.

'I hope you don't lose too much money by having to close this morning to move house,' Ray said.

She wasn't going to lose any money if she had no customers anyway. She looked at Ray and knew he'd help her out financially if it really came to it and she ran out of money. She could sell the airgraphs and pay Ray back. But it wouldn't solve her long-term problem – if the shop really wasn't going to support her in the long-term, what was she going to do?

'I bet you'd make a fine wedding planner,' said Ray, loading another box in his car.

'What did you say?'

Ray joined her at the back of her car, parked on the street by the kerb next to his. Ray had parked behind her, backing in so the car boots faced each other. He sat on the ledge of his boot. 'You could plan Lili's wedding. Get everything organised.'

'A wedding planner – you said?'

'Yes – why not?'

Hannah stared at Ray.

'What did I say?'

That was the most ridiculous thing Hannah had ever heard – her, a wedding planner? For one thing, she had never got married herself, so she had no idea what it would be like to have a wedding. She'd have no words of wisdom or experience to offer the bride-to-be. In fact, she had the worst relationship track record. Who would possibly hire her to plan a wedding? *I wouldn't hire me*, she thought. And besides, she had a shop to run.

Hannah didn't hold back. She told Ray all this as they walked back to the shop.

'I don't think the fact that you're not married should bar you from planning weddings. Imagine if all midwives had to have had babies before they could practice midwifery. I know that's a bit of a silly analogy, but you get my point. You're running a business. Here's a better analogy – you don't have to be an artist to sell paintings, or a novelist to sell books. You do not have to be married to sell wedding dresses or run a wedding business – you get my drift.'

Hannah got his drift, but who would hire her to get her business off the ground? Not that she was seriously thinking about it, but she asked Ray the question anyway, looking to him as though he had all the answers.

'Why, your best friend Lili, of course.'

'She said she wanted a low-key wedding at her and Nate's house.'

Ray leaned towards Hannah, and said, 'No woman wants a low-key wedding.'

'How do you know that?'

'I have read enough romance novels to know, believe me. It's their special day, something that they'll hopefully do only once. They want it to be the biggest, most memorable day in a very special place.'

Hannah immediately thought of Lili and Nate's home – their special place. 'Nate has got a very nice house, and a lovely back garden.'

'It won't have the backdrop and majesty of something like Somersby Hall. Talk to Lili. She'll change her mind about the whole idea of doing it at home, believe me. I bet that was Nate's idea, and she's just going along with it.'

'Lili said that she and Nate don't want to spend thousands on a wedding when they can save that money and put it towards William and Maisie's university education.'

'Well, they can still do that if she can have her wedding for free at Somersby Hall, with a little bit of elbow grease on the part of her and her team, sorting out the grounds.'

Hannah sat on the ledge of her open boot, staring at Ray. 'Rupert, Lady Jemima's grandson, mentioned that he was getting married. Perhaps he'd want to marry at the hall too.'

'There you go,' said Ray, as if it was all settled. 'He could marry at the hall and hire your services as his wedding planner.'

'Yeah – right,' scoffed Hannah.

Ray raised his eyebrows.

'Like I told you, we didn't exactly hit it off when we first met.'

Ray shrugged. 'At least think on it,' said Ray. 'It's an idea, especially if your art and craft shop ever goes the way of mine – you'll have premises to run your business from, and you can even stock and sell wedding dresses – or do they still call them bridal gowns?' Ray shook his head. 'No matter. But look, there's the perfect shop across the yard to buy that all-important bridal bouquet.'

Hannah knew Ray still had a fondness for the yard, especially The Potting Shed.

They returned to the yard. Hannah paused in front of her own shop window, suddenly imagining wedding dresses displayed there. She shook herself out of a very strange daydream. 'I bet they'll never agree to it.'

'Who – you mean the grandson?'

'Yeah, Rupert.'

'But it's not up to him – is it? You need to speak to Lady Jemima. And you have the perfect excuse.'

'What's that?'

'You're her tenant. You want to introduce yourself to your new landlady.'

Hannah wasn't sure that she did. 'What if she doesn't like me?'

Ray smiled down at her. 'I think you underestimate yourself. Do you know why I think of you as my very good friend?'

'Because I'm Maisie's mum?'

'No, you weren't listening. If you didn't happen to be her mum, and we'd met under different circumstances, we'd have still become good – no, great – friends, you dear, sweet girl. You've had some rotten luck with relationships, but don't let them get you down. I … we sometimes wish that it was you who was marrying our son. Don't get me wrong, we love Lili to bits. She's lovely, but then so are you.'

'It would have been good for Maisie for her Mummy and Daddy to get married.'

'I know. But life is messy, Hannah, and we all have to just muddle through and do the best we can with the cards we've been dealt.'

'I want to have what you and Sarah have.'

'It hasn't all been plain sailing.'

Hannah knew that. 'I just want to fall madly, deeply in love with someone that I want to spend the rest of my life with.'

'And you will.'

'I wish that person had been Nate, for Maisie's sake. But I know it's not him. I feel bad about that.'

'Don't. If you had got together, and went on to get married, for Maisie's sake, it wouldn't have lasted, and then Maisie would have had to go through her parents getting divorced, and all the fallout of that.'

That scenario hadn't occurred to Hannah.

'It's in Maisie's best interests that *both* her parents find happiness, find love. I have an idea that you'll find him when and where you least expect.'

Hannah frowned. 'Why do you say that?'

'Because of what I said – life is messy, and things don't always fall neatly into place. Take Owen, Kitty and Jemima. We don't know what their story is, but I can tell you this – I bet whatever went on there was not straightforward, and I'd hazard a guess it involved secrets and lies.'

Hannah was inclined to agree. 'I need to see Lady Jemima.'

'About the letters?'

Hannah was thinking about the wedding venue idea. But she'd have to broach it with Lady Jemima first before she approached Lili. The past, and confronting Lady Jemima with the airgraphs, would have to wait. She was thinking about solving issues in the here and now.

Hannah couldn't get Thea's warning out of her mind. What if Thea was right and she got kicked out of Gatekeeper's Cottage when Lady Jemima discovered she was putting her nose into her family's affairs?

Hannah realised too late that by becoming Lady Jemima's tenant she'd added a whole level of complication to an already complicated scenario with the letters.

'Thea said I should just sell the airgraphs to the highest bidder.'

'But you're not going to do that – are you?'

'Not yet.' Hannah was still on the fence about what to do with the letters – whether to confront Lady Jemima or not. She just desperately wanted to know who Owen and Kitty were.

Thinking of selling to the highest bidder brought to mind the auction at Somersby Hall on Sunday. She'd been debating whether to attend or not. A fortnight had passed, and Maisie's weekend with her dad and Lili had rolled around again. Every time it did, Hannah thought the same thing – it had come round far too quicky and she wished Maisie didn't have to go. Although she always tried to keep herself busy, she felt lonely with Maisie gone.

But this weekend, there was one advantage. She had a free weekend to sort out all her stuff and get settled in and organised at Gatekeeper's Cottage. Hannah decided that she wouldn't open the shop the next day. It wasn't every day she moved house. But it wasn't just that – the slow footfall in her shop had made up her mind. Rather than sitting there all day waiting for the odd customer, she might as well spend her time on Saturday in her new home. The fact that Maisie wasn't around meant she'd get a lot organised. The place hadn't been lived in for some time, so there would be cleaning to do.

And there was the auction on Sunday. Hannah didn't want to go alone, but even if Maisie wasn't going to Nate's house, it wasn't the sort of thing Maisie would enjoy. Hannah was going to ask Thea or Lili if they wanted to go. But it was Lili's weekend with Maisie, and Thea, she imagined, would be on her case about auctioning off the airgraphs.

Hannah had another idea. As they carried the last of the boxes to the cars – it turned out they could do the move in a single trip – Hannah said, 'Ray, would you like to come to an auction with me on Sunday?'

45

Hannah drew the car into the little parking space by the side of Gatekeeper's Cottage. Maisie sat in the car with a pumpkin on her lap and a small plastic bucket full of treats from trick-or-treating with William and the other children who'd come to the Halloween yard party. They had all been given far too many treats by the shopkeepers – Hannah included.

When they'd left Cobblers Yard at closing time, there had still been carved pumpkins outside each shop, and plastic skeletons, ghostly ghouls, fake spider webs, and witches' broomsticks decorating shop windows. *Happy Halloween* bunting still hung in shop windows, and black bats that Maisie had cut from card were stuck to the lamppost.

Maisie had offered her skills again with face painting, this time black cats and white ghostly ghouls. Lili had lots of pumpkins, so children and adults could try pumpkin carving. And they hadn't forgotten the all-important raffle for charity, and there was even a competition for the best pet Halloween outfit.

Maisie had said, 'Now we're moving, and I'm getting a pet, I'm going to enter it into the best pet outfit competition at the next yard party. Will we have one at Christmas?' she'd asked.

Hannah thought that she wouldn't be at all surprised if they did. In fact, she'd made a mental note to suggest it to the others at their next yard meeting in her cosy corner.

'Can we go trick-or-treating here too?'

'I'm afraid there aren't many houses around here to go trick-or-treating. Come on, let's get out of the car.' She couldn't wait to show Maisie her new home.

'Mummy, can I take this sheet off now?'

Hannah didn't have the money for expensive Halloween outfits, so they'd improvised, using an old sheet which Maisie had decorated with bats and broomsticks, black cats, and all sorts of Halloween themed drawings. They'd made a witches hat out of felt, and Mabel had lent her a broom. Maisie had dressed up as a ghostly witch.

This was the reason they'd chosen not to have a competition for the best dressed child; it just wasn't fair if a child was chosen because their parents had the money to spend on a ridiculously expensive outfit. It was Maisie who had come up with the idea for a pet competition instead. Hannah wasn't surprised. Once she'd found out they were moving, she'd had pets on the brain.

'Let me help you,' Hannah said as they got out of the car. Maisie was wearing leggings and a t-shirt under the sheet. Together they lifted the sheet and took it off. Maisie put her witch hat back on and reached into the car for the pumpkin and her sweets. Together they walked from the car to the side of the cottage, round to the little path that ran from the gate through the small front garden to the porch door. The porch had a pitched pantile roof, and although small, it would be perfect for when the weather turned; they would be able to leave wellies and wet coats there to dry.

She smiled as she watched Maisie set the large pumpkin with the crooked grin outside the porch. With Maisie there, it was beginning to feel like home. However, Hannah was a bit worried about what Maisie would make of it when they walked inside. There were old, mismatched pieces of furniture – pine chests of drawers and bookcases, some distressed painted furniture, and even a grandfather clock in the hall, chiming on the hour. The rooms were small but cosy, the lounge painted green, the dining room the same, both with one wall covered in pretty wallpaper with a floral print from a bygone era.

Both receptions rooms were furnished with G-plan furniture – Hannah hadn't known what that was until Ray pointed it out. Apparently, the light mahogany furniture had been all the rage back in the seventies, although Hannah rather thought the house gave off a forties vibe, especially the downstairs. The lounge had two old-fashioned faded patterned sofas, two tall floor lamps with large, frilly shades, and an open fire. The kitchen had old hand-made kitchen cabinets hanging on the wall, and little curtains below the worktop. It wasn't exactly a fitted modern kitchen, but it felt cottagey.

Ray loved the dining room with its mahogany table opposite the old fireplace. There were two easy chairs at one end of the room under another floor lamp with the same sort of shade she'd seen in the lounge. They'd set up Maisie's easel by the French doors that led out into the overgrown cottage garden.

There was a G-plan cabinet, which looked like a dresser, with a selection of wine and pint glasses, along with some plates and dishes that had been left behind in the glass cabinet. Below, they'd opened the wooden sliding doors to discover a selection of very old boardgames.

'Hey, I remember this from my childhood,' Ray had commented, taking one out and examining it. There were some jigsaws with pictures of animals – kittens and puppies in front of an Aga in a cottage – that Hannah thought Maisie might enjoy doing. It occurred to her that they'd never sat together and actually finished a jigsaw. Hannah had put the children's books and games she'd found in Maisie's bedroom.

Together, she and Ray had cleaned Maisie's bedroom from top to bottom and made up her bed with freshly laundered and ironed bed clothes – Hannah had washed and ironed them the night before. She'd unpacked Maisie's stuff, her clothes and toys, arranging things in the wardrobe and on the bookshelves. They both had bedrooms in the eaves with dormer windows. Hannah's bedroom was a double, Maisie's a single. Maisie's bedroom overlooked the grounds of Somersby Hall.

While Hannah was unpacking, she realised she wouldn't get everything unpacked and organised before she had to return to Cobblers Yard for the Halloween party.

Ray had been very thoughtful and had brought over a bag of shopping. He'd prepared a casserole and put it in the oven before following her back to Aldeburgh in his car for the yard party. And now there they were, standing outside Gatekeeper's Cottage. Hannah stared at her daughter, wondering what she was thinking.

'Come on, Mummy, I'm so excited. I can't wait to see inside.'

Hannah wondered if Maisie's enthusiasm would quickly disappear when she saw how old-fashioned the place was inside. It even had patterned carpet. The cottage they'd rented before had been completely renovated with brand new carpet, freshly painted walls and a new kitchen. Gatekeeper's Cottage couldn't be more different.

Hannah still wondered what she was going to make of it.

As soon as they walked in, the comforting aroma of Ray's casserole cooking on a low setting in the oven made her smile.

'Can I go and explore, Mummy?'

'Of course you can.'

She took off her coat and hung it on the old-fashioned coat stand by the front door, watching Maisie go in and out of the rooms downstairs before she started up the stairs. 'Which is my bedroom?'

Hannah followed her up. 'You'll see,' she said, smiling. So far, Maisie hadn't said she didn't like it. At least that was something.

Maisie sat on the bed and bounced up and down as she looked about her, taking in her new bedroom.

Hannah leaned on the doorframe looking around the small, cosy bedroom. The bed was under the dormer window. One wall was papered with a lovely vibrant print of different birds – parrots and songbirds. She'd spent a bit of money buying two lovely patchwork throws, one double and one single. They looked lovely on the beds – very cottagey.

'What do you think?'

'I love it here. Can I have a pet now?'

Hannah sighed. When they'd had to move out of the cottage in Aldeburgh back to the flat, she'd made Maisie a promise – when they next moved into a new home, she'd get Maisie a pet.

She'd said it on the spur of the moment, feeling guilty about the move. Trust Maisie to remember.

'You promised,' Maisie reminded her.

'Yes, I know. Let's get settled in first, and then—'

Maisie frowned at her. 'But you promised!'

'Maisie, I did not say you weren't getting one.' Actually, that was exactly what she was saying, but now she realised she wasn't going to get away with delaying tactics forever. 'All I'm saying is that we can't, you know, go and get one right now. We need to prepare.'

Maisie brightened. 'You mean like going to buy dog bowls, and a bed, and a collar and lead?'

'Um, er … yeah.' *Or a hutch and some straw.* Hannah was thinking perhaps they could get a small pet, like a hamster or a rabbit. It didn't have to be a puppy. Hannah really didn't have time to look after, walk, and train a dog, although she knew that was what Maisie wanted.

Maisie climbed on her bed. Kneeling, she looked out of the dormer window. 'What's that big house through the trees?'

Hannah sat on the bed next to her and looked out of the window too. 'That is Somersby Hall.'

'Somersby Hall?' repeated Maisie. 'Who lives there?'

A horribly rude young man called Rupert, thought Hannah. Although he didn't actually live there, thank god. By the sound of things, he was down from London to organise and oversee the auction.

Hannah replied, 'Lady Jemima.'

'Lady?'

'Yes, she's a lady. It's a title, sweetheart.' Thankfully Maisie didn't ask her anything more about the title.

'She lives in that big house all on her own?'

'Well, not on her own. I think she must have *some* staff to help her, and her grandson, Rupert, is visiting.'

Maisie had taken her witch hat off. She slipped it back on her head and picked up her bucket. 'Can I go trick-or-treating there? I can put my sheet back on.'

'I think Lady Jemima is quite old, sweetheart, and I can't imagine she'd take too kindly to a ghost with a bright orange plastic bucket full of sweets knocking on her door and scaring her witless.'

Maisie sniggered into her hand.

Joking aside, Hannah decided not to mention that the other occupant of the hall probably wouldn't take too kindly to them knocking either – the good-looking guy she was having trouble getting out of her mind. *Well, you'd better stop thinking about him*, she told herself. *He's got a fiancée, and you didn't like his attitude – he was just rude.*

'What's she like – Lady Jemima?'

'I don't know. I haven't met her yet.' Hannah hoped Maisie didn't ask if she'd met Rupert, and what he was like. 'But I'm hoping to meet her on Sunday at the auction.'

'What's an auction?'

'Lady Jemima is selling some of their things. Lots of people will come, I expect, and we'll all sit in a room, and the auctioneer – that's the person conducting the auction – will sell one piece at a time. They'll open with a starting bid – a low price – and then if people are interested, they'll offer what they want to pay, and people can outbid them; that means offering a higher price. And that will go on until nobody in the room wants to offer anymore. Then it will sell to the highest bidder.'

'Sounds boring.'

Hannah smiled. 'I bet you're glad you are going to Daddy and Lili's tomorrow.'

'No, I'd rather stay here in my new house.'

Hannah almost cried when she heard that. 'You like it that much?'

'Oh, yes,' Maisie turned from the window. She bounced off the bed and ran over to the rocking chair in the corner, beside a small bookcase. She switched on the small lamp on the bookcase and scanned the bookshelves.

Hannah had placed a pretty cushion on the rocking chair, and a throw, just to make it look cosy, not expecting Maisie to choose a book, sit in the chair and snuggle under the throw. 'I'm going to read a book,' she said, rocking back and forward.

'All right,' Hannah said slowly, looking at her, puzzled. She hadn't expected Maisie to settle into her new home so quickly.

As she walked to the door, Maisie asked, 'Are you going to buy something at the auction at the weekend?'

'I don't think I could afford anything.'

'Why are you going?

'To meet our landlady.'

'You mean Lady Jemima?'

'Yes. Your grandpa is coming too, so perhaps he might buy something.'

'Do I have to go to Daddy's this weekend?'

Hannah would be quite happy if she didn't, even though she had lots to do, including finishing unpacking and meeting Lady Jemima at the auction. But she was also thinking of Nate. He only got to spend time with Maisie every other weekend.

Sometimes he popped into the shop, if he could, in between his shifts at the hospital to see Maisie after school, and then there were the times Maisie had tea with Sarah after school once a week, and William came too, Nate popping in if work allowed.

But every fortnight was his time to spend with his daughter. She couldn't renege on that arrangement – especially not after how unreliable she'd been recently. 'I'm sorry, sweetheart, but I can't let your father down. He looks forward to your visits.'

'I know,' Maisie said with a sigh. 'It's all right. I'll go.'

Hannah smiled. 'Good girl. I'll call you when the casserole is ready.' She lingered for a moment, her eyes drifting from her daughter – who was sitting rocking back and forward, engrossed in her book, looking as though she'd lived there all her life rather than having just moved in that day – to the dormer window and the ivy-clad house she could see across the lawn.

As she turned from the door and walked down the stairs, the only blot on Hannah's seemingly perfect move to their lovely new home was the thought that the hall might be sold, along with Gatekeeper's Cottage, and in no time at all they'd have to leave. If the hall was sold, anything could happen – some developer might even tear down the gorgeous hall and the cottage and build a housing estate. Hannah wouldn't have that. She was determined to save the hall. Even though she knew this was a rental, it felt like her home now. It was her home now.

Hannah felt a new chapter in her life was just beginning. Her painting, *Sunrise Over Seashell Bay*, had taken her there, but there were still unanswered questions about the whereabouts of Seashell Bay, and the mystery of those airgraphs, the love letters from Kitty, Owen and Jemima.

Hannah paused halfway down the stairs and stared out of the small landing window, catching a glimpse of the hall. What secrets lay hidden within its walls? Hannah chose to ignore Thea's warning about opening Pandora's box. She couldn't wait to meet her new landlady and find out the secrets of Somersby Hall.

The Sunrise Coast Series continues in

The Secrets of Somersby Hall

Paperback and Kindle eBook available from Amazon

I hope you enjoyed *Sunrise Over Seashell Bay*, and would be grateful if you would leave a review on Amazon.

For further details about the author and her novels, visit the author's website.

www.elisedarcy.com

Also by Elise Darcy

The Scottish Highlands Series

Winter in the Scottish Highlands

The Secrets of the Glen

Return to the Lake House

The Boathouse by the Loch

Summer in the Scottish Highlands

Coming Home to Aviemore

The Living Apart Together series

Living Apart Together

It Takes 2 to Tango

Dear John

Love on the Rooftop

Standalone books

Lola & The Man

A Mallorcan Affair

The Villa in Sicily

We'll Meet Again

Printed in Dunstable, United Kingdom

70359501R00211